UPTOWN

J.T. Riggen

In collaboration with Matt Berthiaume

First published by Dog Ear Publishing
4010 W. 86th Street, Ste H
Indianapolis, IN 46268
www.dogearpublishing.net

ISBN: 978-1-4575-1956-7

This book is printed on acid-free paper.

Printed in the United States of America

CHAPTER 1

MARK KENNEDY

Routine

Mark Kennedy awoke with the first beam of light shining through the small window of his solitary confinement room like he did every morning. He stood up and manipulated his neck, forcing three distinct cracks to sound out, the same three joints that he realigned with each new day. He then reached to his face and satisfied the itch within his long, unkempt beard, which always brought some early morning satisfaction. After ten years of prison life, he had grown accustomed to the monotonous routines. Embraced them even. One characteristic he never could adjust to was the cold coming off the stone walls. It never failed to remind him of a simpler time, as a young child when he would play cops and robbers with the other kids in his neighborhood in the frigid winter woods; an innocent and uncontaminated memory that often tormented him given his far less desirable life circumstances. He always caught himself trying to recall how old he was in those days but would inevitably become frustrated with his inability to do so and move on. This was another one of the many features of prison life that Kennedy disliked. His previous life before the incarceration had become muddled. Only a few recollections were still of vivid quality in his mind.

April 19, 1990. He was looking at himself in the mirror before his graduation from the academy, dressed in his New York Police Department brass and formal wear. His father, Detective Greg Kennedy, put his large hands on his shoulder and said how proud of him he was. It was the first time Mark had ever heard those words. He also remembered well his father's death: December 24, 1995. Tragic, but not surprising. He worked the NYPD major crimes unit and wound up on the receiving end of a mob hit. It was his death that opened the door for Kennedy to fill those rather large shoes in the same division. There was only one date, however, that Kennedy thought about one way or another every day: May 21, 2001.

The slightly overweight but powerful Guard Liam Robbins appeared outside Kennedy's small cell, his distinctly high voice piercing the morning peace. "Yo, you awake?"

"Yeah, Robbins, I'm awake."

"You got a letter."

Kennedy sighed. "Great, gonna be a rough day then."

"Speaking of how your day is going to be, good news—you're headed back to your home on Block-E. I'm here to take you. Something to look forward to, eh?"

"Do me a favor and keep this cell warm for me. Chances are I'll be back."

"Could you try to stay out of trouble for just one day?"

"No promises," he responded dryly. "Before we go can I have a minute to read that?"

"Sure thing, Kennedy."

Robbins' incongruently tiny hands appeared at the drop slot, and a moment later the letter fell softly to the ground. Kennedy picked it up, knowing exactly what it was and who it was from. He held it up to the small slit of light creeping into his cell. No return address, as usual. He withdrew the letter, lifted it to the light, and read it to himself:

Mark,

I think about you all the time. I hope that sooner than later I get to be with you again. 359389. Nazi Tattoo. Don't worry about finding him, I'm sure he'll find you. Please be careful.

-J.R.

Kennedy finished reading. Emotionless, he repackaged the letter and called for Robbins. "Hey, I'm ready."

"All set to get out of here?"

"Yeah, take me home."

The door opened and he stepped out backward. Before placing him in restraints, Robbins took the letter from him.

"Burn it?" Robbins asked.

"As usual."

"No problem," he replied as he put it in his pocket.

The two made their way out of the isolation unit and along the hallways back to Block-E. Other inmates passed by and were careful not to look Kennedy in the eye. He thought he had reached somewhat of a legendary status outside the jail walls, but he had become an even bigger legend on the inside. It had only taken him a couple of weeks to show some of the most devious criminals in New York that he wasn't going to put up with intimidation. He wasn't going to deal with disrespect.

The short hike back to Block-E felt great on his legs. He was sure that it would be the best he'd feel all day. Kennedy was dropped off in his single-bed cell. He immediately went over to the mirror, grabbed a razor, and went to work against his beard. The resulting smoothness of his skin was a welcome feeling relative to the thick facial hair growth of the last several months. He looked himself over. His usually well-maintained, wavy dark hair had grown long and shaggy; small tufts of gray had begun sneaking in. Reviewing his body, he was glad to see he hadn't lost much of his bulk. Diligence in maintaining his agility and strength meant the difference between life and death for him. He tossed himself onto his bed, lifted the corner of the mattress, and ran his hand beneath the frame. He looked around to be sure no one was watching before popping off the item he was searching for. He examined it carefully. It was a scalpel blade secured between two tongue depressors that had been taped together.

Whenever a letter showed up, Kennedy could always count on Liam Robbins to deliver. He had been taking good care of him since his first day. He kept an eye on Kennedy and acquired for him the necessary tools so he could conduct his ongoing work. Perhaps most importantly, he disposed of the letters that came to him. Robbins was invaluable.

Kennedy heard footsteps approaching. A guard walked by just as he hid the weapon in his pants.

"Kennedy, back just in time for breakfast," said the guard.

"I don't suppose French toast and bacon are on the menu?" "If you close your eyes and tell yourself that over and over, it might just be."

The guard tipped his hat and walked on. The buzzer sounded for the doors of the cell block to open, and one by one the inmates stepped out in line. When it was Kennedy's turn, he, too, stepped out. No one acknowledged him. Now that he was back on the floor, it created a more somber atmosphere. He took notice of all the new faces that had arrived as he walked up to the food line and grabbed a tray, pausing for a moment to survey the crowd.

Two inmates from behind shoved him out of line. He looked back and saw two younger men standing there. Both had shaven heads and wore flagrant Nazi symbols tattooed on their necks. He thought back to the letter he had received just a few moments earlier.

The inmate who pushed him brought himself chest to chest with Kennedy. The taste of BO swarmed his senses. The only thing worse than the man's stench was his arrogance.

"Sorry, old timer, but this is my spot."

Kennedy chose not to say anything. He went to step back in line behind them, but the other inmate thrust his hand out.

"Sorry, not there either, your spot is in the back." The two inmates high-fived each other.

He looked at them both intently. He noticed one of their prison suits bore the number 359389.

"Your number there," Kennedy said calmly, pointing. "On your clothes..."

"Yeah, you have one too, retard, very good."

He grinned. "That number you're wearing just got you killed."

"Fuck you!" shouted the inmate closest to him as he put his hand in Kennedy's face. Kennedy took his tray and drove it hard against the man's elbow. Briefly stunned, he lifted the tray again and struck the young man squarely in the face, forcing him to stumble backward and fall. All the other prisoners backed away from the scene except for the other offending inmate, who took a swing at Kennedy's head. He blocked the punch, grabbed his arm, twisted it, and snapped it with his forearm. With both men on the ground, he took out his spike and stabbed the man wearing 359389 repeatedly until blood poured to the ground and the life from his eyes melted away. Three guards came running up and tackled Kennedy to the ground; he immediately surrendered while the other bystanders were secured.

Robbins came running up from behind. "Go easy on Kennedy, he was attacked. I saw it."

The guards zip-tied his hands behind his back.

"Goddamn it, Kennedy!" one of them said while picking him up. "Do you *want* to spend the rest of your life in isolation?"

"One less Nazi to worry about."

"Yeah, yeah, they deserved it, right? That's what you always say."

A group of guards walked him back to isolation, where Robbins took over. He took the restraints off, and Kennedy willingly entered the cell.

Robbins looked at him before closing the door. "You're lucky you have so much respect in here. You better be careful though, Mark. Things change quickly."

Kennedy turned back toward the door. "Hopefully I'll be out of here before that happens."

"Yeah, right."

Robbins closed the door, then leaned down to the open slot. "I'll see what I can do to get you out of here as soon as possible."

"No rush," he replied indifferently.

The door locked. Back into the darkness. Kennedy sat down in the same bed he had woken up in less than an hour ago. He sighed as he began rubbing his fingers across a series of scars on his ribs. He was all about routine, and every time he came back to isolation, he couldn't help but think how he ended up in prison in the first place, as well as his first couple months at Firerock Maximum Security Prison. He allowed his mind to drift off to even darker times.

. . . . . .

It was May of 2001. Detective Mark Kennedy was found guilty of five counts of first-degree murder and one count of voluntary manslaughter of an Internal Affairs officer. The latter had been an accident, but he couldn't deny that it had looked intentional. One of the only people who knew the specific details of that night was his partner at the time, brand-new to the NYPD, Officer Will Sutherland, who tried to talk him out of it. He was a rookie. An idealist. The other was Victor Caprizzi, who was a nationally wanted felon. He convinced Kennedy it had to be done. Caprizzi was more than an unofficial partner; he was also a friend, and the two had done some impressive work together in disrupting organized crime in the state of New York. Their run ended with what was titled by the press as "The Mob Massacre." Caprizzi set it up, Kennedy executed. Five of the Atlantic Coast's top mob bosses were murdered. It was the first time he had ever taken justice into his own hands; it certainly would not be his last. His incarceration was immediate, with a sentence of twenty-five to life without early parole.

From the beginning of his imprisonment, his job was far from over. Caprizzi was going to continue to change the world from the outside, and Kennedy agreed to do his part to help him from the inside. He was given an assignment within the first couple months of his arrival. A man by the name of Jordan Rickstein had been arrested for raping the daughter of Brent Waters, the head of the Human Trafficking Division of the FBI. He would never forget that first letter that Guard Robbins delivered to him. A piece of paper with the rapist's name written on it. Kennedy knew what it meant. Jordan Rickstein had to go.

He thought it would be easy. Snatch him from the rec yard and break his skinny neck like a twig. Rickstein's face had been plastered all over the TV, and Kennedy was able to spot him almost immediately. He was tall and skinny, really skinny. His nose looked more like a beak. Everything about the man irked Kennedy. As he approached him to take care of business, a group of three white men, the shortest of whom was 6'2", 250 pounds—two inches taller than Kennedy and about fifty pounds heavier—surrounded him. Their names were Tomas, Kirk, and Smitty. Well-known bodyguards for hire.

Smitty, the biggest of the group, was quick to be verbally aggressive. "Keep your hands off Jordan or we'll break your fuckin' legs."

"You guys are speaking for that piece of shit?" Kennedy responded. "Why don't you let him tell me that to my face?"

"Because money on the outside gets you protection on the inside from punks!"

"Cop punks!" chimed in Rickstein loudly for all to hear.

Smitty continued, "Seeing as how you don't have any friends here, you might as well just walk away. Or stay and get your ass beat."

"Don't think I've forgotten about you, Kennedy!" spat Tomas. "Stay away from me, stay away from Jordan, or I'll make your life a living hell!"

Kennedy turned around. He was outmatched at the moment and didn't have much of a choice. He could hear the jeers behind him. "Dead man walkin'!" Another shouted, "Free pack of cigarettes for the first guy to rape the cop!" The inmates watching the scene could smell fresh blood in the water. Kennedy had failed to make the right first impression.

He went to bed that night thinking about how he was going to take Rickstein. Not following through wasn't an option. If Caprizzi needed this guy dead, then it had to be done. He fell asleep in deep thought without revealing a solution.

The next day he woke up at first light, cracked his neck, and exited his cell when prompted. The cell floor was busy that morning. He had walked by a dozen or so rooms when he heard his name softly spoken. He stopped and listened carefully. He could hear inmates babbling about something and then again, as clear as day, his name was whispered. He turned around and took a few steps toward the cell where the talking seemed to have come from.

"Don't think I won't tear you apart, motherfucker!" he said in his best voice of intimidation as he stepped up to the room.

He gazed in to see a tall inmate by the name of DeMarius calmly standing against the wall. He knew something bad was coming. From behind, Tomas, Kirk, and Smitty tackled him into the cell. Several other taller inmates, including DeMarius, stood in front of the scene so as to obscure anyone's view of the beating. Tomas got behind Kennedy, put a plastic bag around his head, and picked him up clear off the ground. The other two grabbed his flailing arms. Instantly the bag filled with moisture from his attempts at gasping for air. Rickstein's shadow approached him from the front and punched him hard in the stomach, stealing from him the last bit of breath he had managed to hold on to. Rickstein then took out a shiv crafted from a piece of wood and quickly stabbed Kennedy three times along the right side of his ribcage.

Desperation setting in, Kennedy forced his heel directly into Tomas' groin, a lucky shot. As soon as his feet touched the ground, he lifted his left foot and with a swift kick broke Kirk's leg just below the knee. He then grabbed and pulled the very powerful Smitty on top of him, preferring the goliath's punches to Rickstein's shiv.

From across the cellblock, Robbins could make out what was clearly a skirmish behind a line of inmates. He scanned the block for Kennedy and couldn't find him.

"Code black 218-E!" he screamed into his radio. He and several other guards sprinted to the main floor. The inmates blocking the cell quickly disbursed as the guards arrived on scene. Robbins got there first and without hesitation he dove into Rickstein, knocking the shiv away from him. The other guards grabbed Smitty and separated him from Kennedy with a couple of well-placed baton hits.

"Kennedy!" Robbins yelled. "Kennedy, are you okay?"

He couldn't respond. Between the deficit of oxygen and the acute loss of blood, he was left too weak to talk.

The last thing he remembered was Robbins' voice over the commotion calling for medical. Not able to fight the urge to sleep, he closed his eyes and passed out.

. . . . . .

Kennedy awoke to the sound of heart monitors and a sharp pain on the right side of his chest. He looked down to see an attractive younger nurse changing the dressing over the puncture wounds.

"Can you finish that later?" said Kennedy groggily.

The nurse looked up, startled. "Sorry, I, uh, I'll just be a minute, I promise."

Kennedy ignored her for a moment before asking her the next question. "How am I doing?"

"You've been pretty out of it for a couple days. But you're stable now."

Kennedy was lucky to be alive and he knew that. He was surprised he had been out for that long.

"You should get hurt more often," said the blushing nurse.

"What?"

"Well, only if it means I get to help you for a few minutes. It's kinda cool treating someone with the reputation you have."

"Oh. Well, fuck, in that case I'll do my best to get the shit kicked out of me a few more times, just for you."

Offended and a bit scared, the nurse fled the room as Robbins entered.

"Kennedy, you're awake."

He motioned for Robbins to come closer and spoke in a soft whisper. "I'm sure I'll be getting discharged here in a day or two. You have to get those four cocksuckers in a room together. Make sure they're alone."

Robbins looked around cautiously. "C'mon, Kennedy. One near-death experience is enough. You can't take those four guys—it's a death wish."

"I'm going to die anyway if I don't destroy them for everyone to see. Just set it up. Please."

"It's suicide, and I'm not going to be the one to make it happen. Besides, do you know what Caprizzi would—"

"Shhh, don't say that name out loud. Look, this is my call. Don't forget what I did for you. You owe me this."

Robbins stood back up and walked to the door.

Before leaving he turned around. "I'll see what I can arrange. I hope it's worth it."

Kennedy nodded at him and thought, *You and me both.*

. . . . . .

Much to Kennedy's chagrin, he was discharged back to Firerock the next day. Robbins personally met him at the transport van. He stepped down and they locked eyes. Kennedy's look was uncompromising. At first Robbins directed his attention away as if to avoid the silent conversation, but then he looked back and gave him a nod.

"You're late for laundry detail, Kennedy," he said loudly in front of several other guards. "Better get you over there."

Kennedy glanced at them to see how they would react to the strangely out-of-place comment. One by one they, too, silently nodded.

Kennedy chuckled. "Okay then, laundry detail it is."

Robbins took his restraints off and escorted him down a series of back hallways away from the main cellblocks and straight to the laundry room. Kennedy, relaxed and calm, followed behind. As they walked in silence, he became acutely aware of the stitches still in his side; there was no time to worry about that now. After winding halfway across Firerock, they arrived at their destination. He looked through the small window of the laundry room door and saw the four men who had nearly killed him. They were laughing and enjoying the easy day's work, cleaning clothes and folding linens as Rickstein cackled with glee over something. He wouldn't be so happy for very long.

Robbins stepped in front of the door.

"Take this." He handed him a knife.

"No, I might accidently kill one of them quickly with that."

"You're insane, Kennedy."

"Get out of my way," he said sternly. "I will be fine. Those four in there I can't say the same for. Don't come in until I come out."

Robbins subtly shook his head and stepped aside. Kennedy entered.

Rickstein was the first to look up. "Well, well, well. It must be my birthday," he chirped with his deep southern twang. "Ladies and gentlemen, Detective Mark Kennedy!"

Tomas and Smitty walked in front of Rickstein. Kirk limped in last with a cast around his leg. Looks of disbelief on all their faces.

"You really do want to die, don't you, pig?" snarled Tomas.

Kennedy didn't respond, his palms moist with anticipation.

"I'm sure Smitty over here will be happy to finish the job," said Kirk.

Smitty, the biggest and ugliest of the three, smiled through broken teeth. The three men spread out and began their predatory descent upon him. Kirk grabbed a sheet and wrapped it around both of his hands, creating a weapon of strangulation. Tomas picked up a broom that was lying on the ground and broke it to create a sharp edge. The three encircled him. Once they were maximally spread out, Kennedy ran directly up the middle at Smitty. Smitty charged back as the other two closed in from behind. Kennedy grabbed himself a sheet, and as Smitty went for a knockout swing, he slid to the ground, wrapped the sheet around one of Smitty's feet, and popped up behind, pulling the sheet as hard as he could, which sent the large man tumbling to the ground. Kennedy quickly stomped once hard on his face as Tomas took a jab with the broom handle. Kennedy dodged the swing, grabbed Tomas' arm, and shattered it while taking the sharpened broom handle away from him. Kirk managed to get behind Kennedy and wrapped the sheet around his neck. Kennedy quickly shoved the sharp end of the broom deep into his stomach. Kirk stepped back in shock while Rickstein made a desperate run for the door; it was locked. From the hallway Guard Robbins peered inside. He looked at Rickstein for a moment, then turned his gaze away from the massacre.

Kennedy grabbed on to the broom handle lodged inside Kirk and half ran, half carried him across the room to the adjacent wall. He then ripped the wooden handle out and shoved the sharp end of it into his throat. Blood sprayed the wall behind him as Kirk slowly sank to the ground.

Kennedy focused his attention at Tomas, whose useless arm was greatly impeding his efforts at crawling to the back of the room where the other half of the broomstick lay. Kennedy walked over to him and grabbed his legs. He began kicking and screaming.

"Don't hurt me! No! I'm sorry!"

"You're sorry? That's pathetic."

Kennedy pinned his right leg to the ground with his own and broke his ankle. Tomas was left screaming in the corner. Kennedy pondered how he was going to kill him when Smitty, who had regained his ability to stand, landed a punch to the back of Kennedy's head, then bear-hugged him from behind. Rickstein, realizing the advantage had shifted, came running over from the door to help. Kennedy lifted his legs and kicked Rickstein in the face, sending him head first to the ground. As Kennedy's legs came back toward the floor, he used the momentum to snap his head back into Smitty's mouth. Kennedy turned around and with all his body weight tackled him to the ground. He began punching. And then he punched more. Over and over again he ruthlessly smashed Smitty's head in to the concrete. Covered in blood, he wiped a splatter away from his eyes and stood up. He casually walked over to the last of the living bodyguards writhing on the ground. He recovered the broomstick, still in Kirk's neck, on his way over. Kennedy straddled him, pinning him to the ground.

Tomas tried to speak but stumbled over his words. "Pl-pl…I…swear… Kenn…plea…"

"Shhhh," he responded gently.

He wound his arm up and plunged the broomstick down just behind his collarbone. The man let out a bloodcurdling scream, so Kennedy put his hand over his mouth and sat there for a moment until his body went limp. Kennedy stood up and took a deep breath. He turned to face the door and saw the white-faced, trembling Rickstein wedged into the front corner of the room.

"Whoa!" Kennedy shouted out. "You scared me! I forgot you were still here."

"Look," responded Rickstein in a trembling voice, "I can get you things, anything, I promise."

"Is that the line that Brent Waters' daughter used to try to stop you from raping her?"

In between sobs Rickstein pleaded for his life. "I'm sick, man… I need help, you know… Please, just don't…don't hurt me."

"Yes, Jordan. Yes, you are sick. Just think of this as me curing you of your illness."

From outside Robbins could hear the desperate screams of Rickstein as Kennedy went to work on him. The torture lasted for several minutes. The screams turned into a series of whimpers, then silence. Robbins sighed and wiped a bead of sweat off his forehead. A knock from the door sounded. He opened it to reveal a blood-covered Kennedy.

"I'd like to go to solitary confinement now," he said with apathy. "Just till things settle down."

"Uh, yeah, I can arrange that," said Robbins. He radioed in: "Robbins to Johnson, come in…"

"Go ahead, Robbins."

"I've got a prisoner transport from laundry to iso, prisoner 454811."

"Copy that; we're ready for you."

Robbins gave his attention back to Kennedy, who was calm as could be. "I need to put you in restraints."

"Of course." Kennedy complied and allowed himself to be cuffed. "Can we walk by the other cells? Let people see me."

"Yeah, that's, uh, no problem. We'll take the scenic route."

Before leaving, Robbins peeked into the laundry room. Rickstein was propped up on a chair in the middle of the carnage-filled room. There was a sign written on his lap. *Mark Kennedy was here.*

Robbins closed the door and radioed in once more. "Transporting prisoner now, laundry room is open for general detail."

. . . . . .

Although the thought of spending more time in solitary confinement was anything but cheerful, the memory of ending Rickstein all those years ago came with a sense of accomplishment. It was dark out. He had been lost in thought for quite some time. He crawled over to his bed, pulled the blanket up around him, and started thinking about all the things he was going to do when he got out, thoughts that were a part of his everyday routine.

CHAPTER 2

RACHEL DAVIS

New Beginnings

"Dad! Let's go! I don't want to be late!" yelled Rachel from the foot of the long marble stairs leading up to her parents' bedroom.

"I'm coming, I'm coming!" he shouted back. "Just looking for the camera."

Rachel turned to her mom. "Is he going to stall all day?"

"Go easy on your father today. He feels like he's losing his daughter. You'll understand when you're a parent."

"No one's losing me," she responded as she pulled her long chestnut brown hair into a ponytail. "I'm going to be twenty minutes down the road."

"Yeah, but you're a college girl now. He no longer sees you as his 'little girl.'"

Rachel rolled her eyes.

"Just cut him a little bit of slack. He's going to miss you. We're both going to miss you."

"Okay, I'll ignore the meltdown," she said to her mom but then raised her voice so her father could hear, "but if I'm the last one in the dorm, I'm going to look like an idiot!"

Mr. Davis came down the steps with the camera. "Found it, I'm ready. Oh, you know what though; I think I left my Harvard hat upstairs."

Mrs. Davis put her hand on her husband's shoulder. "Forget about the hat, honey."

Mr. Davis sighed. "You're right, we should go. I would hate for Rachel to become the least popular student at Boston University after just one day."

"Ha, ha, very funny," Rachel said sarcastically. "Everyone in the car though, seriously, chop chop."

The three of them exited the massive home as their chauffeur pulled in front to pick them up. Rachel grew up in a small suburb of Boston called Jamaica Plains. Her father, a doctor at Massachusetts General Hospital, and her mother, the vice president of a large advertisement agency downtown, had moved into the home right when Rachel was born. With their hard-earned money they lived very comfortably. The 2.5 million-dollar home they lived in was complete with a jungle-themed outdoor pool and Jacuzzi, a personal chef, and a bedroom for Rachel the size of most living rooms.

As she silently looked back at the house to give a silent good-bye, she found it hard to believe she was off to college. Her father was a Harvard Medical School graduate, but she refused to ride his coattails. She wanted to make her own legacy, find her own path. Boston University was perfect: beautiful campus, great law program, which was her true passion, and a whole new life. Even with the excitement of her first day of independence, she couldn't help but think about her time in high school. She truly had loved the last four years of her life. She was prom queen two years in a row, 3.8 GPA, star player for the Jamaica Plain's High School varsity soccer team. The whole high school experience came to a perfect end with a graduation bash at her parents' house. She had been playing hard to get with the crush of her life, Caleb Gauge, the captain of the boys' soccer team, and that very night they had slept together. In her mind it was the perfect end to high school and the perfect beginning of being an adult college woman. She was going to miss the old days.

They climbed into the Town Car and pulled away from her home. The car smoothly traveled down the long, winding cobblestone driveway as the house disappeared from sight.

As they turned the corner to head toward downtown, the chauffeur was forced to slam the brakes abruptly, sending everyone in the car lurching forward. A black Mustang had nearly rammed into them. Most of the windows in the car were tinted, but she did get a good look at the driver. His hair was slicked back, and he had a pale complexion. His eyes hid behind tiny round sunglasses.

"What a jerk!" exclaimed Mr. Davis. "Classic asshole Massachusetts driver."

"Dad, you're a classic Massachusetts driver."

"When I drive, I'm an assertive driver, not a Masshole like that guy."

"Whatever you say." Rachel took out her phone and started flipping through pictures: her friends dressed up for prom, her golden retriever Dexter dressed up as an elf for their annual Christmas party, her and her parents at their lake house.

"Look at this one," she said, holding the phone out to her father. "Do you remember that?"

"I sure do, last summer. How great was that weekend?"

Her stroll down memory lane was interrupted as they drove by a sign standing across the street: *Boston University, 1 mile.*

Mr. Davis began to get emotional. "Now, Rachel, I just want to tell you a few things before we get to campus."

"Are you crying? Mom, is he seriously crying?"

She looked at her mom, who also had tears forming in the corner of her eyes.

Mr. Davis continued, "You are going to do great things here. But just be sure to be careful. Don't trust any boys who seem interested in you. They only want one thing."

"I know, Dad, you've been planting that thought in my head since junior year. You know how responsible I am." The thought of Caleb Gauge flashed back into her mind and she blushed. She didn't like to lie to her parents, but they just didn't understand what it was like to be a young adult. *Besides,* she thought, *my life is my life at this point.*

Her father continued, "I know, it's just, college is different, and you have to keep your head on your shoulders. Don't ever lose touch of who you are."

The Town Car pulled up to her dorm room. "I know, but really, I'm super late. My other two roommates probably already have all their stuff moved in."

Mr. Davis nodded. "Okay, yeah, let's get you moved in."

Mr. and Mrs. Davis took a moment to regain their composure while Rachel quickly began unpacking the trunk with the help of the driver.

A moment later Mr. Davis got out of the car and grabbed a nearby cart. He helped her load it to the brim. "Geez, did you pack the entire house? You didn't take the plasma TV, did you?"

"No, I left that behind with a video from my third-grade dance recital cued up so you would have something to remember me by," she said, flashing a pearly white grin.

Mr. Davis had to smile. "Point taken."

Once everything was packed, the Davis family made their way into the dorm and to the room that Rachel would be spending the next two semesters in. Just as she had suspected, her two roommates had already moved in all their belongings and were busy chatting about the boys down the hallway. Mr. Davis was first to the door.

"Knock, knock, the Davises are here!"

Rachel pulled her mom close. "You need to get control over him."

"I will, just let him have a moment and then I'll whisk him away, I promise."

Mr. Davis walked right up to the girls. "I'm Stan Davis, it's a pleasure to meet you both." He shook their hands.

The two girls stood up. "Hi, Mr. Davis," said the first. "My name is Alicia. It's really nice to meet you." She extended her hand for a shake. "And this must be Rachel the roommate?"

Rachel responded, "That's me! Sorry about my father, he's having a bit of a rough day."

"That's okay." She laughed. "You should have seen my dad, far worse, I promise. Cute dress by the way, love the flower print."

"Ahem," Mr. Davis coughed. "I'm still in the room, so no trash talking us fathers of the world."

"Sweetie, let's grab your allergy cover and get that on the bed and then we'll go," suggested Mrs. Davis.

The two roommates giggled while Mr. Davis clumsily began taking the mattress off the frame. "That's a great idea, we can help you with that," he said enthusiastically. "We wouldn't want to make Rachel and Alicia and…" he said, looking at the third roommate.

"Betsy. I'm Betsy. Sorry, I'm awful at introductions."

"No problem. Betsy, what a nice name."

Rachel buried her head in her hands for a moment while Mrs. Davis then got introduced to everyone in the room.

Finally she had had enough. "Okay! Dad, Mom, thank you for all your help. I think we got it, so let's head back to the car, I'll grab the last of the stuff, and then I'll see you guys soon."

Mr. Davis, realizing the extent to which his daughter wanted to start her college career, finally submitted. "Yeah, we don't want to overstay our welcome. You three have a lot of gossiping to do." He turned to the roommates. "It was great meeting you two, have a great semester. I'm a doctor at MGH, so if you need anything let me know. I'm sure we'll be seeing more of you guys, I mean girls, or whatever you'd prefer to be called."

Again the girls giggled as they waved good-bye.

The Davises walked down to the car and loaded the final cart. As they finished with the last few items, a group of freshman boys began cheering and yelling from the top window of the dorm. The three of them as well as some scattered onlookers took notice of a large sign with the words: BRING US YOUR DAUGHTERS!

"I think I'm going to be sick," Mrs. Davis said. Up to this point she had held herself together quite well.

Rachel snickered at the sign.

"It's a joke, you two," reassured Mr. Davis. "Probably some immature bet. Eighteen-year-old kids unsupervised for the first time, I'd expect nothing less. Make sure you hang out with boys from the math club and stay away from whatever floor that is."

"You got it, Dad, I promise."

She went over to him and gave him a big hug and a big kiss on the cheek.

"So this is it, eh?"

"Don't worry, I'll be home sometime in the next couple weeks, I promise. I'll tell you about all my classes and friends and how great a job you two did raising me."

"I'll look forward to it." He gave her a big squeeze back.

"I love you, honey," said Mrs. Davis.

"I love you too, Mom." They hugged for a moment and then Rachel was off toward her room.

"Don't forget to carry your key on a lanyard; you don't want to lose them," shouted Mr. Davis.

"No worries, Dad."

"And, honey, make sure you wear sandals in the showers here. God only knows what ends up on those floors," shouted Mrs. Davis.

"Yeah, I can't imagine. I'll be sure to wear 'em."

She gave one last wave and disappeared into the housing complex.

"There goes our little girl."

"There goes our college girl."

Not being able to be any prouder of their daughter, they hugged each other, got back in the car, and with their driver made their way back to their grand home in Jamaica Plains.

CHAPTER 3

DETECTIVE WILL SUTHERLAND

Frustrations Part I

It was 2:33 a.m. and Detective William Sutherland had just gotten called to the scene of a double homicide in the woods along the eastern edge of Brattleboro, Vermont. The scene involved one male victim in his mid thirties and one female victim around the same age. He had been informed on his way that they had been stabbed a combined sixteen times, and the male victim had a gunshot wound to his right kneecap. He pulled up to where the bodies had been dumped along a back road. It was below freezing out, and in his haste to get to the scene, he had grabbed the wrong jacket. The one he brought was fleece; no way it would hold up against the cold for very long. He reached across the seat and pulled an insulated skull cap to cover his shortly trimmed blond hair. *God, I hope this doesn't take too long,* he thought. He stepped out of the warmth of his car and into the brisk early morning air.

Detective Sutherland wasn't the most intimidating member of the Vermont State Police, but he was thought of as one of the best. Physically fit, agile, he modeled himself more like a Marine than a cop; but everyone knew it was his passion for the law and unmatched motivation that were his greatest assets.

The snow overlying layers of ice made it difficult for him to reach the bodies, but as he crunched through the woods, it became immediately apparent that the murder had taken place elsewhere. Although the area would have allowed for enough privacy to commit such a violent crime, there was not a drop of blood at the scene. Stories like this had become increasingly routine throughout the region. A lot of his investigations led back to narcotic trafficking as the trade between Montreal and the Eastern Seaboard seemed to be making a disturbing push. Sutherland was intent on curbing the amount of felony level activity throughout the state, and his eyes were set on Uptown, the massive state-of-the-art casino that was erected in 2003 in the southern part of Vermont. Not everyone saw eye to eye with him on the legitimacy of his Uptown theory. The vast majority of his colleagues and other local and federal agencies believed the correlation between Uptown's existence and the increase in criminal activity to be a combination of coincidence and the simple fact that the casino attracted a very diverse group of people. As it was explained to him, time and time again, this would naturally increase the crime rates in the area. Sutherland wasn't convinced the coincidence was so benign. He did know one fact for sure: The casino made the state a lot of money, and the men making the decisions far above his pay grade weren't keen on his aggressive slant toward Uptown. Even the DA's office—led by Dan Peterson, who was his theory's most adamant naysayer—felt it a waste of time and resources. Sutherland was fortunate to have been given clearance from his direct superiors on sending in an undercover unit there. The only reason Officer Ryan McDonough was able to be deployed undercover was due to his painstaking efforts to reveal that there were a number of employees who had ties to organized crime, mostly out of New York and New Jersey, as well as a couple who ran with the disbanded Uptown Gang nearly a decade ago. So far the operation had yielded very little pertinent information.

As he approached the bodies amidst about a dozen other law enforcement personnel, his phone rang.

He answered, "Hey, how's it going, Jules, sorry, Ms. Romano? Just getting done with work? That's a long day... What are you up to tonight? Busy? Okay, we'll hook up sometime later in the week... Sound good? Perfect, see you soon, sexy."

The other officers eavesdropped and couldn't help themselves from giving him a hard time.

"Hey, Sutherland!" one of them shouted. "Is this one old enough to drink yet?"

The murmur of laughter was interrupted by another officer. "How much are you payingfor her company? Is it by the hour or by the day?"

Sutherland was fine with the criticism. Although he normally hated bringing up women in front of the other men, this one he was actually pretty invested in for more than one reason. Yes, she was gorgeous and they had a great time when they spent time together. But more important to him was the fact that she was an employee of Uptown and her connections there made his access much easier. Jules Romano was his ace in the hole should he ever need to use it.

On the coldest of nights, he could always distract himself from the numbness of his toes with the first official encounter he had with her. He was investigating a petty theft at the Uptown casino. She greeted him at the front door and told him if there was anything he needed not to hesitate to ask. She gave him a look that gave him goose bumps, a look he would never forget. From that day on he couldn't stop thinking about her: Her wavy, burgundy-red hair, sexy figure, exotic eyes. Her confidence was tangible. Two days later he went back to the casino pretending to follow up on the investigation, she saw right through it, and the next thing he knew they were on date number one.

"Hey, Jimmy," he called out to the senior trooper, Jim Konine. Konine had transferred from the Boston Police Department the year he was promoted to detective. "What are the details here?"

"Two bodies, man and a woman, both wearing wedding rings so presumably married. No tire tracks coming in, no tire tracks going out, not a shred of evidence around, but we'll get a better look in the woods at first light."

"Identification? Wallets?"

"Nothing like that, no."

"Any sign of a struggle?"

"Nope, bodies were definitely dumped here. The wounds suggest either a hell of an overkill with the gunshot to the guy's knee, probably to prevent him from being mobile, or—"

"Torture scenario," Sutherland interrupted. "Maybe trying to get information or justtrying to send a message. This looks exactly like that body we saw a couple months ago, you remember?"

"Yeah, the Italiano with the big beard, beat up pretty bad. You think it's drug related like that was?"

"Narcotics or not, I think it's Uptown related."

Another trooper came up from behind. "Uptown the casino? I thought that investigation had come and gone."

Sutherland gave him a once-over. He was about six feet tall, trim, and baby-faced. He didn't have a spot of facial hair, and Sutherland was convinced even if he tried to grow some, he'd be unsuccessful. "And you are..."

"Sorry, sir, Trooper Dominick out of the Brattleboro barracks, just started a few weeks ago. Trooper Konine is my training officer."

"Well, listen to everything this man says," Sutherland replied, pointing at Konine. "He'll teach you a few things."

"Speaking of teaching a few things," said Konine. "I'd like to piggyback the Uptown comment."

"Go on."

"We pulled one thing from the body, a receipt tucked into his boxers."

"A receipt? Okay, tell me more."

"A thousand dollars withdrawn from an ATM at Uptown."

"It's a good thing I hate coincidences; otherwise, I'd be able to convince myself to let that go like Trooper Dominick probably would have."

Konine gave a chuckle. He didn't laugh at much, but he and Sutherland had been close for several years. Konine had helped him with a lot of investigations, including those revolving around Uptown, despite the many migraine-producing obstacles they had to—and continued to have to—jump through to get cooperation from the state's side. Usually by now Sutherland would have made some sort of jab at his thick mustache, but the fact was that he was so cold he really just wanted to get the details of the murder and get back in his cruiser.

Sutherland strolled around the bodies, closely analyzing the scene. They had been dumped one on top of another, lying underneath a tarp. He exposed their brutally assaulted faces.

"Wow, you weren't fucking around, that's pretty bad. This certainly seems like more of a message."

"I agree, but what's the message?"

"Fuck with us and you're dead."

He pondered the layout of the crime for a moment.

"I don't suppose there could have been any witnesses out here, nearby homes, cabins?"

"What do you think?"

"Nothing's easy," he replied. "How about the bodies, find anything besides the receipt?"

"We checked both the bodies out. Nothing on either of them to give us any other clues so far. Not a hair, not a fiber, nothing but a little dried-up blood."

"Let's get them packed up and identified. As soon as information comes in from the autopsy, I want it in my hand. What's the date on the receipt?"

"Last night," chimed in Dominick.

"Okay, clearly the investigation starts there. I want to sit down with Mr. Fontaine, see if he has anything useful to say."

Konine gave a stern look. "You know I hate that prick as much as you do, but the Sergeant said to leave Fontaine alone unless he signs off on it."

"You can take the backburner on this one if you want."

Konine wasn't going to miss the opportunity to ruffle some feathers at Uptown.

"I'm with you until we're forced into early retirement, Will. You haven't been wrong since I've known you. I think if we're going to make a play though, we better make it a hard one."

Sutherland agreed. The clock was ticking and it was time to start making some bolder moves.

"Okay, I'll pick you up first thing in the morning. In the meantime, Trooper Dominick, I want you to personally see to it that these bodies get to the medical examiner. I want to know what type of knife was used. I want this scene combed over again at first light. The smallest details are what I'm looking for. Get this tarp to our crime scene guys."

"The tarp, sir?" questioned Dominick.

"The tarp is the only thing we have that the murderer graciously gave to us. If there's a clue somewhere on it, under it, within it, I want to know about it."

"I'll keep you updated, sir."

Sutherland briskly walked back to his cruiser to escape the cold. Wide awake, he decided to head to the twenty-four-hour gym to fully process the murder scene. Besides that, the excitement he had over going to Uptown the next day would prevent him from anything resembling sleep.

Micky Fontaine's balls are mine, he said to himself as he drove off toward town.

CHAPTER 4

MARK KENNEDY

Freedom Comes at a Price

The sound of the heavy solitary confinement door unlocking startled Kennedy. Seeing the warden's wrinkled face appear in the doorway was equally as startling. Kennedy stood up and waited to be addressed.

"Mark, nice to see you. I was a bit disappointed to hear about the incident in the cafeteria but glad to see you're okay."

"Thank you, sir."

The warden walked into the cell with Guard Robbins following behind. He could see four other guards waiting outside the cell.

"I have some news for you, Mark. I think you're going to like it."

He had Kennedy's full attention.

"You're getting released."

"W-what?" he stumbled.

"Released from Firerock."

"Really?" He could barely contain his emotions. Caprizzi had somehow finally come through. He took a moment to recompose himself. "When?"

"Today, right now. Would you like me to come back later?"

"No, no. This is…good. Just…"

"Unexpected?" said the warden, finishing his sentence.

"Yeah, unexpected. Who do I owe a favor to?"

"We here at the correctional facility are on a need-to-know basis on matters like this. All we were told is that a representative from the Federal Bureau of Investigation is here to speak to you, and he will be taking you into his custody."

"The FBI?"

"The FBI," repeated the warden. "Mark, you should know that this is a temporary release. They need your help for the next undetermined amount of time with something, if you're willing. If you're not, you don't have to go."

"I'll help in any way I can."

"Okay, let's get you over to holding, get the papers worked up, and get you introduced to the Bureau liaison."

Kennedy, still in a small degree of shock, looked at Robbins, who gave a subtle shrug. He was made to put on the icy, rugged restraints once again for transport through the facility. Along with the warden and the group of guards, they walked back toward the general cell population. The last section of hallway was A-Block. It housed some of the more lethal prisoners. They traveled it in silence to the sound of other inmates' perverse threats. The jailhouse was ablaze with energy as those who were incarcerated still wanted their opportunity to physically, if not at least psychologically, harm him.

One prisoner slammed himself against his jail cell. "You better PRAY you don't come back here, Kennedy. I'll fuckin' torture you!"

"You think they'd be happier that I'm leaving," he said under his breath to the entourage of guards.

The group chuckled as they escorted Kennedy to the end of the hallway and through a set of secured doors. On the other side he was led to a holding room so his possessions could be collected and brought to him. The smell of sanitized grime from the prison was replaced with the scent of artificial raspberry air freshener. Kennedy honestly didn't know which one he preferred.

"So, Mark," said the warden, "you wait here. I'm going to let the FBI come in and explain the situation to you. Just sit tight."

Kennedy was left alone. In the far corner of the room, a video camera caught his eye. As he looked at it he could see the lens zooming in on him. He slowly raised his hand and gave it the middle finger.

The door to the holding room opened and in walked a well-dressed man in his forties. Kennedy immediately felt he recognized him. His hair was neatly combed with a side part. He had about a day's growth of facial hair, and he looked rugged and tired, or maybe that was just his face. He had a very serious way about him. This was clearly not a friendly visit.

"Mr. Kennedy," he began. "I am Agent Brent Waters. It's a pleasure to meet you."

Once he heard the name, it immediately registered who he was talking to. Brent Waters, the head of the Human Trafficking Division for the FBI. The man whose daughter's rape he avenged ten years ago. This visit was very intentional.

"Agent Waters, it's a pleasure to meet you," replied Kennedy. "I was told an FBI liaison would be here, not the head of an entire Federal division."

"Well, the nature of the opportunity you're being given is a bit sensitive. A bit over the clearance of a liaison."

"Is that my stuff?" he said, pointing to a bag that Waters had brought in with him.

"It is, not much here. The clothes you came in with, a watch, a wallet. If you decide you'd be interested in helping us, I'm sure we can get you some better clothes and accessories."

"So exactly what is it that I can help the FBI with?"

"I understand you know quite a bit about a man named Victor Caprizzi. Is that correct?"

Where is this going?

"I did, yeah, a long time ago."

"He's dead."

Kennedy was floored. He had no idea, and the dozens upon dozens of letters he had received for the last decade hadn't given any clue to such an event. It was possible he had missed it amongst the many hidden messages and codes.

"Any idea how?"

"A criminal informant of the Bureau shot him in the head. He then fell one hundred feet off a bridge into the Connecticut River. There are sections of that river that are notorious for aggressive whirlpool formations. Bodies get sucked in, they don't get found, so it wasn't a huge surprise when his didn't turn up."

That stupid prick. He never knew when enough was enough.

"Sounds like he got what was coming to him. What does it have to do with me? I clearly didn't do it."

"It is the belief of the FBI that Mr. Caprizzi was involved in some pretty serious crimes."

"How serious?"

"Human trafficking."

"No way," Kennedy was quick to answer. "Victor was a lot of things, but human trafficking? No fucking way."

"Like I said, it is the belief of the FBI that perhaps he was. With his death, we lose the only lead we had."

"So let me repeat myself; how can I help?"

"First I need to know if you want to help, Mr. Kennedy."

Kennedy leaned forward in his chair.

"Of course I do. My hands are at your disposal." He lifted his restraints.

Waters looked at the one-way glass on the wall behind him. "Let's get the restraints off of Mr. Kennedy please."

A security guard walked in and unbound Kennedy. He rubbed his wrists. "So, let's get to business."

"Not here. We have a transport vehicle waiting for you. Fresh clothes, an air-conditioned car, coffee if you want it. You'll be debriefed once you've reached the secure location."

Kennedy, confused by what the details of his release could possibly be, went to stand up.

"One more thing," said Waters. "You need to sign some papers defining the terms of your release. Also that I will be personally taking responsibility for you and that once we have what we need, you will return to this facility to serve out the rest of your sentence, which I hear has grown quite long."

Kennedy peered into his eyes. "Yeah, I've added a few years doing some favors for some people."

Without a reaction, Waters stood up and handed Kennedy a pen and put the papers in front of him. He signed the documents.

"Your car will meet you at the front gate in ten minutes. Say your goodbyes, get changed, and don't keep them waiting."

Waters grabbed his briefcase and left the room.

Kennedy reached into the bag he had left behind. He sorted through his old clothes and from the bottom he pulled out the gold and silver watch his father had given him many years ago. Robbins entered the room.

"Released, eh?"

"For now." Kennedy's attention returned to the paper bag. "So this is it? This is all I own in the world?"

"Here's a few more things, at least while you've earned some temporary freedom," Robbins said, handing him a stack of clothes. "Make sure everything fits. Take advantage of your time."

Kennedy gave a half smile. "Why take care of me all these years? After the Rickstein thing you didn't owe me anything further."

"You remember that kid you took care of for like five years, what was his name?"

"Alonso Vega."

"That's right, Alonso. He was a good kid. You saw that and you helped him survive this place. You're a good man, Mark. You may not fit into this system we have, but in your own system that you have created? You're a hero."

"Thanks, Robbins."

"So anyway, you hear that I'm getting transferred?"

"Really? Thank God I'm leaving. What would I do without you?"

"No shit."

"Where you headed?"

"Vermont, smaller prison there, better benefits, less hours."

"Good for you, Robbins."

"Good luck, Detective," he said with a warm handshake. He then left the room.

Kennedy took the tan slacks and white button-down shirt and put them on. He neatly tucked the shirt in and headed down toward the secured main front door to the prison.

"Enjoy your time, Mr. Kennedy," came the distorted voice of the gate guard over the speaker. The door opened and he walked down the last little bit of Firerock territory. His anxiety was on the rise as he hadn't had any meaningful time to analyze the situation that was unfolding. He walked up to the front gate and made the satisfying, albeit terrifying, step into freedom.

For a savory moment he took in a deep breath and filled his lungs with fresh air. For the first time in years, he genuinely smiled. Not a moment later a black Lincoln Navigator pulled up with Vermont license plates. Immediately Kennedy's smile melted and his mind went racing back to the reality of his circumstances.

The man driving the Lincoln was a younger Italian-looking male, well dressed. He had a big smile on his face and was clearly talking to whoever was in back.

Well, this certainly has a bad feeling to it.

The car came to a stop and the back door opened. From the poorly lit rear the familiar, unforgettable voice of Sammy Sorenteen rang out from within.

"Kennedy, get in the car," he commanded in a thick, monotone, New York accent.

Sorenteen was the dirty work, hands-on, extremely talented, and personal bodyguard of the now deceased Victor Caprizzi. The last time Kennedy had seen him was the night before the mob massacre. He couldn't stand Sorenteen, but Caprizzi always swore by him.

His arrival to pick him up on an FBI-mandated release was nothing short of mind numbing.

"Sammy Sorenteen, anyone else in there with you?" Kennedy asked.

"Just me, get in."

"At this point I'm seriously debating just going back to my cell."

"You have five seconds to get your ass in the car," Sorenteen replied. "Don't be fucking stupid; we play for the same team."

"What team is that?"

He didn't respond. Kennedy stalled for a moment, and without any other choice he entered the car. Sorenteen was sitting facing him. He wore a black trench coat with a nice-looking gray suit under it. His completely bald head looked polished from rubbing against the top of the car. Sorenteen was a machine.

"Where are we off to?" Kennedy asked, knowing there wouldn't be a clear answer.

"You can't know where you're going; however, you have one opportunity, right now, to decide not to go where this car is headed. Do you understand?"

"Is there another option?"

"Run. Run as fast as those legs can carry you and pray that the snipers hit you square in the chest and that you don't suffer for very long."

Kennedy shook his head and looked out the window.

"Good choice. Roderick, let's go," he said to the driver.

The car started up and began pulling away. The Firerock State Penitentiary slowly disappeared from the horizon.

"You hear Victor's dead?" asked Kennedy.

"Old news."

"Who?"

"Who what?"

"Stop fucking around. Who did it?"

"We're not here to discuss Victor."

"I thought that was exactly why I was here."

"No more talking until we get to where we're going."

Kennedy's anger flared. Caprizzi had promised him that he would be the one getting him out of jail when the time was right. Now Caprizzi was dead, the FBI was involved, and Sorenteen was keeping his mouth shut.

"You're not in charge here, Sorenteen."

"Did I say I was?"

"You're sure as hell acting like it."

"A lot has happened in the last ten years, Kennedy—"

"Yeah, a lot has happened! I've murdered my way through a decade of living! I sacrificed EVERYTHING! I'm the guy that's been on the FRONT LINES! So how about a little respect!"

"You don't know what you're talking abo—"

"Do I look like I'm someone you're going to be able to trust at this point? Do I seem like I just spent the last ten years living in paradise?"

Sorenteen merely crossed his legs and stared at him. Kennedy had nothing more to say. His instincts told him that leaving the prison was a poor decision. His burning curiosity kept him in the car.

Within twenty minutes they pulled up to a small air strip. A large private jet was waiting and the engines running.

While pushing Kennedy from behind Sorenteen ordered, "Get in the plane."

"Don't fuckin' touch me."

"Just get in the plane," he said with more force.

Kennedy got out of the car. There were four men dressed in suits, their hands neatly crossed in front of them.

Earlier that day Mark Kennedy was walking out of jail cell 102 on E-block, and now he was stepping aboard a Bombardier Global 5000 private jet to an unknown location, to have an unknown conversation with an unknown person. He took a brief look around at the surreal scene in front of him and then climbed the steps of the plane. Sorenteen was close behind with a duffel bag in one hand and a silver Glock .22 in the other.

. . . . . .

As soon as the plane lifted off, Sorenteen handed him a drink. He gladly took it. Excited to smell alcohol for the first time in ten years, he closed his eyes and lifted the glass to his nose. He quickly set it down and almost vomited.

"Gin? Are you fucking kidding me? I hate gin."

"I know," Sorenteen responded, taking his seat on the opposite end of the jet.

Kennedy poured himself water instead. Peering out of the window, he reflected on Victor Caprizzi. He certainly did not come from the usual mobster story. He used to work for his father's beer company as a child. He worked there right up until he left for college. That's where Kennedy met him. He double majored as an engineer and in business and finished top of his class in both without much effort. Towards the end of his time in college, he developed a special technique along with the advanced machinery to make high-quality alcohol for very cheap. The major beer companies caught wind of this and started making some impressive offers.

Upon graduation he took over his father's company and with his ideas and inventions sold it for millions of dollars. After a small period of investing the money, he began to get bored with his extra time and started obsessing on new mental exercises. He found his niche in the business of outsmarting people; that became his new obsession. He naturally steered himself toward developing ways in which he could cheat criminals out of their own money. He always said it was "true service work." It didn't take him long to develop a long list of frustrated enemies, so he hired Sammy Sorenteen and began using him as big muscle for some of his more "hands-on" endeavors.

Shortly thereafter a man by the name of Rick Valentino, a well-known crime boss in New York, hired him to open up a bar as a front for illegal mob deals out of the back. He agreed, not because he wanted to work FOR a well-established, well-connected crime family, but because he wanted the challenge of TAKING OVER a well-established, well-connected crime family—something Kennedy had never heard of before in his career up to that point.

For the first time since college, Kennedy ran into Caprizzi while investigating a string of suspicious murders that led back to Rick Valentino. When questioned about the bar he was running, he swore that he was just a pawn, just dabbling in the world of organized crime, and that he could hand deliver times and dates of huge drug shipments coming in if Kennedy let him go free. After a few big cases that he closed with Caprizzi's help, Kennedy had a very quick rise to detective and then lead detective for the major crimes unit after his father's untimely death. During that time Caprizzi also rose to power.

Kennedy had spent a long time in his career playing it straight with just the occasional bending of the rules. Later, it became clear that it wasn't enough. His tactics changed. His goal no longer was to put criminals in jail; that was cushy. It was to make the thought of being a criminal terrifying. Through torture and brutality, he made them fear him. He used the system to his advantage just like they did. Caprizzi's job was to manipulate the gangbangers and thugs into fighting with those involved in organized crime. It was a brilliant effort, and it made New England's biggest crime syndicates squirm. Inevitably their actions led to retaliation against law enforcement and their families. They had declared war against organized crime, and organized crime had declared it back. It was at that point that

Caprizzi and Kennedy, much to his partner Officer Will Sutherland's dismay, came up with the mob massacre. The rest was history.

Kennedy had just closed his eyes to take a nap. It seemed as if he had fallen asleep for only moments when he was awoken by the pilot's voice. "All right, everyone, we will be making our final descent here. Buckle your seat belts."

CHAPTER 5

MARK KENNEDY

The Boundary Waters

Kennedy looked out of the window of the plane as it landed on a man-made airstrip. A few hundred feet away he could just make out a log cabin nestled along the shoreline of a lake. He didn't know where he was. He figured he was somewhere north judging by the cold temperature and abundance of pine trees, but there were no other discernible features. On the descent he did take care to notice that there were no other residences within eyesight. It was dense forest and small lakes as far as the eye could see.

Sorenteen escorted him out of the plane. The crisp air felt great against his face. He could smell smoke from a wood fire and hear the sound of waves gently washing up against the rocks. His senses became overwhelmed with the sights, sounds, and smells that at one point were second nature to him. The smallest bit of a headache started tingling behind his left brow, but he didn't care.

About fifty yards away he noticed a boat down on the lake, fully rigged, motor running.

"Please don't tell me we're going on the boat."

"Safest place to talk," replied Sorenteen.

"It's fucking cold out!"

Sorenteen pulled out the duffel bag and handed him a coat.

"You have an answer for everything, don't you?"

Sorenteen ignored him.

"Just give me the coat," he said, snatching it out of his hands. Kennedy looked at the snow on the ground.

"I don't suppose you have boots in there, do you?"

Sorenteen reached in once again and withdrew a pair of boots. As Kennedy reached out Sorenteen gave them a toss out of the plane. Kennedy felt the impulse to punch him in the throat but resisted. His capacity for remaining calm had greatly diminished over the last ten years. He swallowed the urge, tracked down the boots, and made his way carefully down the stone steps toward the boat. He found he had forgotten how to manage ice effectively and almost fell flat on his back on the last step, much to Sorenteen's merriment.

"Kinda feels like that Valencia hit, doesn't it?" asked Kennedy.

Sorenteen glared.

"Clearly still a sore subject," he muttered to himself.

"Kennedy! Holy shit is it good to see you!" called out an Irish-accented voice from the boat.

"Kevin O'Shea. Still running with these guys, eh?"

"Of course. Never stopped. Sorry I never visited you in uh, well, you know. Probably wouldn't have been very smart of me to put myself in prison."

O'Shea hopped out of the boat wearing flannel and a golf cap. He shook Kennedy's hand with a viselike grip.

"Agent Waters in there too?"

"No, he's not here. His job is more than done. You're out of jail; he gets to go back to his regular job."

"I'm headed back to the house," said Sorenteen.

"Go ahead, Sammy, I'll get Kennedy up to speed."

Sorenteen made his way back up the steps toward the house, the sun gleaming off his bald head. All the way up the stairs his tall frame gingerly dodged puddles of water.

"He still hates boats?"

"Motherfucker never got over the Valencia hit."

Kennedy had to smile. "I just made a comment about that a second ago."

"Not surprised he's pissed then. But hey, fuck 'im, we have a lot of catchin' up to do. Come on board, get yourself a drink as a free man."

Kennedy obliged. He liked O'Shea. A true-bred Irishman to his core. Back in the old days he was fired from the NYPD after just a couple of years on the force for tampering with evidence in a major trial. He picked up extra work as security detail for some of the larger concert venues in and around the New York area. Kennedy knew him from the NYPD and hired him shortly after he had reconnected with Caprizzi for a couple of lucrative "off the record" jobs. Whereas Sorenteen was more for intimidation and brute strength, the much smaller O'Shea was more of an untrained pit bull. You would never guess it based on his overly calm demeanor, but push him the wrong way and his short temper would ignite him to go from docile to street fighter without warning. O'Shea had been a consistent part of the Uptown Gang for a long time, and Kennedy was glad to see an ally.

"When was the last time we worked together?" asked Kennedy.

"Jesus, probably thirteen, maybe fourteen years ago."

"Long time."

"That's for sure. Look, I'm sure you've got some questions," he commented while getting the engine started on the boat. "So have at it."

"For starters, why do we need to be in a boat?"

"It is not a secret if it's known by three people."

Kennedy looked perplexed as he usually did with O'Shea's little philosophies.

O'Shea elaborated, "There are people inside who don't need to know everythin'. This will give us some privacy to talk. And besides, not a whole lot of grocery stores around here, so we're catchin' lunch."

"Fresh fish, that actually sounds all right." The thought of it made Kennedy's mouth water.

"It's the best."

Kennedy laughed.

"What's so funny?"

"Nothing, just hard to believe how much has happened in the last couple days."

O'Shea walked over to some fishing poles to store them. "Indeed."

"So, who is ultimately in charge of my release?"

"Victor is."

"So he's alive?"

"I didn't say that."

"So he's dead?"

"Victor is dead, yes. And with his death he had explicit instructions to cash in on a favor that Agent Waters owed him. I think you know what the favor was for."

"Yeah, I do."

"So Agent Waters held up his end of the bargain. Caprizzi said if he died or became compromised, to spring you from jail as quickly as possible. So congratulations, mate, you're the new Caprizzi."

Kennedy digested the information while O'Shea was still busy around the boat.

"I hope there's more information about this plan I know nothing about."

"I can assure you, the plan he put in place is very much alive and healthy."

"Is this the same one that was supposed to have me out of jail several years ago?"

"It's complex. It took longer than any of us expected, and Caprizzi didn't want to involve you too early. Make no mistake, your contributions in jail were important, Kennedy."

"I never saw the benefit of any of it."

"We had to make deals. Deals with important people who had enemies on the inside. It took a lot of fuckin' effort just to make sure those people ended up at Firerock."

"So, what important Jew were you talking to that wanted a young Nazi dead?"

"Some tasks were done as favors. Others needed to be done to intimidate. He was connected with a group of bad characters that were creatin' some problems for us. They thought we were jokin' when we warned them they wouldn't be safe anywhere."

"What's the end game here?"

"It's big. This makes the mob massacre look like a petty theft."

"I'm listening…"

"A handful of us have been left in charge of following through on ten years of work. Ten years of sacrifice. Caprizzi has trusted us to execute."

"I need you to stop being so vague."

"It takes time to build castles. Rome wasn't built in a day. In time, you will come to know everything. There's more information waiting for you in the cabin. To start you need to focus on the primary priority."

"What's that?"

"We're having a problem with undercover cops and leaks. Secrecy is everything for this operation, which is unfortunate because the venue for it is flagrantly loud."

"What's the venue?"

"A casino, in Vermont."

Kennedy gave a look of impatient curiosity.

"About seven years ago Vermont's first and only casino was built. Every wall, every floor panel, every security camera was put in place and constructed by Victor. It is a fully functional casino, it brings in a lot of money, and it also brings in a lot of crime."

"Why's that?"

"Because we have invited it there. A lot of illegal operations are run from the casino. Crime groups, big and small, organized and unorganized.

They all use it for different reasons. We have become the major hub for illegal activity in the Northeast. Hell, the whole Eastern Seaboard."

"And you don't get fucking caught?"

"Like I said, Caprizzi handcrafted it."

"How many undercovers are there?"

"Not sure, but they're there. Nothin' can move forward until they're gone."

"I'm not killing police officers."

"No one's asking you to. Find them and do whatever you want to get them out."

"Inevitably, when the police come knocking on my door, what's my title in all this?"

"Head of Security. So you have to make sure the casino runs smoothly as well. It still has to operate as a casino, you know."

"Who's working there now?" pried Kennedy.

"Micky Fontaine, a connection of Caprizzi's, runs the place on the surface level. He's perfect for the job. You'll meet him tomorrow. The people working the regular security detail are a combination of some of the old boys from the Uptown Gang and a few trustworthy randoms that we've picked up along the way. The important thing to understand is that no one knows the full extent of what is going on except for you, me, Sorenteen, Micky Fontaine, and an unknown contact person we use when we need big favors. Caprizzi very specifically wanted it that way."

"You can't really include me in that group 'cause I don't know shit."

"Patience, you will."

Kennedy continued to process the large amount of information, and O'Shea took advantage of the pause in conversation.

"Let's get off the shoreline. There's a great fishing hole a few minutes away—what do you think? You can grab yourself a whiskey if you want. I know that's your favorite."

Kennedy agreed. He got up to pour himself a drink and the boat took off. He once again closed his eyes and brought the glass to his nose. This time it made every muscle in his body relax. Ten years without a drink. He took a tiny sip. The tip of his tongue to the back of his throat burned. It was perfection. His mind began to wander and he wished he could have spoken to Caprizzi one last time. Being brought into an operation so late in its development seemed ill advised, but he was happy to be out of jail and being put to better use than merely as a tool of intimidation.

The boat came to a stop. Kennedy looked around; it was a beautiful lake. The spot they had chosen was tucked away in a large cove, and pine trees and oaks reached far over the water's edge. The water lay perfectly still. The peaceful moment was disturbed by the sound of O'Shea tossing the anchor into the water.

"We're here. We can continue to talk, but keep your voice down. Don't want to disturb the dinner," he said, pointing to the water.

"So what do you know about this unknown contact person?"

"Uh, not a whole lot; he's unknown."

"I mean, that doesn't scare you a bit, having an unknown person playing a big hand in all this? Maybe that's your leak."

"It concerned us, many years ago. But the bloody man is fuckin' resourceful and has done some risky things for us. So as long as he continues to do what he does, we'll continue not to ask questions."

"Fair enough," he replied not fully satisfied with the answer. "What about money?"

"Money?" He laughed. "We'll all be walking away rich, but this isn't about money for anyone, and the casino gives us all the revenue we need for everything we need."

Kennedy's mind intermittently drifted from Uptown. "What about Jules?"

"I knew that question was comin'. She'll be here tomorrow mornin'."

"Really? At the cabin?"

"Yeah, she's pretty anxious to see you, mate. The letters aren't quite cuttin' it for her anymore. She needs a good poundin'. I'm sure you'd agree," O'Shea said, tossing his line in the water and jigging it back to the boat.

"That's the first bit of real good news I've heard today."

"Look, I'm going to tell you somethin' only because you're going to find out sooner than later."

Kennedy looked at O'Shea inquisitively; he didn't look back.

"Jules has been dating a detective for the Vermont State Police."

Kennedy's face contorted with confusion.

"I shouldn't say she's datin' him, she's just keepin' the police close without letting them in too close. She's gained a lot of intel for us."

"Who's the cop?"

O'Shea didn't immediately answer.

"Who's the cop, O'Shea?"

"Will Sutherland."

Kennedy choked on his whiskey. He put his hand through his hair.

"What? What?!"

O'Shea placed his pole down. "Easy, Kennedy. Like I said, it doesn't mean anythin'. Sutherland has been a thorn in our side since Uptown went operational. We have the appropriate safety nets in place to keep him under control, but her role in this is key."

"Even a thorn can cause a fucking infection. If Sutherland is there, why are we even in Vermont in the first place?! This is crazy. Besides us, he knows more about Uptown than anyone. This is fucking crazy!"

"Sutherland transferred there after Uptown started being built. Caprizzi made the calculated decision to keep pushin' forward 'cause he knew you would be able to handle him when the time came."

"No. I'm not buying that. Sutherland is too big a variable, O'Shea! We're all going to end up in jail or dead. And to involve Jules? She's capable of looking out for herself, but Jesus, Sutherland KNOWS who she is and who she is connected to!"

"Hey, keep your voice down. Everythin' is fine. Sutherland knows shit. Once you do your job and get those undercovers out of Uptown, we'll be in the clear. We've got Sutherland by the balls—"

"Once I do my job?!" yelled Kennedy. "I've been doing my job! I've had my ASS on the line for ten fucking years!" He turned his back and began pacing.

O'Shea got closer to him. "You think you've had it so tough? You've had one job and the help of a whole guard system behind you. We are the ones who have been bleedin', sweatin', doin' horrible things to do what we had to in order to get this project to where it is! We were the ones sacrificin'; you don't know the half of it! So get your fuckin' facts straight!"

Kennedy spun around angrily. "Okay. Okay, fine. I want money. I want a lot of money for whatever the hell is going on. In cash. I will be making my own arrangements when this is over and getting myself to a safe location because I'm not going back to jail for you, not for Caprizzi, certainly not for Uptown!"

O'Shea had heard enough. "You know, Sorenteen said you wouldn't be fit for this. Ten years in the can has melted your mettle! You have no perspective anymore. We should have gotten you out and then sent your ass away!"

Kennedy crouched down and threw himself with a burst of energy into O'Shea, who took the blow around the waist. O'Shea tried to keep his balance but tripped over a tackle box and Kennedy landed directly on top of him. He took a big swing with his right hand, which O'Shea caught and held on to. With his other hand O'Shea frantically felt the ground around him for something to hit Kennedy with. Kennedy grabbed O'Shea by the hair and planned on slamming his head against the ground but found himself being flipped on to his back from a forceful push of O'Shea's powerful lower body. As soon as they both were back on their feet, a red laser emitted from the woods and came to rest on Kennedy's chest. He looked up and saw Sorenteen on the shoreline, rifle pointed at the boat. Kennedy raised his hands in surrender. The laser turned off.

The two men were left panting for air on the boat.

O'Shea spoke first. "Are we good?"

"Yeah," responded Kennedy, rubbing some blood away from his nose.

"I'm sorry about some of the things I said. I, uh, just get heated, ya know."

"Shut up," demanded Kennedy, lifting his hand for silence.

"Don't tell me to shut up, Kenne—"

"No," he responded emphatically. "Look."

O'Shea followed his finger to the fishing line still sitting in the water. The very tip of the pole was ever so gently ticking. The two froze, completely fixated on the line. The pole violently shot down toward the water. Both O'Shea and Kennedy dove for it instinctively and started reeling. Simultaneously they ordered each other to grab the net. They started arguing over who should do what, both barking out commands on how to reel and set the hook. A few moments of chaos passed in the boat and finally they pulled up a forty-three-inch northern pike.

Both laughed at the sight. After a quiet moment and some heavy breathing, the same red dot appeared on the fish, and with a deafening gunshot from the woods, the day's lunch blew up in their hands. They looked at the shoreline where Sorenteen was standing, waving and laughing.

"Glad to see the Uptown watchdog developed a fucked-up sense of humor," commented Kennedy.

"He's definitely got a few screws loose. Remind me to slap him for that one. My heart almost exploded."

"By the way, what did you say the name of the casino was?"

With a sly smile O'Shea responded, "There's only one name fitting for a casino run silently by the most elusive group in the country… Uptown, mate… Uptown."

CHAPTER 6

VICTOR CAPRIZZI

August 2, 2001
Manhattan, NY

Victor Caprizzi inhaled a mouthful of smoke from his cigarette and blew out rings one at a time. He had never smoked before; he was just curious about the physics behind it.

"You need anything else, hon?" asked his waitress.

"A little more espresso would be great, thanks," he responded, handing her a generous tip and eyeing her through his expensive sunglasses.

It was a beautiful day in downtown Manhattan. Caprizzi sat at an outdoor Starbucks café just outside the FBI headquarters. People-watching was one of his favorite things to do to pass the time. He took out a newspaper and began reading the headline news:

Just three weeks ago Theresa Waters was raped and bound in her apartment in Greenwich Village. Her father, Brent Waters, a ranking member of the FBI, found her alive but severely beaten and traumatized after several failed attempts to get in touch with her. The heinous act resulted in a highly focused investigation involving local and federal authorities that quickly led to the arrest of the offender, Jordan Rickstein, an individual with heavy ties to organized crime in the state of New York. He pled guilty to the charges and was sentenced to what some would say a modest 15-20 years to be served at the Firerock Maximum Security Prison, a sentence which has local authorities outraged.

Brent Waters, playing the role of distraught father, took a leave of absence from his position with the FBI and had this to say about the sentencing, "Today, the justice system has failed. It has failed one of its own who has sacrificed so much to defend this country from monsters like Jordan Rickstein. When an unremorseful thug like that gets to hand over a few names of "high interest people" and then gets to live a cushy sentence in a prison where half the inmates work for his father, a known criminal of this state, you know that the justice system has truly failed." Through tears, the director's anger was clear, and his future with the FBI not as clear.

A bell above the door rang as a new patron arrived. Caprizzi's attention was stolen away from the article. Brent Waters had just walked through the door.

Right on time.

Caprizzi had been watching Agent Waters since the day the story broke. Although a known outlaw in the United States since his well-documented involvement in the mob massacre, Caprizzi wasn't one to shy away no matter what the circumstance. Besides, he had paid good money to change his external appearance. He buzzed his hair, grew a well-trimmed goatee, and surgically remodeled his nose, making it rather large. He also allowed himself to gain twenty-five pounds, and where he used to wear secondhand clothes despite his wealth, he now sported top-line designer ware. Along with the new look, he bought himself a flawless fake passport, false ID, and credit cards, and he made sure that the majority of his assets and money were stored internationally.

He watched as Waters ordered his usual dark chocolate mocha with an extra shot of espresso. He then watched as he sat at an outside table and slipped a healthy portion of whiskey into his cup. Waters had been the epitome of what you would expect a federal agent to look like just a month ago. With all he had been through, he now looked more like a degenerate.

Caprizzi stood up. He folded the newspaper under his arm, finished off the last sip of his espresso, and walked over to Agent Waters' table.

"Excuse me," Caprizzi began. "Would you mind if I joined you?"

Waters looked up, disinterested. "I'd really rather you didn't."

"I understand. But I think I may be able to cheer you up, Brent."

Waters looked up again. "Do I know you?"

"I think you probably have heard of me, but no, you don't really know me."

"You do look very familiar," he said, giving him a once-over.

"Can I have a seat?"

Waters nodded approval of his seemingly benign request. "So, does the friendly stranger have a name?"

"I do. Victor Caprizzi."

This caught Waters' attention. He looked at Caprizzi, then around the restaurant. He slowly put his hand in his pocket and withdrew his phone.

"Easy does it," said Caprizzi dramatically. "Don't shoot me with your phone."

"I have the direct number to connect me to my agency right now. So, you better talk fast."

"I come bearing good news. A gift to you, Agent Waters."

"You don't have anything I want. What I want has already been taken from me."

Caprizzi put the newspaper article on the table, which caused Waters to look away. Caprizzi then leaned across and quietly spoke to him. "Fifteen to twenty years?" he asked, tapping the newspaper methodically with his finger. "For raping the daughter of one of the most powerful people in our nation's federal law enforcement system? Wow."

Waters was in between sadness and anger. Tears welled up in his eyes. "What do you want? You aren't busy enough running from the police? You have to fill your morning with harassing me? That's a big mistake."

"Slow down, Agent. Like I said, I'm here because I am equally appalled at every little aspect of what's happening right now. You know why I'm famous, yes?"

"The mob massacre. Don't think I don't also remember the things you did to set that up. You're wanted for a reason well beyond sending Mark Kennedy in to execute a handful of assholes."

"Mark Kennedy is a hero for sacrificing his freedom so that others could enjoy theirs. That's something we could all learn something from," he said with conviction. "And far more important than that, you need to know that the thought of an individual like Jordan Rickstein being alive and dare I say, happy while reminiscing with the other animals like him, getting props for doing what he did to your daughter gives me a heartache." He put his hands up to his chest.

"Well, he's already in jail. He'll have his people protecting him. What's done is done."

"What if it wasn't done?"

"What do you mean by that?"

"Mark Kennedy is currently residing at Firerock Maximum Security Prison, the same prison that is currently housing Jordan Rickstein. Kennedy is still on the clock. And I have direct access to him. One call, Agent Waters. One call and Rickstein will get his, I promise you that."

Waters fell silent, methodically swirling his mocha.

"I suppose you need something in return? Something from me?"

"I need you to go back to work. I need you to find peace with what has happened, not to forget it, but to harness the anger it has caused you. I need you to continue to do what you do best with the FBI. I need you to go back to your big corner office like it's just another week. And, I want you to make yourself available to help me when I call on you for a project I'm putting together."

"I'm not getting involved with illegal activity. Just talking to you makes me supremely uncomfortable."

"I'm not asking you to do anything illegal. I'm asking you to help me and my associates where you can to help us make a difference. As time goes on you can choose to stay as far away from this as you want, or, what I'd prefer, you'll dive in head first with us. The mob massacre did exactly what Kennedy and I wanted it to do. It humanized organized crime. It made it vulnerable. It made this country safer. This new project will do that plus a lot, lot more. All you have to do is tell me to make a phone call, justice will be served against a horrible person, and you go back to work. Do we have an agreement?"

Waters stared at Caprizzi from across the table. He put his Irish coffee down.

"Make it happen," he said coldly.

Caprizzi stood up. "We'll be in touch, Agent." He slipped his sunglasses back on and exited the café. He approached the street and lifted his arm. Within seconds an Escalade pulled up and he got in. Sorenteen was in back; O'Shea was driving.

"Did he go for it?" asked O'Shea.

"Gentlemen," he announced, "Project Uptown is a go."

CHAPTER 7

DETECTIVE WILL SUTHERLAND

Frustrations Part II

Sutherland and Konine sat comfortably in the heated interior of an unmarked Vermont State Police cruiser in the parking lot of Uptown.

"Where is that rookie of yours?" asked Sutherland in between sips of his coffee.

"No clue. He said he'd meet us here at nine a.m. sharp."

"Not impressed. He's got ten minutes."

They listened to the morning AM radio for a few moments. Konine nervously scratched his moustache.

"Something bothering you?"

"Me? No." Konine paused. "But…did you hear the news this morning?"

"No, why? Good story?"

"One I think you'll be interested to follow up on."

"Well, let's hear it," Sutherland said, taking another sip.

"A friend of mine works as a guard at Firerock. He called to tell me that your boy Mark Kennedy was released."

Sutherland choked on the coffee. "Mark Kennedy…like Mark Kennedy my partner ten years ago Mark Kennedy?"

"Well, it would be a ridiculous lie to make up, wouldn't it?"

"That is really…surprising. What did he get released for?"

"He didn't know. Just heard it through the grapevine, and then sure as shit he saw him walk out the front gates the other day."

"I'll definitely be following up with that once we're done here today. Should we go over the plan again for how we're going to approach this?"

A loud series of knocks on the driver's side window made Sutherland jump. He rolled the window down.

"Jesus, Dominick, a little more tact next time."

"Sorry, sir."

"Why are you so late, Trooper?"

"On the phone with the medical examiner and the crime scene team."

"Some of the reports are back?"

"You told me to stay on 'em, so I've been harassing them since early this morning. Preliminary results are in."

"Good," said Konine. "What do you got for us?"

"It's a little cold out here."

"Well, then you better talk fast."

"First and foremost, out in Greenfield, Massachusetts, just south of the Vermont border, a report came in from a neighbor that the thirteen-month-old daughter of a John and Audrey Marineau was shrieking for hours. The neighbor went to the house to check on them and noticed forced entry through the back door. There was a big mess inside, blood at the scene. Pictures found in the house are matches to our two bodies. We got them identified and looked up their names on our system. We got a hit on both. Looks like they have dealt with the Scapparzi family in the past."

"The Scapparzi family?" asked Konine.

"Organized crime group based in the southern part of Massachusetts," answered Sutherland. "They keep a pretty low profile, but we've pinched a couple of their drug mules recently running ecstasy up into Canada. Any important evidence at the house yet?"

"No, we're waiting on info from the crime scene guys who are out there now."

"How about the bodies?"

"Couple things. Looks like sometime prior to the dump they had their mouths duct taped. Examiner also said that the woman's arms were both dislocated, and with the extent of the damage done to her wrists by the restraints that were used, they're thinking she was probably hanging by her arms over her head for a prolonged period of time."

"Damn." Sutherland winced. "So that torture scenario is seeming more and more likely."

Konine nodded in agreement.

"The tip of the knife that was used broke off in the man's femur," Dominick continued. "Based on the depth and width of the stabs and the makeup of the recovered blade, our evidence guys are pretty confident it came from a Ka-Bar knife, army standard issue."

"There are a couple of Uptown employees that are former army, military, or whatever. And I'm sure they have access to a lot of different weaponry, so that doesn't narrow it down all that much. That having been said, I still want to know who over there has an army background. How about the tarp?"

"Nothing, totally clean."

"Okay, decent work. You've earned the right to tag along this morning."

"Thank you, sir."

"Let's head in there. Follow my lead. Dominick, you stand in back, straight face. Don't talk to Fontaine, don't even look at him."

"Got it."

The three of them headed toward the front doors of Uptown. Jules wasn't in town, which was unfortunate. She could have arranged a meeting without too much of a hassle. Now they would have to go through the proper channels to get a meeting with Fontaine.

The size of the casino always impressed Sutherland. It was shaped cylindrically and stood twenty-five stories with a total glass exterior. Equally as impressive as the dimensions was the slick layout. There was only one way to access the casino: a side-by-side inflow/outflow driveway. The rest of the casino was surrounded by dense forest. This driveway was intended for pick-ups, drop-offs, and people using the high-priced valet services. Along the driveway was also a walkway for people who chose to save a few dollars and park in the main lot, which really was only an option four to five months out of the year due to the lengthy winter, which was fast approaching. At the beginning of the road stood a rock wall about seven feet high. It was draped in sparkling lights and extended across the front perimeter of Uptown until it met with the wood line. The wall also turned in and ran the entire length of the 100-foot-long main entrance road. Modern lampposts lined the cobble path. It always gave Sutherland the feeling that he was in 19th century New England. Upbeat band music played from invisible speakers embedded into the wall. The further in you walked, the more you could begin to hear the action of the casino and hotel. Huge monitors came into sight, advertising the featured act of the day and all the different amenities the hotel guests had at their fingertips including the casino, outdoor/indoor pools, and top-of-the-line restaurants. By the time one reached the end of the walkway, it felt like a different world. The narrow path opened up into a vast adult playground—a large interlinked system of shops and bars. Despite how early and cold it was, people were littering the grounds. As you transitioned to the inside of the hotel, the look drastically changed. There were thousands of flowers, tall trees, and a trickling brook. They all weaved in, out, and around the main lobby like a modernized version of the Garden of Eden. The best view was from three stories up overlooking the central indoor courtyard, which boasted a dozen or so boutiques and high-end bakeries and restaurants arranged around a rather large koi pond and fountain. The rooms themselves were scattered throughout the upper floors of the hotel, but if you had the money, the interior rooms overlooking the courtyard were the best of the best.

Once the three of them walked through the main lobby, they approached an attractive woman named Summer who stood in front of a remarkably tall, cascading waterfall overlying a pristine cut of onyx. The ultra-illuminated word "Uptown" was written obliquely within the centerpiece. With the water gliding over it, the emblem shimmered and danced.

"Good morning, I'm Detective Sutherland—"

"Oh yes, Jules' boyfriend, right?"

Konine and Dominick broke smiles.

"Something like that, yeah."

"How can I help you today, Will?"

"Let's keep this formal."

"Sorry, Detective Sutherland. What can I do for you?" she said with what he was sure was a forged smile.

"I need to speak with Mr. Fontaine."

"Hmm, I know he's really busy…" she said, flipping through an appointment book. "There's a very popular band playing here tonight, which has him short on extra time."

"Well, this hopefully won't take long, and I'm afraid it pertains to a very important investigation."

"Oh," she said, more serious. "Well, I'll call right up to his office then. Wait right here please."

Summer walked away and flagged a man over. They chatted for a moment. He looked over at them and didn't seem particularly happy. He got on his cell phone and then said some more words to Summer. She returned.

"Okay, he'll see you in his office. I'll have security bring you right up."

"Great, thank you for your help."

The casino was fairly dead as he expected it would be that time of day. There were just a few chain-smoking clients feeding their gambling addictions. With their security escort they walked through the array of different slot machines and table games. Sutherland noticed the impressive system of video cameras. With some of the more advanced security technology that Uptown flaunted, he was sure their movements were being tracked. They made it to an elevator in the back. The security guard swiped his card and the door opened. He pulled out yet a different card and swiped again once inside the elevator to allow admittance to floor thirteen. Sutherland had never been to any of the Uptown offices before.

"So is floor thirteen where the business side of the casino is run?" he asked.

"Yes sir, very private area. Casinos often don't have a floor thirteen because guests consider it bad luck to stay there, so Mr. Fontaine thought it would be a neat idea to make floor thirteen the operations floor. Conferences, meetings, different heads of the different departments all have their offices up here."

"I'm sorry and you are?"

"Joshua."

"Joshua, I don't suppose the name John Marineau rings a bell, does it?"

"No, sir. I don't really interact with any of the guests. Though Mr. Fontaine, he knows just about everybody."

The elevator reached its destination. Straight in front of the elevator was a sliding glass door. "Office of the President of Operations" was neatly displayed in front. The receptionist sat just inside. She was another exceptionally attractive woman.

"Detective Sutherland?" she assumed.

"Yes," he replied, raising his hand.

"He's ready for you; follow me." She got up and walked rather sensually over to the door of Fontaine's office. Sutherland caught Konine staring at her long and smooth legs.

"Focus, please," he whispered.

"Fuck you," he retorted.

They made their way in.

"Mr. Fontaine, Detective Sutherland, and Troopers Konine and Dominick," introduced the assistant just before she left the room and closed the door.

Micky Fontaine, "The Face of Uptown," was a frustrating man to deal with. As far as Sutherland was concerned, he was fake from the top of his perfectly combed hair to the tips of his overly manicured nails. Despite how young he was, thirty-seven, the local politicians loved him. His ability to be dangerously charismatic made him think he was invincible, and in some arenas he was. Sutherland never saw him wearing anything less than top-of-the-line, name-brand clothes and accessories. His polished look was impressive.

"Detective Sutherland," he started, pointing to a chair in front of his desk. "I can't say it's all that nice to see you again given our last couple meetings, but I'm always willing to help the local police in any way I can."

"I'll stand," Sutherland replied. "And just so we're clear, I'm a state trooper, not a local police officer."

"My apologies. Would you mind if I sat?"

"You can sit, stand, lie down, it's all the same to me."

Fontaine took a seat and crossed his legs.

Sutherland continued, "I want to assure you that I'm here to work with you, not against you, to solve a particularly brutal murder that occurred earlier this morning."

"Oh my," Fontaine announced. "And you believe that the Uptown has something to do with it?"

"I didn't say that."

"You didn't have to. You implied it. Was he an employee here?"

"Not as far as we know, but we recovered a receipt from his pocket from an ATM withdrawal here last night."

"Well, this is good news, yes?"

"How do you figure?"

"I'm sure our recently upgraded security system will have him on camera. We can see who he was with and maybe what the circumstances of his visit were."

"You'd be willing to let us take a look at your security footage?"

Fontaine flashed a wide smile. "Of course, Detective. The safety of my casino is my priority. Let's go straight over to the security office."

Fontaine's enthusiasm in wanting to help made Sutherland nauseated. He looked up at Trooper Dominick and signaled for him to walk with Fontaine. He and Konine walked a few steps back.

"Keep your eyes open," he said to Konine.

"Always."

They made their way down the floor to the large security suite. Inside there were dozens of computer screens showing the action around the casino mixed with programs running that were a part of standard-issue casino security. Sutherland didn't understand most of what he was looking at.

Fontaine walked up to one of the men working there.

"Lucas, I need eyes on a potential guest from yesterday."

"You got it, sir. Details?"

Fontaine looked at Sutherland. "Detective? He's all yours."

Sutherland walked up to the computer while retrieving the information from the receipt. "John Marineau, he was at ATM number 1029 last night at 10:33."

"Okay, let me pull that ATM up."

Lucas went to work on the computer, pulling up footage from a camera nearest the specified ATM. At 10:33 p.m. on the dot, the image of John Marineau appeared.

"Okay, stop right there. Rewind a couple minutes, and can we do a wider shot? I want to look at everyone around that area."

"Sure thing."

"Can we ID these people?" asked Konine, pointing to the image of the bystanders.

Lucas looked at Fontaine.

"Whatever they need, Lucas."

"Okay, running facial recognition. The limitation here is that it only picks up those people who currently are or who have been guests here before. The nice thing is that if we can ID them, we'll instantly know if any of them have priors."

"Amazing technology," commented Konine.

"Top of the line. Cost me a pretty penny too," said Fontaine from the back of the room.

A list of names appeared on the side of the main screen.

"Dominick, go ahead and write down all those people's names; we'll need to interview as many as we can."

"Looks like no one in that frame has priors except for Mr. Marineau. Seems like a pretty violent guy," commented Lucas.

"Can you look at how many times Mr. Marineau has been a guest here?"

"Yup." His fingers quickly went to work on the keyboard. "Looks like he was a regular, came in every other month or so."

"He's on screen," announced Fontaine.

Everyone looked up. Sutherland carefully watched as Marineau walked up to the ATM. Very casually he withdrew the money and then walked back the same way.

"Can we start this footage from the second he arrived to the second he left?"

"Yeah, let me compile the info. It will just take a few seconds."

Sutherland turned to Konine and spoke in a loud voice. "Another mob-connected guy hanging around Uptown—not surprising."

Fontaine made his way closer to Sutherland.

"This upsets me as much as it does you, Detective."

"Does it? Does it also surprise you that someone like this is visiting your casino?"

"No, not really."

"And what do you attribute that to?"

"Look, Officers..."

"Troopers!" barked Konine.

"Right, Troopers. We've been down this road a dozen times already. I'm not wasting time going on this ride again."

Sutherland turned his back on the conversation.

"Besides, I think you'll all be impressed with some of the changes we're making here."

"What kind of changes?" asked Konine.

"Well, for starters, with our new security system, we will be hiring a new head of security."

Sutherland returned to the conversation. "Oh, you mean the thug that you have running the show now isn't doing a good job?"

Fontaine shook his head and gave a dramatic sigh. "I've always understood and appreciated your accusations, Detective. However, Mr. Sorenteen has been an exemplary employee. His presence here alone has vastly impacted the security of this casino and has allowed the Uptown to flourish as it has."

"Mr. Sorenteen is a gangster. He has connections to a man that was an international felon. He along with a handful of other employees that you directly hired."

"Detective Sutherland, I wish you wouldn't offend me and my colleagues like this."

"And I wish you and your colleagues wouldn't offend my intelligence, Micky." He stepped up to Fontaine's chest. "You...offend...me."

"As I've said before during the many investigations you've pursued against Uptown," Fontaine began as he retreated back to his chair, "I have given second chances to brilliant people who are excellent at what they do. They are businessmen, they are professional, they believe in this casino, and most importantly they believe in being better people. Have you ever been given a second chance, Detective?"

"I'll choose not to answer that."

"So what about the new employee?" Konine redirected. "Another criminal?"

"In fact, yes, I have gone out of my way to hire a rehabilitated man. His abilities will be the missing link this casino has required since its inception. I have great faith he'll help give us a better name."

Sutherland laughed. "You think hiring a criminal will help give this place a better name?"

"Humor us," said Konine. "What's his name?"

"I think you've probably met him before. His name is Mark Kennedy."

Sutherland looked at Konine, who returned the same look.

"You hired Mark Kennedy? How did you know he was getting released?"

"I have eyes and ears everywhere. No one deserves a second chance like he does. Don't you agree, Detective?"

Sutherland glared back at Fontaine, his mind rapidly processing the information.

"Detective, Mr. Fontaine!" called out Lucas from his computer. "I have the footage you need."

"On the big screen please," Fontaine ordered.

They all watched Marineau's arrival from the previous night. Lucas had managed to create a montage of his every step and outlined him with a bright neon green circle. He arrived in a shiny blue BMW convertible right around the time the withdrawal occurred.

"Dominick," called out Sutherland.

"Yes, sir?"

"What kind of car does Marineau drive?"

"That's not any car registered to him, sir."

He and his wife got out as the valet took the keys.

"I want to talk to that valet driver," called out Sutherland.

Dominick was scribbling down notes.

The two victims made their way into Uptown. The wife waited at the front door, nervously checking her watch as the man walked straight to the ATM and withdrew the money. They then both walked straight back out to their car and left down the well-lit driveway.

"Go back to the last couple frames there," demanded Konine.

"You catch something?"

"Maybe."

The footage went back to the couple getting into the car. As the car pulled away frame by frame, sure enough, there was movement in the backseat.

"That's our killer," said Konine.

"Or at least the guy who'll lead us to him. Are there any other angles you can get us?"

"Straight in front of the casino doors, we have cameras that can identify all passengers within a car. But…doesn't look like he makes himself visible until well beyond those cameras."

"Dominick, get an APB out on a blue BMW convertible. Can we zoom in on the plates, Lucas?"

"Yes, we can."

"AJAX 313," Sutherland read aloud. "I want that car found."

"I'll get right on it once we're done here, sir."

"We're done here now."

As Sutherland made his way to leave the room, Fontaine stepped in front of him. "I know we don't see eye to eye," he said, reaching his arm out and patting Sutherland's shoulder. "But we can work together amicably. I hope this new information yields results. If you need anything else, my hands are your hands."

"I think that will be all, Mr. Fontaine. I'm already going to get an earful from my office for being here."

"No, you won't. I won't tell anyone you were here. A bit of a peace offering. I am not an enemy of the state; I am a friend."

"Do whatever you'd like," Sutherland responded coldly, taking Fontaine's hand off of him.

Sutherland, Konine, and Dominick walked out of the room and back to the elevators. Once alone inside, Sutherland addressed the troopers using a soft voice.

He looked first at Dominick. "Like I said, I want that car found priority one."

He then looked at Konine. "I need you to do me a favor."

"Name it."

"Get in touch with Mass State Police. See if they can't drop in on some of Scapparzi's people, see what they can tell us about John Marineau."

"I'll get right to it."

The three left the casino. Sutherland couldn't shake the feeling he was being watched.

"Have a great day, Will!" said Summer, the Uptown hostess, with a bright smile and a wave.

Will returned a half smile back.

On their way out the door, Sutherland muttered, "This place is laughing at us."

"Or they're helping us and there's nothing to find here," said Dominick.

Sutherland and Konine scowled at him.

"I'll keep my opinion to myself from now on."

"Good idea. You two ride together," ordered Sutherland. "I'm headed to the office to put some pieces of this together. Get back to me with that info ASAP."

The three parted. Sutherland got into his cruiser and headed to the barracks. Something Fontaine had said stuck with him. *Has anyone ever given you a second chance?*

In fact he had received a second chance at the hands of his mentor, Mark Kennedy. He was working under him as a rookie officer in New York. It was common knowledge throughout the department that he had been assigned to Kennedy as an extra pair of eyes because of the Internal Affairs investigation happening at the time. His first day on the job could have easily been his last. He was running late to the initial meet and greet. Kennedy decided he wasn't impressed and left from where they were supposed to rendezvous. About an hour later, convinced he was going to get reassigned, he got a call from Kennedy, who gave him an address and said to meet him on the second story of the business office there. When he arrived, there was no one to be found. Instead of a business office, there stood an old, broken-down apartment building. He climbed to the second story, gun drawn; still there was no one. As he reached the end of the floor, he heard a scuffle coming from just outside the hallway window. He looked over the edge of the broken glass and saw Kennedy, who had a man's face trapped with his forearm against the side of a wall. Things seemed relatively under control until he tried to pull handcuffs out, and the man tactfully wiggled free and headbutted him in the jaw. Disoriented, Kennedy pulled his gun out, not realizing the safety was on. His firearm made a series of empty *clicks*. The offender took the opportunity and tackled him against his squad car, delivered a devastating knee to his groin, and then hopped behind the wheel.

Sutherland, in a desperate effort to contribute, jumped from the second-story window. He landed squarely on the roof of the car and predictably felt the acute pain of a broken ankle upon impact. The car darted out of the alleyway and sent Sutherland tumbling headfirst to the ground. Kennedy, having gathered himself, gave a brief look of confusion in Sutherland's direction, released the safety from his sidearm, and emptied the clip into the back two tires of the car, sending it sliding into traffic and straight into a stop sign. Sutherland could remember, half in a fog, watching Kennedy sprint over to the car and drag the man out headfirst through the shattered driver's side window. He cuffed him and brought him back over.

Kennedy loomed over Sutherland, a dry look on his face. "The only reason why you will get to show up to work tomorrow is because I need you to be my chauffeur."

Sutherland, not knowing what to say, gave him a default "Thank you, sir."

"It wasn't a compliment. And if you entertain me anymore like you just did, I'll send you packing myself. Get your shit together."

"Yes, sir," he replied, defeated.

"We'll get him processed and then I'll take you to the ER."

"That won't be necessary, sir. We'll be there all day for an ankle problem, no need."

"All day? I have a few connections there; we'll be fine. In and out in an hour."

He helped him up, brought the perp to holding, then cruised to the hospital. It turned out the man he had arrested was one of the heads of an organized crime group in New York at the time and only ended up with a slap on the wrist. A year later he would be shot in the head by Kennedy.

. . . . . .

Sutherland was in disbelief that Kennedy was out, much less back in his state and working for Uptown. He was hopeful this would get him some more leeway with his Uptown investigation. If nothing else, perhaps he could gain access to Kennedy, talk with him. The break he was looking for had just fallen into his lap, and he had a lot of work to do to catch up on what Kennedy had been up to the last ten years in prison and what the circumstances of his release were.

CHAPTER 8

MARK KENNEDY

Up to Speed

For the first time in over a decade, Kennedy slept in. He woke every thirty minutes with the feeling of impending doom that the guards would be storming into his cell, just to realize that he didn't have to answer to anyone, not that morning. So time and time again, he drifted off to sleep, nestled into his quiet, private room.

Around 11 a.m. he felt another body slip into his bed. The light aroma of strawberry perfume filled his nostrils. An arm wrapped around him; it was smooth and soft. He could feel the butterflies in his stomach clamoring. He turned around and came eye to eye with one of the most beautiful sights he had ever seen. Jules Romano lying in bed next to him. They kissed, a long, tender kiss. The saltiness of her lips was addictive. He ran his hands over her back.

"I missed this body so much," he whispered into her ear.

"Not as much as I missed yours," she said as tears of happiness rolled down her cheek.

They kissed again. She was even more beautiful than he remembered. She looked as if she hadn't aged a day. He knew she couldn't say the same about him. He was glad he had decided to shave his face smooth and cut his hair back to its short and wavy style; the way he used to wear it. He also had the opportunity to color it a deep dark brown to abolish the infiltrating gray.

Jules flickered her infectious smile. "Things haven't been the same without you. It's just a relief to have you back."

Kennedy smiled. "Have you gone soft on me there, Jules?"

"Fuck you," she said playfully. "I'm as hard as I've ever been, and so are you by the way."

Kennedy's ego flared. He went in a third time for a long kiss when a knock on the door sounded.

"C'mon, you've got to be kidding me."

"They can wait." She winked at him.

The two spent the majority of the morning in bed behind locked doors. The men downstairs occasionally came to see if they could get access to Kennedy, just to be turned away in between moans and groans emanating from the master suite.

Around lunch time Kennedy and Jules rejoined the group downstairs. Kennedy was dressed in a pinstriped black suit, looking much sharper than he had the previous day.

"Thanks for giving us your time this morning," said Sorenteen in his vintage flat affect. "You enjoy yourself?"

"Give him a break," said O'Shea. "The man's been without the company of a woman for ten fuckin' years. How are ya, Jules?"

"Better now." She gazed at Kennedy.

"Glad to hear it. We have some things we have to go over before we head out."

"Head out where?" asked Kennedy.

"To work. We have to get back to Uptown and get you introduced in."

Kennedy took a seat and grabbed some fruit off the table. Jules sat on his lap.

"So, what exactly happens from here?"

"It's simple, mate, we go to Uptown today. Now, your release is going to be big news. So for the first little bit of time, it's just about gettin' you established. You will focus on being the head of security, and off the record you'll be figurin' out the snitch situation. Any ideas on how you're going to do that?"

"Haven't thought about it, but I'll come up with something."

"Well, that's real fucking encouraging," said Sorenteen.

"Okay, calm down," said O'Shea, trying to keep the peace. "Jules, as soon as you can, get in touch with Detective Sutherland. He's going to want to meet up with Kennedy sooner than later; might as well get that out of the way."

Kennedy looked around awkwardly at the mention of Jules' and Sutherland's fabricated relationship. Jules gave his forehead a kiss and scratched his head.

"Don't worry about me. I'm yours. This is just business."

"Yeah, don't worry about sharing Jules' body with a fit, younger guy."

"I will fucking end you," snapped Kennedy.

"Jesus, you two are fuckin' impossible," remarked O'Shea. "Just don't look at each other for now. If we can't work together, there won't be an operation."

"You're right, I'm done," said Kennedy, calmly looking at Sorenteen.

Sorenteen shook his head and said nothing else.

"As I was going to say," started Jules, "he already knows. He texted me last night about it. I told him it was true and that I'd set up a sit-down between them."

"Perfect," commended O'Shea.

"Beyond distracting Sutherland," began Kennedy, "it's not impossible that I may need help with what my job is at the casino. So whose my team?"

"Well, a trade not properly learned, is an enemy. That is to say once we've got you fully integrated to the casino, then you'll be the one callin' the shots. For now, the three of us are in this together, and Jules is pretty much the messenger if you can't get to us immediately. No one else is to know anything about anything unless we all deem it necessary."

"Did Caprizzi deem it necessary for someone to tell me anything about anything?"

"He prepared files for all of us. Yours is upstairs in the office. None of us have looked at it."

"Good, I'm going to go check it out. When do we leave here?"

"One hour."

"In that case, I'm going to go freshen up," said Jules, unabashed. The lower half of her well toned bottom peeking out from under the long-sleeve button up shirt she wore.

"I bet you are," said O'Shea, chuckling.

"Go fuck yourself, Kevin," she said as she disappeared from the room.

Kennedy grabbed a cup of coffee and another apple; the first one had been far too delicious. He headed upstairs straight to the office. He slowly opened the door. The room was huge. Four computers were set up on the far desk. There were three televisions set up and a conference table arranged off to the side. A lot of business had been conducted in this room.

He scanned the rest of the area and came across multiple volumes of notebooks neatly stacked and organized on a bookshelf with dates and times ranging from the day Kennedy was sent to Firerock to as recent as June of 2010. "The Uptown Project" was titled on everything. On the desk was a sealed manila envelope. *For Mark Kennedy's eyes only* was clearly printed. Kennedy retrieved a letter opener and took a seat at a chair overlooking the lake. It was a heavy envelope. He withdrew a large stack of papers full of people's pictures, documents of pertinent Vermont State Police investigations, and blueprints of Uptown. The last page within the envelope was a plain, single white piece of paper with *The lives of a few for the lives of many* neatly handwritten in the center. This was a slogan they lived by in the days leading up to his imprisonment. He leaned back in the chair, took a sip of coffee, and started from the beginning.

. . . . . .

As Kennedy walked to the foot of the private landing strip, he could see Sorenteen and O'Shea waiting. They were dressed in the same suit that he was, same thousand-dollar watches, and same designer sunglasses.

"Are you fucking kidding me?" Kennedy yelled out, feeling a bit ridiculous.

"Things have changed, mate," said O'Shea. "We're representin' a multimillion-dollar company now. We have to look the part."

"I think you all look fantastic," said Jules.

They looked back. She, too, had made her way to the landing strip. She wore matching pinstriped pants, although hers hugged the curves of her body. She had a white blouse with a pinstriped vest over it, and her cleavage was flagrant. Her burgundy-red hair was as wavy and gorgeous as Kennedy had ever seen it.

O'Shea gave a whistle. Kennedy didn't hesitate to look her up and down more than once, and she returned a flattered smile. The plane door opened and steps descended.

"Everybody in, we're going to be late," said Sorenteen.

One by one they entered and took their seats. O'Shea broke out a bottle of champagne.

"Everybody gets some, no room for pussies," he looked at Jules, "with one exception of course."

She gave a sarcastic grin.

"This is a celebration before things get serious," continued O'Shea. "Might be the last time we have to not think about the future."

O'Shea poured them all glasses. He raised his own. "The lives of a few for the lives of many."

The four of them raised their glasses and took a sip as the plane took off.

As soon as they hit cruising altitude, the party amongst old friends and acquaintances began. The group reminisced of the old days.

"What about St. Patrick's Day in Times Square, 1996 I think it was?" asked Kennedy.

O'Shea shook his head. "No, no. I drank you under the fuckin table that night."

Kennedy swatted his hands in the air in disagreement.

"I'm Irish, Kennedy. No one on this planet is going to out drink me on MY day."

"Well, one thing is for sure," said Jules.

"What's that?" asked Kennedy.

"We're going to put that night to shame tonight."

"Ya know there are many good reasons for drinkin'," sang out O'Shea, "and one has just entered my head: If a man doesn't drink while he's livin', how the hell can he drink when he's dead?"

The four clinked their glasses again.

Kennedy could feel his face starting to go numb. The alcohol was hitting him harder than he wanted it to. He preferred to keep a clearer mind but didn't want to seem like he had lost any of his edge in front of the others.

"Are you fucked up already, Kennedy?" O'Shea called out.

"Fuck you. I'm been in prison for a decade. I don't get fucked up. This pussy over here though," he said, pointing at Sorenteen, "he's starting to look a little sloppy."

Sorenteen stared back at Kennedy, took a knife out, slammed it into the back end of a can of beer, which sprayed all over them, and chugged the remains of it in one gulp. He casually tossed the empty, mangled can to the ground.

O'Shea choked on his drink from laughter. Kennedy wiped the beer from his face, not as entertained.

As the flight went on, one by one they each went to a quieter seat to rest. Kennedy couldn't sleep. For well over an hour he sat staring out into the dark nighttime sky. He felt nervous, an emotion he wasn't used to. It bothered him. Made him feel vulnerable. The taste of freedom was his to have, and yet this plane brought him closer and closer to what he felt was his very probable return to prison. He didn't want to think about it anymore. He walked up to the front of the plane where Jules was. He sat down next to her and scratched her thigh gently.

"How you holding up?" she asked groggily.

"There's a lot to adjust to. And I get the feeling I haven't seen anything yet."

"There is a lot to take in, and the casino is wild. Stick with me though, you'll do all right." They kissed.

"I'm going to ask you something. I want you to be honest."

"Okay," she said, allowing herself to wake up a bit more.

"Tell me that there is nothing between you and Sutherland. I mean, I don't give a shit, I really don't. I just need to know."

"I'm only going to say this once." She looked hard into his eyes. "There is nothing between me and Detective Sutherland. We get to stay in the loop with some of the things the police are up to, I make things more complicated for him, but I am with Uptown. I am yours. This body is yours. Good enough?"

Kennedy smirked, "That's all I needed to hear. You come find me if anything ever happens or you get cornered in any way by the police. I'll deal with Sutherland my own way if I have to."

"I thought you two were pretty close at one point."

"We were. But he chose his path. I chose mine."

Kennedy caught a glimpse of large lights amongst the darkness.

"What the fuck is that?"

"That is Uptown," said O'Shea, making his way to the front of the plane. "Welcome to Caprizzi's playground." He reached for the music control and put on some hard rock as the plane took its final descent and landed in a small airfield a little bit south of the casino.

From the airstrip they hopped into a helicopter with the word "UPTOWN" printed across it.

"You've got to be kidding me," said Kennedy, astounded at the resources they had access to.

"The best for the best," said Jules.

The chopper took them on a twenty-minute ride to a helipad atop the casino. From the exterior he was amazed at how out of place it all seemed. Surrounded by such a rural area, it was hard to believe anyone would visit. But sure enough, the parking lot down below was packed.

In the back of the Uptown there was an outdoor pool area. It was a warmer late fall night in Southern Vermont, and the party below had clearly spilled out onto the pool deck. The chopper landed.

Sorenteen was the first out and headed straight for the rooftop entrance. O'Shea and Kennedy were next.

"You're going to meet everyone tonight!" yelled O'Shea over the propeller of the helicopter. "But the only people that matter are the ones from the portfolio in Caprizzi's office! We're the ones that matter! We're the ones that know the extent of the plan, so keep it that way!"

"Let's go, you two!" Sorenteen shouted, waving them in.

Once inside they were greeted by three waiters each holding 5,000 dollars in cash and a bottle of Don Julio tequila. They took their complimentary gifts and walked to a private elevator where they were escorted by two security guards.

"Follow me," said O'Shea. "We're headed to the Uptown club, Energized, then we'll hit the casino for all it's worth."

"You really think all this is a good idea? I feel like there's a lot to be done."

"As far as people know, we are a bunch of thugs who all have big-time jobs for a legit casino. If we don't party, that will look strange. Enjoy yourself tonight; tomorrow the party's over."

They made their way through a series of back hallways and came up to a private entrance. The door swung open and revealed an exquisitely decorated club. There were three bars, loud music, and what seemed like an intergalactic light show spinning out of control. About a hundred people crowded the inside. There were some women walking classily around in full-length gowns, while others were classlessly running around, drunkenly crawling on men every chance they were given.

When the four of them stepped in, the music stopped and the crowd turned toward the door. An eruption of applause and cheering began. O'Shea and Sorenteen were celebrities here and by proxy so was Kennedy. His face turned a shade of red. He couldn't stop his eyes from roaming wall to wall, taking in the sight.

They headed to the bar arm in arm while O'Shea was listing off names that would be important for Kennedy to know, "This is Nicky Deez; he helps run floor security, and he also runs the clean-up crew. We make a mess, he's an expert in disposing of the garbage."

"Got it," replied Kennedy.

"These three guys over here are Billy BonBon, Johnny Lamposte, and Roderick Beamer; they oversee the pit managers on the floor and help with transportation. So you'll be working with them regularly to start out with."

Kennedy nodded.

"You see that guy hanging off the pole?"

"Hard to miss."

"His name is Zippy," O'Shea continued. "I don't think he'd be able to pass an IQ test if his life depended on it. He's got a few screws loose, so just be careful around him."

"Why does he work here?"

"Because when push comes to shove, that guy will bite a man's testicles off. I like havin' a guy like that in my corner."

"I suppose better to fight with him than against him."

O'Shea went on with the onslaught of names. "Over there is Lucas; he's the surveillance captain in the control room. That stoic man standing by the middle bar, you see him?"

"Yeah."

"He is the head attorney for the Uptown, the Beast of the East, Danny Icon."

Kennedy was overwhelmed by the name game and had to take a swig from the tequila bottle.

"That a boy, Kennedy, the night is young. Just one more introduction for now, I promise."

"Outstanding," he replied.

"Here is a man that you will get to know very well. Micky Fontaine. He is the owner of the Uptown."

Kennedy could literally smell him from across the room. He reeked as if he had just sat in a bathtub full of cologne. He looked more like a doctor from a soap opera than an owner of a casino.

"Yo, Micky!" O'Shea shouted. "Come meet Mark Kennedy. Our new boss!" He then turned to Kennedy. "Well, see you at the bar."

"Wait! O'Shea, don't—"

"So, you're the infamous Mark Kennedy," Fontaine yelled enthusiastically.

Kennedy watched as O'Shea disappeared into a sea of people as he halfheartedly shook Fontaine's hand.

"Kevin and Sammy have been talking about you for the better part of the last year. You have no idea how happy we are that you could join the team. I'm sure you're anxious to get going, learn about how the Uptown functions—"

"But we will save all of that for tomorrow," interrupted a short and stocky man. "Tonight we drink like the gods. One thing, Kennedy, stay away from the Brazilian chick. She calls herself 'Lola.' Just a ridiculous fuckin' name but whoa! What a wildcat. She's mine."

Kennedy turned around and saw the unmistakable figure of an old acquaintance. "John Billings, holy shit," he said with some surprise.

He certainly hadn't expected to see anyone else he recognized. Billings had just come aboard the Uptown Gang the preceding year before his incarceration and helped him out quite a bit with some of his investigations. He had never been the most attractive member of the group. Beady little eyes, receding hairline, sketchy-looking tuft of hair under his bottom lip, and a jagged scar left behind on his left cheek from the disaster that was the

Valencia hit many years ago. He could be a little much at times, but his quirky, outspoken ways were usually fun to be around.

"She's all yours, Billings," he said, thrilled to not be talking to Fontaine anymore. "This ocean doesn't seem like it's running out of good-looking fish any time soon. I'll throw my line out on someone else."

"First of all," Billings drunkenly spat, "don't think of it as throwing a line out. It's more like tossing dynamite into a bucket. Secondly, I imagine you're just going to end up givin' it to Jules. Am I right?" he said, thrusting his hips in the air.

"Let's find the others."

"Let's hit it!"

Kennedy scanned the room. Sorenteen, Jules, and O'Shea were sitting at a private table in the back. Although there were many people gawking at them in awe and gossip, no one dared approach their table. Jules caught his eye, so he made his way over. The crowds of people gave him anxiety. He could feel his shirt soaking in the sweat from his neck. A guest stumbled in front of him, and he shoved him to the floor.

"C'mon, Kennedy, push forward," commanded Billings from behind him.

It seemed the more he pushed people out of his way, the more crowded it got.

"Hey!" boomed O'Shea, grabbing a couple of people and tossing them aside. "He said to get out of his fuckin' way!"

The crowd quickly dispersed, giving them easy access to the table. He caught Sorenteen smirking and shaking his head.

"You good?" asked O'Shea.

"Yeah, I need a drink."

O'Shea leaned into one of the bouncers by the table. Moments later a bartender appeared.

"I'll take a Macallan 12."

The bartender nodded and looked at Billings. "What are you drinking?"

"What do I want? I want a fuckin' martini!"

"Yes, sir. Dirty?"

"Do I want it dirty?" He looked at Kennedy. "Can you believe this guy? I've been coming here for years, and he wants to know if I want it dirty." He looked back at the bartender. "Yeah, I want it real fuckin' dirty. I want that damn drink so fuckin' dirty I have to shower after I drink it!"

The people within earshot laughed. "Hey! Bartender!" he yelled again. "I want it so dirty that the drink itself gives me a rim job and then spits in my face! Dirty! If you fuck this up, I'm going to break the glass across your fuckin' face."

Not sure whether he was being serious, the bartender scurried off. Billings was as inappropriate and entertaining as Kennedy remembered him. Their drinks came back almost immediately. Billings got his martini and made quick work of it, putting it down in a couple of gulps.

Shortly after, the men, with their chosen women, hit the casino floor. They gambled away hundreds of thousands of dollars as they moved from table to table. Roulette, craps, blackjack, poker. The alcohol was being thrown around like water. By two in the morning, their group had tripled, full of employees from the Uptown and miscellaneous friends of the group.

As the evening turned to day, the sun started to rise, and the night became a blur. The last thing Kennedy could remember was being escorted back to his room by Billings, arm in arm, and Billings throwing him onto his penthouse suite bed.

As he left the room he said, "Good luck getting sleep."

The door closed and from the bathroom walked out Jules. She was wearing nothing but a skimpy see-through negligee. She peered straight into Kennedy's mind with those exotic eyes of hers and slowly made her way to the bed. Starting at his feet she seductively and intentionally made her way north.

Kennedy's last thought of the night: *This beats the hell out of jail.*

CHAPTER 9

RACHEL DAVIS

First Night Out

Rachel took a big gulp from a can of Red Bull. She had been studying for hours. First week of college and she already had two papers assigned. She knew that if she received anything less than an A on her first collegiate paper, she would be devastated, so she was pouring herself into the assignment.

"Rachel, you in here?" called out her roommate Becky.

"I'm in my room," she shouted back.

Becky came skipping in with a smile on her face, wearing a red skirt that revealed far too much skin and a black top to match.

She flicked her short dark hair dramatically. "It's Friday night and you're coming out."

"I caaan't," Rachel groaned. "This paper is so far from being done it's ridiculous."

"I don't care about that," Becky said, bouncing over to the mirror to make some adjustments to her outfit. "What I do care about is your reputation in this dorm."

"But I—"

"And I won't take 'no' for an answer."

She strutted over to her desk and snapped her laptop shut.

"If I come out tonight, you have to promise not to bother me tomorrow."

"Do I seem like the type of girl to peer pressure my roommate into having fun all weekend?"

Rachel smiled.

"Besides, we've all picked out the boys we want to hook up with, so you need to get on it before all the good ones are taken."

"Okay, I have to get ready quick."

"Sounds good, we're gone in twenty."

Rachel ran off to the bathroom to get ready. The last week had been exhausting. Between classes, advisor meetings, and studying, she hadn't interacted with a lot of other people besides Becky. Truth be told, she was glad to be getting away from work for the night. The girls on her floor were headed to Avalon, a club notorious for its Friday Night Ladies Night party. She thought about calling her father before going, then thought better of it. She'd call him first thing in the morning.

"You ready, bitch?" Becky called into the bathroom.

"One second!"

She grabbed an extra spray of perfume and slipped a heart-shaped necklace over her head that her parents had given her as a graduation present.

All the girls going out met in their room. There were seven of them total. Rachel walked in with her tightly curled brown hair, black short shorts, and blue tube top with matching heels. The other girls all whistled at her as Becky entered from the common room kitchen and broke out a bottle of rum for them all to take shots of.

"Here's to being single, seeing double, sleeping triple, and having multiple!"

Becky cheered.

The rest cheered with her and they all took their shot down.

"Let's get to the club. I don't want to wait in line all night."

"I don't think we're going to have to wait very long—look at this group!"

The girls all laughed.

"Well, I don't want to be late because I don't want to miss out on the guys from Sigma Pi," said another.

"That's a better reason," announced Becky. "Let's call the cabs and take a couple more shots before we go!"

The seven girls took down a couple more rounds of rum and then made their way downstairs to the idling taxi. A campus police officer walked by.

"Where are you ladies headed?" he asked.

"Club Avalon, sir. It's eighteen-plus night there," Becky answered.

The officer looked dubiously at them. "You all know how to keep yourselves safe, right? Don't leave each other's side, don't walk a long distance home, use good judgment."

"We will, we promise. Have a good night, Officer." Becky winked.

"You can come with us and keep me safe," said one of the girls.

They all giggled as they piled into their transportation for the evening. The taxis brought them straight to the club, and one by one the girls got out, fixed their dresses, and walked directly up to the main entrance to the dismay of the long line of men outside being forced to wait.

"You ladies on the list?" asked the bouncer.

"Do we need to be?" asked one of the girls.

The bouncer looked at the group. "I suppose not. You don't have any dudes with you, do you?"

"Hell no!" several of them said emphatically.

"And you're all eighteen?"

"C'mon, look at us, we are a group of sexy girls looking to party."

"All right, just wait one minute and we'll get your group."

Singing and dancing, they waited for the bouncer to usher them in.

. . . . . .

Two large Russian men pulled up outside Club Avalon in a midnight black Mustang. The driver took off his perfectly round glasses and cleaned them off before placing them back gently on his long nose.

"Is that the group?" the driver asked.

"Yes, for sure. Marcus was very specific."

"Why these girls?"

"They are young, seventeen and eighteen. College age. They are here alone."

"Should be easy then."

The driver pulled out a small mirror and lined up a hit of coke. He snorted it all down in one long line.

"Take it easy. We don't want any slip-ups. Tell me about the girls again."

The driver pulled out a series of pictures of each individual girl.

"Rebecca Johnson, goes by Becky, eighteen, dark hair, her family owns a diner in New Hampshire. She is loud, confident."

"Not her, who's next?"

"Lindsay Cooperman, seventeen, blond hair, nice body, her father is a cop in Maine—"

"Next. C'mon, you know the rules, no cops."

"Rachel Davis, seventeen, dark hair, also very nice body, she's quieter, in her room a lot, rich family from here in Boston. Dad is doctor, Mom is vice president of some company."

"Let me see her picture."

He handed over a picture taken of her on her first day moving in. She had been wearing a flowery dress, a strand of hair being blown across her face.

"Yes, she is the one. Inform Antoni."

"Are you sure Marcus will be happy?"

"I know Marcus, and I know she will be perfect."

"Okay, I'll make the arrangements."

While the passenger of the car watched the whole group of girls be let in the club, the driver pulled out his cell and sent a text:

Antoni:

Rachel Davis, blue top/blue heels, wearing a heart necklace. We'll be waiting.

"Now what?"

"We wait patiently," responded the driver. "It won't be long."

. . . . . .

The group of girls headed straight for the dance floor. Like ants to sugar water, a group of men tried to smoothly infiltrate their group. Amongst the flirty few were some of the boys from their dorm who had managed to sneak in several flasks past the bouncers. The girls readily shared the remaining alcohol they offered. Rachel could feel one of the boys come up from behind and start dancing with her. She looked at Becky, who checked him out, then gave the thumbs-down. Rachel awkwardly danced away.

"Thanks for the honesty!" she yelled over the loud techno.

"That's what roomies are for!"

Rachel noticed Becky looking over her shoulder toward the edge of the dance floor.

"Look at that guy, he's gorgeous!"

Rachel turned around and saw the man she was talking about. He was very attractive. Short, spiky hair, athletic body, dressed nicely with black dress pants, a white undershirt, and a style vest. He looked like he was about their age.

"Go talk to him right now. He's looking over at you."

"How do you know that? Maybe he's looking at you," Rachel said back.

"Are you kidding me? Look at you. You look hot tonight. Besides, I'm working on the president of the Sigma Pi house. That one is all yours."

Rachel looked timidly toward him. Becky flagrantly waved her hand and got his attention, then signaled him over.

"You're such a bitch."

"You love me. Don't do anything I wouldn't do," she said sarcastically as she danced away.

The man approached her. "Hey there, my name is Antoni, what's yours?" he said loudly in her ear with a hint of a Spanish accent.

"Rachel! I love that vest! Very trendy!" she said playfully.

"I thought so too! My roommates said to leave it, but I knew what I was doing!"

Rachel laughed. "I love the accent. Where are you from?"

"What's that?!" he asked over the commotion.

"I said I love the accent!"

"I can't hear a word you're saying," he said with a smile. "Let's go to the bar!"

"I'm not twenty-one!"

"I am, just turned. I'll get us a drink!"

He reached his hand out and she took it. He led her to the bar and ordered them a drink.

Luckiest night of my life, she thought to herself as she racked her brain for good conversation starters.

"This is much better," he said once they reached the quieter bar area.

"Totally. So where do you go to school?"

"Boston College, love those Eagles."

"Oh nooo," Rachel said, pretending to choke.

"What's that?"

"I go to Boston University, not sure we can be friends."

"Well, I know we just met, but we'll have to go to counseling, work through our differences." They both laughed.

The bartender reached over and tapped him on the shoulder. "Hey, buddy, here's your drink."

"Thanks, mi amigo."

"What is that?" she asked.

"It is delicious and strong. You can have it. I'll tell the guy I dropped mine and get a new one," he said, handing her the drink.

"Thanks."

He looked at the bartender and ordered another. Rachel took a big sip.

"Wow! I need a chaser with this!"

"It could be the only drink you have tonight, and it'll still get the job done."

Antoni got his drink and the two made their way back to the dance floor. They had spent about a half an hour dancing when Rachel started to feel light-headed.

"Hey, do you know where my friends are?" she asked him.

He looked around. "No, I don't see them. What's up?"

"I'm not feeling well. I feel a little nauseated."

"Oh shit, for real? I'll get you to the bathroom, make sure you're okay, then I'll get you home if you want. My friends were going to pick me up in a little bit anyway."

She thought for a minute about the offer. Putting coherent thoughts together was becoming an increasingly difficult task.

"Yeah okay, thanks," she replied, just wanting to be back in her dorm room.

He put his arm around her and helped her toward the bathroom. With every step of the way, she felt less and less in control. She desperately wanted her feet to stop moving, but they kept stumbling forward against her will. She thought about telling Antoni to stop for a minute but couldn't find the words to communicate. In her mind she began to panic.

What is going on!? If only I could call my dad.

Antoni escorted her to the hallway where the bathrooms were but then kept walking beyond them straight to the side exit. He opened the door and helped her down the steps. Confused and exhausted, she allowed herself to be taken deeper into the alleyway. The last thing she remembered was seeing a black Mustang pull up and Antoni telling her he would get her home safe and sound.

CHAPTER 10

MARK KENNEDY

New Beginning

Kennedy woke up to a knock on the door of his suite. His headache from the previous night's alcohol binge felt like an elephant crushing his head. He checked his watch; it was 8 a.m. He had only been asleep for four hours.

"There better be a really good fucking explanation for this," he muttered, half asleep, as he dragged his feet over to the door and opened it.

"Sorry to bother you, sir," said the offending young bellhop. "Micky Fontaine had me specially deliver this to you for your first day of work. He said to pass on the message: *This will help you look as good as I do.*"

Kennedy stared at the bellhop through bloodshot eyes. "I'm going to count to three, and if you're not gone, I'm going to become violent."

The bellhop took the hint, laid the suit down, and walked away quickly. Kennedy took an ice-cold shower and reluctantly put the outfit on. He made his way to the conference room on the thirteenth floor adjacent to Fontaine's office. The main players of Uptown were already there.

"You're late," said Sorenteen.

"Go fuck yourself, I haven't been hungover in a decade. But if you want, I'll make your head feel like mine."

"It's possible your headache is due to the two punches you took last night, mate," said O'Shea.

"That explains a lot about how I feel this morning."

"Hey, chatty Cathys, work time, let's go," commanded Fontaine, who had just entered the room.

O'Shea stood up. "So let me begin by introducing you to a few baseline details. Then we'll hit the floor and you can tell us what you think."

Kennedy nodded.

"You are the head of security for this casino. Everything going on within the casino you are in control of. Drunk guests, cheaters, scammers, robbers. Those are your focuses. We need to make you visible to people, and we need to make people know that you're just a regular guy working in a regular casino. You have Fontaine, who can help you with anything you need. I'm relying on you two to get that part of the job done."

Kennedy rolled his eyes at the thought of working with Fontaine.

"We are bleeding money right now, and if we're going to look like a legitimate casino, we need to not only plug the holes, but we need to fix them as well so we don't bleed in the future when more important guests arrive. Any questions?"

"What's Billings doing here?" Kennedy asked, looking at Billings in the corner of the room.

"He's your right-hand man for security-related issues. Anything else?"

"No."

"Good. Let's head downstairs and take a look around."

O'Shea put on a fedora and aviators.

"What the fuck look is this?" joked Kennedy.

"What do you mean? I look great."

Billings chuckled. "He means that people from Vermont don't look like this. They wear flannel and John Deere hats." He looked at Kennedy. "I've been telling him that for fucking years."

"Oh. I didn't know you two were such fashion icons. One of you has been in prison for a dime, and the other is a fuckin' fat, retarded Italian."

The banter continued as the four of them made their way to the main floor. As usual, Fontaine out-flashed them all. Every day he made sure to live up to his name, "The Face of Uptown." It amazed Kennedy how he knew just about everyone who passed by, guests and employees alike. He caught Kennedy looking his way.

"It's all about appearance, my friend," he said in a low voice. "Everyone in this state loves me because everyone perceives that I love them."

"How in the hell do you manage to keep everyone's name straight?" replied Kennedy. "It took me two years to learn the front office assistant's name back when I was working."

"Check it out." He pointed to his ear. "Virtually untraceable earpiece. I have a guy whose sole job is to video ID people that are around me. Then he tells me their name and something about them while I'm saying hello. Watch and learn."

Bored by the topic of conversation, Kennedy was sorry he had asked. Fontaine walked up to a man and a woman who appeared to be his wife.

"Great to see you, Pete. How was the concert last night?"

The man responded with a big smile. "It was awesome! So much better live. Thanks for the recommendation!"

"Drop my name at the bar," Fontaine replied with an obnoxious smile. "They'll give you and your friend there any drink you want on the house. Have a good one!"

He turned back to Kennedy and gave him a thumbs-up. "No idea who that guy was, but now he thinks the president of Uptown personally knows him, right down to the very important detail that that slut he's with ain't his wife. If you're going to work on the floor at any time, I would highly recommend you pick up that doctrine. People come here because everyone is royalty here. And besides that, the guests won't want to fuck with you if they know you. Don't mess that up."

"Look, Fontaine, I'm sorry, I just don't care," Kennedy replied. "If I was fifteen years younger, I could do your job and my job. Unfortunately that's not the case. So you do whatever it is you do, and I'll do whatever it is that I do. Sound good?"

Fontaine stopped, red in the face. He shook his head, confused, and veered off toward the high-end restaurant, Augusto's, greeting people along the way.

Kennedy caught up to O'Shea. "So as I was saying, right now we have one of the most sophisticated video surveillance technologies that exist; it has a couple holes in it, but for what we need it for, it's perfect."

"If it's good for you, it's good for me."

"We have different table games like roulette and poker that we separate by stakes, and they all exist centrally and then our rows of slots come out from the center. In the back are the live poker table rooms A-G. We have the largest selection of casino games on the Eastern Seaboard."

Kennedy scanned the room as O'Shea talked.

"There are two stationary 360-degree cameras that exist on each corner of each table, and most of them overlap. There are blind spots that exist on certain tables though."

"Okay," said Kennedy, paying close attention.

"So in those instances we have two pit managers who work those sections to keep a better eye out. Let's move on to the vault."

The group of men walked to the far corner of the casino. Kennedy's previous thoughts of nervousness became more anticipatory anxiousness as he focused in on all the guests of the hotel. He was excited at the thought of investigating possible scams and cheaters; putting his old skills to use. He had all but forgotten the fact that there was something more sinister happening within the bowels of the casino.

They came to a door that blended into the wall perfectly. To access it, Billings swiped a key card. It led them to a hallway that led straight to the vault. Two large men in Uptown suits stood outside. Both with sidearms on their hips. They acknowledged O'Shea and Sorenteen and stepped aside. To enter the vault, there was a complex system of simultaneous thumbprint approval and iris recognition, two different codes that had to be entered, as well as a swipe from the same card used to gain access to the restricted hallway.

"Mr. Kennedy, welcome to the second most secure area of Uptown," announced Billings proudly.

"The second most secure? Can't wait to see the first most secure," Kennedy said as they moved inside. The interior more resembled an international bank. There were thousands of lockboxes spread out between multiple rooms. One of the walls contained a large, metal door that housed the cash deposits. A central platformed area, protected with multiple trip sensors, housed the most precious guest possessions. Every inch of the room was under surveillance by cameras both stationary and revolving. Two guards stood post on the inside at all times.

"How often does cash get brought in?"

"Once a week. Armored cars that work exclusively for Uptown come and switch out the cash. As they are employed by us, there's never a problem with unknown personnel coming and going."

"Well, this area definitely seems secure."

"You haven't seen anything yet," said Billings.

He walked to the rear of the vault to some more lockboxes and inserted a key into one of them. It opened, and implanted inside was yet another keypad. Billings entered a code and the central portion of the wall opened into another hallway.

"Holy shit," said Kennedy aloud. "Fucking Caprizzi."

O'Shea patted him on the back. "This is called A-Wing, the most secure place inside Uptown."

Right away Kennedy noticed a door off to the right. "What's this?"

"It's under construction for now. When it's done I'll personally give you the tour."

They continued their tour down the short, well-lit hallway. At the end there were two more doors. Kennedy peered into the window of the door off to the left. It could only be opened from the other side. There was a steep, spiraling staircase.

"Where does that go?"

"It's one of the back hallways that only we have access to," answered O'Shea. "It dumps out into the main stairway of Uptown. It also dumps out on floor thirteen, where all our offices are."

Kennedy looked at the other door.

"And this one?"

O'Shea gestured to Billings. He opened the door and flipped a switch. One by one the ceiling lights turned on.

Kennedy couldn't believe his eyes. The room was a mess, with different groups of boxes and crates scattered throughout. The far half was made up of ceiling-to-floor shelves all packed with stores of guns, drugs, delicate art pieces, and what appeared to be evidence boxes. Further in he saw expensive cars and what was clearly an area for money cleaning. There were enough felony-grade items being held to put everyone who worked for Uptown in prison for life. As they walked in further yet, he saw a series of interrogation rooms in the back of the warehouse. Outside one of the rooms sat a chair that stood in front of a wall with shackles dangling down. The wall itself at one time had been white but currently was spackled red. Memories of Rickstein propped up against a single chair amongst the slaughtered remains of other inmates made his gut wrench.

"What is that, over there?" He pointed.

Sorenteen responded, "You can imagine we deal with some pretty dangerous people. People who want what we have. In order to have become so well respected by the people we work with, we had to show that we don't fuck around. That corner oftentimes is where we end up spreading that message."

"The lives of a few for the lives of many," O'Shea said delicately.

Kennedy nodded in agreement. He scanned the back wall of the room. On the opposite end was the entrance to a roughly engineered tunnel. It looked just wide enough and tall enough to fit a bus. The dark hole extended away from the A-Wing warehouse. Kennedy couldn't see the end of it. He walked toward it.

"That's how we bring this stuff in," explained O'Shea. "It leads out to a pathway in the woods. It's virtually unfindable unless you know where to look."

"So how exactly is this all set up? I'm sure you don't just let anyone drive themselves in here and drop their shit off."

"Fuck no," said Billings. "Clients come in the front door, and they meet in one of our conference rooms. The arrangements are set. Off site they are in charge of loading up whatever they need help with, whether it's disposal, holding, cleaning, selling, distributing, whatever. Then our people meet them in one of our many locations. The swap occurs once we're sure there's no tail, and our people drive the goods here through that tunnel. Every shipment that comes in, all hands are on deck. The video surveillance of the casino has nothing to do with the video surveillance of A-Wing. Two different systems. Sorenteen personally assists with the pickup, and O'Shea, myself, and a couple of the security guards make sure everything goes down smoothly on this end."

"What if something does happen? Gunshots, someone gains access, security system fails?"

"The whole casino was designed by Caprizzi to literally shut down like a giant jail cell if that ever happens. No one in, no one out. And this whole area burns from the inside and collapses. If we ever were desperate, A-Wing gets incinerated, then gradually the rest of the hotel, and we disappear."

"Which would be a big fucking waste," said Sorenteen. "So instead we're careful in what we do, and those that put us at risk get a special seat in the corner." He redirected once again to the bloodstained chair.

Kennedy shrugged. "All right."

"All right," repeated O'Shea. "Kennedy, go with Billings back to the main security office. Get a feel for the system and get a feel for the casino, then go play security guard. We'll touch base later."

With that he nodded at Sorenteen and the two went out one of the many well-hidden side doors leading to the back hallways of Uptown.

"Follow me, Kennedy," said Billings. "You gotta check out the system we're workin' with."

. . . . . .

Kennedy and Billings made their way back to the control center on the thirteenth floor. As they passed by the slot machines, he saw Jules walking toward them.

"Oh great," said Billings.

"You don't like Jules?"

"She's fuckin' mean to me."

"You're such a pussy."

Jules gave Kennedy a hug. "You boys have a nice morning?"

"It went well," responded Kennedy, "about as well as my hangover would allow anyway."

"Yeah, last night was a fuckin' riot, wasn't it?" chimed in Billings.

"Johnny, why don't you go to your room, take the forty seconds you need to jack off, and meet Mr. Kennedy upstairs in just a moment."

Billings looked at Kennedy for some support, but Kennedy avoided eye contact with him. Billings, with a scowl on his face, muttered a few inaudible phrases directed at Jules and headed to the control room.

"So you're not feeling that great, eh?"

"Not in the least. I must say A-Wing perked me up a bit. I've never seen anything like that before."

"Funny, those are the exact two things you said about me last night."

Kennedy chuckled. "So what is it you do when you're not running around with the state police?"

"I'm a floor manager. Keep clients happy, keep the big spenders spending. My craft is getting men to burn their money away. I'm quite good at it."

"I don't doubt that in the slightest."

She leaned in and kissed him.

"Dinner tonight?"

"I can't tonight," she said, looking upset.

"Do I want to know why?"

"You probably don't, no. But can I ask you a question that will give it away?"

"Sure."

"What day would be good for you to sit down with Detective Sutherland?"

Kennedy rolled his eyes.

"Don't make this any harder please."

"Anytime is fine," he submitted.

"'Kay, I'll set it up." She leaned in and kissed him again. "I love you, Mark."

"I'll see ya."

She walked away to greet some newcomers.

Kennedy took the elevator to the control center. Upon arrival he took a look at all the camera stations and began familiarizing himself with the computer system. The face recognition software was impressive. He had never seen something so advanced.

"I can't believe this shit," said Kennedy. "Ten years ago we were still pretty much submitting names and fingerprints and waiting indefinitely for the results to come back."

"Yeah, I bet. Technology has gone about a light-year and back since you were poppin' gangsters."

Kennedy shook his head and ignored the comment. "So these cameras see every corner of the casino except A-Wing?"

"About 95% of it, yeah," replied Billings.

"And Caprizzi did *all* of this?"

"Everything you see. And as a result, he put himself in too deep. He was into some heavy shit."

"He was always into some heavy shit. That's what happens when you live by the mantra 'The end justifies the means.'"

"He pushed the envelope too fucking far. Look where it got him."

"Am I disappointed he's dead? Absolutely. Am I surprised? No. But if he was willing to die for this project, then the least I can do is see it through to the end."

There was a pregnant pause in the room.

"So, how well trained are the pit managers in each table section?" Kennedy asked, breaking the silence.

"They're good enough. One per section. They usually oversee about four to five tables at a time."

"What about people who want to cheat the casino? You'd think that they could use stealthy devices for communicating. How do we monitor that?"

"Wireless signaling devices have been used a lot in different ways in casinos, and we have a brand-new electronic detection system. Now it's the least of our worries. One of Victor's hand-made inventions."

"Nice," Kennedy said, giving the room one last look over. He looked out the security glass to the chaos of the main floor. "So what do we do now? There's so much happening at once here, it's hard to see where we would be needed."

"That's what Lucas is for, him and the rest of the guys up here," Billings responded. "They know what to look for, and when they see something that needs attention, they'll call."

"What do we do in the meantime?"

"Well, there's the occasional paperwork, documenting, checking in with employees. Ya know, making sure everything is running smoothly."

The last thing Kennedy wanted was to be sitting alone with his thoughts, staring at paperwork.

"Anything else we could be doing?"

"Fuckin' around the casino?"

"That sounds better."

The two of them began their walk around the grounds, starting at the front entrance, which could only be described as majestic. Two red carpets encircled the main *Uptown* waterfall. Behind it they became one and led to the front desks and concierge. Behind the front desk and running up the wall to a domed ceiling was a media screen.

"Jesus, look at the quality of that screen."

"It's HD."

"HD? What the fuck is that."

"Oh yeah, you don't know shit anymore." Billings laughed. "HD means high definition. Which means the picture quality on things like this are sharp."

A picture of Micky Fontaine wishing everyone luck flashed on the screen.

"I don't know what it is about that guy; he just annoys me. Even more so in HD."

"He grows on ya."

"Doubtful."

Billings chuckled. "Let's hit the shopping up on the second floor. There is almost always some prime Northeast ass up there."

"You really haven't changed a day since I saw you last."

"I'm a little bit shorter than I used to be. Not sure what happened there."

"It's called estrogen. Clearly you have more of it than most."

"Ha. That's a good one. Real funny fuck, aren't ya."

"Just lead the way."

As they weaved their way through the casino to the elevators, Billings tapped Kennedy on the shoulder. "That pit manager over there is flagging us over."

They approached a blackjack table toward the east end of the floor. The man stepped out to greet them.

"Good afternoon, Mr. Kennedy."

"What do you need, Marco?" he asked, taking an unnoticed look at his name tag.

"You know my name?"

"That's my job," he responded. He hated it that he had just used one of Fontaine's tactics.

"Sir, I just wanted to let you know there's a gentleman on the end of table four who just left to go to the bathroom, said he would be back in five. I'm almost certain he's cheating. His hands are all over the place, so it's tough to see exactly what he's doing, but he gets every big card he needs when it counts. What do you think?"

"We'll look into it." Kennedy turned to Billings. "Call upstairs to the control room, let's video ID this guy. I want to know how many times he's been here in the last month, how much he's won or lost overall. Then I want to get the closest live shot we can of the next couple hands he plays."

"Done and done," said Billings as he stepped away to make the call.

Kennedy addressed the pit manager. "Open up a spot for me at the table. I want to play the next couple hands with him."

Kennedy waited a moment for Billings to return. It felt good to give orders after having taken them for such a long time.

"Okay, we got a Steve Goodwin from Mystic, Connecticut. He's been kicked out of Foxwoods in Connecticut two times in the past for cheating. He has frequented this casino once a week for the last three months. He's left with over twenty thousand dollars in winnings."

"Well, all right," said Kennedy with a smile. "Let's get to work."

Steve Goodwin returned to the table, and Kennedy stumbled up behind him, pretending to be drunk.

"Can I have a seat here, buddy?" slurred Kennedy.

The man looked him over and, unimpressed, responded, "Sure thing. Try not to throw up on me though, okay?"

"That's a good one." Kennedy let out a loud, fake laugh.

The man didn't respond.

"Ya know I've been drinking all day? Hell, I've been gambling too. Can you believe how much I've won?"

The cards were being dealt. Kennedy repeated himself. "Can you guess how much I've won, pal?"

"Hey, I'm trying to concentrate here; you should do the same," the man responded sharply.

"Oh, whoa, fine. So sorry to be a distraction." He looked at the other players. "I can remember a time when people talked with one another. Rode their hot streaks with other gamblers. Drinking and celebrating…"

Watching from afar, Billings was getting a kick out of the bizarre tactic.

The dealer spoke to Kennedy. "Ten and another ten for you, sir."

"That's twenty! That's pretty lucky! I better ride the lucky streak. I'll take a hit!"

"You have a thousand dollars on the table, and you're hitting on a twenty?" the man spoke angrily.

"Well, yeah, it's called pushin' the limits, man. Dealer, hit me!"

The card was laid down. "A two—that puts you at twenty-two. You bust."

"Oh man!" Kennedy exclaimed. "Did you see that? One off, almost nailed it!"

The dealer dealt Goodwin a ten and a five.

"You ever just start throwing out random numbers to the universe, hoping Mother Earth will be so kind as to return the cards to your hand?"

"Would you back off?" Goodwin shouted, redirecting his attention to the dealer. "I'll just stay."

"Very good, sir," said the dealer. He turned his card over. "Dealer has twenty-one. You lose."

In a jeering voice Kennedy leaned in close to his ear. "Should of went for it, eh?"

The man looked up at him. "Good thing I only lost fifty bucks to your thousand. You wanna play in the big leagues?"

"I'm the biggest leaguer around, bro," Kennedy responded in a heavy drunken accent.

Billings laughed out loud in the background.

"Okay then, old timer, here we go." He took a wad of bills out. "Let's do five thousand."

Kennedy figured if he was going to cheat, there was a decent chance he'd go for it now that he was playing with a large amount of money.

"Five large? I'm in!"

"You just keep playing the way you've been playing. I think I'll be fine."

"Oh, I'll keep my strategy. Don't you even worry about it."

The dealer dealt to the five people sitting at the table. Kennedy was dealt an eight and a ten, while Goodwin was dealt face-up a ten. Just as Marco the pit manager had noticed earlier, the man made some movements with his hands that looked like some sort of tic. Kennedy grabbed his arm, which elicited a scream of surprise.

"What are you doing, you fucking drunk?!"

Kennedy was able to flip his right hand over to reveal a card sitting in his palm. It was an ace, which would have given him twenty-one. The man took the vodka tonic he had been drinking and swung it at Kennedy, who moved backward out of the way and pulled the man into a choke hold. Some of the other players scrambled out of the way while Billings came running up and assured everyone that everything was fine. Kennedy maintained his grip until the man gracefully passed out.

"Shit!" exclaimed Kennedy.

"What's up?"

"I ripped my suit."

"We'll get you another. Help me get this schmuck to our regular interrogation rooms."

With the assistance of a couple of security guards, they brought him to a small room. Without much time passing, Goodwin regained full consciousness.

"W-w-what the hell happened?" he stammered.

Kennedy positioned himself right up next to his face. "You're going to really wish you hadn't pushed your luck here today. You've stolen money from the wrong people."

"What are you going to do, arrest me?" he mocked.

"It's unlikely that that will be the outcome." Kennedy left the room and Billings stayed behind.

Outside Sorenteen was waiting.

"Nice work," he said.

"I have a problem."

"Not surprised," Sorenteen said, folding his arms in front of him.

"As much fun as it is wasting my time dealing with petty shit like this, I want more."

"I don't know how many times we have to say it, but getting you established as a legitimate employee is important. You going all fucking Rambo from the get-go is going to attract too much attention."

His confidence soaring from the recent scuffle, Kennedy took the conversation further.

"I don't mind playing the role of a grade-B security guard, but I need to know what else is going on, in full, so I can better make a plan for what's to come."

"Trust in the plan, Kennedy."

"Easy to say when you know the fucking plan."

Sorenteen sighed. "Fine, we'll sit down with O'Shea tomorrow and get you up to speed. I don't want to hear another word about this till tomorrow."

"That's fine."

"And, Kennedy…"

"Yeah?"

"Change your fucking jacket. You're making this place look bad."

Kennedy glared at him until he left the room. Sorenteen always had to get the last line in. He looked back into the interrogation room to find Steve Goodwin had been badly beaten. He was bleeding from at least two wounds on the top of his head, and his hand was swollen to the size of a basketball; Billings must have broken it. He had two black eyes, and his face was bruised all over.

He ran into the room. "Billings, that's enough!"

Billings turned back to Goodwin. He grabbed him by the hair. "We will require you to return the full amount of twenty thousand dollars within one week…you hear me, you stupid fuck!"

"That actually won't be necessary, John."

Billings looked up in confusion mixed with skepticism. "What the hell are you talking about?"

"I'm in charge here," said Kennedy confidently. "This is my decision. I'm telling you we will let him keep his winnings and kindly ask him not to come back to the Uptown."

Billings tried to interrupt, but Kennedy raised his voice above him. "That way Mr. Goodwin won't go to the police about being assaulted since he gets to keep his illegally obtained twenty thousand dollars. And I assume you won't be coming back to the Uptown ever again?"

Goodwin nodded.

Billings gave Kennedy a look.

"Do we have a problem?"

"No," Billings answered as he pushed Goodwin off the chair. "No, we don't. Of course not," he said, starting to laugh. "I do get carried away sometimes, you know, blood pumpin', getting all jacked up on lettin' someone have it."

"Yeah, very empowering," replied Kennedy sarcastically. "Call Nicky Deez and have him clean this room up. I don't want any evidence left behind."

"Consider it done, boss."

Kennedy went to leave the interrogation room.

"Where you headed?"

"I think a little hair of the dog might be a good option for me right about now."

"All right, boss."

Kennedy left the room and made his way to the closest bar. The bartender he approached was large. Based on his look alone, Kennedy figured he was one of the guys connected to Uptown. He had long, scraggly hair.

His scruffy beard suggested he hadn't shaved in several days. His right forearm was covered in tattoos. The one that demanded the most attention depicted a bright red dragon setting a church on fire.

"Bartender, whiskey on the rocks."

"Sure thing, Mr. Kennedy," the bartender responded.

"And what is your name?"

"Roderick Beamer."

"That's right. I remember you from the party last night?"

"Yes sir," he said, handing him his drink.

"Okay, well, keep up the good work."

"Will do, Mr. Kennedy, have a good one."

"Oh and Mr. Beamer..."

"Sir?"

"Shave that beard, get some control over that hair. We're trying to run a casino, not a 7-Eleven."

"Absolutely sir, sorry."

Kennedy sipped on his drink and took off to do some more surveillance of Uptown.

CHAPTER 11

VICTOR CAPRIZZI

June, 2002, Brooklyn, NY

Dan Peterson sat in his plush leather chair looking out his window toward the New York skyline. A little over a year ago, many would have considered him next in line to become a district attorney; however, after the scrutiny over being too harsh with Detective Mark Kennedy, and then the scrutiny of being too soft with Jordan Rickstein, that position melted right out of his hands along with his old job.

He took his glasses off and rubbed the bridge of his nose. He lifted a plaque off the windowsill: *Best Lawyer in Town, Best Husband All-Around.* It was a recent gift from his wife and fifteen-year-old son for his fiftieth birthday. He wished he could believe the inscribed words. Taking in the full view of the city for one of the last times from his office, he caught a glimpse of himself in the window. His hair had made the full transition to gray just in the last year. He had always been careful to watch his weight, but lately he had gained several pounds.

He sighed heavily. It was only a matter of time before the eight years he spent in law school, and the two decades he spent submersed in his work, would all be for nothing. His wife didn't even know a fraction of the extent of the situation. His time as a New York prosecutor was coming to an end.

His intercom buzzed in. "Mr. Peterson, a Will Sutherland is here to see you."

"Will Sutherland? As in Officer Will Sutherland?"

"Yes sir, he says he just needs a minute."

"Send him in."

Peterson took a seat behind his desk. He hadn't spoken to Sutherland since he took a statement from him subsequent to the "mob massacre." His door opened and in stepped a uniformed officer.

"What is this?" Peterson said angrily.

"What's what?"

"You're not Will Sutherland!"

"Oh, right. That's my fault. I accidently gave your assistant the wrong name."

"What is the meaning of this intrusion..." Peterson took a closer look. "Wait a minute, you look familiar to me."

He glanced at the officer's name tag: *Caprizzi.*

"You! You stay right there. I'm calling the police."

"Mr. Peterson, I have come here for some benign legal advice; the real police won't be necessary."

"911, what's your emergency?"

"This is Dan Peterson, I'm a prosecutor for the state of New York. Victor Caprizzi has just walked into my office."

Caprizzi casually took a seat in front of the large cherry wood desk.

"*Okay sir, you're going to want to calm the fuck down and listen to Mr. Caprizzi for just a few moments. Love those glasses by the way.*"

Peterson walked to the window and peered down. A white van was sitting outside the office. The man driving, a tall, bald man, waved up at him. Peterson nervously sat back down.

"What do you want with me?"

"First of all, relax. I need you to really think hard about what I'm about to ask you, and I don't want you distracted with fear. I'm not here to hurt you in any way."

"How do I know that?"

"I didn't get to where I am by killing good people. Important people anyway. I'm just here to offer you a job."

"A job?"

"Yeah," Caprizzi responded, grabbing a pear off his desk and biting into it, "a job. I heard you've had a rough year, I mean, yikes."

"Just tell me what you want and please go."

Caprizzi took his authentic NYPD hat off and placed it on the desk.

"How old are you, Dan?"

"Why does that matter?"

"Your question is counterproductive to what I'm trying to achieve. Please, just answer my questions."

Peterson thought for a moment at the angle being taken. He eventually answered, "Fifty."

"So basically, if you're lucky, you're at the halfway point of your life, right?"

"What are you driving at?"

"Right. So, you were on track for some serious career jumps. I heard that you were so close to becoming the lead DA for the Manhattan office. Is that true?"

"I might have been."

"Look, I don't blame you for what you did to Kennedy. Hell, he deserved it. Quite frankly I deserve to be in there with him."

"Mark Kennedy was a great detective. But he lost his mind and now he's paying the price. I was sorry to see his career end like that, but it had to be done. You, on the other hand, I would have loved to see you rot in prison."

"You see? Yes! That's the fire! That's the intensity you'll need!"

"Need for what?"

"I have something I'm putting together. Something big. Something that will truly change this country for the better. Something that Mark Kennedy would have fought for and died for. Something that will easily erase the memory of Jordan Rickstein off your portfolio. Does that sound good to you?"

"Why me?"

"Because I've read the majority of your case files. You're good. You know the law frontward and backward, and I need someone with that skill set to help me."

"I don't need flattery."

"In that case, let me speak with candor. You're smart and you have a license to practice in the state of Vermont which is vitally important to me right now."

"Get to the point."

"What's the most heinous crime happening in this country today?"

"I don't know, there's a lot."

"Humor me. What do you think is number one?"

"Sex trafficking."

"I knew you'd say that. You took an impressive stand against sex trafficking and child abductions here in the state of New York a few years back. How would you like to make an aggressive push to end sex trafficking in this country?"

"From Vermont?" He snickered. "How?"

"The human species makes its more difficult decisions based on one variable: Is the relative amount of effort, pain, and suffering worth the financial gain? I will make it so the answer to that question for all sex traffickers is a simple 'no.' I will send a message that will shred through the people who are the most responsible, all the way down to those who are least responsible, and everyone in between."

"This is a hoax. You don't have the resources to do that, and if you're planning anything like that…that…heinous mob massacre, I'd prefer to stay far away from such an act."

"This is real. And your career is over. You have done amazing things in your time, and after a couple controversial decisions they shove you aside? You are in a position, right now, to make some real change. To help ensure that we do have the resources we need. I'm not asking you to kill anyone. I'm asking you to help give us an opportunity to not only punch sex trafficking in the mouth, but to set it on fire afterward and watch it burn."

Peterson stood up and paced back to the window. He noticed the white van was gone.

"I can sense your interest in the phone," Caprizzi remarked, lifting the handle off the lever and dialing a nine and a one. "You have two choices: You can push that last number, and I'll bolt out of here—who knows, maybe I'll get caught."

"Or?"

"Or, you let me and my associate take you to my lake house in the country to discuss the specifics of what we need. I have a jet waiting. We'll have you back by dinner, and if you don't like what we talk about, no hard feelings."

"Who's your associate?"

Caprizzi stood up and walked to the door; he opened it and waved his arm. A man entered. Peterson couldn't believe his eyes.

"How did you…"

"Not important. You can call him Mr. X for now. You never know who's listening."

"Back by dinner, right?"

"Back by dinner," he replied.

Peterson walked over to the phone and hung it up. He took his jacket down from the coat hanger as well as his hat.

"Let's not waste any more time then."

CHAPTER 12

WILL SUTHERLAND

The Financier

Sutherland waited patiently outside Sergeant Jennings' office. He had filed a request at the DA's office over a month ago for more invasive surveillance at Uptown and was hoping with the most recent murder investigation and Mark Kennedy's release, it would be granted. The sergeant had called him that morning to tell him that he wanted to discuss some things.

If his request was denied, again, he knew exactly what his next move was going to be. It didn't take a mastermind to know that Kennedy's release and expedited hiring at Uptown was no coincidence. He had called Firerock and tried to access Kennedy's ten-year-long file, but it had been completely sealed. After hours of digging around, making phone calls, and begging for favors, he was able to determine that it had been made classified by the Federal Bureau of Investigation. *Could Kennedy be somehow working as an informant?* He wanted to have a sit-down and find out.

While waiting outside his sergeant's office, a news story came on over the television in the breakroom that caught his attention. The headline news of the day was a story about a young girl named Rachel Davis who was reported missing. Her parents were on the morning news issuing a statement through sobs and moments of complete emotional breakdown:

"Please, to whoever may know where our baby is, come forward with information. She's a good girl, a great girl, and we are so worried about her."

The dad came on:

"If someone has taken her, we beg of you not to harm her. We have money. We will find a way to pay you whatever you want. Just please, I am begging you, bring our daughter back to us!"

The father was then ushered off the stage, and Agent Brent Waters took his place:

"At this time, her last known whereabouts were at Club Avalon two nights ago. She was last seen with this man, identified as Antoni Bortega. We believe this to be an alias, but if you recognize this man or have any information regarding this case, please contact us at..."

"Sutherland, let's go," commanded Sgt Jennings.

Sutherland got up and entered the office.

"Have a seat."

"Did you hear this news story?"

"Yeah, just awful."

"So, what do you have for me, sir?"

"Look, Detective, I'm not going to beat around the bush. Your request for extra surveillance got denied."

Sutherland rolled his head back and sighed deeply. "Very predictable, another month of my life gone. What a waste of time."

"You gave it your best shot, again, and now it's time to move on, again, unless something else more concrete presents itself. If the extraordinary level of illegal activity is going on there, like you believe, they'll slip up."

"Not if it's Victor Capr—"

"That's enough muttering the name of that deceased man around here," the sergeant interrupted. "You get people all worked up and it never leads to anything. No evidence equals no case, which equals a waste of taxpayers' time and money. So that's it. On to new cases like the murder you're working on, for starters. It's not a recommendation, it's an order."

"Yes sir."

Sutherland excused himself and sauntered off to his desk. Konine was waiting for him. "How did it go?"

Sutherland shook his head.

"Damn it, you've got to be kidding me."

"I know, believe me, I fucking know."

"So that's it then, eh? Focus on that Marineau murder maybe?"

"The Marineau case is a good one." Sutherland lowered his voice. "But I'm not done here. I want to run over Micky Fontaine's story one more time."

"Fontaine? We've covered that angle. He's clean."

"We're missing something. Something with the way he got named the CEO of Uptown. Get Dominick to bring the file up."

"All right," Konine responded halfheartedly.

Sutherland poured himself a cup of coffee. Fontaine had been the subject of Sutherland's first investigation against Uptown. He came from no money, no fame, no formal business background, and had shit for credit. A major loan company had come along, decided to be generous, and all of a sudden Fontaine was the president of a casino, hiring ex-cons and criminals. Over time he became one of the most popular characters in the state of Vermont. Fontaine was the weak link, and hidden underneath thousands of pieces of paper was the answer. Files from the casino licensing and zoning, construction permits, the loan agreement, bank accounts; the connection was there somewhere.

Konine came up the stairs and brought the investigation report to Sutherland. "I'm going to take a vacation; let me know if anything turns up."

"I'll be sure to send it in a memo, you lazy ass," he said as Konine walked across the office to Dominick's desk.

Sutherland started flipping through the papers, running the chronological story through his head. Jonas Rockerford, the vice president of a major New York-based loan department at National Summit Bank, signed off on giving Fontaine a sizable start-up loan. Absolutely no connection between Fontaine and Rockerford. They had never even lived in the same city. Rockerford, three times married, had a great life. His current wife was a younger woman, a real trophy. Together they had one biological daughter. All three of them had crystal clean backgrounds. Sutherland picked up the file of his first ex-wife, Karla Montsey. They were married a total of six months when he found out she was having an affair with her boss, and they split shortly thereafter. No kids, no criminal relatives, nothing of any significance. Lisa Summit was the second wife. She was the daughter of the founder of National Summit Bank. They were introduced to one another at a work retreat. After being married for twelve years, they got divorced. It was Rockerford's turn for the adultery. Mr. Terrence Summit, the father-in-law, was retired by the time their marriage fell apart, and based on Rockerfords superb stats with the company, he retained his job and she had somewhat of a breakdown. She moved away to Arizona. She was remarried to a Latino man named Tomas Vega. He was a "business owner" found to be connected with a local gang, Los Lobos Rojos. Tomas had been visiting New York "on business" per his statement when he was arrested for sexual battery and assault of a young girl. He was given five to ten years at Firerock around the time Kennedy was arrested. He only made it a few months before he was murdered; he had been stabbed in the neck with a broken broomstick.

Sutherland called out, "Hey, Jim! Get over here."

"On my way."

Sutherland continued to read the report. Tomas had two estranged sons. Sutherland put their names into the computer: Alonso and Jorge Vega. There was nothing local that came up except for Alonso's last known address, which happened to be in Vermont. He expanded the search to the national database. Alonso, shortly after turning eighteen, had gotten into some serious trouble with possession of cocaine and a DUI resulting in manslaughter. He spent five years at Firerock and then moved to Vermont shortly after. There was nothing else about the boy, who was now about twenty-eight, nor his brother Jorge, who at this point could be living anywhere.

"You solve the case already?" asked Konine as he approached Sutherland's desk.

"Did you know that the guy that Fontaine got the loan from…"

"Rockerford?"

"Exactly, Rockerford. His second wife, the one whose father owned National Summit Bank, she was remarried to a guy who ended up at Firerock."

"Yeah, that's all in the initial report, isn't it?"

"It is, but check this out. Read this to me." He pointed to a line from a Firerock report log.

Konine read aloud, "At approximately 1100 hours inmate number 410087, Tomas Vega, was found deceased in laundry room B. The medical examiner placed cause of death secondary to a lethal upper extremity vascular wound involving both the subclavian artery and vein as well as part of the descending thoracic aorta via a sharp broken edge of a broomstick. Also involved in the murder was inmate number 296310, Smitty Dreyfus; inmate number 401946, Kirk Johnson; and inmate number 891120, Jordan Rickstein. See individual reports for further details on the deceased. At this point in time person of interest is inmate number ******, **** *******. Guard Liam Robbins was first on scene…"

"Does anything strike you as strange about that report?"

"The blanked-out name?"

"Exactly. Now, look at this." Sutherland licked his fingers and flipped through a different stack of papers. He withdrew a checkout log from Firerock. "This is the time and day of Kennedy's physical release from Firerock. This is the only piece of information I was able to have access to from his file. Read it to me."

"10/13/2012: 0822. Prisoner number ******, **** ******* is released under the supervision of the Federal Bureau of Investigation."

"You see? His name is etched out. Tomas went to prison right around the time Mark Kennedy went to prison. If Kennedy is responsible for his murder, there's the connection."

"Firerock is one of only a couple maximum security prisons in New York. Odds are actually pretty good they'd end up at the same one."

"And you're aware that one of Tomas Vega's kids lives here in Vermont now?"

"I didn't know that, no. But what connection could these kids have to anything?"

"I intend on finding out as long as you agree that there's a possibility that these coincidences are interrelated."

"It's a stretch, but sure, also a possibility," Konine said, lowering his voice. "But Sutherland, Sergeant said to lay off. You sure you want to go down this road?"

"Only if you're in," he said, pointing to Konine.

"What's the son been up to recently?"

"Nothing. No police reports, no convictions, no jail time."

"Name and address?"

"Alonso Vega. Last known was a shitty neighborhood just outside Rockingham."

"That's only like twenty minutes away."

"Yup," replied Sutherland, clicking and spinning his pen quickly in his hands, an anxious tic he picked up during his career.

"I'm driving," remarked Konine. "Dominick, you're coming with!" At the sound of his name, Dominick poked his head up from his desk. "Get in touch with the Rockingham Barracks, let 'em know we're on our way. And if any of the troops who know the area are available to assist, we need 'em."

"After you, Trooper," said Sutherland.

"Lead the way, darling," he replied.

. . . . . .

Sutherland pulled up to 4333 Sunshine Avenue, Rockingham, Vermont, with Troopers Konine and Dominick behind him, as well as Trooper Lance Smith, who was available from the Rockingham Barracks. Sutherland had made it clear to all of them that this was a "friendly" visit, but they should be prepared for anything.

The street name was clearly an oxymoron, as it looked as if this particular part of town had never seen a ray of sunshine in its existence. Dusk was settling in and storm clouds made their presence known with rolls of thunder in the distance. Drops of rain slowly turned to heavy downpour. The three cruisers rendezvoused before heading down the dark, windy road, which was overrun with dead, towering maple trees and untrimmed bushes. Half the lights on the street were broken, which created a darker than usual environment for that hour of the day. As the three cruisers quietly crept down the street, doors to houses closed and locked, and people scurried off their porches. They reached the address.

"Hmm, nicest house on the street by far," said Konine over a private radio channel.

"Not saying much given what the rest of the houses look like," returned Sutherland.

Smith radioed in, "I'll be curious to see what the inside looks like."

"We're going to find out. Konine, you take Dominick and go around back."

"On it. I love playing sweeper."

Konine got out of his cruiser with his trainee, and they inched their way around the back of the house. Sutherland noticed that a drape shuttered from one of the side windows.

He and the other trooper exited their vehicles, and the storm instantly soaked them. They quietly walked up the front steps and positioned themselves along the side of the door. Sutherland pushed the doorbell. He followed it with three loud knocks. No answer.

He knocked again. "Alonso Vega, this is the Vermont State Police. We would like a word with you!" he said in a booming voice.

Again, no response. Sutherland peered in through the front window. He could just make out a sliver of the inside of the house. A marijuana pipe sat on the edge of a nearby table.

"Possible narcotic paraphernalia; let's go inside."

Smith smiled. "I couldn't agree more."

They both drew their guns. Sutherland gently turned the door handle. It slowly opened a couple of inches before the latch stopped it.

"On three," commanded Sutherland. "One, two, three."

Trooper Smith kicked in the front door, and Sutherland moved inside. They entered only a few steps into the first room.

"This is the Vermont State Police..."

Three young men huddled together in the next room bolted for the back of the house.

"Runners!" screamed Sutherland. He could hear their footsteps and what sounded like pots and pans clamoring to the ground two rooms away. He cleared the first room while Smith ran up and secured the next doorway. Sutherland caught up and waited a moment.

The back door shattered and the three men went roaring out of the house.

Konine and Dominick were waiting. "Out back, out back!" yelled Konine.

As one of the men leapt down the four stairs extending from the back patio, Dominick speared him in the chest just before his feet hit the ground. They both slammed to the lawn and slid several feet through deep puddles of mud. Konine ran over to assist with the first arrest.

Sutherland and Smith sprinted for the back of the house. The back door was broken and two of the unknowns were running for the fence on the other end of the yard.

"Smith, get back to the cruiser and head up to the next street," Sutherland ordered. "Make sure they don't cross over into another neighborhood. Call for backup!"

"On it!"

Sutherland ran after the two men. The one in front was small but superbly agile. He easily hopped over the fence; the other larger one was struggling. Sutherland caught up as he was trying to hoist his other leg over the top. He holstered his gun and took aim with his Taser. He shot the loaded prongs, landing a direct hit. He sent 50,000 volts of electricity into the young man, who dropped off the fence instantly in a heap of convulsions.

"I got him, I got him, you go!" yelled Dominick from behind.

Sutherland dropped the Taser and hopped the fence. He listened for a moment and heard rustling up ahead through the dense forest. About thirty yards away he could see lights to another house. Smith's police cruiser went speeding by to get the adjacent road secured. He made his way through the woods quickly, dodging in and out of trees and bushes, stopping every now and again to listen for more footsteps. As he approached yet another fence, the sounds of the fleeing suspect dissipated. All was noiseless save the steady beat of the rain. He pulled up behind a tree.

Smith's voice came over his radio. "In position, no sign of the suspect."

Sutherland took a step out into the open.

BANG! A gunshot went off nearby, followed instantly by the side of a nearby tree shattering. He retreated back a few steps, withdrawing his gun.

"Shots fired! Where's the backup?"

Off in the distance he could hear sirens. Help would be there any second, but with the vast woods and scattered neighborhoods, Sutherland felt he had no time to waste. He pushed forward once more, his Glock ready. He heard more rustling and spotted the man sprinting toward the fence, which he hopped over once again without much effort.

"Fuck!" he exclaimed.

He ran up to the fence himself and smashed his foot through it to create a window. He peered through, and two more bullets ricocheted nearby. He took cover to the ground. He slowly lifted his head and looked through the hole just in time to see the suspect running for the side of the house. Sutherland unloaded three rounds, making contact with the suspect twice. Even with the injury, the suspect managed to jump up and into a window of the neighbor's home.

Sutherland jumped the fence and carefully moved toward the outside back wall.

"Konine, position?" he whispered.

"Just arrived to the adjacent street, Hawthorne and Walnut."

Sutherland leaned away from the house to get a view of the address.

"Come to house one twenty-eight on Hawthorne. The suspect is inside. Tell me when you're ready."

"Ten-four."

Sutherland waited for Konine to get everyone organized. Although it took just a few moments, it felt like hours.

"Sutherland, we're ready at the front door. Backup is here, but it doesn't look like anyone's home."

"I'm going in. On my mark you storm the front."

"Got it, we're ready."

He looked at the window the suspect had jumped through. There was blood streaked up the side of the house. He gauged the height of the window and decided it was too high and too dangerous to attempt. Instead he crept up the rear staircase leading to the back entrance. Each step creaked when he walked. He pulled up just outside the door, took a deep breath, and lifted the handle. It was open. Silently he stepped in. In the next room over was a family of four watching TV with the lights off. The kids jumped up, startled, and the mother screamed. Sutherland motioned for them to be quiet and flashed his badge.

He quietly asked, "Is this your whole family?"

The mother nodded in affirmation. As they tried to calm themselves, Sutherland moved to the room that the outside window led to. The door was closed.

"Konine, move in. Come to the rear of the house. Be careful—there are friendlies in a room off to your left. Get them out of here."

Konine, Dominick, Smith, and two other troopers entered. One of them veered off and coaxed the frightened family to safety.

"Alonso Vega," Sutherland called out in a thunderous voice. "Or friend of Alonso Vega, you are about to make this very difficult for yourself. We have troopers outside the window, outside the door here, surrounding the house. We know you're alone. Throw your gun out the window, and surrender yourself!"

No response.

"Okay, we're going in," said Sutherland over his radio. "Guns ready."

The team inside and out positioned themselves.

"Here we go!"

He kicked the door in and took cover. It didn't take long to realize that the man had passed out, most likely already dead.

"Suspect down!"

"Ambulance is on the way," Konine responded.

Sutherland ran up to the young man, felt for a pulse. There wasn't one.

"Starting CPR!"

Sutherland gave two rescue breaths and began going to work on his chest. Blue lights flooded the house as several EMS and local sheriffs showed up on scene. Two paramedics came running in and took over the resuscitation effort.

"Is that your guy?" asked Smith.

Dominick answered, "One of the guys we picked up is Alonso Vega. He said you were chasing his brother, so this must be Jorge."

"Holy shit, Sutherland," scolded Konine. "Sergeant Jennings is going to flip the fuck out."

Sutherland turned to Smith. "Would you mind if we used one of your interrogation rooms?"

"Not at all, Detective, shouldn't be a problem."

"Sutherland, it's time for damage control!" pleaded Konine.

"All we need is some degree of pertinent information. We can't go back to the sergeant without having something. Let's see if there's any information to recover; then we'll go from there."

"Your instincts on this better be right," Konine replied as he walked off with Dominick close behind.

It was a lonely, short ride to the Rockerford Barracks. Sutherland pounded the steering wheel in frustration over the shooting. *Fuck! I shouldn't have fired,* he thought. He decided to focus on more important details. Smith had gone ahead and put the suspects into an interrogation room, giving Sutherland time to think about what angle he was going to take. Alonso was not going to be happy about the news of his brother.

Smith drove the two suspects to the Barracks and placed them in an interrogation room. Just before Sutherland stepped in, Trooper Smith pulled him aside.

"Jorge Vega died on the way to the hospital."

Sutherland sighed. "Okay, thanks for the update."

He opened the door and entered. One of the suspects was Latino, the other white.

"Okay, you two, my name is Detective Sutherland. Remind me again how you know Mr. Vega?"

"We're friends," they both said. He knew at least one was lying.

"Names?"

"Alonso Vega," said the first.

"Pete Gardner," replied the second nervously.

He focused on Gardner.

"How well did you know Jorge?"

"You mean George?"

"Yeah, George. How well?"

"I just met him a few days ago."

"And you?" he asked, pointing to the other.

"I'm his brother, so I've known him awhile."

"So you and your brother both live here in Vermont?"

"Yeah."

"Trooper Smith?" called out Sutherland.

Smith appeared at the door.

"Escort Mr. Gardner out of here; take a statement from him."

Pete Gardner was taken from the room.

"Okay, Alonso. So we recovered some cocaine and some non-prescribed narcotics from the house. This leaves me with a series of questions for you, and I can assure you it is in your best interest to answer honestly and truthfully because this is going to go one of two ways. You cooperate, I will mention that in my report, and I'll do you the favor of leaving out the part where you tried to run away. I'll do everything I can for you. You don't? I nail you for so many offenses that I promise you will end up with a maximum prison sentence. Capiche?"

He didn't respond.

"Good." Sutherland took a seat across the table. "You know, I traveled here from Brattleboro just to talk to you."

"Fuck you," Alonso said angrily as he slumped down in the chair and focused his eyes on the ground.

"HEY!" barked Sutherland, slamming his hands on the table. "Sit yourself upright in that chair and give me some fucking attention!"

He did as he was told.

"You know, I would love to be talking to you and your brother right now, but he's not around to answer any questions. You see, right after he tried to kill me, I had no choice but to put him down. Can you help me understand why he would have done that?"

Alonso grew quiet. Tears welled up in his eyes. "Man, fuck! No man, c'mon. He's dead?"

Sutherland turned his tone more somber. "He's dead, Alonso. He could have easily kept running or surrendered, but instead he wanted a shootout. This has a lot of us confused."

"You're lyin', man," he said with a shaky voice.

"I'm not lying to you. Whatever he was into, or whatever you had him into, he was spooked, man, bad. I want to know what had him so scared that he had to end his life over it. Forget want, I *need* to know. Now he is no longer with us, so the responsibility to communicate falls with you."

Sutherland was silent for a moment. Alonso continued to quietly cry.

"Why did you run?"

"Dude, I don't know. I was told if cops ever showed to get my ass in gear no matter what. I told Jorge to make sure he did the same thing."

"Who told you to do that?"

Silence.

"You and your brother were close, right? Grew up together? Had to deal with that deadbeat dad of yours together? Made it out of New York together?"

"Yeah."

Sutherland leaned forward in the chair. "Well, did you guys talk? You know, about your past? About your jail time? Real personal type stuff?"

"Yeah, we talked. Not when he first moved in, but eventually. I would have been fine not talkin' about anything from before, but he wouldn't leave it be. And I couldn't hold in the secrets no more."

"I need to know those things you told him, Alonso. The things you talked about with him, I need to know."

"Like what?" he said angrily.

"Let's start with your father."

"There's nothin' to tell that I'm sure you don't already know. We was given up by our mom. Dad was pissed that he had to take us and mess up his great life with that rich banker bitch. So he started takin' it out on us.

We bolted to New York first chance we got and ended up gettin' into trouble."

"You mean you got into trouble, with that DUI."

Silence.

"Don't bury yourself. And if you are burying yourself, I really hope you're not doing it for Jorge. Because if that's what you're doing, some sort of brotherly honor code, I promise you, there's no honor in screwing yourself out of a life for someone who already took his."

Alonso squirmed uncomfortably in his seat.

"Let me ask you bluntly the question I came here to ask. Had Jorge, or you, ever had a run-in with a man by the name of Micky Fontaine, Mark Kennedy, or Victor Caprizzi?"

Alonso stopped moving at the sound of the names.

"C'mon, Alonso, if you know something, I can help you."

"Why you askin' 'bout those names?"

"Because those names are linked to a murder investigation. That is why we're here. If you know something and refuse to talk, that will look really bad."

Sutherland allowed the thought to sink in before continuing. "You know, I can tell you're not a bad guy. You're a victim of your circumstances. You've been living under a rock with your brother for close to five years. Now you have a chance to start over. Help us. Help yourself."

Alonso's leg started shaking up against the table. Sutherland kept his gaze on him.

"Look, man, all I know is this. We was approached by that Caprizzi dude in New York. I don't know how he found us, and I ain't ever seen him since. He told us what we already knew, that our dad was pushin' around and takin' money from his wife's ex-hubby. That chump Rockman, or Rockstead…"

"Jonas Rockerford?"

"Yeah. Then that Caprizzi dude tells us that he knew our dad pushed us around. He offered to set us up here, give us nice things, keep us protected, and all we had to do was to get our old man up to New York. So we did. Told him we was in trouble, begged him to come up. Next thing we knew he was gettin' arrested for beatin' on some chick. He was killed right after that in prison. Before we got to live the life we was promised, I got picked up for that bullshit DUI charge. But Kennedy? Man, he got me out of some shit at Firerock. He looked after me. I owe that dude my life."

Boston's heart was thudding inside his chest. "And Micky Fontaine?"

"Never heard of him."

"One more question: Why did Jorge fire at us?"

"When Caprizzi first talked to us, he said no cops should ever show up. But if they did, we was to run, fight, shoot. Whatever we needed to do to get away. You cops had no business showin' up at our doorstep. We didn't do nothin' to no one!"

"For what it's worth, I'm sorry today ended like it did. Trust me, I didn't want this."

"I can't believe he's dead." Alonso buried his head in his hands.

"Okay. Okay. You did good, Alonso. Thank you for your help. I'll make sure this all goes in my report. Konine?" he called out.

The interrogation room door opened. "Yes sir?"

"Get the state's attorney on the phone and let's get his witness protection set up through the marshal service."

"Absolutely, sir, I'll get on it."

"No, no!" shouted out Alonso. "I ain't doin' no witness protection. You think I'm safe out there? You're kiddin' yourself, man. I'd rather be in prison then go into witness protection and get dragged further into this. I'm not testifyin', I'm not gettin' involved!"

"Alonso, I really think—"

"NO! I'm…not…goin'!"

"Fine."

Tears welled up in his eyes again as Sutherland left the room.

"Where do you want him?" asked Konine.

"Until we can convince him to testify, the safest place for him to be is prison. Get a solitary room set up; we'll work on him once he's spent some time there. We need that testimony."

"I'll take care of it."

Trooper Smith walked up to Sutherland.

"Your sergeant is on the phone. He wants to speak with you. He sounds rip-shit pissed."

"Could you cover for me? Tell him I'm on my way back to the barracks right now. Oh, and also tell him to get the DA's office ready for tomorrow. I got a witness that can connect Victor Caprizzi to Uptown. Make sure you use those exact words."

"Will do, Detective."

"How exactly can you definitively connect what he said to Uptown?" asked Konine.

"He said that his father, Tomas Vega, was stealing money from Jonas Rockerford. Uptown was looking for a legitimate loan. So they find this guy, Rockerford, and find out he's got some problems they can help with. Victor Caprizzi then finds and convinces Alonso and his brother to get their father to come to New York. Next thing that happens? Tomas is arrested. I was the arresting officer."

"What?"

"The connection obviously didn't come to me until just now. Kennedy was my T.O. back then. He put me in the right place at the right time. I saw that dirtbag going at it with a young girl. I broke it up and arrested him. He then winds up dead in prison, and I bet it was Kennedy's name in that blacked-out Prison Fatality Report. I guarantee you that Caprizzi set up a deal with Rockerford that if he approved a big loan to a clean guy, Fontaine, he would take care of his problem with Tomas. The deal goes down, Tomas is taken care of, the sons are set up in a safe place for getting Tomas to New York, everything is set up. But Alonso ends up in prison. Who ends up taking care of him? Mark Kennedy. He kept him safe because it was the fulfillment of the deal that Alonso and Jorge made with Caprizzi. It's not rock solid, but it's enough for an extensive investigation by anyone's standards, including Dan Peterson's."

"We may have dodged a big ol' bullet on this one."

"You bet your ass we did. Make sure Alonso is okay. I'm going to have to take a leave of absence while they investigate the shooting, so just keep me updated."

"Will do."

Sutherland left the barracks. He got into his cruiser and started the engine. He pumped the air with his fist. The day had been a good day.

. . . . . .

Agent Waters knocked on the door of Stan and Deborah Davis' house. Mr. Davis was quick to answer. His hair was disheveled and he had deep, dark circles under his eyes. His face was devoid of emotion. The news of his daughter's abduction had broken him.

He cleared his throat. "Agent Waters, thank God you're here. Is there any update on Rachel?"

"May I come in?"

"Of course."

Waters stepped into the massive home. "Mr. Davis—"

"Oh, Agent Waters," interrupted Mrs. Davis, "is there any word from anyone?"

"I'm afraid we haven't heard anything yet. No demands have been made. No one has reported seeing her after the night at the club."

Mrs. Davis became weak-kneed. She fell to the floor and began to sob.

"If she was taken by that man, why wouldn't anyone have called for a ransom? I just don't understand," said Mr. Davis, his voice quivering with frustration.

It broke Waters' heart to see them so distraught, so lost. He knew the feeling all too well.

"What if...what if our little girl is dead?" shrieked Mrs. Davis between inconsolable sobs.

"We can't think like that, honey," encouraged Mr. Davis, who had begun crying as well. "We just can't think like that. I won't stop searching for her. We won't give up hope until she is back home."

"Mr. and Mrs. Davis, I want to assure you that the FBI is working hard on this. I promise that I will personally do everything in my power to find your daughter. You have my word."

"Just find her, please!" begged Mr. Davis with his last bit of energy as he sunk to the floor alongside his wife, rocking her back and forth.

Waters nodded and stepped into the other room. He wiped away his own tear and centered himself. He felt lower than dirt but knew there was little he could do right then and there to help the Davises.

His phone rang; it was the Bureau.

"This is Agent Waters."

"Good morning, sir. I have a Detective Will Sutherland again from the Vermont State Police on hold; he says he needs to speak with you."

"Tell him I'm in the middle of something, I'll call him back when I can." He hung the phone up. From the other room he could hear the Davises talking gently to each other as Mrs. Davis continued to cry. He left through the main door and addressed the agent standing outside.

"Make sure you screen all phone calls coming to the house. Who knows, maybe someone will call."

"Yes sir," the agent responded.

Waters slipped into his company car and gazed back upon the house.

The young agent sat down on the leather living room couch next to the house phone and began the day's wait for the ransom call he knew would never come.

CHAPTER 13

RACHEL DAVIS

Fear

Rachel ran down the driveway of her home in the small suburb just outside of Boston. On the other end of the long, curving road sat her beautiful home. Everything was in full blossom, including the bright white flowers that grew within the hedges that lined the entire length of the driveway. They were her favorite. Far ahead, her parents both appeared at the door. They had ear-to-ear smiles painted on their faces and were waving emphatically to her. She had just seen them a week ago, but it felt much longer. She had never been more excited to hug them. After several long strides, her happiness turned to frustration as she realized the faster and harder she ran, she came no closer to wrapping herself in her parents' loving arms. The smooth cobblestone road became choppy. As she tripped and stumbled along the path, she quickly fatigued.

"Dad! Mom! Help!" she screamed. They just continued their absent waving; her father blew her a kiss.

"Please! Help me!" she screamed again.

Without warning Antoni, her captor, stepped out in front of her and violently threw a black cloth bag over her head.

She awoke. Startled at first. Then the unnerving sensation that something was horribly wrong moved her toward panic. She couldn't see anything; something had been tied around her eyes, and she was sitting in what felt like a comfortable chair, but her hands were tightly secured along with her feet. Her heart began to pound, her breathing shallow and fast.

Where am I? What happened?

Some voices off in the distance spoke in what sounded to Rachel like Russian or German. Thrashing about, she made a desperate attempt to tear her arms free, but to no avail. Her mind began to race.

Should I be silent? Should I say something? Beg for my life? Do my parents even know I'm missing? Who is doing this? Am I still in Boston? How long have I been here?

She began crying.

No Rachel, c'mon, no time for tears. Deep breaths. Just keep breathing.

She began taking deep, controlled breaths. One at a time. It was her only focus. A door opened and a series of footsteps shuffled toward the chair. She wasn't expecting the man's voice to be so soft, comforting even.

"Rachel Davis. That is your name, yes?" said the man with a Spanish accent. She didn't respond.

"If you tell me your name, I would be more than happy to take that blindfold off of you. I know how distressing it is to not be able to see. I promise it will help you be more calm."

She thought for a moment on what to do. Although she didn't want to be trading favors with whoever this was, she felt having her eyesight back was a priority.

"Yes, that's my name," she squeaked, her voice weakened from a prolonged period of silence.

"Very good. Thank you for your honesty. You will find that honesty and trust are very important to me."

The man pulled the material from her face. It didn't take long for her eyes to adjust as she was in a dark room. The first thing she noticed was that she had been dressed in expensive clothes, different from the ones she was last wearing. She expected to be dirty but found quite the opposite was true. She had been cleaned from head to toe. It took a moment for her eyes to focus on everything else going on around her. She was in a small room that more resembled a dungeon. The walls were made of stone. There were no windows. A single light bulb attached to a wire was suspended from the ceiling and provided the only light in the room aside from a man who was taking pictures in the corner. The flash from the lens temporarily blinded her with each and every snap. There were four men in the room besides the one talking. They were large and wore all black. Three of them wore black ski masks. The fourth she immediately recognized. His sleazy, slicked hair and dirty glasses that sat at the end of his nose were unmistakable, *the man from the car who cut them off.* She looked at the man who was addressing her. He was surprisingly small, barely taller than she was. He had delicate and soft features, curly dark hair that was well maintained. His hands matched the rest of his body, diminutive and feminine-looking. He wore dark sunglasses, hiding his eyes, cargo pants, and a white v-neck T-shirt with what appeared to be an expensive diamond necklace dangling around his neck. As she continued to look over her captor, he smiled.

"My name is Marcus. It is so nice to meet you."

"What are you going to do with me?"

Marcus chuckled. "Yes, this is a very common first question. I can assure you that it's not as bad as you're probably thinking."

"My parents have money; they'll be looking for me. I'm sure they'd give you anything you wa—"

"Sh, sh, shhh," he interrupted, lifting his fingers to his lips. "I know your parents have money. It means they took good care of you over the last seventeen years of your life. It makes you perfect."

"P-p-please let me go."

"I cannot do that, Rachel. I am sorry, but you have been chosen, and so you are with us now."

Panic gripped her once again. She began to scream for help. Her shrieking sent stabs of pain through her throat and head.

If only someone could hear me.

Marcus, unaffected, clapped his hands twice. The door opened and another girl was brought into the room. Rachel stopped screaming. The girl was young, nine or ten years old. She didn't look frightened. She merely stood there, still as a statue, gazing upon Rachel. She wore rags and was filthy.

"There will be no more screaming," Marcus said calmly. "Every girl gets to have one outburst. But that is it. And I'm going to teach you the consequence for your action."

He walked over to the girl and kneeled down beside her. "Rachel, this is Theresa. Theresa, can you say hello to Rachel?"

"Hello, Rachel," she quietly said.

"Now, Rachel, in this new family you've been brought into, everyone is held accountable for how they behave. You do as you are told, everyone is treated well. You do things that are not acceptable..."

He reached his arm back and slapped the young girl across the face, knocking her to the ground. She hit the floor and then scampered into the corner of the room, curling into a small ball.

Rachel was somewhere between acute fear and rage. Marcus stood back up and motioned to the other men in the room. They walked up to Rachel and unbound her from the chair. For the first time she noticed that across her hands was a rope that traveled along the ground and then up to the ceiling. Marcus began pulling on the other end, which was attached to a system of pulleys. It yanked her off the chair, but she didn't resist as she didn't want the other girl to have to suffer another hit. She was led to the front of the room where the rope pulled her arms above her head and lifted her to the tips of her toes. Marcus secured the rope and walked over, holding her gently around the waist.

"I do hope you will cooperate. You are my prized possession. But if you'd rather be treated like a piece of meat, I can certainly arrange for that as well. Something to keep the men entertained. Something to keep their hunger satisfied. Would you like that, Rachel?"

"No," she quickly responded.

"Good. That is good." He turned to the large man guarding the door. "Bring Theresa back."

The man walked to where she lay and led the submissive girl out of the room.

"You cooperate with me, I am not only cordial with you, but I will be cordial with the others. It's that simple."

"What is going to happen to me?"

"Like I said, honesty and trust are very important. So I will be honest. It is hard to say what will happen to you. Whoever buys you for the most will get to decide that. It is unlikely you'll be staying here in this country for very long though."

She felt her body involuntarily begin trembling. Tears welled up in her eyes once more.

"You are doing a good thing, Rachel. You'll make a man very happy. And much more important than that, you'll keep your family safe."

He reached into his pocket and withdrew a series of pictures of her parents. One was of her father taking a jog. Another was of her mother laughing with a friend.

"Don't hurt them, please."

"I would hate to hurt them. Rachel, I don't want to do anything like that. But that is up to you to decide. You think you can behave for me?"

She nodded.

"Will you behave for the men who want to have you? Do anything they ask?"

Rachel hesitated, but nodded once again.

"And, Rachel, whatever you do, don't ever run, because that would hurt me very…very deeply."

She nodded once more. Marcus let her feet back on the ground and got so close his lips touched her ear.

"You are beautiful. I will be sure to take care of you." He kissed her cheek. Nausea filled her insides.

He turned and left for the door. "Take her to the others."

Two of the other men walked over quickly. One took the rope down while the other placed the cloth back around her eyes. They led her down a series of hallways, her feet catching on the uneven ground from time to time. Eventually she came to a stop inside another room. They took off her restraints. She waited to take off the blindfold until the door had closed behind her and a few extra moments had passed. She was in a smaller room, but it had the same general look to it. The only real difference was that her new quarters had a small window on two of the walls. She walked up to the closer of the two and saw it led to another room. It was the girl from before.

"Hey," she whispered. "Hey, Theresa?"

The girl slowly lifted her head, a bit of fresh blood still smeared on her cheek. She looked at Rachel, her eyes cold, loveless.

"My name is..."

"Rachel. You told me already."

"That's right. How long have you been here?"

Theresa thought for a moment. "I'm not sure."

This poor girl. Rachel felt stabs of emotion but knew she needed to hold it together.

"Wow, you must know a lot about this place."

"We travel all over. Where am I now? Do you know?"

"I think Massachusetts. But I can't be sure."

"What's that? Massa...Massatoo..."

"Massachusetts? It's a state up north."

There was a pause.

"Where are you from?" Rachel asked.

"I don't remember."

"Theresa, you have to stay strong for me, okay? We're going to be fine. My parents will have everyone looking for us. Okay?" she said, her voice beginning to crack.

"That's what the last girl said."

"What last girl?"

Theresa pointed to the opposite wall. Rachel walked to the other window. She gazed in and could make out a body slumped over on the bed. The sheets were stained a deep red; she had been beaten to death, or maybe she beat herself to death.

Rachel's legs became wobbly; they refused to hold her body weight any longer. She allowed herself to fall to the ground. She looked back at Theresa, who had already retreated back into the darkness of her room.

Rachel rocked herself back and forth. She couldn't help but think about her parents and about what they would do if they were in her situation. For the first time in her life, she didn't have an answer. She was alone. She had no one. Her life was over.

CHAPTER **14**

MARK KENNEDY

The Rabbit Hole

Kennedy inserted his keycard to activate the secured employee elevator. As he waited for it to descend, he saw Billings walking toward him.

"Yo, Kennedy, what are you up to? Problem upstairs?"

"Morning, John. No, no problems. Just heading up to thirteen to talk with a few of the Uptown guys."

"Oh. Well, should I come? I mean, I didn't get a fuckin' invite, but I've been a part of the team here longer than you. It's startin' to feel like I'm getting kicked off the baseball team here."

"John?"

"What?"

"Relax. It's just a brief sit-down, nothing important."

"Yeah, yeah. Go to your fuckin' meeting. If anything important comes up, let me know."

"Sounds good."

The elevator door opened. Kennedy stepped inside and made his ascent to thirteen. He had been called the night before by Sorenteen. O'Shea and Fontaine agreed that it would be better for him to know what was going on beneath the surface of Uptown sooner than later. He was anxious to hear more about this greater plan that was so complex and fragile. The plan that resulted in the death of Caprizzi.

The elevator came to a stop. Two guards were waiting outside. "Mr. Kennedy, nice to see you."

"Gentlemen."

"They're waiting for you in Mr. Fontaine's conference room."

"Thanks."

He stepped forward through the sliding glass doors of Fontaine's office. Lisa, the assistant, was there with a welcoming smile.

"Good morning, Mr. Kennedy, you're looking excellent today."

"Don't I always?"

"I meant, exceptionally excellent."

"I appreciate it. They're in the conference room, yeah?"

"That's right, just follow this red carpet all the way around to my left." She winked at him as he passed by.

He entered through the main conference room doors. Fontaine spared no expense on his private office. The long table was made of a rich agar wood, and expensive, colorful paintings hung on the walls. The level of cleanliness in the room made Kennedy think twice about wearing his shoes on the carpet. O'Shea was sitting on top of the far end of the table, talking with Jules. On either side of him were Fontaine and Sorenteen. A speakerphone sat in the middle, the red light indicating it was in active use.

"Kennedy, top o' the mornin' to ya," exclaimed Fontaine.

"Isn't that supposed to be his line?" Kennedy asked, pointing at O'Shea.

"Fuck you, Kennedy, no one from Ireland actually says that to one another, you profilin' bastard."

Kennedy made his way across the room to a chair nearest the group. He took a seat.

"Do you want anything to drink?" asked Fontaine. "Coffee? Water?"

"Coffee, thank you. Nice to see you're earning your paycheck."

"Well, you're just on fire today, aren't you?" Fontaine hit a button on the table. "Lisa, can you bring us a round of coffees?"

Within a few seconds she arrived and dropped off the smoldering hot beverages. She gave Kennedy a flirtatious smile.

"Don't tell me…" O'Shea said, shaking his head.

"No. She's half my age."

"That never stopped ya before."

"I'll pretend I didn't hear that," chimed in Jules.

"Are we ready to get to business here?" blurted out Sorenteen.

"Aye. Who wants to begin?"

Kennedy raised his hand.

"Kennedy, you have somethin' to say?"

"Who's on the speakerphone with us?"

"That's our contact, Mr. X. He wanted to formally meet you since you're going to be in the inner circle here." O'Shea stood up and grabbed a portfolio from under the table. "You know, Kennedy, Caprizzi spoke very highly of you. He always did. He was connected to you, believed in you, believed in your focus and abilities to get things done no matter what the circumstances."

"Well, we spent a lot of time together in the old days. Loyalty was important to us."

"It showed. As soon as you went to prison, he was workin' on his next project. He recruited the guys and girls he felt he could work with until you got released. But you proved more useful in jail than on the outside, until recently, for obvious reasons."

"Go on."

O'Shea walked over to Kennedy and placed the portfolio down but kept his hand over the top. "You've seen A-Wing. That part of Uptown has been fully active for over five years. More illegal transactions have occurred here than any federal or local agency could possibly fathom. People can suspect all they want, but there's flat-out no evidence that A-Wing exists, and we've gained so much popularity and so much respect that we've earned the right to house what will prove to be one of the largest underground operations that this country has seen." He lifted his hand off the portfolio.

Kennedy opened it. The first file he saw was a picture of a man. His name was printed below: *Marcus.*

"Who is this?"

"Can't you read?" asked Sorenteen.

"I can read, but all it says is Marcus. What is that? An alias? No last name?"

"We only know him by that. His face doesn't match any databases, and believe me, we've checked nationally and internationally."

"What are we holding for him?"

"It's not only what we're holdin' for him. It's what we're doin' for him."

Kennedy closed the portfolio without reading any more. "You are the king of drawing out suspense, O'Shea. Can someone just pull the trigger and tell me what the plan is?"

Sorenteen spoke. "Human trafficking. More specifically, girls being sold to the highest national and international bidders."

The room was silent.

"Kennedy? Did you hear him?" asked Fontaine.

"Human trafficking?" he asked in disbelief.

"Aye, mate."

"Human trafficking!?"

Sorenteen casually took his gun out and placed it on the table.

"Put your gun away, Sammy," O'Shea demanded. "Kennedy, what are ya thinkin'?"

"Girls? Being sold as sex slaves and worse?! Have you guys lost your fucking minds?!"

The speakerphone crackled. "Mark," rang out a distorted voice.

"Oh, great, Mr. X decides to give his two cents."

"Listen to me, Mark. What was the purpose of your mob massacre?"

"To put an end to bad people who knew how to manipulate the law to their advantage."

"This is no different."

"This is really fucking different!" Kennedy shouted, getting closer to the receiver. "We're talking about helping innocent people get hurt, abused, their lives destroyed! That's not what we do! It's not what I do!"

"Kennedy," said O'Shea calmly. "Sit back down."

"I'll sit when I'm ready to fucking sit."

Jules reached over and grabbed his hand. He looked at her; those deep hazel eyes instantly cooling him down. He sighed and took a seat.

O'Shea continued. "These people, these monsters that run this trade are far more above and advanced than the standard law. Their connections run so deep that they are truly invincible. Now, there will be a group of girls comin' here, and things will happen to them that make me sick to my stomach. And we are going to let it happen because when the time comes and we eradicate this Earth of these monsters and their connections, not only will we be disrupting human trafficking along the East Coast, but throughout the world."

"How is this going to affect the world?"

"Some of the clients that will be involved are international. Political leaders, local and abroad. Warlords, high-ranking militants, and higher-up distributors and traffickers of the global sex trade."

Kennedy sat quietly contemplating.

"Well?"

"No," responded Kennedy, not fully convinced. "This is crazy. It's too big. And when it inevitably fails, we will have only contributed to horrific crimes. No fucking way."

"Caprizzi put his trust in ya, mate," said O'Shea.

"Caprizzi wasn't speaking for all of us," barked Sorenteen. "I told you he wouldn't have the spine for this. Deep down he's afraid. I've seen it in him since he got out of Firerock. He's afraid of going back to jail. He's afraid to make the necessary sacrifices so that others don't have to suffer. He's lost his edge."

"Shut your fucking mouth, Sorenteen. Stop pretending like you're some sort of freedom fighter. You're an over glorified thug, so back the fuck off."

Sorenteen raised his gun. "We should kill him now. He knows too much and he's not going to cooperate."

"Sammy, I told you to put that fuckin' gun away!" yelled O'Shea.

"Don't do something stupid," said Jules.

Sorenteen reluctantly tucked it back in his suit jacket. O'Shea nodded at Jules, who walked over to the large flat-screen TV and turned it on. She accessed a prerecorded newscast. "Mark, take a look at this." She pressed play. A female reporter showed on the screen.

It has been five days since the disappearance of Rachel Davis from a club in downtown Boston. Her parents, Stan and Deborah Davis, who initially gave several adamant public statements, have not been available for comment the last two days nor have they been seen outside of their Jamaica Plains home. The FBI have aggressively investigated the disappearance and have uncovered very few leads. A family distraught, a daughter whose whereabouts are unknown, and according to Brent Waters, the head of the Human Trafficking Division for the FBI, the only lead they did have, her captor Antoni Bortega, has so far led to a dead end.

The newscast paused.

"That is real," she said, pointing to the still shot of Rachel Davis on the television. "We have everything set up. And let's not forget all you've sacrificed for this already." She sat down next to him again. "Now the day of retribution is knocking on the door, it stares us in the face, and you're going to stand in the way?"

Kennedy peered at Rachel Davis. Cases of old ran through his head; kidnappings and rape. Investigations tied to human trafficking.

"How much of a safety net do we have? How in control are we?"

Fontaine answered. "Uptown is a proven safe haven. The only problem we have is Will Sutherland. He continues to snoop around despite being ordered not to."

"How do you know he's been ordered not to?"

"Do you know who Dan Peterson is?"

"I do. He is, or at least was, a prosecutor in New York."

"He's working with us."

Kennedy laughed. "C'mon, Dan Peterson?"

"No joke. He is the senior DA in the state of Vermont now. He's on board. No major investigation is going to happen under his watch."

"Unless Will has something to do with it," said Jules.

"You really think he'd go above his superiors? Act on his own?"

"I don't just think he will. I know he will."

"And that's where I come in?"

"That," said O'Shea, "and if you're in, 100%, not an ounce less, you'll be making the decisions around here. That's what Caprizzi wanted."

"And this Marcus is coming here with girls who have been abducted. With this Rachel Davis?"

"It's all but sealed."

"What do you mean by that?"

"He's coming within the next week, unannounced. He wants to see the place, meet us again, make sure everything looks and feels okay before he green-lights it. But make no mistake, he's ready to sell. There's only one variable we absolutely have to control."

"Sutherland?"

"Exactly."

The speaker to the room buzzed and Lisa's voice sounded out. "Mr. Fontaine, sorry to interrupt. Detective Will Sutherland is here to see Mr. Kennedy."

"That is not under control," Sorenteen jabbed.

"Mark," announced Mr. X, "are you on board? Will you help us finish this?"

Kennedy leaned back in his chair. He returned his gaze to Rachel Davis. "I'm in."

O'Shea and Fontaine gave a nod. Sorenteen maintained his scowl of disapproval.

"But if we're going to do this, we're going to do it my way. No innocent people get hurt by our hands. And as soon as possible we end this."

"I think we're all on board for that, mate. Remember, the lives of a few, for the lives of many. Very few people are built to be able to do this sort of thing. We are obligated to at least try."

"Very good, gentlemen, call me if you need anything," said Mr. X before the receiver clicked off.

"One other thing, O'Shea."

"What is it?"

"I want John Billings working directly with me."

"Caprizzi left him off the list for a reason."

"Billings will do as he's told and I trust him. That's more than I can say about some of the people in this room right now."

"Okay, you can have Billings with you, but if anything happens it's on you to take care of it."

"Nothing is going to happen."

"You should get downstairs and talk to Sutherland," said Fontaine. "Get him out of here."

Kennedy got up to leave. He turned around as he reached the door. "How the hell did Caprizzi put this all together?"

"It's Caprizzi, mate. He wanted it done, and so it was."

CHAPTER 15

VICTOR CAPRIZZI

December 18, 2003, Atlanta, GA

Caprizzi, O'Shea, Sorenteen, and Billings pulled up outside a small diner. It was an unusually hot day in Atlanta for December, and the only thing worse than getting out of the air-conditioned SUV was standing next to the exterior tin of the establishment, which elevated the temperature yet another several degrees.

"Billings, you wait in the car," ordered Caprizzi. "Keep your eyes out for any trouble."

"You got it, boss."

The rest of them made their way into the diner, sweat and humidity drenching their shirts. The inside wasn't any more comfortable as there was no air-conditioning. They seated themselves and ordered a round of ice waters.

"What's that look on your face, Sammy?" asked Caprizzi.

"What look?"

"You see it, Kevin? He looks worried."

"Aye, I see it. Not exactly the most intimidating look I've seen you give."

"Billings looks more intimidating than you right now," Caprizzi commented as they all looked at him in the driver's seat outside; he was picking his teeth in the rearview mirror.

"I don't like that we're meeting this guy on his terms."

"There's no other choice. He's a big-name client, so he gets what he wants. That's why I brought all three of you. We'll be fine. Just follow my lead."

Sorenteen looked around the diner. He returned his attention to the table, where Caprizzi was staring at him.

"What?"

"You're killing me."

"What are you talki—"

"Go wait in the car with Billings."

"I was just look—"

"Sammy, trust me, just go wait in the car, keep an eye out from there."

Reluctantly he stood up and left. As he exited, a group of men walked in.

"That's them," said Caprizzi, looking in their direction.

The five men who entered carried themselves confidently. The one in front, who solely went by the name Marcus, was small, unintimidating. He hid behind designer sunglasses and colorful pastel clothing, but the four other men around him looked more like highly trained military officers. They sat at a nearby table. Marcus took a seat with Caprizzi and O'Shea.

"Marcus. It's nice to meet you."

"Indeed," he said nonchalantly while his arms moved dramatically in the air for emphasis. "We're very excited at the thought of conducting business of this scale in the United States and with such nice accommodations."

"We are happy to have you."

"If you don't mind me saying, your reputation makes me and my associates just a bit nervous. How do we forge the level of trust necessary to push forward?"

"It's very simple, Marcus. I can assure you that I act for financial gain only. You're a businessman, one of the best in the world, I hear."

"Flattery won't be necessary."

"Well, it's deserved. And I say that because I, too, am a businessman, and I would consider myself an excellent one."

Marcus let out a quiet laugh.

"I will be dedicating my life to this casino and everything that happens inside it. I would never ask you to trust someone you didn't know just like I wouldn't appreciate being asked the same thing. Just pay attention to us for the next six or seven years. See what we do and how we do it. Words don't mean anything; it's actions that speak the loudest. I'm sure you'd agree?"

"Mr. Caprizzi. I do agree. I also must emphasize that trust is everything to me. I have put down my own family members in the past because of my issues with trust. I am willing to build a relationship between your people and my people to hopefully one day conduct the level of business you claim you can provide. But let it be clear, if you decide to go down this road, if I ever get the sense that you are untrustworthy, whether I'm alive or not, I can promise that you and your people will learn the true meaning of pain."

"As much as I don't like partnerships based on threats, I am willing to let that one stand, because I have sacrificed so much already to put myself in this position, and I know that there is a great potential for great business here."

They shook hands.

"There will be one more thing that must be done, something I require in order to begin our empire today."

"What can I help you with?"

"The diner we sit in has a room downstairs. One of my girls is down there as we chat, spending some time with a rather untrustworthy client. A lesson must be taught. I would like you to take care of this problem for me. You do this, our friendship can begin."

Caprizzi looked at O'Shea and signaled for him to take care of it.

"How hard a message would you like me to send?" he asked.

Marcus took a small sip from his water. "An Irishman. I like that. As hard as the moment calls for."

O'Shea put his cap on and excused himself from the table. Two of the bodyguards also stood up and brought him to the kitchen. The cooks didn't seem to care about their unwarranted presence and went about their daily routine without so much as a glance in their direction. They stopped and the two escorts knelt down, removing a section of floor from beneath them; no one would know it was there unless they knew what it was they were looking for. There were narrow steps leading down into darkness.

"Down there?" O'Shea asked.

The Russian bodyguard pointed down. "End of hallway," he instructed.

He stepped as lightly and slowly as he could, using the walls as crutches. His hand ran over a light switch. He flicked it and a series of dim lights illuminated the underground hallway. There were several doors on either side. A digital timer clicked above each room. The one on the end had an hour and twenty minutes left. He walked cautiously toward it, pausing to listen at each door along the way. He couldn't hear any activity. He pulled up outside the last room, where he had been instructed to go. Gently he pushed on the handle. It was locked. He knocked hard three times.

"Time's up!" he announced.

"Fuck you! I have over an hour left!"

O'Shea looked back to the staircase, which seemed further away than before, and then back to the door. He knocked three more times.

"C'mon, mate, time is money."

"That's it!" belted the man.

A sliding lock sounded and the door swung open.

"I paid for..."

O'Shea tackled the man around the waist and drove him to the edge of the bed. Without much effort the man threw him off and into the adjacent wall. He went for a knockout swing, but O'Shea was able to dodge the effort. The man's fist took a chunk out of the rock wall. O'Shea slipped behind him, grabbed one of his arms, and with his other hand grabbed his hair to gain better control. The man pulled his head forward so hard, the hair ripped out of his scalp. Having more mobility, he pounded O'Shea in the face with his free arm. O'Shea lost his grip and the man pinned him back up against the wall and kneed him twice in the thigh. On the third effort O'Shea caught his knee, picked him up, and body-slammed him into the corner of the room. Using the heavy nightstand table as a weapon, he crushed the man continuously until his movement ceased.

O'Shea stood up, panting for air, his leg seared with pain. He looked toward the bed and saw the beaten and battered, half-naked girl strapped down. She was blindfolded and freshly bruised all over her face and arms. He undid her restraints and took the blindfold off. She simply lay there, half in a daze. O'Shea covered her up with some blankets. He had the unshakable sense that he was just as guilty as the man in the corner. He wanted to get out of the basement as quickly as possible.

The lives of a few for the lives of many, he reminded himself. The thought left him no more comfortable with the scene he had just become a part of.

He went back to the man's body and felt his pulse. There was none. He had killed him. Uncaring about the well-being of the abuser, he knelt down and took his wallet. He flipped it open and revealed an Atlanta Police Department badge.

"Oh fuck!" he exclaimed.

He quickly left the room and ran up the stairs. The bodyguards were still there.

"Did you know he was a fuckin' cop?"

They smiled at him.

"Just make sure you clean the room up."

O'Shea stormed back to the table where Caprizzi and Marcus were making small talk.

"That was quicker than I thought it would be," commented Marcus. "Were you successful?"

"Not exactly the encounter I thought it would be."

"Looks like you were struck in the face, and I noticed a limp. Are you okay?"

"I'm fine," he said sharply, flipping the badge on the table. "The cop is dead."

"Good. I don't very much like men who depreciate the value of what is mine."

O'Shea returned an angry glare.

"Don't worry, Irishman, we'll take care of the mess. You can trust us. You did me that favor and now the friendship can begin." He raised his water glass. "To friends and success?"

Caprizzi lifted his and kicked O'Shea under the table. O'Shea copied.

"To friends and success," they both repeated.

CHAPTER 16

MARK KENNEDY

Meet Will Sutherland

The moment Kennedy had heard Sutherland was a detective in Vermont, he knew there would come a time he would have to confront him. He had already mentally prepared himself for the encounter, and yet, faced with the moment, he felt less than confident. His feelings toward his former rookie trainee were complex. He had no respect for him. Yet deeper down he was jealous. Pains of betrayal still stung him, but he knew at one point in his young career, he would have made the same decisions that Sutherland had.

From across the floor he saw Jules was with him; they were chatting away. Sutherland spotted him and came over. Jules followed.

"Mark Kennedy. I had to see it to believe it. It's a pleasure to see you again!"

They shook hands.

"Officer Sutherland, or I suppose Detective Sutherland now. Jesus, last time we spoke I was just a few hours from my sentencing. You look different, grown up. You still jumping off of rooftops and doing things the hard way to catch your suspects?"

Sutherland let out a hearty laugh. "I only did that once, and maybe if you hadn't let the guy drive away with the car, I wouldn't have needed to jump out of that window."

"That was a brand-new company car. I loved that car."

"Unbelievable," said Sutherland. "I still can't believe I'm talking to you right now. I was really glad to hear the news of your release."

"Honestly?"

"Honestly, I was shocked, but still glad for you."

Kennedy noticed Sutherland touch Jules in the small of her back.

"Jules, this is Detective Will Sutherland, my old partner."

"I know Will. We're actually, uh, seeing each other." She gave Kennedy a mean look.

"I learned far too much from this man," said Sutherland.

"Like what?" she asked.

Kennedy answered, "I taught him to see through things, understand situations for what they are."

"Exactly what I was going to say."

"Well, I guess I'm just impressed how many people know you," said Jules. "It seems like everyone has heard of the great Mark Kennedy."

"Well, I'm famous for my sins. What can I say? Not everyone knows of Mother Teresa, but everyone's heard of the devil, right?"

There was a pause in the conversation.

"So, Will, you're here to catch up or on business?"

"As much as I'd like to be here to catch up, I am here for business."

"How can I help?"

He turned to Jules. "Would you mind giving Mark and me a minute to talk?"

"Of course not." She squeezed his hand and went to the nearest bar and had a seat.

Sutherland continued. "Are you familiar with the name Alonso Vega?"

Kennedy thought for a moment. "Yeah, I am. He was an inmate at Firerock, great kid, dealt a rough hand in life."

"What was the extent of your relationship with him while you knew him?"

"Am I being interrogated?"

"No, Kennedy, c'mon, just a courtesy conversation. Your name came up as someone he knew from prison. Just wanted to get some info on him."

"Fair enough. He was getting beat on pretty badly—he was a smaller kid, you know. So one day I decided enough was enough. I started standing up for him the best I could. By the last couple years of his sentence, people generally knew he was off limits."

"Why take care of this kid? Why put yourself in harm's way for a drug pusher?"

"You know all too well that I hate assholes."

"Yes I do."

"He wasn't one of them. But the other assholes who got off on pushing him around? I wasn't going to stand by and watch it happen. I had seen it too many times before. What is this all about anyway?"

"I can't get into too many details, but he's involved in a current investigation. He ran from us. Had his brother take a few shots at us. We ended up having to put him down. It's in all the newspapers."

"You killed his brother?"

"He killed himself when he took the gun out; you know what that's like."

"Yeah, no, you're right. It's been awhile since I've been in the action like that. I'm glad to hear no one on your team got hurt. Am I allowed to ask what the investigation was about?"

"I can't really discuss it with you, Mark. But I do have an unrelated question for you. It's actually the real reason why I came out here."

Kennedy felt a lump in his throat.

"When I heard you got released, I couldn't help my curiosity, so I looked into it. It turns out your file is sealed by the FBI. Your entire time at Firerock is locked out of the system. Any thoughts on that?"

Kennedy lowered his voice. "Between you and me, I don't know much. I was released into the custody of the FBI. I have no idea why or who I should be in touch with, but next thing I knew Mr. Fontaine reached out to me and asked me to come work for him. I'm thinking that they might be running surveillance or something on this place. So until I'm told what to do or who to report back to, I'm just working and doing the best I can to blend in. Do you have any idea why they would pull me from prison to work here?"

Sutherland looked inquisitively at Kennedy. "Not entirely, no. I'll have to try to get in touch with them. Maybe I can figure out some more details. I would think the more you know, the better for your safety."

"My safety? Am I not safe?"

"As I'm sure you've picked up on, there's a lot of shady business happening in this part of the state, and I know you know there are some shady characters working side by side with you, including some, uh, old colleagues of yours."

"So far, I haven't seen anything bizarre or inappropriate besides the amount of partying that goes on. I'm aware there are some guys from the old days around, Sorenteen, O'Shea, but they keep to themselves. They all do their part to contribute to the success of the business here."

"And what is your role exactly?"

"I've been asked to help run an honest casino. That's what I'm doing, you can count on that."

"Can I count on you to tell me if anything pertinent comes up?"

"I will, but I'm not even sure what it is I'd be looking for."

"Well, for starters, I don't suppose you've seen your old friend Victor Caprizzi hanging around, have you?"

"Victor? You didn't hear?"

"He's dead. Yeah, I heard. You know they never found his body, right?"

"I did, but I also heard he got shot in the head. Tough to heal from that one, don't you think?"

"Would be tough, but if someone could figure out a way, it'd be Caprizzi."

"I'll keep my eyes open for him, but it's a waste of energy."

"If I was a trainee, I'd drop it because you're telling me to. But now, gotta go with my gut feeling. So just let me know if you see anything suspicious. And if you're ever in trouble or want to tell me anything, you let me know."

Sutherland peered straight into Kennedy's eyes with such intensity that Kennedy had to avert his stare. He didn't expect Sutherland to have so many things to say.

He wrapped the conversation up quickly. "Okay, Will, we'll be in touch. Let's grab lunch some time and catch up officially, sound good?" he asked while walking away.

"Kennedy!" said Sutherland loudly. "One more question."

Kennedy turned around. "Shoot."

"What are you doing tonight? You want to grab a drink with me and Jules?"

Kennedy smiled. "It's not a matter of what I'm doing, it's who I'm doing."

Jules, eavesdropping on the conversation, got Kennedy's attention with an angry expression.

"You've already picked up a piece?"

"Yeah, maybe you've met her. Her name is, uh…" he looked back toward Jules, "Lisa Holt. She's Fontaine's assistant." He winked at Sutherland.

"Much deserved fun for you. All right, Mark, we'll talk soon."

Kennedy waved and made his way over to a coffee kiosk to decompress for a minute. He looked back just in time to see Sutherland lean in and plant a kiss on Jules' lips. She withdrew, clearly a bit embarrassed, and then left with Sutherland hand in hand. Kennedy, not happy with Jules leaving with him, was just glad the interaction was brief. He breathed a sigh of relief. He would have to keep a close eye on Sutherland as he was never one to shy away if he felt something was wrong. Caught up in the intensity of the conversation, he didn't realize Fontaine had also been within earshot of the meeting.

"That was brilliant work, Mark." He gave Kennedy an overly hard pat on the shoulder. "You handled that perfectly. I didn't realize you used to be partners; I just thought you worked in the same division. How perfect is that?"

"It was a long time ago."

He couldn't quite put his finger on why Fontaine rubbed him the wrong way. He thought it was probably the laugh. It reminded him of Jordan Rickstein's cackle.

"Okay, good talking to you, Micky," he said, walking away.

Fontaine ditched the smile. "Hey, Kennedy. I can't figure you out. We're all on the same team here. So what's with the attitude toward me?"

"Let's get something straight. I might to some degree answer to O'Shea, maybe even at times I'll answer to Sorenteen, but there's no way I will ever answer to you."

"I'm the CEO of this casino."

"Fake casino," he whispered.

Fontaine took an aggressive step toward him, and in sync with the step, Kennedy grabbed Fontaine's testicles as hard as he could. Fontaine let out a stifled yelp as Kennedy whispered into his ear, "You don't ever, ever come at me in any way. Clear?"

Fontaine managed a whimper for a response. "Clear."

"Good!" said Kennedy loudly while releasing him from his grip. "I'll see you later. I would put some ice on those."

Fontaine gave him a thumbs-up and they parted ways. Kennedy was anxious to get into the portfolio O'Shea had given him in anticipation of Marcus' arrival. His role had become much clearer to him. Although the pieces were all in place, they all had to be glued together. So that's what Kennedy was going to do—be the glue to ensure that everything fit together as Caprizzi had intended it.

. . . . . .

Nightfall had come and Sutherland and Jules had just finished dinner. Sutherland had some time off with the ongoing investigation of the shooting, and he was taking full advantage of it. After a couple of bottles of wine, they went back to his place. Jules strolled over to the couch, sat down, and gave him a seductive look. Sutherland's heart skipped a beat as he made his way over to her. She let out a short squeal as he picked her up and began kissing her. She reached her feet back toward the couch and was able to shift her weight enough to pull him down. She situated herself on top of him. After a few more moments of foreplay, he undressed her and she undressed him. The sex was passionate, intense. It sent multiple waves of numbness through both of them. Afterward she lay on top of him, her hair spread over his chest.

"Shall we go to bed?" he asked.

"I'll be up in just a minute. I'm going to clean up in the bathroom down here."

"Okay, don't be long."

He kissed her and headed up the stairs to his bedroom. As soon as he disappeared up the steps, Jules jumped off the couch and slipped her dress back on. She quickly and quietly made her way through the dark downstairs rooms and into his office. She flicked the light on and sat down in front of Sutherland's desk. There were dozens of Vermont State Police files sitting there but none revolving around Uptown. She opened a couple of drawers. Nothing important. The bottom file was locked.

Fuck. Where would he keep the key?

She ran her hands beneath the desk and knocked something over. She bent down to see what it was: a long cardboard tube. She popped the top off to examine the contents.

Blueprints. After a moment she realized the pages included more than just standard blueprints. Inside was every possible schematic angle of Uptown. There were even some bird's-eye views of the whole exterior area that showed before and after pictures of the land. Extensive notes had been taken on floors he had visited and ones he hadn't. Doors he had opened and ones that were locked and restricted. He had two clear circles drawn with question marks. One was the casino floor door to the vault. The second was the woods out behind Uptown on the aerial map. He noted a small dirt road that seemed to run through the woods that hadn't been there before.

While taking as many pictures as she could, she heard footsteps coming down the stairs. She packed everything back up and placed the tube back under the desk. She crossed her legs and spun the chair around just as Sutherland appeared in the doorway.

"I thought you were getting ready for bed?"

"I got lost, then thought it would be more fun to play hide and seek." She stood up and took her dress off again. "You found me, you win." She ran at Sutherland and jumped into his strong arms. Holding her tightly he walked out of the room and made his way upstairs to the bedroom.

. . . . . .

Rachel Davis had just fallen asleep on her cot when the sound of a girl's scream awoke her. Her heart rate immediately jumped as her ears adjusted to the night. A guard was muttering something a few cells away. She got up and quietly made her way to the small window of her cell door. Trying to breathe as lightly as possible, she peered up in time to see a large guard dragging the limp body of one of the girls down the hallway. Afonos, the man from the Mustang, was close behind. His hair was disheveled, but all it took was one stroke of his hand through his greasy hair to put it back in place. He was zipping his pants back up.

"Fucking stupid girls. Worthless products. Weak like puppies," Afonos grumbled.

Rachel had become familiar with this scene. The men would often come down and "test the product." Sometimes it was over quickly, sometimes not. It wasn't unusual for things to get out of hand either. When that happened, the girl of the night would end up badly hurt. For the most recent victim, Silvia, it meant her death. No one had visited Rachel yet. Marcus wasn't lying—she was a star item and there was an order for no one to bother her.

As days became weeks she had made it a point to get to know every girl in the dark cellar they were held in. There were only a few moments a day when no one was in earshot, and this was the only time they had to converse. There was Silvia, who she would never hear from again. She was an exchange student from Guatemala and had been doing a semester at Rutgers University in New Jersey. She was kidnapped only a week ago. Theresa was in one of the cells next to Rachel. She had grown very fond of the little one. By far the youngest, she was priceless to the guards as she was the punching bag that kept the rest of the girls in line. Jessica and Gina, both fifteen, were from Italy. They had been shipped here months ago. There was Katrina and Susan; Lisa and Autumn. The girl who had resided in the cell next to her, the one who was already dead when she arrived, was Christine. She was the oldest at the time and had reached a point where she felt there was no other choice but to beat her head against her cell wall until she felt no more. Now a girl by the name of Dawn was imprisoned there. She was quiet, didn't talk much. In total there were twenty girls in this particular cellar. Rachel was sure there were more cellars out there.

Together they feared all the guards, but none more than Afonos. His name meant "immortal" in Russian. She knew this because he always bragged about it as he beat and raped the other girls.

"Who's next, let me see, who's next?" he excitedly said to himself. He stopped outside of Gina's room. "You. You didn't think I'd forgotten about you, did you?"

A lot of the girls had grown accustomed to the routine. Others were so drugged up that they didn't even know what was happening to them. But the worst was when they came to have their way with the "prime products"—the girls who were not to be drugged because their value depreciated on the market.

Rachel heard Gina begin to cry and beg for his mercy. The heavy door opened to her cell, and her voice went quickly from clear and strong to muffled. She was being choked.

Enough was enough.

"Hey!" Rachel yelled before thinking of what the consequences would be. "Hey! Stop hurting her!"

The sounds of her gasping for air continued.

Rachel became infuriated. "Hey, you stupid fuck. Who are you kidding? Your dick is too small to actually break any of us in."

Gina started coughing and taking deep breaths. He had let her go. She looked out her small window for signs of Afonos. Silence. Then footsteps. Soft at first, then louder. And louder. Then nothing again. She gripped onto the bars of the window and leaned her head as far to the side as she could to try and get a glance at Gina's room. A belt buckle violently whipped across her knuckles. She stumbled backward, her hand filled with searing pain. She looked down at her hands, which bled deeply. His face appeared behind the bars.

"What did you say to me?"

"I'm sorry, I just…I didn't want you to hurt her."

"You're sorry? You're not sorry. But you're about to be. You just broke the rules. Your defiance just made one of the product's nights very long. Just feel lucky that you're off limits, and that the others have to suffer for your fucking loud mouth."

He disappeared again.

"Wait! Don't go! Are you so weak that you have to fill up on young girls to make yourself feel like a man?!"

He came running back to the door and unlocked it.

"You are supposed to be off limits, but I suppose Marcus wouldn't mind if I taught you a lesson in respect." He ran up to her, grabbed her by the hair, and threw her as hard as he could against the door of her cell. Her face smashed up against the window.

"You will not soon forget this night, you bitch." He stepped back and whipped her as hard as he could with the metal of his belt. She screamed out; tears of fear built up in her eyes.

Don't show him you're afraid.

She stood up straight as she could. She kept her eyes forward. He again forced her face against the window hard. He spread her legs. Rachel kept her gaze toward the other cells, all the girls' faces peering toward hers. Rachel was one of the oldest in captivity. She had taken it upon herself to do everything she could to protect the others. If the opportunity ever presented itself, she would do anything she needed to get them out of that dark, cold cellar. But tonight was about getting through her punishment. She let her mind drift to memories from her past. She erased her conscious mind and let Afonos have his way.

CHAPTER 17

MARK KENNEDY

The Meet and Greet

Kennedy looked out from atop the Uptown helipad over the rolling hills of the Green Mountain State. It was shaping up to be a nice morning; chilly, but blue skies as far as the eyes could see. Jail had become a distant thought. He hoped it would stay that way. He checked his watch: 9:38 a.m.

"Got somewhere to be?" asked O'Shea.

"He's thirty-eight minutes late. Clearly he doesn't care about other people's time."

"Well, I've met him once before, long ago. I can assure you, he doesn't give a fuck about other people's time but his own."

"Great, so we're working with a felon who's also a narcissist?"

"It's just like working with Caprizzi all over again."

Kennedy laughed. "Good point."

The faint sound of a helicopter got Kennedy's attention. He looked around and saw it off in the distance.

"Call Sorenteen and Fontaine. He's here."

O'Shea took his phone out and gave a quick call to the others.

"They'll be up in a minute," he informed.

"Good. So just like we talked about last night, we need to treat this guy like royalty. He's used to having his way; he's not the type that's gonna play well with others."

"Fontaine is going to play his role of making sure he's comfortable, but you're going to be the man that works directly with him. He knows of you, and your background, so you'll have to convince him that you're legit. Remember, the more he sees you as a black-and-white businessman, the better off we'll be."

The door to the roof opened. Billings, Sorenteen, Jules, and Fontaine came out and joined them in a line as the helicopter made its final approach.

"Looking good, ladies and gentlemen," said Fontaine. "Image—"

"Is everything. Yeah, we got it," Kennedy interrupted. "Just don't forget our individual roles. Fontaine, you're the spineless charmer."

"Can we not call it that?"

"Okay, you're the gutless pretty boy."

The others smiled.

"O'Shea and Sorenteen, you guys are the muscle. Go toe to toe with his muscle. I'll keep his confidence in check, make sure he's here to play ball with us, not take over our whole operation."

"Here we go," said Sorenteen as the chopper made contact with the roof.

A set of stairs dropped and out stepped two huge bodyguards, one built like a linebacker the other like a sumo wrestler. They each carried sidearms on their hips. They turned toward each other and extended their hands. Marcus gave each one of his hands and stepped down slowly like an old man. Behind Marcus stepped three more bodyguards. Two looked to be Hispanic, the other European. Kennedy noticed the European's face was bruised and battered. They walked as one unit to where they stood.

Fontaine was the first to step forward. He shook Marcus' hand. "It is a pleasure to finally meet you, sir," he said with a perfectly manufactured smile.

"The pleasure is all mine, I can assure you."

"How was the trip in?"

"I hate flying. Happy to be on the ground."

"Can I get you anything to start? Perhaps a drink?"

"I am fine for now." He looked everyone over and stopped on Jules. "A woman handling the sale of women? Absolutely not."

Jules looked like she was about to punch him.

"Marcus," said Kennedy, "Ms. Romano is irreplaceable. She is the best at what she does and quite frankly is more of a man than any of us."

Marcus lifted his hand for silence. "This is not negotiable. She can help from the distance, but I do not do business directly with women."

Kennedy leaned into Jules and whispered, "Go ahead and leave for now; first impressions are everything. I'll let you know how this goes. Maybe for now just focus on Sutherland."

"You owe me," she said before leaving the group.

"I would very much like to step away from the noise of where I stand."

"Absolutely," said Fontaine. "Let's head inside. Just one thing: We don't usually allow weapons in the casino."

The five bodyguards stiffened up, and one took a step closer to Fontaine. This prompted Sorenteen and O'Shea to take a step forward as well. Kennedy noticed that with the exception of Sorenteen, the bodyguards towered over everybody, including him. It was his turn to be introduced.

He pushed forward and cut in front of Fontaine. "Sammy, Kevin, it's okay. You can relax." He looked at Marcus. "It is our policy that we don't have firearms in the casino, for everyone's safety. But I want to make it clear that Victor Caprizzi trusted you and your professionalism, and so do I. So as a courtesy, your men are welcome to keep their firearms until you feel more at ease."

"A most kind gesture. Thank you."

"Let's head inside."

Marcus nodded and waved at the helicopter. Four more men got out. These men were a different breed altogether. They were all thin, wore heavy eyeliner, piercings in every imaginable piece of skin. Some were disfigured, and all carried with them an aura of evil. As far as an unnerving group of individuals, they set the bar. The whole group entered through the rooftop access door.

Kennedy introduced himself. "My name is—"

"Mark Kennedy. I know. I've done a lot of research on you. I must be honest, I was disappointed, saddened even, by your friend Victor's death."

"So was I. I'm just glad he completed his vision for this place before he died." He did a double-take of the last four individuals off the plane. It was impossible not to be distracted by them. "If you don't mind me asking, who are these gentlemen joining us?"

"They are the handlers. I give them their basic needs, including the occasional woman for their more carnal requirements, and they make sure the product is ready for the showing, behaving properly, that sort of thing. They can be shown their rooms at once."

"Micky, you want to show them their rooms?"

"Actually," interjected Marcus, "if it's all the same, I'd like them to stay in the girls' rooms."

Kennedy felt extremely uncomfortable with the idea but had to swallow his feelings on the matter. "That will be fine."

"Afonos, you go with them."

"Yes sir," replied the guard with the bruised face.

Fontaine left down the stairs with the handlers. Marcus redirected his attention.

"Mr. Kennedy, I do have some things I need to get off my chest."

"Call me Mark."

"Very good, Mark. Victor has spoken very highly of you in the past, and with the number of favors he has done for me in the last several years, I am hoping that we, too, can establish that level of partnership."

"Well, there's nothing I like more than a businessman. A true businessman. You have a product; it needs to be sold in a delicate and safe way. We specialize in that here. You could not have chosen a safer place to conduct your business."

"I will make that assessment before long. I am less concerned about Uptown itself, and more concerned with your background, Detective."

"Ex-detective. And quite frankly I'd be more concerned with the fact that I shot six people to death at one point in my life."

"I, too, have killed those who have hurt me, or those who tried to disrupt my line of work. I would never judge you for such an act."

Kennedy stopped. "I want to get one thing clear. My being a detective eleven years ago has no bearing on who I am today. I will not be going back to prison, nor will I live my life as a poor ex-convict. Victor left Uptown to me. I have my second chance. I don't care what the product is; I care about the smooth and safe handling of the product and its distribution. If someone gets in my way, I will put them down. If someone puts me or my men in harm's way, I will put them down. If our operation is questioned by someone, or I feel the reputation of Uptown is in jeopardy, I will put them down."

Marcus lowered his sunglasses. "Threats?"

"Not threats, facts. I don't doubt that I have to earn your trust. However, through Victor, you already have mine. You have it until proven otherwise, and I hope it never gets to that point."

Marcus nodded and slipped his sunglasses back up. "I like that and I think I feel the same way. We have both invested a lot in this. I suspect this will all go smoothly. May I see the showing room?"

"That's where we're headed."

The group slithered back and forth through the secret hallways of Uptown. Kennedy explained the layout of the casino and hotel, went over details of where they would all be staying, and gave Marcus a keycard to get into wherever he needed. They arrived at the vault. Sorenteen walked up and opened it for everyone. They stepped inside.

"I hope we have a better setup than this vault," said Marcus.

"Of course we do, mate," O'Shea answered.

"Lead the way, Irishman."

He walked to the back of the vault, opened the secret lockbox, and entered the code. The wall fell away like it always did. Marcus let out a couple of claps.

"I love it, very dramatic."

Instead of walking the length of the hallway to the warehouse, they stopped outside the door immediately off to the right. Kennedy hadn't viewed the showroom yet. He was anxious to see the layout.

O'Shea knocked on the door. "Coming in!"

He waited a moment. From the other side the door swung open. There was an Uptown guard present who waited for them all to enter, then closed the door behind them.

The group walked down a flight of stairs and into a dimly lit room. A hallway wrapped around the central viewing area. Every twenty feet or so there was a door to a private room. On the inside of each room was a small bar, a handful of expensive chairs bolted to the ground, and a one-way mirror. The viewing stage was set up like a fashion runway. Different lights stood above to accent the product in different ways. On the other side of the rounded hallway was a series of holding rooms; spaces where the girls would sleep and men could "test" the product. The room as a whole was decorated well with expensive chaise lounges and fine sculptures scattered throughout. The hardwood floors blended nicely with the taupe-painted walls.

"This is extravagant," commented Marcus.

"The best for the fuckin' best," blurted out Billings.

Everyone in the room looked at him.

"And you are..."

"Oh, sorry, I should have introduced myself earlier. I'm John Billings. I help Mr. Kennedy out...and uh...Mr. Kennedy is helping you out. So I suppose indirectly I'll be helping you out."

"John, perhaps you could leave the talking to us," said Kennedy.

Billings lifted his hands up in apology, but Marcus cut in. "No, no...I rather liked that. John Billings, you say?"

"Yeah."

"I like your energy."

Billings looked around awkwardly. "Uh, thanks?"

"Well, gentlemen, I still have to see the rest of the grounds. I may even make a few suggestions, but if everything goes as well as this tour, then I think we're in business."

"Okay then," said Kennedy. "Assuming everything goes smoothly, when do you want the product delivered?"

"In three days' time. We can drive it straight to here?"

"Absolutely. But before we move to the next step, we'll be taking a few precautions."

"I'm listening."

O'Shea and Sorenteen gave confused looks. Kennedy was talking off script.

"I know that everyone in this room is in for the right reasons. But when we are talking about so many people involved with the security and planning, I think safety is the best policy."

"What do you recommend to ensure the safety of my girls?"

"I won't even bother you with the details. Just let it be known that I will be taking careful measures so that there are no surprises on our end."

Marcus thought about his words carefully. "No surprises would benefit all of us. Do what you must, just do it carefully please."

"One more thing."

"Yes?"

"We need access to the names and profiles of the buyers coming in. Those sorts of details are usually pretty important for making sure everyone's needs are met."

Marcus thought a moment. "No. I cannot reveal the names of my buyers. I will get you their information as far as the amenities they prefer and the types of girls they desire, but I can't let you meet them until the day of the show. Fair?"

"Actually, I'm afraid I wasn't asking. I was telling."

"The anonymity of the buyers is of the utmost importance."

"Ensuring that the buyers are who they say they are is of the utmost importance. Victor wouldn't have taken 'no' for an answer on this."

Marcus thought for another moment. "Very well."

"Excellent. On with the tour?"

"I would very much like that."

"I'll escort you out of here, and my associates Sam Sorenteen and Kevin O'Shea will bring you around the grounds. Make sure you walk around our courtyard and try a blueberry muffin from our New England Culinary Academy bakery. It's a must-have."

"Where will you be?"

"I have a casino to run. I want to make sure everything up top is okay."

"Very good."

They left the showroom and exited through the vault back to the casino floor. Kennedy saw Jules talking with some high-roller casino guests.

"Enjoy Uptown, gentlemen." He departed the group and made his way to Jules.

"Can I borrow you for a moment, Ms. Romano?"

"Sure thing, Mr. Kennedy." She turned to the wealthy man she was speaking to. "Just excuse me for one second."

They took a few steps away from the table.

"How'd it go?" she asked.

"I think it went as well as it could have. Sounds like he's in."

"So I'm seriously out of the loop on everything?"

"I really don't think he's going to go for you being an integral part of this."

"That's such bullshit. I'm getting a bad feeling about all this."

"How do you mean?"

"Can I be honest with you, Mark?" she said, lowering her voice.

"Of course."

"Something about Marcus. He's not…human. He's playing by our rules now, but that will change, I know it. Not to mention Will is getting closer and closer. He knows more than he's letting on. We can take care of this right now, clean it up, and move on."

Kennedy ushered her to walk with him. "Believe me, I would love nothing more than for this to end. I feel like my soul has already been shredded. But O'Shea was right. Now that the payoff is so close, the difference between bringing down Marcus compared to destroying a major chunk of it all at once, the ringleaders, the traffickers, the buyers. That's the payoff."

"I just hope everything goes the way it's supposed to. I don't…I can't see you go back to jail, or worse…"

"Hey, I'm here to stay. I'll figure something out. You stay focused on Sutherland."

"One thing is for sure, he's very focused on you, trying to figure out your angle."

"My secrets are safe. You want to get dinner tonight, maybe even just order some room service in my suite?"

"I can't, I have to meet Will tonight. There's some sort of party going on for some of the troopers."

Kennedy shook his head. "This is killing me, you know?"

"I know, but I can't just walk away from my job either. I love you, Mark."

She stepped up close to him and planted a kiss on his lips.

"Take care of yourself, please. I don't need anything else to worry about right now," he pleaded.

"I will. I have to get back to work."

"Okay, we'll talk later."

As he walked away he took his phone out and dialed Fontaine. He got his voice mail.

"Micky, it's Kennedy. As soon as Marcus is settled in, let's get everyone together. I have an idea to make sure the product makes it safely and to weed out any leaks we may have. Just let me know when you're all available."

He headed off the floor to catch up with the others. The bait was hooked, the hook was set, and barring any slipups, it was just a matter of reeling.

CHAPTER 18

WILL SUTHERLAND

Calm Before the Storm

Jules adjusted her clothes outside the door to Sutherland's house. She pulled a small mirror from her purse and made some last-minute touch-ups to her makeup. She hadn't been sure what exactly one wears to a police barbecue, so she decided to go with her favorite casual outfit: jeans and a red strapless top. The unusually beautiful fall day extended into the evening hours. The air had actually warmed some, the sun was setting, and the smell of grilled chicken emanated from around the house. She rang the doorbell and Sutherland promptly answered.

"Jules, I knew it was you." He leaned in and gave her a kiss.

"Fashionably late, you know me too well," she joked.

"You look…wow."

"Thanks. Are you going to invite me in?"

"Of course, come on in, everyone's out back."

She entered the home. She realized this was the first time she had been here during daylight hours and completely sober. It was nice. The interior was well decorated with the light brown walls blending with the rugs and furniture, professionally organized throughout the rooms.

"I didn't know you had such an eye for decorating."

"I have to impress the ladies somehow, don't I? How else could I be named sexiest trooper in the state every year?"

"First of all, it's the biggest sex addict award that you win every year," commented Konine from the kitchen. "And secondly, you didn't tell us that you were dating a model for God sakes."

Jules blushed.

"Save your sweet talk for Fontaine's assistant, who you recently eye-fucked to death."

"I wasn't eye-fucking, I was eye-lovemaking."

Jules let out a laugh. "Well, regardless of what it was, she's single, so if you want I'll put in a good word for you."

"I thought Kennedy was hooking up with her."

"He wishes he was hooking up with her."

"I'm sure he wishes he was hooking up with you more."

"I'm Jules Romano by the way..." she said, redirecting the uncomfortable conversation toward Konine.

He shook her hand. "I have heard so much about you. The guys can't wait to meet you."

"Well," said Sutherland, "I'm not sure the next opportunity we're going to have like this to just hang out, so I'm glad we could all get together tonight. Is Dominick coming around?"

"He should be by. He's on duty but he said he'd make it for some salad and rice or whatever that vegetarian swallows."

They laughed their way to the backyard. It was a small area but had enough space for a patio, grill, and some grass. The other troopers were playing catch with their respective significant others.

"Everybody, this is Jules. Jules, this is everybody."

One by one each trooper came up to meet the woman Sutherland had been talking about for the last several months. They were all very flattering.

Sutherland went over to the grill to turn the food, and Konine followed along with Trooper Smith.

"So, Jules Romano, you weren't kidding. She is a hottie," said Konine.

"I think I scored pretty good on this one, eh?"

"Redhead? I'm shocked you went with that. That's...different."

"Isn't your wife a redhead, Smith?"

"She is, and like I've said before, she's fucking crazy."

"It's great to spend some time with her around other people. She seems like she's having a good time already."

They looked over and saw she was with several of the troopers' wives and girlfriends. They were chatting and pouring themselves drinks.

"What are you going to do about her if we get our opportunity to take Uptown?"

Jules waved at him from across the yard. He waved back.

"She'll have to make a choice. Me or Uptown. Until then, I don't really want to ruin a good thing."

"Ballsy, Will, ballsy."

"I don't want to be here all night talking about things that frustrate me, so this is my last question, I swear," said Konine.

"Let's hear it."

"Have you heard from the DA's office?"

"Nothing yet."

"So what's the next move with the casino?"

Sutherland looked up again to make sure Jules was busy. "I made contact with my undercover yesterday. He's going to be able to get free for a little bit this coming Sunday. I'm meeting up with him; he says he has some information."

"Nice. I'll come with."

"Sounds good. You want some of this chicken?"

"Hell no, I'm holding out for the burgers."

"Sutherland, heads-up!" yelled one of the other troopers as a football came flying toward them. He leapt up and grabbed it out of the sky.

The trooper who threw it made a cat whistle. "That was hot!"

The troopers and the girls laughed as Sutherland tossed the ball back.

Jules walked over to Will and tried to guard him as the ball was returned to him from across the yard. She didn't know what to expect when she had gone out on a date with a state trooper, but more and more each day she fell in love with the non-Uptown related lifestyle. The group of people was amazing. They all led relatively stress-free and normal lives. And Will, he was a dream come true. Uptown was the last thing on her mind for the first time in a long time. She leaned in and whispered into his ear, "You are so getting some tonight."

He looked back. "I don't know what I did, but I'll take it." He kissed her as she knocked the ball free from his grasp and went running across the yard with Will chasing behind to the cheers of the other troopers.

. . . . . .

"So what's this plan, Kennedy?" asked Fontaine.

He looked at the usual crew sitting around the conference room table.

"Today is Thursday. In three days a bus filled with women of varying ages will be dropped off at a to-be-decided location. From there, one of our guys will pick them up and bring them to Uptown under the guard of Sorenteen and Marcus' men. The fear this whole time has been that there is an active leak within our group."

"Are you going to be able to fix that in three days?" Fontaine asked.

"I will. And here's how. I would bet that the leak is coming from one of the mid-level guys working here. Any lower level guy than that, who gives a shit. They don't have access to any information."

They all murmured in agreement.

"Each of us is going to approach one of them and tell him he's getting a promotion, that, uh, we need him for some more risky operations and that he has to pick up a bus full of girls. We give each a different pickup point. Each of us will wait at each address at the time we specify from afar to see if any of the points get hit by the police. If one does, that's the leak."

"Then what?" asked Sorenteen.

"Then we get that person in a controlled environment, make sure they're disarmed, and secure them until this whole thing is over."

"Why do we have to tell everyone the nature of the product coming in? That doesn't seem smart to me. The whole point of this is to keep it quiet."

"If it gets leaked to Sutherland that a human trafficking ring is possibly sweeping through Uptown, he will get his hopes up, he'll call in a raid, and then have it end in failure. His office will restrict him even more with what he can and can't investigate, which will free us up when it matters most."

"Why not make up something equally as illegal," commented Fontaine.

"Like what?"

There was silence in the room.

"I think it's a great fuckin' idea," said Billings.

"You would, little Kennedy," said Sorenteen.

"I agree with the plan as well," said O'Shea.

Kennedy took the conversation back over. "That's the plan, it's the best we got on short notice, and it will work."

"Okay, let's set it up," O'Shea commanded.

"I have written down here the addresses to five different discreet spots that are easily scoutable from a distance. Each person takes one. Billings and I will talk to Nicky Deez; Sorenteen, you take Roderick Beamer; O'Shea, you leak the info to Zippy and Kendall; Fontaine, you talk with Donovan."

The group got up and went off to find their respective potential rats. Kennedy knew where his would be. During the day he was usually a bartender at one of the main casino bars. Kennedy noticed on the way to the main floor Billings was quieter than usual.

"Is something wrong?" he asked.

"Nah, just...still wrapping my head around the fact that we're dealing with a human trafficking ring. It's pretty heavy."

"Yeah, I had a tough time with it as well. But we're being careful and the right people are going to pay for it. We're doing good here. It's hard to see it sometimes, but we're doing good."

"If you say so, Kennedy. I trust you."

"Let's not have too much of a pussy moment here, okay?"

"Yeah, sounds good. Where's Nicky?"

He pointed. "Over there, bar three."

"Let's go."

They walked up to the bar. Nicky Deez was hard at work. He was twenty-seven, had a classic Italian look. Despite the fact that he was in constant motion all day behind the bar, his perfectly spiked hair never moved out of place. Its defiance of gravity always amazed Kennedy. The ladies apparently loved it.

"Kennedy! Billings! You need the usual?"

"Not now, we're actually here on business."

"We need to talk to you about something," said Billings. "Have someone cover ya for a few minutes and join us at this table over here."

"Will do."

Kennedy and Billings took a seat that had the fewest people around it. Nicky was close behind.

"So what's up, guys?"

"We have good news. You're getting promoted."

"From what to what exactly?"

"Cleanup crew to transporter. And if everything goes okay, we'll have you play some bigger roles in some things coming up. Details to follow."

Nicky nodded his head with confidence. "Thank you for giving me the opportunity! What are my orders?"

Kennedy handed him a piece of folded paper. "Don't lose this. This is the address that you will go to at the specified time. There will be a bus waiting there. Get in it, don't ask questions, drive it straight to the warehouse."

"Can I ask what it's carrying?"

"Girls. Don't bother yourself with who they are or what their purpose is."

"You got it. I won't ask anything more."

"Just so you know, we're going to have you wear a wire so we can hear everything going on, just as a precaution. You understand, right?"

"Yes sir."

"You up for this, Nicky?" asked Billings.

"Of course, I'm ready. I won't let you guys down."

"Good. Don't tell anyone about this," ordered Kennedy. "In fact, don't even bring this up again with me, John here, Sorenteen, Fontaine, nobody!"

"Sounds good, Mr. Kennedy."

"And in the meantime, I'll take that cocktail. Make it a whiskey, neat."

"Make it two."

"You got it, gentlemen, coming right up." He disappeared behind the bar.

Kennedy gave a nod. "Now we wait."

"I hope this works."

"Me too. Otherwise it all might be over sooner than later."

Nicky returned with the drinks. Kennedy and Billings clinked their glasses.

. . . . . .

"Oh, Will! Oh, Will, yes, yes..."

Just looking at Jules look down at him sent shivers through his body.

"Mmmmm!" she moaned loudly, collapsing on top of Sutherland. The perfect previous day had turned into a cold and rainy next morning at Sutherland's house.

As they lay there in each other's arms, Jules let her subconscious slip. "Do you love me, Will?"

Sutherland was quick to answer. "I do. I can't believe I actually feel this way about anyone. It has always been about work. It's good to have something else to focus on."

She smiled. "That was the right answer."

"I will tell you one thing though. This is very important."

"You can tell me anything."

"I know I sound like a broken record, but I have a bad feeling about Uptown. If anything ever goes down there and you get hurt, I don't know what I'd do."

She thought about Kennedy. "I know, I..."

"You what?"

"It's...nothing."

"You sure?"

"Yeah, positive." She smiled at Sutherland and there was a moment of silence as the rain came down, tingling on the rooftop.

"So what do you think of Mark being back?" she asked. "I know you two go back quite a ways."

"Mark Kennedy. The best mentor a guy could have. I looked up to him in every way, and for a long time he pushed me aside. He really resisted my efforts to get to know him."

"Really? The way you guys talk now I'd have thought you were old friends."

"No, not the case. He used to ask me if I had a younger brother in high school looking for a part-time job so that he could have a partner that would actually function on an adult level."

"Ooo, ouch," she responded, wincing.

"And then, once we did start to be a good team, he forced me into a decision I couldn't make." His mood became more serious. "I basically screwed him to save my ass. I still don't know what the right thing to do was."

His pager went off, which he glanced at. He set it back down.

"Nothing important."

"Do you ever work?" asked Jules, sensing he didn't want to talk about Kennedy anymore.

"I'm always at work. You see this here? You and me? This is work, I'm interviewing a key witness."

"Witness to what?"

"Witness to the greatest lovemaking machine Vermont has ever seen."

"Ohhh." Jules laughed. "Well, if that's the case I'm moving back to New York."

Will laughed with her. "All joking aside, if something was to ever go down there and I wasn't around, you find Mark. He'd probably be the safest person to be around."

Jules could feel the pangs of guilt settling in, given her current situation between the two men. Sutherland's phone went off, indicating a text. He looked at it and jumped out of bed.

"What's wrong?" she said, startled.

"You stay here as long as you want, get some sleep. I gotta go in."

"It's your day off I thought."

"Me too."

He took off out the door and looked at the text again as he got into his cruiser.

Sunday 7AM, Human Trafficking movement. 41 Dixie Hwy, Bethel.

The number was blocked but he knew exactly who it was: his undercover. Sutherland was confused. He was supposed to be meeting his contact on Sunday around three in the afternoon. Something big must have happened to prompt a page and a text. He called Konine and told him to get Dominick and meet him at his desk. He buckled his belt and hit the gas. He had a lot of planning to do.

. . . . . .

Kennedy awoke Sunday morning early to make sure he got to his site before anyone else would be showing up. The night before he had Billings driving vans and buses all over town to set up the individual traps. Inside each transport vehicle, the front was separated from the back by a wall, and the windows were tinted so as not to reveal the empty seats. Sorenteen was due to meet Marcus just outside the county line, where he would take the real bus to the warehouse of A-Wing with heavy protection from Marcus' guards.

Kennedy had already polished off his third coffee. He put his windshield wipers on high. It had been raining since the night before, which didn't help his visibility of the van down below from where his car was parked. He peered through binoculars. Nothing yet. Over his headphones he could hear Nicky Deez's radio blaring through the wire he was wearing. He was due at the pickup point any minute.

He closed his eyes for a second. The picture of Rachel Davis still vivid in his mind. He wished they hadn't shown him the picture. A car door slamming shut startled him. He opened his eyes and leaned forward. Nicky was there. He walked up to the van and as he was told, without looking in the back, he climbed into the driver's seat. He started the engine and drove off. No sirens. No helicopters. No SWAT. Kennedy pulled out to follow him. He was careful to take note of any suspicious-looking cars around. He turned down the same road the van did, keeping his distance. His phone went off.

"Hello?"

"It's Billings."

"What's up?"

"I can see some unmarked cars off in the distance. I think it's about to go down with Beamer."

. . . . . .

Sutherland had been holed up in an auto garage since early that morning. He had units securing a mile perimeter around the address he was given. There was a van parked in an empty lot, but there had been no movement in or around it yet. The downpour made visibility difficult. He took a sip of his coffee.

A car pulled up to the lot and out stepped Roderick Beamer. He jumped out of his car and got into the van and pulled away.

"Two twenty-four, this is two thirty-one."

"Go ahead, two thirty-one," returned the voice of a focused Sergeant Jennings.

"I've got my undercover pulling out in a large van. I'm thinking he is headed for Route Fifteen. All available side streets are secured for a mile."

"Does anyone have visual on the cargo?" Asked Jennings.

"Negative," he responded.

"Us either," chimed in Konine and Dominick.

"I got nothing," reported Smith.

"Okay, at the next light take him."

Sutherland sped forward and around several other cars to get behind the van. Two more unmarked cruisers pulled onto the road in front. The group approached a traffic light, which turned yellow, then red. All three cruisers turned their lights on.

Sutherland got on his cruiser megaphone. "Driver, turn off the van, roll your window down, and toss the keys outside the vehicle! Keep your hands outside and within our view!"

Beamer did as he was told.

Sutherland then ordered, "Get out of your vehicle slowly."

Four troopers ran up to the side. Beamer got out and crossed in front of the van. They secured him and placed him on the ground. A few others ran up to the back, clipped the padlock to the rear entrance, and slipped inside.

Each team member ran down the hallway yelling "clear" with each seat that held nothing.

Several moments later they checked in over the radio. "Nothing, sir. No one's here."

"What?" said Sutherland, confused. He looked at Beamer, who had a look of defeat on his face. "Are you sure?"

"Am I sure there isn't a bus filled with prostitutes?" responded the team leader sarcastically.

"Okay," said Sutherland. "I want the van torn apart."

He picked up and walked his undercover, Trooper Ryan McDonough, to his cruiser to get out of the rain. His long hair was sopping wet, and he looked stressed.

"Should we talk now? Or should we talk at the barracks?"

"What is this?" McDonough shouted. "This is harassment. There's nothing to talk about. I was told to pick up a van. I did. I thought it was a shipment of food or something for the restaurant. So I'm not going anywhere but back to work."

Sutherland looked at him, trying to decipher the message being given to him. He figured McDonough wanted to be let go back to Uptown.

"Fine. Rest assured I'll be dropping by though, real shortly, you piece of shit, and you tell your boss that I'm coming for him too."

"Fuck you!" he shouted back.

Sutherland got out of the cruiser and dragged McDonough out.

"Unleash him, impound the van."

"How am I going to get home?"

"Not my problem."

Konine came up to Sutherland as McDonough began walking back the way he came in the pouring rain.

"What the hell was that all about?"

"I don't know. He's not safe though. We're going back today, same time we agreed upon a week ago. We'll pick him up with a warrant. I'm sure he's got good information for us."

"Sound's good. Jennings wants to talk to you."

"Fuck. What the hell am I going to tell him?"

"Just take your licking, let him know you've got your undercover giving you details later today. Like you said, he must have something useful."

Sutherland nodded. "I'll see you at seven tonight in the Uptown parking lot."

"I'll bring Dominick."

"Perfect, see you then."

. . . . . .

For the first time in days Rachel actually felt mildly comfortable. The soft cushion of the bus that she sat on was a welcome change to her cold cell. Of course if it was her choice, she probably would have preferred to stay where she was. Having a bag over her head was the worst feeling in the world. She could hear two men talking somewhere in front of her in a different language. She could also hear a girl somewhere behind her whimpering.

"Be strong," she said aloud, hoping it would bring comfort to whoever was crying.

"Hey!" yelled a loud voice. "No talking! You can't even follow that one rule?!" His voice got clearer as he walked toward her. Expecting to be hit, she clenched up and was momentarily relieved to hear his footsteps walk beyond her. That relief quickly came to an end when she heard the sound of skin on skin. He had struck the girl behind her. The crying stopped. She had gathered since her abduction that there were at least two dozen other girls in the cellar with her. It was difficult to tell ages because she never really caught more than a glimpse of the others at any one time. Despite that, she had grown to consider herself like a big sister to the other girls. She did what she could to protect them. She gave them extra food when possible. She made promises to the men so that they wouldn't hurt the others. Just the other night she had given herself, again, to one of the guards who was on the prowl.

Afonos was the only man that Marcus had assaulted after finding out what happened the night she antagonized him. Other than that she didn't think Marcus knew the men used her. Most of the girls had to perform at one point or another, but he kept telling her she was special and that he didn't want anyone touching her until she was sold. He couldn't possibly know what went on down in that dungeon. Rachel hated herself for thinking that Marcus actually cared about her. For unexplainable reasons she couldn't help it.

Through the last several weeks her hopes had dimmed and erased, as there had been absolutely no opportunity to escape. Her captors were very careful. Multiple girls had decided not to follow the rules. They were now dead. She got by, day to day, thinking about home, her family. Her memories always betrayed her though and would quickly turn to the face of her original captor, Antoni. He haunted her at her core.

The bus came to a stop.

"All right, girls," sounded out a Russian voice, "wait until you are grabbed. You will walk single file and be inspected. Then you will be brought to your new homes for the next bit of time. Same rules—don't test us or I promise you and your families will be brutalized."

The sound of scuffling feet could be heard. After a few moments someone grabbed her by her clothes. She stumbled initially but was yanked back on her feet hard enough to rip her shirt. They had her come to a stop just outside the bus. She could feel two girls on either side of her. Then she keyed into new voices, American; she hadn't heard an American man's voice since her capture.

I must still be in the United States, she thought. The idea gave her hope.

"Do you want to see the girls?" Marcus asked someone softly.

"I don't need to," responded a man's deep, strong voice.

"I'm surprised, Mr. Kennedy. I figured you always inspected your product before holding it."

"I've found that sometimes not knowing anything about the product helps me focus on its proper care."

"Well, at least let me show you my prized possession. She is going to sell for so much, I can promise you that."

"Hey, he said he didn't want to fuckin' look at the product," rang out a different man's voice.

"It's okay, Billings, I'll look at the one. Make it quick though, then we'll get them to their rooms."

Footsteps. This time they didn't pass by; they stopped directly in front of her. Her mask was taken off. The light pierced through her head, making her turn away briefly. But then she was able to look up at the new group of monsters. There was a shorter, larger man standing next to a taller man with wavy salt-and-pepper hair. A hard exterior, but compared to the animals she had been around the last bit of time, his eyes told a different story. They stared at each other briefly. She half expected him to jump to her rescue the way he looked at her, cut the ropes off her hands and tell her everything was going to be okay.

"Very nice. Let's get these girls to their rooms," he said.

Marcus put the bag over her head once more and led the group of girls away, down a hallway, then through a door and down some steps. Cold chains were wrapped around her wrists and then her mask was taken off. Her new room was much nicer than the one before. A queen-sized bed with soft and colorful accent pillows. The room decorated in white with a chandelier overhead. A series of scandalous dresses hung in a closet. There were no windows. Then her eyes came across a shadowy corner. She nearly screamed when she saw the eyes of someone staring back. A skinny man with bright white skin emerged, with pierced ears, nose, and one of the corners of his eyes. His arm looked like it had been badly burned, and he wore contacts that made his eyes look like those of a snake.

"I am your handler. I'll be here to prepare you for your great moment."

She crawled into the corner of the room, feeling that was the safest place to sit.

The next chance you have, you run.

Death no longer frightened her. The thought of being sold did. Even if it meant her family being put at risk, they would want her to try, no matter what.

CHAPTER **19**

MARK KENNEDY

The Promotion

Kennedy took the last bite of his filet mignon, savored it for a moment, and washed it down with an expensive cabernet. He was having dinner with O'Shea and Sorenteen at Augosto's. They were anxiously waiting for Fontaine to show up. As Kennedy polished off his glass of wine, Fontaine finally arrived.

"You would not believe some of the requests Marcus' men are making. Absolutely fucking ridiculous."

"They get whatever they want. The more distracted they are, the better," replied Kennedy.

"So, Mark," said O'Shea, "you have us all here. Where do we stand with our leak?"

"We found it."

"Are you sure?"

"Without a doubt. Beamer got pinched; he's the undercover."

"What's your plan with him?"

"Nonlethal," Kennedy quickly answered.

"As long as he goes quietly," said Sorenteen calmly.

"No, I meant nonlethal period," he shot back. "Everything we're doing is meaningless if we don't do our best to minimize unnecessary casualties. Like our original plan was, we get him to a secure location, we get him locked up, we release him when the whole thing is over."

"All I'm saying is that if push comes to shove, his life is not worth risking the whole operation. We have to have that mind-set."

O'Shea butted in, "The lives of a few—"

"I'm really getting tired of hearing that line," Kennedy interrupted. "Enough have sacrificed. It's time to get this thing in motion and execute."

"Look, we have an old sayin' in Ireland. 'The inevitable never happens and the unexpected constantly occurs.' We have to be ready."

"Okay, Kennedy" chimed in Sorenteen. "So how does this go down in your mind?"

"We commend Roderick for dealing with the police. Tell him the bus pickup was a test and that he and everyone else involved passed and that we're having a big party for them tonight."

"And who's going to tell him that?" questioned Sorenteen.

"Fontaine, you up for it?"

"Well, well, you actually need me to do something?"

"It's a yes or a no."

"It's not a problem."

"Are we going to do this upstairs in the employee bar?"

"No, we need to be away from Uptown. In Caprizzi's files he mentioned something about a hole-in-the-wall bar he set up to be used as an extra spot to take care of private shit like this. What's the name of that place?"

"The Shack," replied O'Shea.

"Is that a good spot?"

"Aye, it'll do."

"That's where we'll do it then."

"When we get there, I'll be the one to take care of it," commanded Sorenteen.

"Why you?"

"We need someone to drive, someone to secure the outside, and someone to initiate contact with him. I'm the fucking biggest, so I'll be the one with first contact."

"Fine. That work for everyone?" Everyone nodded. "Okay, let's get Billings and Jules up to speed and get this done."

As they left the restaurant, they all put on their Uptown suit jackets and earpieces and headed for the casino floor. Kennedy and Sorenteen stopped by Nicky Deez at the main bar.

"Hey, Nicky," called out Kennedy. "You know where Roderick is?"

"Yes sir, right over there, bar number five. He's packing up early though, taking the afternoon off to see some girl."

"Thanks."

As Kennedy and Sorenteen made their way across the casino, Sorenteen called Fontaine. They spoke briefly on the phone.

Sorenteen stopped short. "Let's wait here for a minute."

"Why's that?"

Sorenteen pointed to where Roderick was working. Fontaine appeared.

Fontaine was damn good at what he did. Despite Kennedy's dislike for him, he was the most charismatic person Kennedy had ever met. If he wanted, he could not only convince a bovine to go to the chop house, but the cow would be excited about it.

"The Face of Uptown" went to work for a few minutes, and from where they stood, it looked like Roderick bought it. Fontaine walked away, and Sorenteen and Kennedy both heard over their earpieces, "The fish is thinking about it; go set the hook, Mark."

Kennedy walked over to the bar a few minutes later.

Roderick waved to him. "Good afternoon, sir."

"Hey, Roderick," he responded coolly. "Did you hear about the party tonight?"

"I did. Mr. Fontaine was just telling me about it. I'm pretty excited, just not 100 percent sure I can make it."

"I see. Well, let me tell you, it's not just a staff party going down."

"What do you mean? What else is it for?"

"They're promoting you. Big raise on the other end of tonight."

"Are you serious? How do you know that?"

"I spoke with Fontaine this morning. I recommended you after I heard that you were able to shake the police today. We need more people like you, and I think you'll be very interested where your career goes from here," he said, shaking Roderick's hand.

Roderick accepted the handshake with an apprehensive smile.

"So, you want to ride with me and Sammy, now that you're entitled to do so? We'll take the Uptown high-roller limo."

"Uh, yeah, sure, that's amazing. Thank you. I'll just have to call my girlfriend and let her know what I'm doing tonight."

"No problem, we'll pick you up around seven. Black tie affair, by the way, so dress accordingly," Kennedy said while walking away.

He nodded at Sorenteen and Fontaine, and they nodded back. It was on.

. . . . . .

At 7 p.m. on the dot, Kennedy and Sorenteen pulled up in the nicest limo that Uptown had to offer outside of Roderick's apartment. Both wore black slacks, black button-up shirts, and black coats. Sorenteen's head was as shiny as ever. He was sitting all the way in back of the limo facing the front, while Kennedy was sitting on the side bench facing the door. Roderick got in with a big smile. He also looked very dapper with his usual disorganized scramble of hair neatly slicked back.

"So this is what it's like to be on the upper payroll, eh, Kennedy?"

"Exactly right," he said with a wink.

Sorenteen spoke. "Just so you know, when we get there we're going to be early. Everyone else is coming in the Uptown party bus, and they had to make a stop to pick up some entertainment."

"It's still going to be a big event, right? Everyone will be here?"

"I can assure you the plans won't be changed in any way, shape, or form," said Sorenteen, staring first directly at Kennedy and then giving a reassuring smile to Roderick.

. . . . . .

Sutherland, Konine, and Dominick parked their cruisers outside Uptown. It was seven o'clock and time to "arrest" undercover Trooper Ryan McDonough to get some much needed intel out of him given the morning's disaster. Sutherland had texted Jules earlier to meet him at the front door, and she didn't disappoint.

"Hey, Will, Jim, new guy—so what's going on?"

"We're here to have a word with one of your employees, Roderick Beamer. Any idea where he is?"

Jules hesitated for a moment. "Um, he's not here."

"Okay…Where is he?"

She once again stumbled over her words. "I…I'm not entirely sure."

"Hey," said Sutherland a bit more firmly, "this isn't a joke here, Jules. He could be in a lot of trouble. We need to talk to him."

She knew Will would see right through any lies from her. She panicked. "I think someone said something about he was headed to a party at a place called 'The Shack.'"

"The Shack? Never heard of it."

"It's about twenty minutes north on I-89 off of exit two, and then just another minute or so. It's your first right, kind of a long dirt driveway back along the tree line. I could be wrong though, just what I heard."

Sutherland looked at Jules, concerned. "Is everything okay? You're acting…off."

"I'm fine, long day, sorry to not be more helpful."

"Okay, Jim, let's head to this place, see if we can't spoil the party."

They left and got back into Sutherland's cruiser. "Fuck!" Sutherland exclaimed. "Just what I was afraid of."

"You think they set up McDonough to flush him out?"

"Yeah. If we don't get there in time, it may be too late for him."

They bolted out of the driveway, and as soon as they hit the main road, threw their blue lights on.

Jules peered out of the front doors. Torn on what to do, as soon as the car was out of sight, she texted Kennedy.

. . . . . .

Kennedy, Beamer, and Sorenteen cruised up I-89 for several miles, champagne flowing. Roderick was seemingly clueless. Sorenteen sat there the whole ride with an eerie sense of calm despite knowing what this was all leading to. Kennedy was doing the opposite and overcompensating for his own anxiety by being overly talkative and friendly.

Kennedy's phone went off, and he took a look at the text that had just come through: *Sutherland +2. On the way.*

"Something wrong?" asked Beamer.

"No," responded Kennedy, smiling. "Why?"

"Just seemed like you got bad news."

"Nothing like that. I'm having some very frustrating girl problems. That won't get in the way of tonight though, I promise."

They drove for another several minutes and parked outside the small bar. There were lights on inside, but it seemed empty.

"So this is the place, eh? Everyone is on their way?" asked Roderick with a hint of nervousness in his voice.

"Should be here any minute," responded Sorenteen. "Mark, why don't you give them a call, see how long they'll be." He turned and looked at Roderick. "Rod and I will head on in and start the drinking. Get a head start. How does top-shelf bourbon sound to you?"

"Sounds good. We'll see you in a minute, Mark."

Kennedy had a sinking feeling in his stomach as he realized how little room for error there was, especially now with the state police on their way. All reservations about the plan had to be put aside; the ball had been set in motion, and no one could stop it now.

Roderick and Sorenteen walked into the bar while Kennedy pretended to make a call.

Once inside, he pocketed his phone and made his way around the building. He noticed a door leading to the back of the bar. He pulled on it and it opened. He listened for a moment and heard nothing so he closed the door, grabbed an industrial-sized trash can, and dragged it in front to ensure no one was going in and no one was coming out of the rear entryway.

As he made his way back around the building, he noticed how quiet it was. A few car headlights shone through the trees and continued on their way. Every light made him a bit more paranoid. He went to the front of the door and removed his Glock, loaded it, and cocked it.

Just in case.

A solid minute went by, which he spent in silence, heart racing, keeping an eye out for anything resembling a police car. Despite how grimy this particular part of town was, the unobtrusive nighttime sounds were soothing compared to the bells, sirens, yelling, and regularly over-noisy environment of the Uptown casino.

Kennedy turned around and put his hands over his eyes to see inside better. Without warning, a bullet came shattering through the front glass door and soared within inches of his left ear. Kennedy dove to the ground and quickly made his way to the door handle. He could see Sorenteen and Roderick were wrestling for control over a silenced 9 mm pistol, so he wasted no time to slam through the front door, gun drawn.

As he ran in, Roderick managed to fire a couple of shots in his direction, which sent Kennedy diving over a table. He stood up poised to shoot.

"Don't fire, it's too loud!" Sorenteen yelled.

He gave a powerful tug on the silenced weapon as Roderick let go. He stumbled backward and tripped over some stacked chairs. Roderick pulled his own .40 caliber from his ankle and began shooting rounds toward the both of them while moving further into the bar.

Kennedy had to take cover once again as Sorenteen flipped a table over for protection. Roderick ran into the back. Kennedy made a run for the bar, slid across the top, and hustled to the entrance of the kitchen. He tucked his gun away and slowly grabbed a silver serving tray. He looked at Sorenteen and signaled for him to leave the bar. He understood.

"Kennedy, let's get out of here!" he said aloud. He then ran loudly across the floor and slammed the door shut behind him.

Kennedy could feel his heart thumping in his chest as he crept as close as he dared to the kitchen. He heard someone attempting to open the back door and then nothing else. The silence was deafening as every sound seemed amplified. A clock ticking. The wind blowing outside. A piece of shattered glass from the front door as it fell to the ground. Then Kennedy became acutely aware of a different noise. Roderick's breathing on the other side of the wall. It drew 100% of his attention.

The breathing began getting louder. Kennedy readied the tray to strike at the right moment. He heard him take one last deep breath. He bent his knees as Roderick slipped around the corner, his .40 caliber in front of him. He batted the tip of the gun with the tray as Roderick fired a round and missed. Kennedy dropped the tray and grabbed the wrist wielding the gun. They both ran each other into the wall, where the struggle for the .40 began.

"Kennedy, please don't do this! I'm a cop, for Christ's sake!"

Roderick let go with one of his hands and frantically wrapped it around Kennedy's waist, almost grabbing the sidearm right out of his belt. Kennedy put pressure on Roderick's neck with his elbow, which made him bring his free hand back up to try to relieve the force.

"Sammy, get in here!" Kennedy yelled. "Get control of his hands!"

Sorenteen came sprinting back in and grabbed the .40 caliber away, squared himself up, and kneed Roderick hard in the stomach. Doubled over, Roderick took a deep bite of Sorenteen's forearm, tearing a chunk of flesh off. Sorenteen screamed and slammed into Kennedy hard enough so that they both lost their grip. Roderick made his last desperate effort to run for the door.

"Shoot him! Fucking shoot him!"

Kennedy withdrew his gun, aimed it, and shot a round directly into the back of Roderick's head. His body instantly went limp and hit the floor, sliding a few feet before coming to a rest.

Sorenteen ran over to the body, making sure he was dead.

"W-what…the fuck…j-just happened!?" Kennedy stuttered.

"He was ready for me to make a fucking move. I turned my back for a second; he must have seen my gun and went to grab it. I knew we should have just killed him!"

"What do we do with the body?"

O'Shea came running in. "I hear sirens! We gotta get the fuck outta here, NOW!"

Kennedy drifted from what O'Shea was saying. He could see his lips moving, but the only sound he heard was the voice of Roderick begging for his life.

Sorenteen shook Kennedy. "HEY! Time to go!"

Kennedy snapped back to the present.

"Hang on one second," he said.

He ran over to the body and started searching all the pockets. In the inside of his jacket, he found a small device: It was a wire. He yanked it out.

"No more time!" said Sorenteen angrily. "Let's go!"

The three of them sprinted out to the car. As they got in, the sounds of sirens made it seem like the police were right on top of them. Blue lights reaching through the woods reflected off the white wall of the bar. Once inside the car, O'Shea floored it through a side alley and on to a back road.

"What the hell happened in there?" asked O'Shea.

"Just drive!" responded Sorenteen.

"What happened to your fuckin' arm?"

"The motherfucker bit me!"

"Is your blood at the scene?"

"Hello! He fucking bit me! My blood will be all over his face!"

O'Shea and Sorenteen continued yelling at each other. All Kennedy could do was see the look in Roderick's eyes when he had him pinned against the wall. He wished he still had the ability he forged while in prison to kill and forget. It was easier knowing the people he was sentencing to death were bad people. This was much different.

"What are we going to do now?!" yelled O'Shea. "What are we going to tell everyone?!"

"Just shut the fuck up and let me think," retorted Sorenteen.

"Both of you shut the fuck up!" Kennedy roared.

Both the men fell silent.

"A cop is dead. We killed an innocent man."

"He was the one who started—"

"Shut up, Sorenteen! Fuck!" he said as he ran his blood-tinged hands through his hair. "Everyone stop talking. Just get us to Uptown. There is a casino filled with more innocent people and girls that we are in charge of because we brought them into this. So let's just be quiet and think about what needs to happen next."

The rest of the trip back to Uptown was spent in silence.

. . . . . .

Sutherland pulled up to The Shack, with Konine and Dominick close behind. Another squad car pulled up with them. Reports of gunfire in the area prompted several units to be en route. The three of them jumped out of their cars first. Sutherland ran up to the door, gun in hand.

"This is the Vermont State Police, drop your weapons!"

There was no response. He took notice of the shattered front window.

He gave a nod to the other troopers and slowly entered through the front, with Konine and Dominick following. There was no one there. The other troopers who arrived circled in back. Sutherland spotted a pair of legs behind a knocked-over table.

"I got a body!" he yelled.

"Get him. I'll sweep the kitchen." Konine ran off to secure the rest of the bar.

Sutherland went running over to the corpse. He knelt down and turned the man over. The face had some of the features of Trooper Ryan McDonough, but the head shot made it impossible to confirm. He lifted up the right sleeve of the jacket the corpse was wearing. It revealed a forearm tattoo of a dragon breathing fire onto a church. It was McDonough.

"No! Fuck!" Sutherland yelled as he scrambled to take a pulse. There was none. There was a bullet hole in the back of his head with a large exit wound, and blood surrounded the body. His hands began to shake involuntarily. A wave of nausea punched him in the stomach.

He stood up and threw a table over. "Goddamn it!"

Konine returned as the backup came in the front door.

"The back is clear." He glanced at the body. "That's not…"

The look on Sutherland's face said it all. Konine pounded his fist against the bar.

"We should have picked him up when we had the chance."

Sutherland didn't respond. Dominick came out of the kitchen as well.

"Hey, I got something here."

Sutherland stood up and rushed over. "What is it?"

"It's a note. It was left on the oven."

"Let me see it." He grabbed the note out of his hand and read it aloud.

Sutherland, check my right shoe.

Sutherland immediately ran back to the body. He grabbed the right shoe and tore it off the body. A small tape recorder fell to the ground.

"Son of a bitch hid the tape."

"What do you want to do, Will?" asked Konine.

"Every inch of this bar gets dusted for prints, every drop of blood gets tested. I want McDonough searched stem to stern for more evidence he may have brought with him. You see this blood all around his face? I want his mouth swabbed; match it to known convicts in the area and Uptown employees. If there are video cameras anywhere, I want the videos. Whoever came here tonight blew it, and we need to capitalize."

"Where are you going?"

"I can't be here right now. I'm going to head back to listen to the tape."

"Okay," said Konine. "What do you want to tell the sergeant?"

"Exactly the truth. Maybe this will help light a fire under his ass. We are not in control; we need to regain it."

"Anything else?"

"Yeah, I don't know what this bullshit was of a human trafficking group rolling through, but I'm taking it seriously. I want to talk to Brent Waters with the FBI first thing in the morning."

"Sounds good."

Konine walked over to the body and put his hands on the shoulder of the fallen for a moment and then left to call the crime scene team. Sutherland walked over and knelt down. He did the same.

"Let's get these motherfuckers and everyone who may have even remotely contributed."

Konine and Dominick nodded as Sutherland stood up and headed for his car.

. . . . . .

Upon arrival back at Uptown, Kennedy went straight to his room. He walked to a chair tucked into the corner of his suite and slumped into it. He was finding it difficult to concentrate. His hands trembled as he grabbed the wire out of his pocket. He put it on the ground and crushed it. After a moment he stood back up, grabbed his gun and a bottle of whiskey, and headed to the bathroom, where he disrobed and ran the bath. He set the gun down next to him on the ledge of the bathtub. As he slipped into the boiling hot water, he took a long pull from the bottle. Across the room he could see his bloody clothes. He became fixated on them. He took another pull from the bottle and then another. The harder he tried to clear his mind, regain his focus, the more the reality of the situation sunk in. As if to play an even crueler joke, his mind involuntarily shifted to the dirtied, terrified face of Rachel Davis looking at him through watery eyes, silently begging for help. Of course, he had done nothing.

After close to an hour of sitting quietly in the red-tinted bathwater, listening to the drip of the faucet, a knock came at the door. He picked his gun up and pointed it toward the sound.

"Mark!" came Jules' voice. "Mark! It's me, I'm coming in."

He put the gun back down. Jules cautiously walked into the bathroom and saw him lying there, a look of distress painted on his face.

"Baby, are you okay? Oh my God, what happened?"

"Shh. Please just…sit here with me."

She sank to the ground outside the tub, slowly moving the gun off the ledge and taking the whiskey away from him. She wrapped his arm around her and put her head on his shoulder.

"How did Sutherland know where we were?" Kennedy said after several moments of silence.

"What?"

"How did Sutherland know we took Beamer to The Shack?"

"Will showed up asking questions, wanted to talk to Roderick. I panicked, so I told him he was out there because I didn't want him snooping around Uptown, and I didn't want to lie to him because he would have known. I figured you guys could take care of it quickly. But I never said you were there with him. You're safe."

"You…you told him? Whose side are you on, Jules?"

Jules removed herself from under his arm. "You know the answer to that," she said, offended.

"No, I don't. You've been spending all your time with him. Now you're giving him information against us. Our prints are all over that bar. Sorenteen's blood is all over that bar! We are fucked!"

"Don't say that, that's not true."

"Sutherland is ready to pounce! And it's because of you!"

"Will is ready to pounce because of you!" she shot back. "He's obsessed with you and your involvement. That's what keeps him coming back."

The room phone went off. Kennedy reached over and picked it up.

"What is it?"

"It's Billings, A-Wing warehouse, ten minutes."

"Okay." Kennedy hung up.

"Who was that?" asked Jules.

"Don't worry about it," he responded, wrapping a towel around his waist. "When I get back, you better not be here." He stormed out of the bathroom.

"Why? Why are you doing this?"

"Because!" he yelled. "I am losing my fucking mind! I just killed an undercover cop! I have teenage girls locked in the basement! I have a casino full of monsters that look to me like I'm a friend! This isn't what I signed up for, but now it's my fucking reality! And then while all this bullshit is happening, I have you, the only person I would actually trust, and you're fucking the man that could make all of this, everything we've done, not matter. So I'm simplifying things for you, Jules! Get the fuck out of here! One less variable I need to worry about! Leave Uptown! Don't come back! And if you tell Sutherland anything—ANYTHING!—I will kill you."

Jules wiped a tear from her eye as Kennedy stormed off into the other room. She grabbed his gun and tucked it into the back of her pants.

"You want to see where my allegiance lies?" she yelled. "You want me to prove myself?!"

Kennedy didn't respond. He threw some pants on and a shirt. He came back into the bathroom, but Jules was gone. He sighed deeply, grabbed his phone off the desk, and made his way to the conference room.

CHAPTER 20

MARK KENNEDY

Sammy Sorenteen's Turn

The Uptown gang all met in the back of the warehouse. O'Shea and Fontaine were arguing over a variety of topics. Billings was checking Sorenteen's wound. Kennedy himself was flat-out exhausted. He hadn't bothered to comb his hair. His body ached.

"Are we going to conference in Mr. X?" he heard Fontaine asking.

"I don't think that's a good idea," argued O'Shea. "We keep this one close to home. Besides, there's nothing he can do."

"So now what?"

"Chances are they'll be coming for one of us if not all of us," said Kennedy.

"What do they actually have for evidence?"
"How about my DNA spilled over the whole fucking bar," Sorenteen said.

"Okay," started Kennedy. "Let's all think about this. Your blood work from an evidence standpoint isn't going to be available for quite some time. Let's assume they have a list of decent evidence against any of us, and let's assume that someone actually comes by for the arrest. No one says a word. We are only a few days from the payoff. It's going to take Sutherland at least that long to put together the pieces."

"Kennedy's right," said Fontaine. "There's no other option but to assume we still have time to pull this off. Let's call Dan Peterson, see if he can delay some things. If worse comes to worst, if this whole operation is sinking, I say Kennedy tells Sutherland exactly what's going on. Only tell him it's all going down next week. Hopefully he buys it."

"Or they'll shut down Uptown and that'll be that," combated O'Shea.

"One step at a time," said Kennedy. "Let's deal with the fact that some of us might be getting arrested tonight."

"What about my arm?" asked Sorenteen.

"We're going to have to do something about it. You've got Roderick's teeth imprints there. You've got his saliva all over you, not to mention you're still bleeding."

"What are you suggesting?"

"Back when I was a detective, there was a guy this one time who needed to get rid of some evidence just like this. He burned it off his arm. It was actually really effective."

Sorenteen sat back in his chair. "What did you have in mind?"

"Fontaine, do you have anything hot in here?"

"Yeah, there's an iron in the interrogation room. I'll grab it."

He got it and brought it back. He plugged it in. Sorenteen squirmed in his chair. Kennedy had never seen him nervous before.

After a few moments Fontaine spoke. "It's ready."

Sorenteen walked over toward it. He grabbed a chair and Kennedy grabbed the iron. "O'Shea, Billings, Fontaine, better hold him down."

Fontaine grabbed the opposite arm. The two others both held onto to Sorenteen's affected arm.

"Take this," said Kennedy, putting O'Shea's hat in his mouth. "Ready?"

Sorenteen nodded.

"Sorry, mate," said O'Shea.

Kennedy lifted the iron and without hesitation drove it directly into the wound bed of the chunk of arm missing. Sorenteen's body shook with pain, but he didn't make a sound. After several seconds Kennedy let up. Sorenteen sunk in the chair, his face pale.

The warehouse speaker buzzed. "Mr. Fontaine, the Vermont State Police are here."

"That was fuckin' quick," said O'Shea.

"What do they want, Lisa?" asked Fontaine.

"They say they have a warrant for the arrest of Mr. Sorenteen."

The group looked at him.

"Fuck," Sorenteen said in between breaths.

"No, this is a good thing," remarked Kennedy. "We'll wrap your arm up. If anyone asks, you got into a scuffle with a guest here at the hotel. We're all each other's alibis. You got burned during the fight. Just don't give them any other details."

Sorenteen stood up and drank down a glass of whiskey. He put his jacket on.

"Good luck, Sammy," said O'Shea.

"Make sure someone calls Peterson."

"We'll get right on it."

Sorenteen looked at Kennedy. "Don't lose your head, Kennedy. We're too close."

Kennedy acknowledged the words.

Sorenteen left the room to be taken into custody.

"Well, if it was going to be one of us, he's the one I'd want in there," commented Fontaine.

"Aye, mate. He'll give 'em a run for their money."

"I'm going to go," said Kennedy.

"Go where?"

"Get a drink. I gotta think about some things."

"I'll come with you," called out Billings.

The two left the room and made it to the casino floor just in time to see Sorenteen getting cuffed in the main lobby and led out. As Sutherland left he spun around and caught Kennedy's eye. He shook his head with a hint of disgust before shoving Sorenteen out the main doors.

CHAPTER 21

WILL SUTHERLAND

Steel Trap

Sutherland entered the interrogation room. Without so much as acknowledging Sorenteen, he sat down and placed a file on the table. He leaned back in the chair and stared at Sorenteen, who stared back expressionless.

"Are you going to make this easy or are you going to be difficult?" asked Sutherland.

"Make what easy?" Sorenteen replied.

Sutherland waited another few moments before commencing with the interrogation. He eventually tossed several pictures of the crime scene at The Shack and of the deceased undercover, Trooper Ryan McDonough.

"You recognize him?"

"I do. That's Roderick Beamer."

"You don't seem very bothered by these photos."

"I am not generally bothered by anything. And besides that, I'm not surprised to find out he's dead."

"Why's that?"

"He was dealing with some sick individuals. We were all trying to get him to stop, but clearly he didn't."

Sutherland let out a laugh. "He was a Vermont state trooper. But you already knew that, right?"

"A fuckin' cop? Well, I suppose even cops can be dirty criminals too, but you already knew that, right?"

"So where were you last night around seven?"

"Working, like I do every night."

"Where were you working?"

"McDonald's drive-thru."

"This will be a lot easier if you just answer my questions."

"I was working with Micky Fontaine and Mark Kennedy. We were having problems with one of the guests, and we had to remove him from the casino. It's all in Mr. Fontaine's report from last night; you can read it yourself."

"And I suppose you have video footage of this?"

"We have some video of it, but the incident itself occurred inside a room, and there are no cameras in people's rooms."

"Of course not." Sutherland stood up. "I don't think that's where you were last night, Sammy. I think you were at a bar called The Shack."

"You're not a very good detective then, 'cause I haven't been there in weeks."

"We found your fingerprints all over that place. Yours, Mark Kennedy's, and Kevin O'Shea's, along with McDonough's."

"I've been there many times—we all have—just not last night."

Sutherland pulled out a picture of the floor next to the kitchen.

"What is that, right there?" he said, pointing to the picture.

"Not sure."

"Drops of blood. Now Trooper McDonough was shot once in the head, and his body was left right where he fell. He had no other wounds to his body or face, so whose blood do you suppose is way over by the kitchen?"

"I've heard stories of bullets to the head causing an impressive splatter. Maybe start with that theory?"

"Doesn't fit the crime scene. By the way, what happened to your arm?"

"I told you, there was an incident involving a guest last night; he ended up using a hot iron to defend himself."

"Let me see it."

Sorenteen did as he was told. Fresh, deep burn marks were imprinted on his skin.

"What was the guest's name you fought with?"

Sorenteen hesitated. "I don't remember."

"Look, whether you tell me now or the evidence tells us later, you're fucked. So just tell me the truth and I will help you."

"What evidence?"

"What evidence?!" he shouted. "There's another man's skin inside McDonough's mouth; there's another man's blood at this scene. There are bullets everywhere. There is evidence literally all over the bar. Evidence that eventually will link you to the murder of a Vermont State trooper."

Sorenteen fell silent, eyes fixated on the table.

"You think you're pretty tough, don't you? Invincible even?"

"If you say so."

"I'm going to play you a tape. And then I want you to tell me what you think about it."

Sutherland placed a recorder on the table and hit "play." Sorenteen heard his own voice talking to McDonough.

"We are promoting someone internally."

"Promoting to what?"

"We have a large operation coming in, and we need more hands to help with the security. It's big. A lot of money at stake, amongst other things."

"What's the operation?"

"Do you accept your promotion?"

"Of course, I want in."

"Good. We need you to pick up a van. It will be dropped off and we need you to drive it back here."

"What's inside it?"

"Girls. But you may not look in back. Forget about what is going on in the back of that van. You will pick it up and drop it off and that is all. Make sure you don't have any tails. Do you understand?"

"Absolutely."

"Don't let us down."

Sutherland clicked the recorder off. "Thoughts?"

"We were trying to weed out any bad apples. There have been a lot of bad people coming through, some that work for Uptown. Secondly, your undercover cop seemed to have his hand in some pretty illegal projects. I mean, he jumped at the opportunity to transport around girls. We figured we had him as good as caught. We were waiting at Uptown for him. But when you showed up to take him down, his other employers must have found out about it. Killed him."

"Sammy, Sammy, Sammy. You are so full of shit it's disgusting. I hate myself for what I'm about to do, but I'm going to share some knowledge, if you're willing to share some back."

"You can talk. I don't have to listen."

"You tell me who pulled the trigger on Ryan McDonough, you give me a name, and I'll make sure when the world around Uptown comes crashing down, that you don't spend a day in jail. I will cut you that deal, but you need to give me a name."

"How will you do that?"

"I have a witness who can connect Victor Caprizzi to the origin of Uptown. He can connect Micky Fontaine and Mark Kennedy and Kevin O'Shea and you. I will be sure he leaves your name out on his official report. You give me a name, I'll erase one."

Sorenteen was quiet.

"Don't talk yourself out of this. It is your only chance not to live the rest of your filthy life in prison. It's over. This is all happening very soon and very fast. Give me a name."

Sorenteen looked away. Sutherland grabbed his face and forced him to look at him.

"Give me a fucking name! Right now! Spit it out or I'll toss your ass in holding for as long as I can until I can get my witness to drop your name—then off to prison you go."

"Fine! Just get your hands off me!"

Sutherland released him. "Name, let's have it."

Sorenteen opened his mouth to talk as Konine entered the room with Dan Peterson.

"Detective Sutherland, a word?" said Peterson sternly.

"I need one more minute."

"Right now, Detective" came the commanding voice of Sergeant Jennings.

Sutherland stared at Sorenteen, who gave a subtle shrug. He could feel his blood boiling as he stormed out of the room. He waited for the door to close before pleading his case.

"I have him. I have him where I want him, and he's going to give up a name. This could be it!"

"Detective Sutherland, you have time and time again reached out by yourself against the recommendation of this state and those above you. If you would put this much focus into other avenues, you'd be the best detective in the region. But you just won't stop."

"I have a confession coming—"

"Correction, you are coercing a confession, and Danny Icon is going to shred this interrogation apart. When you don't follow the rules, the system breaks down."

"Dan, I have a witness that can link these pieces together. I am on the verge—"

"You've been on the verge now for years. Who is this witness?"

"His name is Alonso Vega. He has connections to Caprizzi, to Kennedy, to the man who originally funded the construction of Uptown, and I can prove it."

"I hope you're not referring to the Jorge Vega shooting. A case where you shot and killed a suspect, and then interrogated his brother the same day."

"Sir, with all due respect, I was the best one to lead that interrogation."

"It doesn't matter. And besides that, you were investigating a documented dead angle without the permission of any of your superiors."

Sutherland fell silent.

"I read that report, several times. You actually connected yourself to Caprizzi in it, Detective."

"What?"

"You said in that report that you were the arresting officer in the Tomas Vega case, the father of the Vega brothers. An arrest that also involved Mark Kennedy in a time when he was working directly with Victor Caprizzi."

"You can't possibly think—"

"It doesn't matter what I think. It matters what is documented; it matters what can be proven. You have shoved this department and the state in between a rock and a hard place."

Sergeant Jennings had heard enough. "Detective Sutherland, until further notice you are suspended active immediately. Trooper Konine will take over the investigation of Ryan McDonough's death. He will take over any residual Uptown investigation."

"Yes sir," said Sutherland coldly.

"Watch that tone with me."

"Sorry, sir. I understand."

"Go home. Take a couple days off."

Sutherland walked toward his cruiser. Pissed off, he slammed the door shut and punched the steering wheel several times. He didn't care what the department did to him. They could take his gun, they could have his badge, and they could put him in jail. As far as he was concerned, he had already passed the point of no return. His phone went off. It was a miracle. It was Brent Waters.

"Hello?"

"Detective Sutherland, I heard you called my office several times. What can I do for you?"

"Agent Waters, you don't know how happy I am to hear from you. I believe I have evidence that there is human trafficking coming through Vermont and that it could possibly be connected to Victor Caprizzi amongst several others."

"What stemmed this belief?"

"One of our undercovers was shot and killed last night. In a recording we were able to retrieve from the scene, something was mentioned about girls being brought through Vermont. Do you have ANY sort of information on that?"

"That's very interesting. It's the belief of my department that the increase in abductions over the last year or so is going hand in hand with human and sex trafficking up the East Coast to Montreal. What else can you tell me?"

"I can't talk about it freely. I don't know who I can trust."

"Okay, I'll meet you in Vermont as soon as I can. I have to take care of a few things I'm working on now. Just lay low—we'll look into this together."

"Thank you, sir."

"No, Detective, thank you."

With a small sense of renewed energy, he knew he had to do one other thing before completely reaching out to the FBI. He had to sit down with Mark Kennedy and have a one-on-one chat with his old partner and mentor. He was either with him or against him, and the time was now to find out which it was.

. . . . . .

Peterson opened the door to the interrogation room. "Mr. Sorenteen, you're free to go."

"Thank you. Sorry I couldn't be more help."

Peterson turned to go and pulled Sergeant Jennings aside. "Get some control over your department."

Sorenteen grabbed his things and left the barracks. On his way out his phone went off. A text had come in from Peterson with the name of Sutherland's witness. He generated a text for the crew back at Uptown.

Prisoner Alonso Vega...Have Robbins take care of him.

CHAPTER 22

RACHEL DAVIS

Escape

Rachel's handler was with one of the other girls he was responsible for keeping track of. It gave her a little bit of time to be alone, which at this point was all she hoped for on a daily basis. She had been able to rip a spring out of the bottom of the bed the day she arrived in the new room. Every chance she got, she went to work on the bolt that held her chained to the wall of the room. She knew she couldn't make it too obvious; she hoped it was just loose enough to eventually break free. The sound of two men talking outside her door caught her attention. Their voices were muffled, but it sounded like they were arguing. She slipped off the bed and put her ear against the door in an attempt to decipher the conversation. The door made a loud noise as the lock was disengaged. She jumped back onto the bed.

Get ready to run, Rachel. Now or never.

The door flung open. She wasn't expecting to see Antoni Bortega on the other side of it, with a sinister look on his face.

"You!" she exclaimed.

"You remember me, baby?" he said with his slick Spanish accent. She would never forget that voice. He staggered over to her, drunk.

"No one is supposed to see me."

"The rules don't apply to me, chica. I never did get my chance with you. Well, tonight is the night. I've been thinking about this since we met."

He went to grab her and she rolled off the opposite end of the bed. She noticed the door was still cracked open. She darted for it, but he grabbed and threw her into the wall. She sunk to the floor. He picked her up and flung her back on the bed, climbing on top and pinning her.

"Just calm dooown. It will feel good, I promise," he whispered in her ear.

She gave one last attempt at getting him off of her, but she was too weak. He ripped her shirt off. Overpowering him wasn't an option, so she did the opposite. She totally relaxed.

"You see? That's what I'm talking about."

Rachel brought her mouth to his ear and whispered, "Fuck you!"

She got her mouth around his entire ear and clenched down as hard as she could. He screamed and tried to pull away, but her jaws were unrelenting. He grabbed her face and pushed so hard a portion of his ear tore off. He fell off the bed with blood gushing from the wound. Rachel ran for the door, but the chain didn't break off the wall. It ripped her arms backward so hard it dropped her to the ground. She gave one last yank and the bolt came free. She hid behind the door just in time as two guards came running in with Tasers ready. They both ran to Antoni, and Rachel slipped behind them out into the open hallway. She ran as fast as she could. Behind her she heard Antoni screaming.

"Get her! Bring her back here!" His voice, distant at first, seemed to be getting closer. And closer. "I'm going to kill you, you bitch!"

She ran around the circular hallway to a set of stairs that led upward.

"There's nowhere to run! You're going to wish you were dead by the time I'm through with you!" he yelled from close behind.

She hopped three steps at a time, not sure where the long staircase led. All she could do was hope that she was taking the right way to salvation.

. . . . . .

Kennedy and Billings were doing their rounds together through the vault. Kennedy felt it important to check out A-Wing often as Marcus' people were partially in charge of guarding it. He wanted to be sure they were doing their job and nothing more.

"So what do you think about that text from Sorenteen?" Billings asked.

"We'll wait till he gets here to act on anything. I want to know exactly what happened."

"You think O'Shea is on board for that?"

"O'Shea is a smart guy. He only does what he has to do. So I'd assume he'd want all the information before jumping on anything as well."

Kennedy swiped his card to the vault and the door opened. The two guards on the inside nodded to him as they entered.

"You guys can take a few minutes," said Kennedy. "We'll be here for a while."

The guards left the vault.

"Open up the door to A-Wing, would you?"

Billings walked to the back of the vault and entered the code into the lockbox. The wall separated to reveal the back hallway. He walked by the door that led to the viewing room and froze.

"What is it?" asked Kennedy.

"I don't know. Come take a listen."

Kennedy walked up to the door. It sounded like someone was screaming. They both got closer, trying their best to hear what was being said. They both took a step back when something slammed up against the other side.

"Help! Help me, please!" came the sounds of a young girl.

Billings looked at Kennedy. "What the fuck is going on down there?"

"Open the door."

Billings did as he was told. The door swung open and a girl fell at his feet and wrapped herself around his legs. She curled up into a tiny ball. He caught a glimpse of her face, and even through the mask of blood she wore, he immediately recognized her: Rachel Davis.

"Please help! They're going to kill me!"

Kennedy looked back at the hallway. A younger man with blood all over his face as well came stumbling up the hallway with two of Marcus' guards behind him.

They got to the top and he let out a laugh. "Of all the people to run into, the man who runs the whole operation here!" He looked at the guards. "You boys can leave us. Make sure the other girls are locked up. Now!"

The guards did as they were told. As soon as they were gone, Kennedy was the first to talk.

"What the hell is this?"

"You're Mark Kennedy, right?"

"That's right."

"This bitch bit my fucking ear off," he said, pointing to the nub that was left. "And now I am going to teach that punta a lesson."

He reached around Kennedy's legs and grabbed her by the hair, dragging her back toward the steps. Rachel made desperate attempts to wiggle free.

"She is a fighter, isn't she?! So much more fun than the dead fish."

Kennedy could feel himself getting angry. Flashes of the anger he had toward Jordan Rickstein danced in his head.

"You're not supposed to be using the product," Kennedy said darkly.

"Don't tell me what I can and can't do. She is my product. I will do with her what I like. Don't worry, I'll have her cleaned up when I'm done."

He picked her up once again by the hair and dragged her to the foot of the steps. Kennedy walked to the door and shut it before he could get through.

Antoni glared at him, an evil look crossing his face. "Get away from the door."

Kennedy looked down at Rachel, who looked back up at him. Terror across her face.

"Please..." she said in a soft voice.

"Shut up!" Antoni yelled as he lifted his hand up to hit her.

Kennedy grabbed his hand midair and with his other hand slammed his head against the wall. Antoni let go of Rachel and she scurried to the opposite wall, where Billings stepped in front of her.

"What are we doing here, Kennedy?" asked Billings.

Kennedy ignored him as Antoni whipped out a knife. He swiped at Kennedy, who dodged the first effort. He took another swing and Kennedy ducked and speared him to the ground, knocking the wind out of him. Billings ran up and took the knife out of his hands. Kennedy started choking him. The much smaller Antoni made futile attempts at hitting him. The hits became softer and softer until he was just about to pass out. Kennedy wasn't done with him. He released his grip and Antoni began coughing and gasping for bits of oxygen.

"Give me the knife," he said calmly.

Billings threw it to him and held Antoni's arms down. Kennedy lifted the man's head up.

"You make me sick. And no one in this moment deserves this more than you."

He took the knife and slowly slit his throat ear to ear, Antoni's eyes wide with pain and panic. After he was done he dropped his head and stood up.

Rachel popped up, no longer afraid, and wrapped her arms around Kennedy. Kennedy held her for a minute awkwardly, then got down on one knee to look her in the eyes.

"Are you okay?"

She shook her head no.

"Look, you have to do something for me, and it's going to be the hardest thing you have ever had to do."

She looked at him, frightened and confused.

"You have to go back to your room downstairs."

She began to tremble, tears flowing freely. "Please don't make me. Please, I'm begging you."

Kennedy held her tighter. "Listen to me, Rachel, I will not let them hurt you. But if you leave here, the men who did this to you will hurt all the other girls, and then they will disappear and never be heard from again. We need to stop these men permanently. We need to make them pay for what they've done to you and so many others. But I need your help. You can trust me."

And in that moment she did. Every instinct she had told her to run. To push herself away and just continue to run. But this man had saved her. He could have stood by and done nothing to help, but he saved her instead.

"Okay," she cried.

"I will check on you every day to make sure you're all right. You have to be strong. You have to make everyone believe that you are a prisoner here and that you are helpless. But when you are no longer a prisoner, when the time comes, you will take all the other girls and you will lead them out of here. And everyone involved, I mean everyone, will pay."

She nodded. "I believe you."

"Okay," he said gently. "Go back to your room. I'll take care of this mess."

She turned around and opened the heavy door. She glanced back. Kennedy felt shame that he had to make her do the unthinkable. Their eyes met once more and then she made her way down.

"Call Nicky," he said to Billings. "I need this cleaned up, thoroughly."

"What about Marcus?"

"I'll deal with Marcus. Just make sure she goes back to her room and that Nicky gets here immediately!"

Billings ran down the stairs to make sure Rachel made it safely back to her room.

Kennedy got a text from Sorenteen. He was back and was calling an emergency meeting. Billings reappeared.

"Okay, we're good here," he said.

"Sorenteen just got back. We have to meet with him."

"Before we do, you and I have to talk," said Billings seriously.

"Let's walk and talk."

The two left the vault as Nicky went running up to them, tools in hand to make Antoni vanish. Kennedy took off his jacket and handed it to him.

"Get rid of this."

Nicky took it and continued down the hallway. Kennedy addressed the guards.

"No one in and no one out except for Nicky Deez."

They nodded. "Yes sir."

Once away from ears he returned attention to Billings. "So what do we need to talk about?"

"Up until this moment I wasn't sure if you were someone I could trust. But I see that this entire thing disgusts you as much as it does me."

"Of course it does."

"It's all gotten out of control, Kennedy."

"There's not much we can do about it until it's over."

"That's not true," he said, stopping.

"What are you talking about, John?"

"There are things I haven't told you, I haven't told anyone. You and I can still get out of this. We can get Sutherland to help us."

Kennedy looked around to make sure no one was listening. "Have you lost your fucking mind? Sutherland is not an ally. He would make this thing way messier than it already is. And besides, we help him, guess where I end up?"

"It's not about you, Kennedy, it's about these girls. What if we weren't there just now? What would be happening to her?"

"What have you told Sutherland?"

"Nothing…yet. But I know you're in this for the right reasons. I know you want what's best for everyone."

"Let me think about it."

Billings nodded. "Think quickly."

The two got into the elevator and met with everyone in the privacy of the conference room.

"Where have you two been?" asked Sorenteen.

"Making sure everything was okay downstairs. Where's Fontaine?"

"He couldn't make it."

"Well, how did the interrogation go?"

"Peterson bailed my ass out."

"So they didn't get anything?"

"No."

There was a collective sigh.

"What does Sutherland know?"

"He has all the evidence in the world. It's only a matter of time before he can use it. He also has a recording of me talking about girls being brought here. The good news is, for now, he got taken off the case."

"Good fuckin' work, Sammy," said O'Shea.

"What about Alonso Vega?" Sorenteen asked.

"We were hoping you could tell us."

"You haven't given the order yet, Kennedy?"

"I need to know what the reasoning is before I just off someone."

"He can put all of us attached to Uptown and Victor."

"How?"

"It doesn't matter. Sutherland has him cooped up in one of the local prisons. He needs to be silenced."

"Fuck," said O'Shea. "We'll make sure it's quick, but he's gotta go."

"I won't have anything to do with this," announced Kennedy. "You want him dead? You make the call."

"Robbins is your connection; you need to tell him."

Kennedy thought a moment. "I get the final say. I'll take care of it as I see fit. You don't know Robbins like I know him. I'll make sure the problem is taken care of."

"Okay then," said O'Shea.

"Billings, why don't you get in touch with the Vermont State Prison system, find out exactly where he's being held. Make sure he's even in the right prison for us to pull this off."

"Sounds good."

Billings left the room.

"Anything else?" asked O'Shea.

Kennedy waited for the door to lock.

"We have a problem."

"Another one?" asked Sorenteen.

"A big one. It needs to be our number one priority. I think Billings has been compromised."

"How do you mean?" said O'Shea tentatively.

"I don't think he's done anything yet, but he's looking for an easier way out. He said something about wanting to get in touch with the police."

Sorenteen jumped up, grabbed a water glass, and shattered it against the adjacent wall.

"We need to get our shit together!"

"Calm down, Sammy."

"Don't tell me to calm down! We are supposed to be in control! When did you find out about this?"

"Just now, on my way up here."

"What are we going to do?"

"I want to sit down with him and see if he's talked more than what he's letting on."

"And if he has?"

"I'm sure he hasn't done anything stupid."

"But if he has?"

"If he's become a risk, we'll put him in one of our holding rooms until it's done. Is everyone on board for that?"

"Fine," said O'Shea.

"He's your problem," snapped Sorenteen. "You better fucking fix it."

"Like I said, I'm sure he hasn't done anything to screw us."

"We'll see, won't we."

"We certainly will."

CHAPTER 23

VICTOR CAPRIZZI

Upstate New York: April 2001

"C'mon, watch the road!" Kennedy yelled at Caprizzi as a car honked at them. "I didn't even know you knew how to drive a car."

"So you knew that I graduated top of my class in engineering and business, but you didn't think I could figure out how to drive?" Caprizzi turned and gave Kennedy a pathetic look.

"Just watch the road. You're giving me an ulcer."

The car took a sharp right-hand turn. It was about 5:00 p.m. on a Thursday, and the streets were getting busy with the working-class population working their nine-to-five jobs.

"Why are we upstate again?" asked Kennedy.

"Because we are securing an important investment this afternoon."

"You know I hate vague answers."

"Just trust me, the more surprised and genuine you are, the better."

"Is everything set up back in Manhattan?"

"Almost, just have to convince Lugo Fernandez to show up. That will complete the gathering of the five biggest mob heads in the same room to discuss how to put an end to you permanently."

"How much firepower are we talking?"

"Well, two different answers. In the room? There should be none, or close to none."

"And outside the room?"

"I don't want to make you nervous, so let's avoid crossing that bridge just yet."

"It won't matter anyway. I'm going to kill all of them."

"I know you will, Mark. I know you will," Caprizzi responded with a sincere glance toward Kennedy.

"Eyes on the road please."

"Yeah, yeah. You can relax, we're here."

They pulled up to a local bar. Just a bit further down the road was Firerock Maximum Security Prison.

"What are we doing here?"

"This bar is where all the guards from Firerock come after their shift ends."

"Did that answer my question?"

"We're waiting for a minute. Just keep your eye out."

Kennedy shook his head and looked out his window. There wasn't much to see. A parking lot with three cars parked in it. A small-town local bar scene with a Laundromat and several closed businesses completing the depressing landscape. A man stepped out of the bar. He was a bit overweight and wore a Firerock Security outfit. He waved good-bye to whoever he had been conversing with inside. As the guard walked to his car, a man appeared around the corner. He kept low to the ground and moved quietly so the unsuspecting guard couldn't see him.

"You seeing this?" Kennedy asked.

"See what?" he replied.

Kennedy situated himself closer to the window to see out better. The man who had slipped around the side of the bar put a mask over his face and jumped into the same vehicle at the same time the guard did. It quickly became evident that there was a struggle happening. Kennedy could see the masked man whaling away on the guard.

"Holy shit!" he exclaimed as he opened the car door and ran toward the attack.

Caprizzi rolled his window down and looked upon the unraveling scene with a smirk on his face.

Kennedy wrapped around the back of the car and with the butt of his gun shattered the passenger side window. The masked man looked up at Kennedy as Kennedy delivered the second blow to his face.

"Ah fuck! My nose, you stupid shit!"

Kennedy grabbed him by the collar of his shirt and dragged him out of the broken window and threw him against the side of the car, kneeing him as hard as he could in the gut. The man dropped to his knees to catch his breath.

"Are you okay?" he asked the guard, who was visibly shaken up.

"Yeah, I think so," he responded, wiping some blood away from his forehead. He got out of the car and came to meet his attacker face-to-face. He pulled the mask off.

"You know him?" asked Kennedy.

"Yeah. He was an inmate up the road. He got released a couple months ago."

Kennedy picked the former inmate up and wrenched one of his hands behind his back. He wrapped his other arm around the man's throat so he had better control of his head.

"Well, eye for an eye. What do you think?"

The guard looked around, first over his left shoulder, then his right.

He cocked his arm back and delivered a hard blow to the former inmate's face, knocking him out cold.

"Nice fucking hit," Kennedy remarked, dropping him to the ground.

The guard looked at Kennedy inquisitively. "Wait a minute, I know you."

Kennedy lowered his sunglasses.

"You're Mark Kennedy, the detective, right?"

"That's correct," he replied professionally.

"Holy shit, you're like a hero at Firerock. Well, amongst the guards, not so much the prisoners."

Kennedy laughed. "Yeah, I wouldn't imagine too many of the local shit heads in there will be sending me any birthday presents." He took out his business card and handed it to the guard. "And what's your name?"

"Liam, Liam Robbins."

"Guard Robbins. It's a pleasure to meet you. I'm glad we were swinging by when all this happened."

"Me too, Detective. That could have gone much differently. What should we do with him?"

"You should call this in. Have one of the local officers come by and pick him up. Leave me out of the story though; I don't want to have to do any paperwork. I'll give you full credit for putting this douche bag back in his place."

"I'll take it, no problem. Have a good day, Detective, and thanks again. I'll never forget this."

Kennedy walked back to the car and got in. "Can you believe it? That guy would have killed that guard if we hadn't been here."

"What was the guard's name?" asked Caprizzi.

"Liam Robbins."

A smile stretched across Caprizzi's face. He started the engine of the car and began driving away.

"Whoa, whoa, what about the investment?"

"We just made it. Nice work, Mark, as always."

Kennedy stared back at Caprizzi and breathed out a laugh of disbelief. "Well, that was easy enough."

Caprizzi laughed back. "You hungry? I know a great Greek place around here."

"Yeah, let's eat, on you of course."

"As always, my friend."

CHAPTER **24**

WILL SUTHERLAND

Who's in Control?

Alonso Vega woke up to his cell being pounded on by one of the guards. "Wake up, Vega! Let's go!"

"Man, are you kiddin' me? What time is it?" he said crankily.

"Are you fucking kidding me, Vega?" yelled Guard Robbins. "This isn't day care, it's prison. I'm flipping your cell, got word you have some contraband, so wake your ass up, get out of bed, turn around, and put your hands around your back."

Alonso mumbled under his breath as he slowly put his feet on the cold ground and shuffled over to the center of his cell, placing his hands behind his back as directed

"Open up cell 105," said Robbins over his radio. The door swung open and Robbins in routine fashion secured Vega's hands and pushed him into the back of the cell.

"Jesus, man, take it easy," said Vega, still half asleep.

"Shut your mouth," Robbins demanded.

Robbins took a minute to flip his bed over and throw the sheets to the ground. He then made sure no one else was watching. There was no one within earshot. He slipped out of the room and ushered a new prisoner in.

Alonso turned around and saw the massive prisoner staring him down. Robbins disappeared from the door.

"What's going on here, man?"

"Nothin' personal," said the prisoner. He cocked his neck back and head-butted Alonso as hard as he could. Alonso's forehead split open like a watermelon. He was left so disoriented he didn't have time to yell. The prisoner dragged him into the corner of the room and wrapped his massive hands around his tiny neck and squeezed.

He spoke in a low voice. "Mark Kennedy remembers you and he's sparing your life, brother. You keep fucking quiet 'cause if you don't, I don't need to remind you what will happen."

He gave one last squeeze as Alonso's eyes rolled into the back of his head. Robbins appeared at the door again and ushered the prisoner out.

"Close cell 105," he ordered. The door shut and locked. Robbins escorted the prisoner that Kennedy had lined up to intimidate Alonso back to his cell.

. . . . . .

Detective Sutherland sat at his house, waiting for an update from the FBI. Although he had been commanded to stay away from Uptown, he knew he wasn't going to be able to stop until he achieved the outcome he wanted. The initial sting of embarrassment from watching Sorenteen skip out of the barracks had passed. The anger and frustration that had built over the last several years grew stronger. He gave a quick call to Jules; she always had a way to calm him down. It rang five times and went to voice mail.

He moved over to a locked drawer in his living room and once again pulled ex-detective Mark Kennedy's file. Comfortable in his sweats, he got himself a diet soda and pulled the video of Kennedy's interrogation from the night that ended him—the last night that Mark Kennedy would be considered an active detective.

"I had every intention to kill that evening."

"Just to be clear, you are admitting to the murder of Lugo Fernandez, Robert Stanley, Joey D'Agostino, Shielah Chumein, Ricky Valdez, and Officer Luke Thompson."

"Officer Thompson was a mistake. As far as the others go, yes."

Chills ran down Sutherland's spine at how lifeless and calm Kennedy was during that interview. He went back to watching the tape.

"Jesus, Mark, why? Why throw your career away?"

"It had to be done. They fucking deserved it. You think those cocksuckers play by our rules? They don't. They only respond to one thing: the fear of death. It was the only thing to do. Can I give my official statement now? I'm getting fucking tired of this."

"Go on, Detective..."

"I was tipped off by Victor Caprizzi of a meeting amongst the top New York crime bosses in a locked-down warehouse thirty minutes outside the city. I was on suspension for an active investigation by Internal Affairs for my involvement with the Uptown Gang. I brought two of my personal firearms from home as well as a state police-issued shotgun and arrived at the scene at about noon."

"The murders didn't take place until almost nine."

"I waited in a false wall underneath the staircase all day. Watched as each individual walked up the stairs to the room. After I was confident all the parties were accounted for, I entered through a rear entrance, south side of the building."

"How many entrances were there?"

"Just two. The way I was entering and the front."

"And you knew that?"

"Yes. I had been over the blueprints of the building thoroughly with Victor the day before."

"So the act was completely premeditated?"

"Yes."

"Okay, go on."

"Upon entering the room I found five men and one woman sitting around a table. The only option for an exit they had at that point was the front stairwell because they sure as hell weren't going to go through me."

"Then what happened?"

"I took both my sidearms out and quickly dropped two of them with single shots to the head. Two of the three remaining made a run for the front door, while the other one scrambled for his weapon. I pulled the trigger of each of my guns again, striking the two running toward the front door, once each. I took cover into the rear stairwell as D'Agostino opened fire on me. I looked around the corner just in time to see the two that had run for the door were pointing their guns at each other."

"Any idea why they would do that?"

"I suppose neither one was sure who was responsible for setting up the hit. Both pulled the trigger simultaneously, and they both dropped dead. I came back into the room ready to open fire on the last man, but he had taken cover under the table and I took a bullet to my chest."

"Just to be clear, you opened fire first. Is that correct?"

"Yes."

"Jesus, Mark. All right, go on…"

"His fire hit my flak jacket. I proceeded to drop the sidearms and handle the shotgun. I unloaded all but two shells into the end of the table where the fifth man was hiding. I saw his body drop to the ground. Someone came up from behind me and started strangling me."

"The driver of one of the cars?"

"Exactly. I blew his foot off, and after he fell to the floor, I put the last shell into his chest and locked the back door to the room to prevent anyone else from coming in."

"What happened to Officer Thompson?"

"I grabbed my weapons and made a run for the front exit."

"Why not go out the rear exit, same way you came in?"

"I was afraid there might be more people coming up from the back. The moment I opened the door, Officer Thompson came rushing in with backup close behind. I wasn't expecting anyone important to be there. All I saw was another body. I killed him. I then immediately put my weapons down and was taken into custody."

Once the interview was over, Kennedy sat there quietly staring at the video camera. Sutherland felt like he was staring right at him. He knew more about that night than most. He was a rookie at that time. He knew what Kennedy was doing that evening, and yet he took no action to stop him or help him. Then he committed the ultimate betrayal; he had been the one who called Officer Luke Thompson from Internal Affairs. He was responsible for his death and Kennedy's incarceration. The thought made Sutherland uncomfortable and ashamed.

His phone rang. He figured it was Jules but the number came up as *restricted.*

"Hello?" he answered.

"Sutherland? It's me, Konine."

"What's up?"

"I'm calling from the St. Johnsbury Prison. Bad news—your boy Alonso Vega got hammered on by one of the prisoners. He's dead."

Sutherland jumped off the couch, spilling the soda he had opened. "What? Are you fucking kidding me? What happened?"

"No one knows. He was in his cell. Guard by the name of Liam Robbins was on his rounds and found him like that. He thinks he killed himself. His body is on its way to the medical examiner now."

"There's no fucking way. He wouldn't have done that. He knew he was in there for safety. What the fuck?!" He almost threw the phone across the room but then regained his composure. "Call me as soon as the report is complete, okay?"

"Will do."

He hung up the phone.

Sutherland put his street clothes on, grabbed his gun, and walked out to his car. The first snow of the season had begun to fall. As his feet hit the sidewalk, he noticed a shadow out of the periphery of his vision. He turned to face it. It was snowing hard enough that it took him a moment to realize who it was.

"Jules," he said softly, "put that gun down."

Jules stood there, arm extended and hand shaking. She pointed the Glock directly at him.

"Whatever is going on, killing me is not the answer. I mean, it's me, Jules. Please, point that gun away from me."

She didn't budge. The tears rolled down her cheeks. Sutherland noticed Trooper Dominick circle her from the back, his gun drawn. A man walking his dog stopped at the sight. Dominick got his attention and had him move away from the scene.

"Ma'am," he said firmly. "Put the gun down."

Sutherland motioned for him not to shoot. He took a step toward her. Her hands trembled a bit more.

"Whatever the problem is, whatever your involvement is, I can help. But not like this. Don't end it this way."

Staring at Will, she wanted to pull that trigger. More than anything in the world, in that moment she would have done anything to pull that trigger for Uptown, for Kennedy. But she couldn't bring herself to do it. She lowered the gun and dropped it. Dominick ran up from behind and placed her in handcuffs.

Sutherland slowly approached her. "Let's get her inside."

Dominick nodded and escorted her up the stairs back into the house.

Once inside Sutherland sat her down in the living room chair. Dominick stood quietly in the back.

"What the fuck, Jules? You came here to shoot me? To kill me after all we'd been through?"

"This isn't about love or feelings; it's about what had to be done."

Sutherland was crushed. Angry and crushed. "You know, after we talked at Uptown, and you told us to go to The Shack, I had Dominick follow you around. Make sure you were okay. If he hadn't been here, then what?"

She looked down at the ground. He had never seen her so vulnerable and confused. Her hard exterior had melted away.

"Listen to me, if you have something to say, now is the time to say it."

She took a deep breath. "I'm in love with Mark. And I'm in love with you."

Sutherland stood up angrily. "And that's why you're here with a fucking gun in your hand!?"

"No, there's more," she said, swallowing hard. "There is some shit happening at Uptown, Will. There are girls there, underage girls, sex slaves or whatever. They are planning on using them to get to a human trafficking group so they can do something like the mob massacre."

Sutherland stepped back a few feet. "What the fuck are you talking about?"

"I'm sorry...it's just...I had a job to do. But everything has gone to shit."

"How does Kennedy fit in to all of this?"

"He's a part of it. He's losing his fucking mind, but he's a part of it." She wiped running mascara from her cheek with her shoulder.

"How did Kennedy go from prison to all of a sudden being right back to what he does best? How did he stay connected?"

"I sent letters, every month or more sometimes. Some of those letters had names written on them. Names that he would erase for Victor."

"Where are those letters now?"

"Gone. The only other person to see them would have been the guard helping him on the inside."

"Who?"

"His name is Liam Robbins."

"Robbins? That piece of shit." Sutherland sat down in a chair. "What else do you know? I want to know everything."

"I don't know everything. They cut me out as soon as some guy named Marcus showed up."

Sutherland wrote the name down. As tears ran down her face, he walked into his office and called Konine.

"Yeah, Sutherland, what's up?"

"I need a favor."

"Name it."

"Pick up Guard Robbins; meet me underneath the bridge right off of Exit 6 in Bristol. Don't ask me any questions. Just know that Robbins may be the key to everything we need to know."

"You got it."

Sutherland walked back into the room.

"So what happens now?"

"You're under arrest, Jules. It's as simple as that. Don't try to get in touch with me, don't try to call me. You're an accessory to a sex trafficking ring, you're an accessory to at least one murder, and you pointed a gun at a Vermont state trooper."

Jules sobbed.

"I don't have a safe place to put you, so you're staying here. If you run, I swear to God I will hunt you down. Stay here, and when the time comes, cooperate. That's that."

She nodded.

Sutherland grabbed his gun and put it in his belt. He looked at Dominick. "Stay with her until I call you." He walked to the door and slammed it shut.

CHAPTER **25**

MARK KENNEDY

The Car Wash

Kennedy walked over to Billings' suite. He knocked on the door twice and waited. Billings answered the door in a bathrobe and looked less than enthused to be disturbed.

"Kennedy, fuck, it's eleven o'clock at night. We kinda have a long day tomorrow. What is it?"

"We need to talk."

"About what?"

"It's private."

"So do you want to come in and we can talk about it?"

"It's more private than that."

Billings stared blankly at Kennedy. "Can you just tell me what the fuck you need from me right now?"

"My car is exceedingly dirty. We should take it to the car wash and get it cleaned up. There's one right down the road from here."

"That's the secret? Your fuckin' car needs to be washed?"

Kennedy stared at Billings with eyes that spoke louder than words.

"Okay, never mind. I won't say any more. Let me grab my clothes and we'll go."

"I'll meet you down in my car."

Kennedy headed back down the hallway to the elevator. He was nervous. He desperately wanted Billings a part of the operation because of the level of trust he had developed with him. But after what Billings had told him in the hallway outside A-Wing, Kennedy couldn't ignore the possibility that he was some kind of narc or that the operation had broken him down completely.

The plan was to take him away from Uptown, go inside the car wash, where the situation could be contained no matter what the outcome. Kennedy would have only a few moments to extract the information he was searching for because if he didn't get in touch with Sorenteen by the time the wash was over, it would be assumed that Billings was a liability. Added to the complexity of the situation was the fact that if Billings were connected to state or federal agencies, he could be wearing a wire.

He idled out front for about ten minutes, the exhaust from the Town Car circling in the brisk air. When he spotted Billings walking outside, he swung around the loop of the main entrance and picked him up.

"So what are we doing? Is 'car wash' code for something? Is this about yesterday?"

"Shhh. We're just headed to a car wash. I didn't want to come alone, dangerous streets out here, you know."

"Dangerous streets? In Vermont? You really have lost your mind, and your balls. I'm disappointed, like a father finding out his son doesn't want to be a mobster. It's fuckin' depressing."

Kennedy drove the rest of the way in silence. He entered the twenty-four-hour car wash slowly until the beacon turned red, indicating to him that the car should stop. He selected the nicest wash option as it took the longest. He would have but a few moments to navigate his way quickly through the interrogation. Once the wash started he turned the music up very loudly to neutralize the efforts of anyone who may be listening in.

"Jesus, Kennedy!" exclaimed Billings. "Turn that down!"

Kennedy was quick to respond. "Listen up, John, we have the length of this car wash to talk, and that is all the time we have."

"What the fuck is this?"

"What you said to me the other day, we should involve Sutherland: What did you mean?"

"I meant we could take a different avenue to end this thing so that we minimize how many more people end up dead."

"Have you lost your ability to carry this thing through to the end? Yes or no?" Kennedy waited a moment, then repeated himself. "Yes or no!?" he yelled, pulling his gun out.

"Would you calm down and point that fuckin' thing away from me? You don't know the whole story, okay?"

"You better start talking then. We only have a minute."

The light wash had just finished its course, and the power washer was now slamming against the side of the car.

"Okay," started Billings. "You want to know? I killed Victor."

Kennedy nearly choked on his own tongue. "What?"

"The FBI got in touch with me years ago; they wanted information on Uptown. Basically they gave me an offer, a way out, and all I had to do was be a low-end criminal informant for them from time to time. Give them basic information. Just enough to keep tabs on Victor."

"Who? Who in the FBI?"

"Agent Brent Waters directly. I wasn't supposed to talk to anyone else."

"Waters?" said Kennedy, confused. "He told me when I got out of prison that there was a criminal informant in Uptown, that he killed Caprizzi and bolted."

"He lied."

"Well, what the hell happened with Caprizzi?"

"He found out, obviously. He invited me out to run some errands late, pick some shit up. We drove for hours. We ended up at a bridge in Connecticut. He pulled the car over and walked up to the edge. He told me to get out. When I asked him what the fuck he was doing, he took a gun out. I thought that was it for me. Instead he put the gun in my hands and pulled it straight to his chest. 'Pull the trigger,' he said. 'Pull the trigger and end this if that's what you want.'"

"And you did?"

"Waters told me to take the opportunity if it ever presented itself. And besides, you think things are out of control now, you should have seen how things were. Trying to gain popularity in the crime world, give me a break. We did a lot of terrible fuckin' things. None of it was worth it. So, I thought I'd take care of shit on my own. I pulled the trigger and he flipped over the side of the bridge."

"I thought you shot him in the head?"

"No," he tapped Kennedy's chest, "right there."

"Did you see his body afterwards?"

"Hell no. I ran. But he was dead, I'm sure of it. Between the gunshot and the height of the bridge, shallow water beneath, no way."

The soaping phase of the cycle began, blasting soap against the windows, which made it dark inside the car. Time was up.

"I'm sorry, Kennedy, I should have told you earlier."

"I need you to focus, John. What happened afterwards with the FBI?"

"They never got in touch with me again. Never heard from them, never saw them. It's like I was never working for them."

Kennedy's mind began to race.

Whose side was Agent Waters on? Did he have his own agenda? What was Caprizzi thinking? Could he be alive? He had so many questions, but it was too late. Locked inside the car, which sat in darkness from the soaped-out windows, it was over for John Billings.

Kennedy felt that something was off. Something caught his attention.

"Did you notice the car wash stopped?"

"Yeah, so?" Billings muttered back, his head buried in his hands.

"The wash shouldn't have stopped," he replied, trying to look out of the windows. "Fuck!"

"What?"

"Just get down."

"Get down where?"

"Just do it, John!" he yelled.

No sooner had he given the command than a small segment of the windshield shattered, followed by the screams of Billings. He looked over and realized he was bleeding from the shoulder.

"What's happening? Is this a fuckin' hit?"

"Just let me think. We're in a fucking kill box right now, and I don't know who's on the other side."

The glass punctured out again and a bullet went soaring between the two of them, missing by just inches and landing in the backseat of the car.

"Get your ass down into the foot space!" screamed Kennedy while shoving him to the ground.

Bullets began raining down. The windshields cracked, splintered, then finally shattered. The front and back of the car were decimated. The barrage went on for what seemed like minutes. Thankfully, down in their respective foot spaces, Billings and Kennedy were relatively safe due to the structure of the car.

The shooting stopped and all Kennedy could hear was the sound of him and Billings breathing heavily and his heart thudding in his chest as he felt all over himself for any blood. He looked over at Billings, who looked to be unconscious.

The driver side door swung open and he was grabbed out of the car by two large men wearing masks. The first one threw him hard against the wall, and the second immediately followed with a punch to his face. Kennedy went down on one knee, and when one of the men went to pick him back up, he jammed his hand up into his jaw, which sent the offender stumbling backward. The other masked man was quick to knee him in the stomach and then again hard in the face, which almost knocked him unconscious. The two men began stomping on his chest and legs. Kennedy was helpless. Although his right eye was already completely swelled shut, he could still see with his left. In his direct line of sight was his car, and he noticed that Billings was no longer inside. At that moment Billings came sprinting around the backside of the Uptown vehicle and tackled one of the men standing above Kennedy, slamming his head into the car wash control, which restarted the cleaning cycle. The power washer came on and drenched all four of them within seconds. Kennedy used the distraction to get himself up and wrap his arms around the other man's waist, picking him up clear off the ground and driving him to the concrete as hard as he could.

Off in the distance the sound of sirens became audible, followed by the voices of men getting back into their cars outside the car wash and driving away. The four men were left inside fighting for their lives. Kennedy dove back on top of the man he had just put to the ground, and as the two grappled for control of each other's arms, Kennedy managed to deliver a blow to his head that greatly reduced the man's awareness of his surroundings. Kennedy cocked his arm back and delivered the knockout blow to the masked man's head. He looked up and saw that Billings was being choked. He ran as hard as he could toward the two, lowered his shoulder, and knocked him off Billings with such force that he felt the man's shoulder crunch and dislocate.

Kennedy went to help Billings up, but he ripped his arm away.

"What the fuck is going on, Kennedy?"

"I don't know. We need to get back to Uptow—"

Kennedy felt a sharp object spear him in the back. Almost instantly his body contorted and he fell to the ground violently. Billings went to run as he felt the prongs of a Taser pierce his side; he was brought down as well. Several moments later the electrocution ended; Kennedy's vision narrowed and became dark until finally he passed out.

CHAPTER 26

WILL SUTHERLAND

Answers

Sutherland cruised off the interstate exit where Konine was supposed to meet him. The snow was still accumulating and had covered the landscape with at least six inches. As he merged onto Route 5, he could see the bridge up ahead. Sure enough, there sat Konine's squad car protected from the weather, two men leaning against the hood. Sutherland pulled his car off a side road to join them. He brought his car to a stop and got out.

"Jim, hey, glad you could make it. I assume this is..."

"Liam Robbins of the St. Johnsbury prison."

"Liam, it's a pleasure," he said, extending his hand.

"The pleasure is all mine. I've heard great things about you."

"Well, I'm sure they're mostly exaggerated."

"So, Detective, if you don't mind me asking, how can I be of help to you?"

"Trooper Konine didn't explain to you why you were here?"

"No sir. Just that you needed my help and it had to be kept a secret."

"Well," started Sutherland, leaning against the cruiser as well, "it does need to be kept very quiet for sure. There is something big happening and I think you may hold the key to it."

"Sir?"

Sutherland put his finger up to silence him and walked back to his car, grabbing a large file which he flopped onto the hood next to Robbins.

"Liam, you used to be a guard at Firerock in upstate New York, right?"

"Yes sir."

"And you kinda looked after a man by the name of Mark Kennedy, is that right?"

"Absolutely. Mark Kennedy was a hero in New York. I wasn't going to let any dirtbags get to him if I had anything to say about it."

"Gotta love the loyalty," blurted out Konine. "The system could use a hundred more like you."

"I appreciate that very much."

"Look, Liam, I need you to be sincere with me. Your answers to my questions could very well be the difference between a disaster happening and a disaster being stopped."

"Okay," he responded nervously.

"Okay," repeated Sutherland. "So you're a guard at Firerock. Mark Kennedy comes, you two work together there, get to know each other…"

"I actually met him before he ended up in prison. He saved my life one day from some degenerate trying to assault me."

"Wow, I didn't realize that. Right place, right time, I suppose."

"Exactly."

"So, you two actually know each other and you help him however you can. He leaves Firerock and comes to Vermont. Right after, you leave Firerock and come to Vermont. Hell of a coincidence."

"I couldn't be more pleased working in the same area as Mark."

"So you two were pretty close."

"I think so."

"He ever give you any letters while he was in prison?"

The question caught Robbins off guard. "What do you mean?"

"What do you mean what do I mean? Pretty straightforward. Did Mark Kennedy ever give you any letters that he received?"

"No, nothing like that. All letters were logged, searched, and then given back to the system."

"Well, that's what's supposed to happen. But I know that Kennedy got letters in prison. Only if you look here…" Sutherland pulled out a log of incoming letters to Kennedy: There were none.

"Well…I mean, that's odd. I don't know what to tell you about that."

"You know who Jules Romano is?"

"No clue, sir."

"Jules Romano. Doesn't ring a bell?"

"No sir."

"Jules Romano is someone I know very well. At least I thought I did."

"What does that have to do with me?"

"She told me that she sent letters to you to give to Mark for something like ten years. Each letter had a name written on it. Those people tended to end up beaten or dead."

Robbins began shaking his head. "No, no way."

"Don't do that," commanded Konine. "Don't shake your head no. You listen to what Detective Sutherland says and you answer his questions."

"Thank you. Now look," Sutherland said, getting closer to Robbins' face, "I don't doubt that you don't know the half of what is actually going on, but you indirectly helped, and continue to help, a manipulative and dangerous group of people. That same group is who Kennedy works for. You know things and I need to know what you know. Right now."

"Am I under arrest?" he asked.

"No, you're cooperating with the state police. Nothing like an arrest is happening here."

"Absolutely not," chimed in Konine.

"Then I'd like to leave."

"We can't let you leave, Liam. Not till you tell us the truth."

"I want to call a lawyer. Call Dan Peterson."

"Dan Peterson? Why would I call Dan Peterson?"

Robbins fell silent. Sutherland's eyes became wide.

"How do you know District Attorney Peterson!?"

"I don't, just a name…I…just a name I'm familiar with."

Sutherland stepped away from the car and then quickly walked back up, bumping his chest into Robbins.

"You listen to me. There are girls being held, fucking girls! Sex trafficking, prostitution, and the death of children. And it's all happening right here. Right under our fucking noses! Did Mark Kennedy or Dan Peterson or God himself ever tell you that what you were doing was directly helping them bring underage prostitution through Vermont?!"

"Mark would never get involved in something like that."

"Mark is involved in something like that. He's in neck fucking deep in something like that, Liam! And my goddamn hands are tied. Trooper Konine's goddamn hands are tied because of people like Dan Peterson and people like you!"

"How can you be sure girls are involved?"

"That same woman, Jules Romano, knows about everything. She couldn't handle it anymore and she came to us for help. Now, I believe that you are the lowest man on the totem pole. So when this thing goes down and the shit starts rolling downhill, are you going to be the guy who is the hero and breaks this thing wide open? Or are you going to be the fall guy for a sex trafficking ring and spend the rest of your life in prison with no one to protect you? I think you know what happens to supporters of underage prostitution in prison."

Robbins looked off in the distance; for a moment he looked like he was going to pass out but then brought his eyes back to Sutherland and Konine.

"Look, I don't know a lot of what's going on. I'm not sure how helpful I can be."

"Let's start with those letters."

"I would get letters for Mark. They'd show up at my house. I'd deliver them, then I'd burn them."

"Any names you can remember?"

"I only looked one time. Mark made me promise I wouldn't look anymore."

"What was the name, Liam?"

"Jordan Rickstein."

"Jordan Rickstein. Like the Jordan Rickstein who raped FBI Agent Brent Waters' daughter and ended up brutally slaughtered in prison a few weeks later?"

"Yes."

"Holy shit," he said, looking at Konine.

"Unbelievable," Konine responded.

"What happened with Alonso Vega?"

"I thought he was just a drug peddler, a worthless nobody causing problems. I promised Mark I'd help wherever I could. I got an order from him saying to make sure Alonso Vega wouldn't want to cooperate with the police anymore. I didn't mean for him to die, I swear." He seemed like he was close to crying.

"Hey!" yelled Konine. "No time for tears; stay focused. Are you telling us that Mark Kennedy got in touch with you and told you directly to harm Alonso Vega?"

He nodded.

"Okay. You're doing good, Robbins. How do you know District Attorney Dan Peterson?"

"I don't. I was told if I was ever in trouble, especially with you, that I should get in touch with him."

Konine scratched his moustache as he concentrated on all the pieces of information. Sutherland looked at him and signaled him away from Robbins.

"Can you believe this shit?" Konine said excitedly. "We have 'em. We finally have 'em."

"Think about this though. Dan Peterson was a prosecutor in New York. He was the one who sentenced Kennedy to life in prison. He then blew it with Jordan Rickstein's sentencing. Rickstein ends up dead. Dan Peterson ends up moving to Vermont just a few years before Uptown is built. Then, Liam Robbins is a guard in New York, Kennedy gets released, they both end up in Vermont."

"How deep you think this goes?"

"I have no fucking idea, but what I do know is that this has Victor Caprizzi written all over it. And if that's true, alive or dead, Caprizzi would have every angle covered."

"We can't go in alone, Sutherland."

"I don't think we are alone."

"What do you mean?"

"Kennedy isn't in this for the girls or the money. He's in it to make a difference. That's what they've set up. He's going to take down this ring and then he's going to run. Maybe I can get him to help us. Or at least try to make a play on him."

"How about Agent Waters? Haven't you been in touch with him?"

"I have. He's supposed to get in touch with me today or tomorrow. He's coming in to help. But can we trust him?"

"What do you mean?"

"He's based out of the New York FBI division of Sex Trafficking. His daughter was raped by Jordan Rickstein. A little bit of a coincidence, don't you think?"

"You think the FBI is involved?"

"I don't know. Until I talk with Waters, we have to assume so."

"Let's talk about this more after we arrest him," Konine said, looking over at Robbins, who was sitting in the dirt next to the car.

"Yeah, go ahead and arrest him, let him know pending his official statement and full testimony we'll cut a deal with him. Then call Peterson's office, tell them you need to talk to him. When he gets to the precinct, you arrest him too."

"And Kennedy?"

"You leave him to me."

. . . . . .

Kennedy awoke to being splashed in the face with a bucket of water. Wherever he was, his arms and legs were bound to an immovable chair, and he had something taped to his mouth. With his first effort at moving, he felt searing pain throughout his ribcage, a potent reminder of the beating he and Billings had just suffered. It was dark in the room, but even through the darkness he could see shadows moving about and a line of several people who also looked to be sitting and squirming in their chairs. The lights came on. In front of him was Marcus with two very large bodyguards on either side of him. One he recognized as Afonos. He wore a sling and looked pretty beat-up as well. Kennedy looked to either side of him. Fontaine, O'Shea, Sorenteen, Billings, and Nicky Deez were all bound to similar chairs. He realized he was sitting in one of the private viewing rooms down in the A-Wing showcase hall. That meant breaking free from the chairs would be impossible. It also meant no one could hear whatever was about to happen: The rooms were completely soundproof.

Marcus began clapping. "This is an impressive bunch," he said softly, pushing his long, curly hair out of his eyes. "I don't fully understand the dynamic here, or who is working for who, or who is against who. But I must say, you're all incredibly fucking stupid for thinking I wouldn't find out."

Kennedy tried to burst himself free from the chair to no avail.

"I'm pretty good at knots. I've grown to be very good at tying down squirming, pathetic girls." He nodded at one of the guards who walked up to Kennedy and grabbed him hard by the face. "Stop fighting or I kill everyone here. Nod if you understand."

Kennedy nodded.

Marcus continued the show. "One of my men, one of my good men, is dead: Antoni Bortega. According to my guards, at least one of you killed him and at least one of you helped clean it up. That is unacceptable. More than that, I have Mr. Kennedy and Mr. Billings here running off in the middle of the night to have secret conversations. I need to know what was discussed."

Billings looked petrified.

Marcus glared down the line. "I believe there is a power struggle happening amongst us. There is only one person in charge. That is me. I am as compassionate as I am unforgiving. Nothing will stand in the way of doing my job." He paused as a guard handed him a stack of photographs. "As added incentive for those who will remain with us, I'm going to show you a series of pictures." He flashed in front of them thirty or so photographs taken of girls ranging from young to very young. "If there is any more fucking around under this roof, they will all be tortured and killed along with each and every one of you."

Marcus once again signaled to his guards, and they took off the tape covering the bound men's mouths. No one spoke.

"Which one of you has betrayed all of us and is causing the problem?"

They all stared forward without answering.

"Let me repeat. Which one of you has betrayed all of us and is causing the problem?"

Again no one said anything.

"Loyalty is important, so the fact that you're all standing up for someone who is against all of us confuses me."

The pregnant silence continued. Marcus stuck his hand out and Afonos gave him a gun. He walked up to Nicky Deez, who was on the far end of the line, and put the gun against his head.

"You all have three seconds to tell me who the problem is. One... Two... Three..." He pulled the trigger. A loud bang went off and Nicky's head snapped back, blood splattering the wall behind. Kennedy looked away, helpless to do anything. He glanced at Billings, who was next. Billings had fear burned into the depth of his eyes.

"Would anyone like to say anything?"

"Marcus," called out Fontaine, "just calm down, let's talk about this."

"That's not a specific name. One..." He raised the gun to Billings' head. "Two..."

"Wait," said Kennedy.

"Mr. Kennedy, you have something to say?"

"Your guy, Antoni, was abusing the product. Rachel Davis in fact. I killed him to protect the product as that is my job. I didn't know who he was, and none of these other guys had anything to do with it."

Marcus thought a moment before lowering the gun away from Billings' face. "I don't doubt that you had the right intentions for killing Antoni. But I know that you and Mr. Billings were both involved, and I know you and Mr. Billings were in that car together. No more lies."

"Billings was thinking about calling the police," said Fontaine. "Kennedy was going to dispose of him before you showed up to take care of both of them."

Billings' eyes stared down; he had no defense for himself.

"Is this true, Mr. Kennedy?"

Kennedy glared at Fontaine, then at Marcus. "Yes."

"Well then, the solution is simple," he said, nodding to his guards who promptly walked over to Kennedy, unbound him, forced a gun into his hand, and had him stand in front of Billings. "Get rid of the problem, show me you can be trusted, and we will move forward."

Kennedy's stomach was paralyzed. The operation was at a crossroads. Billings gazed into his eyes. Kennedy saw only fear in them. The rest of the room held their breath as it was up to Kennedy, and Kennedy alone, to make the decision. He knew what Marcus would do if he refused, but it didn't make the task any easier.

Kennedy silently mouthed to Billings, *I'm sorry.*

He lifted the gun to Billings' head and pulled the trigger. There was a deafening *bang* and Billings' head snapped back violently as Nicky's had. Blood sprayed the wall behind, and Billings' body went limp.

The two guards immediately jumped Kennedy and threw him to the ground. One climbed on top and dug his knee into his spine, sending jolts of pain down his legs. Marcus crawled up to his face and squished his head against the cold concrete.

"Now," began Marcus, tapping Kennedy's forehead, "two are dead. I have four left. I am sorry this had to happen, but I hope there will be no hard feelings. You four are vital to this auction, but from now on you will include my men in everything that you do so that I have eyes and ears on all of you. And if you so much as blink inappropriately, I'll kill the four of you and every living distant relative that you have any sort of connection to. This is a promise."

"Absolutely, Marcus," said O'Shea.

"We didn't need Billings anyway, he was extra weight," said Sorenteen.

"Things will go smoother now without a doubt," chimed in Fontaine.

"Good," replied Marcus, getting to his feet. "Mark, do you have any words of encouragement?"

Kennedy wanted to spring loose and tear everyone's throat out. But like his first interaction with Rickstein in the jail yard ten years ago, he was outmanned and out resourced. Now was not his time. He cleared his throat under the pressure of the guards still on top of him.

"I think we're all on the same page. Everything is in place."

"Bueno, friends," said Marcus. "So back to work. Eugene and Afonos will provide you the files of the men you will be picking up. They will also be working with you, helping you in any way you see fit, and will report everything back to me."

They all nodded in approval. Marcus left. Fontaine, O'Shea, and Sorenteen exited the opposite side of the room with Afonos, leaving Kennedy alone on the ground. Kennedy looked over at Billings, still tied to the chair. The sumo wrestler-shaped Eugene took him down and dragged him across the room and into the hallway. Billings had been the only one willing to do the right thing, to stop things before more people got hurt, and he was the one who paid the price. Kennedy picked himself up, walked to his penthouse on the other end of the casino, and disappeared into his room, which seemed colder and darker than any jail cell he'd ever been stuck in.

CHAPTER 27

FINAL PREPARATIONS

The Uptown gang, with their new babysitters, met up in the warehouse the next morning. Kennedy was sore from head to toe.

Four Escalades were ready and waiting to be taken out for a dry run of the transportation of all the invited guests to the auction taking place in less than twenty-four hours. As Kennedy walked toward the rest of the group, he saw that Eugene and Afonos were off in the corner talking. Everything about the two of them made Kennedy furious, down to Eugene's handlebar mustache. He wanted to rip it off. Of course he'd have had a tough time doing that given the sheer size of the man. His buzzed head held a dozen or so scars. Kennedy approached the remaining members of the Uptown Gang.

"How's everyone today?" he asked.

"Not well, mate. Although you look worse than the rest of us. How are you?"

"I'm a fucking train wreck. We need to talk about last night."

"Absolutely not," snapped Sorenteen quietly. "No more talking. Talking gets us nowhere. It got Billings nowhere, that's for sure."

The bodyguards looked up at them and began walking toward the group.

"All right, gentlemen," said Kennedy aloud. "Let's focus on today's work."

"What is the plan?" asked Afonos.

"Look," responded Kennedy, "you guys are coming in at the last second on all of this. You're not going to play a role. You're just here to watch. Don't get in our way or you'll end up like your boy Antifreeze, or Anthill, or whatever the fuck his name was."

"His name was Antoni, and he was a friend."

Kennedy stepped toward Afonos, and although he only reached his chin, he spoke with icy confidence. "Your friend was a fucking pedophile. He got exactly what he deserved."

"Just like your friend did, yes?"

"How's your arm doing by the way?"

"Okay, okay!" yelled O'Shea. "That's enough. We have a lot of work to do, so let's get to it. Everyone in their cars. Kennedy's giving orders. Let's go over the routes."

Kennedy backed down and they all got in their respective cars. They took the tunnel that brought them to a series of back roads and eventually out to Main Street, where they awaited further instruction.

Kennedy wanted to start off by practicing quick shifts to alternate routes.

"Deviate course to East Harmon Street," he announced over the radio to Sorenteen's car.

"Got it," he responded.

His car swung wildly down the perpendicular road as Kennedy's car continued down Main. He then gave the next set of instructions.

"Car three, route two."

O'Shea's car slammed its brakes just in time to hit Daniellson Avenue. This was the route back toward the private woodland helipad where the buyers would be dropped off.

Kennedy radioed in to all three cars, "All right, everyone, meet back at the wood-side entrance of Uptown. Remember, if something happens to me, your orders come from Sorenteen. See you in a few minutes."

Kennedy was speeding back to the start zone when something bright caught his attention in his rearview mirror. Blue lights.

"Son of a bitch." He clicked his radio back on. "I'm getting pulled over right now. I'll be a few minutes behind you."

Kennedy pulled over to the side of the road and slid his gun into the back of his belt. He turned his attention back to his rearview mirror.

"You've got to be kidding me," he said as he saw Sutherland approaching the rear of his vehicle. He rolled his window down.

"Mark! Well, well, well. I haven't had the honor of holding some legitimate power above you before."

"If you give me a ticket, I will put you down," he said, pointing with his fingers and a half smile on his face.

"You were really cruising through town there. Everything okay?"

"Yeah, of course. I haven't driven a nice car in a while, and I suppose the old lead foot came out for a moment."

"And your face?" questioned Sutherland. "You look like you were the target of a gang hit for Christ's sake."

"Domestic abuse actually," he dramatically responded. "Any other sensitive questions?"

"Where were you headed so fast?"

Kennedy hesitated to answer this time. He pulled his sunglasses down. "Are you interrogating me, Will?"

Sutherland forced a laugh. "No, of course not. I haven't pulled a traffic stop in a while, and, uh, the old habits are coming back, I suppose."

"Fair enough," Kennedy replied, not overly appreciating the sarcasm. "Speaking of which, why are you pulling traffic stops right now?"

Without missing a beat Sutherland responded, "I wasn't, but when I saw a car go flyyyying by me, I couldn't help myself. This is how I usually solve all my big open cases, the bad guy making a mistake."

"Did you just refer to me as 'the bad guy'?"

"No, poor attempt at humor, I suppose. Hey, you want to get lunch?" he asked, changing the subject.

"Lunch? Don't you have some open cases to tend to?"

"C'mon, those can wait, Mark. We haven't had a really great opportunity to catch up. You know what? That's it. I just decided that lunch is happening, right now."

"Look, Will, I agree, we should catch up, but now isn't the best time—"

"Well," interrupted Sutherland, "I can either give you a ticket for a few hundred dollars for speeding or you can buy me lunch with that big casino salary of yours. What do you say? Like old times."

Kennedy sighed at Sutherland's persistence.

"Sure. We can grab lunch. I'll follow you."

"Great!" said Sutherland enthusiastically.

As soon as he left, Kennedy texted Sorenteen: *Need to run interference on Sutherland, head back to Uptown whenever you want, I'll catch up with the team later.*

He followed Sutherland about two miles. They stopped at a small Irish pub and walked in together.

"Hey, Murph," they said simultaneously.

Sutherland looked at Kennedy. "You've been here, what, a month? You already know as many people as I do. Unbelievable."

"Yeah, the boys at Uptown are quite the crew. They know just about everybody."

Sutherland went up to the bar. "Murph, two beers, two Reubens."

"Coming right up, Detective Sutherland."

The two men took a seat at a side booth.

"So how are things at the casino?"

"It's going well," Kennedy responded casually as painful thoughts of Billings bubbled up.

Sutherland pushed further. "How about the guys you work with? I mean, half the guys over there have a criminal background, some with some pretty heavy mob ties."

"I really can't pass judgment on that because I'm also an ex-criminal with some pretty heavy mob ties in my past. They took a chance on me, and I've done nothing but good work for them."

Sutherland smiled for a moment while Kennedy took a sip of his beer.

"Look, Mark, it's just you and me here. Okay? No one can hear us, there's no wires here, no taps. It's you and me. So you can cut the bullshit anytime you want."

Kennedy was taken aback. "I don't like your tone."

"You don't have to like it. I'm watching out for you, and I have a feeling that you're hiding some very incriminating information from me."

"Like what?"

"Like you're working for the FBI, right? I mean, you weren't totally honest with me before when you said you didn't know who to contact or who was ultimately in charge of you, were you?"

Kennedy looked around the bar and lowered his voice. "I'm not working for the FBI. I haven't seen any FBI. So as far as I'm concerned, they have little to do with anything at Uptown."

"You're lying to me. Look, I'm here to help you, but I can't help you if you don't help me."

"Help you with what? Your insanity?"

Sutherland sat back. "I had a really nice talk with Liam Robbins yesterday. You know him?"

"I know of him, yeah."

"Well, according to him you guys are old friends, and he had an impressive story to tell about disposing of secret letters addressed to you."

"Every one of those assholes got what they deserved."

"I also had a chat with a woman I think you're quite familiar with, Jules Romano?"

Kennedy went silent. "What about Jules?"

"Well, as I know you know, we were pretty close. She showed up at my house yesterday, with a gun."

Kennedy aggressively rubbed his eyes.

"Yeah, I ended up having to arrest her. She then proceeded to tell me that you were hands-on involved with a sex trafficking operation."

Kennedy took a swig from his beer bottle.

"You want to know the part that really blew my mind?"

"Sure."

"The very nice but very dull Liam Robbins told me that a man by the name of Dan Peterson was somehow involved in all this."

Kennedy could feel the blood rushing to his face. He took a deep breath to try and keep his exterior calm.

"It's amazing how people can be so in control over their tiny little environments, and how that control can disappear in a second."

Kennedy leaned forward. "You're barking up the wrong tree, Detective."

"Detective? I think we're a bit beyond formal titles, aren't we?"

"You think you know what we do? You think you understand what is going on?"

"Who's we?"

"Shut the fuck up! You should have taken your sergeant's advice and dropped the case. You want to know how I know about that conversation?"

Sutherland didn't have a response.

"I know that because for the last ten years, a highly controlled system has been put in place. The end result is going to be the violent destruction of a group of monsters that would otherwise be free to do the awful and heinous things they do."

"So by endorsing sex trafficking and by killing undercover officers and by leaving a wake of destruction in your path, you actually believe it will have all been worth it?"

"Where you see a wake of destruction, I see a path to true justice."

"Bullshit, what justice? There's no justice being done. You're hoping that this all goes well. You're hoping that you are successful. And what if you're not?"

"Well, it would be a done deal if you had just stayed the fuck away. If you had just listened and really thought about what was happening, this would have all been a clean production."

"Don't blame your failures and your crimes on me. You're sounding more and more like one of them every day. 'No one needed to die if the cops hadn't shown up!' I mean, give me a fucking break."

"This isn't a group of thugs killing crack heads over an ounce of smack."

"No, it's a group of thugs killing cops in order to ATTEMPT to kill other human beings. The way this is supposed to work is that those people go to jail, we cut deals to get to the more important people, then we pass that information on to bigger agencies who work on taking them down legally. It's that simple."

"I've seen your system. I've worked in your system, and it fails. Not this one though. In my world we gather everyone, from top to bottom, from foreign to domestic, and we end it."

They both sat there, staring at each other, neither budging.

"So that's it then?" asked Sutherland.

"It seems like it, kiddo. Where do we go from here?"

"Since I've failed at getting you to come to your senses, plan B is to beg you to just disappear. You and the rest of your people. Just vanish, before anyone else gets hurt."

"I can't do that."

"Well, when this whole thing goes down, and you have to choose between the lives of good people and the lives of bad people, you remember whose side you're really on, Kennedy. Don't blur the lines between what is right and what is wrong."

"And my advice is when this whole thing goes down, you should be somewhere else. Because whatever is going to happen, it can't handle another impromptu drop-by visit by the one and only Detective Sutherland."

"I will put you down. If it means protecting those girls and if it means bringing those responsible to actual justice, I will put...you...down."

"The feeling is mutual."

Sutherland got up to leave. "Bill is on you, yeah?"

Kennedy nodded.

He spun around one last time. "If you change your mind, let me know."

Kennedy put his sunglasses on, dropped cash on the table, and stood up. "Don't hold your breath."

The two of them walked out one after the other, went to their respective cars, and drove their separate ways.

CHAPTER 28

WILL SUTHERLAND

Trust

Sutherland waited at his house impatiently, his leg tapping against the table in his home office. He was racking his brain over and over again with all the details of all the people he believed to be involved. Agent Waters would be there any minute. He needed to make sure he could trust him. Quite frankly Waters would have to be very convincing. He pulled out the blueprints of Uptown. He pored over them, trying to take in every nook and cranny. A knock came at the door. He grabbed a gun from his desk drawer and tiptoed quietly. He peeked through the peephole and saw it was Agent Waters.

"Are you alone?" Sutherland said loudly.

"Yeah, I'm alone, Detective."

He opened the door slowly and motioned him to come in.

"You need a water or coffee or anything like that?"

"No, I'm good for now. So what do you got for me?"

"I was about to ask you the same thing."

"You know the FBI and local authorities don't generally work together quite like this."

"So why did you come?"

"Mark Kennedy."

"What about him?"

"He has information we need."

"What kind of information?"

"I'm not at liberty to tell you that. We just need to get to Mark Kennedy sooner than later; then we can push forward."

"I can't let you do that, sir."

"Why?"

"I already spoke with him. He's involved in the whole scheme, and he denies having any connection with the FBI whatsoever. He's off the grid and out of his mind."

"We've been monitoring Kennedy for quite some time but always from a distance. We wanted him to believe that we weren't keeping track of him.

There couldn't be any contact between us; otherwise, I'm sure he'd have already run or been killed. He knows what he's doing."

Sutherland looked dubious.

"Look, Detective, you called me asking for my help. I've been launching an aggressive sex trafficking campaign ever since my daughter was attacked. I have been following a man named Marcus all over this country, waiting to pounce."

"Did you say Marcus?"

"Yeah, why?"

"His name came up. I was told he's at Uptown right now."

"Marcus has been on our watch list for over fifteen years. He's an international king of the sex trade industry. He dropped off our radar weeks ago; we thought maybe he had slipped out of the country, but with your intel, it sounds like he may very well be holed up at your casino. If that's true, you need to figure out who you trust and who you don't. Either help me or get out of my way as my office handles it."

"Can you just explain how the man who raped your daughter ends up dead at the hands of Mark Kennedy, who you then release ten years later to a casino where this sex trafficking ring is set up?"

"Wow," Waters responded, pacing back and forth. "Let me explain it to you slowly. Like I said, we've been monitoring Kennedy for a long time. Caprizzi had Kennedy kill Rickstein over principle. Admittedly we knew about it as we had access to every letter given to Kennedy from Jules Romano, and we let it happen."

"Why?"

"We had been investigating the possibility of Caprizzi being involved in human trafficking. He covers his tracks well though. Kennedy was our backup plan. We were patiently watching and waiting because we knew we would eventually release him when the time was right to see if Uptown would pick him up. We knew he had connections with Uptown through those letters, and when we let him go without any instruction, sure enough, Uptown calls for him."

Sutherland considered the information.

"Might I add that on top of all this, a detective calls me out of the blue, screaming about the surfacing of a full-blown conspiracy. So here I am, looking for some help from you. And all I'm getting is 'I don't know if I can trust you.' If that's true, then why the fuck bring me here, Detective?"

"Okay, you're right. I believe you. And now, as promised, I'll let you in on some things that I don't think you know."

Agent Waters waited.

"There is a whole system of interconnected players here. For starters, a prison guard who is connected to Mark Kennedy from his time in prison works for our system here in Vermont. We had a witness that could connect Caprizzi to the Uptown, and he ends up beaten to death. That guard will admit to giving the order that was given to him by Mark Kennedy. Then I come to find that a prosecutor from New York who was involved with Kennedy's case and your case turns up to be the next DA in Vermont, and every step of the way, he heads off my investigations, my interrogations, my attempts at a case despite the evidence I compile."

"You think your local district attorney is in on it?"

"I know he is. And I had one of the very few people that I do trust bring him in today, and lo and behold, he wasn't at work. In fact he hasn't been in for two days. He's gone, out of thin air."

"Jesus, Detective, I see where your paranoia comes from. I'll have my people send out a countrywide search for him."

"So Kennedy hasn't been in contact with you at all?"

"No. And we weren't going to move on him right away, but it sounds like they're offing loose ends and Dan Peterson is on the run, or dead. If it's happening, it must be happening imminently."

"We need to jump on this," said Sutherland.

"We need to do it carefully, and we can't call this in to the state, 'cause who knows where the leaks are. We can't blow this opportunity."

"Do you have people you absolutely trust to help?"

"Of course, a few of the best. I'll get them assembled for tomorrow. We'll stake out the entrances of Uptown, and hopefully they waltz right into our lap. You have any guys who can help?"

"Three. Troopers Konine, Smith, and Dominick. I'll get them updated."

"Perfect. We'll meet at 0500 hours tomorrow morning and get ourselves organized. You've done a hell of a job, Detective, you deserve recognition."

"Thank you, sir, see you tomorrow."

"Tomorrow."

. . . . . .

Night time fell over Uptown. The casino was packed with an energy that could barely be contained. The whole weekend at Uptown was a mess. There was a jazz festival going on, and just about every room at the casino was booked. Kennedy had planned it that way with Marcus so that all the ingoing and outgoing traffic would blend better. Unfortunately, it was also the last night that Marcus' men had the opportunity to defile the girls who were going to be sold the next day. No doubt each and every one in some way or another would be taking advantage of that night.

Kennedy made his way to A-Wing under the premise that he was "double-checking everything." He spoke with all of Marcus' guards, who now were solely in charge of security. Kennedy approached Rachel Davis' room. A guard stopped him.

"No, no one sees the main feature tonight. Strict orders."

Kennedy opened up his jacket. From it he pulled an envelope holding 10,000 dollars.

"It's yours, I just want five minutes. I won't leave a mess, I promise."

The guard contemplated and took the money.

"Five minutes. If you do anything to cause any marks, I snap your neck."

"You got it."

The door opened and Kennedy slipped inside. He looked to the bed, but there was no one there. Off in the darkest corner she crouched.

"What do you need?" she said with her head down in her arms, her voice a ghostly rasp.

"Rachel, it's me," he said softly.

She looked up, and her eyes were devoid of life. "You came back…I wasn't sure if I'd see you again."

He walked over to her and knelt down.

"Are you, uh, are you here to save me? Is it over?" she asked drowsily.

Kennedy realized she must be on some sort of drug. He lifted her eyelids; her pupils were severely dilated.

He looked away out of guilt. "I can't, not yet. I wish I could just take you out of here, stop anyone who stepped in our way, but I can't. Soon though, tomorrow, I swear it's over."

Rachel's head slumped backward, then snapped back to attention.

"Look at me, Rachel. Look at me!"

She gazed up. A single tear managed to fall from her eye.

"One more night. Tomorrow morning you let them dress you. You need to look nervous, but not too nervous. Allow yourself to be bid on with the other girls. Are you listening? Rachel! Can you hear me?"

"I'm listening," she said, frustrated, her eyes flickering shut then open again.

"When you start to hear the screams and you see smoke, you run. The same way you ran last time. No one will be in your way though. You run straight out the same way you did before. When you get to that hallway, you take a left and you sprint to the door and you wait. That's where I'll be; that's where you'll be safest. The police will be there soon after and that will be that. Safe and sound and those responsible will have suffered. Repeat back to me what you're going to do."

Rachel was having difficulty staying awake.

"Rachel, what are you going to do tomorrow?"

"Run out the same way I did, take a right at the end of the hallway, and wait for help."

"No. Shit," he muttered. "Rachel, you take a left. Repeat after me...left."

"I'll take a left."

"Perfect. That's perfect. Don't forget." He reached his hand out and went to give a reassuring touch to her hand. In a confused state she pulled away and crunched herself tighter against the wall. She looked at Kennedy like she didn't know him. He stood up and knocked on the door. The guard came and let him out. He walked back to the main casino fuming. All his hatred building. His impatience reaching a peak. The end was within reach and in just a few hours he was going to unleash hell on everyone involved. For himself. For Billings. And most importantly, for Rachel Davis.

CHAPTER 29

JUDGMENT DAY

Snowfall. For five straight days the region had been slammed by the tiny frozen crystals. On this day the snow fell gently. It was serene. Kennedy was once again taken back to those days of old. The simpler days. In no time at all, childhood memories would be forced to the dungeon of his mind and the snow would be covered in the blood of monsters. He drank from his steaming cup of coffee as his Uptown Escalade cruised toward the hand-built helipad deep in the woods several miles northeast of the casino to pick up the guests of honor. He was in the lead car, followed by Fontaine, then O'Shea, and brought up in the rear by Sorenteen. Kennedy was relieved that only two of Marcus' men were assigned to come with, and Sorenteen and Fontaine were the unlucky ones who had to put up with them. Each man was equipped with earphones and the decided-upon weaponry that Kennedy had hand-picked from the stores of options within the A-Wing warehouse. He and Fontaine both had M-16s. O'Shea preferred a shotgun, and Sorenteen was handling a M40A1 military grade sniper rifle. They all carried Glocks for backup as well as heavy bulletproof vests and sunglasses to reflect the brightness of the snow. Fontaine had begged and pleaded to wear matching gray suits, which after much debate they reluctantly decided would suffice.

Several of the local buyers had already been escorted to the casino using the A-Wing tunnel. The three they were meeting were internationals who had flown in to Boston, were transported to a private airfield, and then brought in by helicopter.

As he drove, Kennedy kept his eyes on every subtle movement outside the car to look for anything suspicious. He wondered if Sutherland was out there somewhere, waiting to pounce. Or maybe he had been bluffing. He thought it best to expect the worst and hope for the best.

All four cars followed smoothly behind one another through the rough, snowy terrain of the back roads and finally out to a clearing where an old farmhouse stood. Around back was where Caprizzi had built the small landing pad. Sorenteen veered off as planned to obtain a vantage point where he could see from afar anything undesirable approaching and take down anyone necessary.

As the cars came to a stop in a straight line, two of the helicopters had already landed and the third buzzed over their cars. The chopper banked hard to the right to align itself properly and made its final descent. It was 12:45 p.m., right on time.

Kennedy stepped out first and radioed to Sorenteen, "How we look?"

"I'm in position. Everything looks clear."

"Outstanding," he responded, anxious to get the transfer under way.

The three other car doors opened and the other men stepped out. O'Shea approached the choppers with his shotgun and dropped to one knee to provide a sense of cover for the buyers.

A man by the name of General Javier Alceveda was the first to step out. He exited with two armed military bodyguards, each towering in stature and carrying handguns. No doubt there were heavier arms on board. The general was a portly fellow. He stood about six feet tall. An intimidating aura surrounded him. His sunglasses reflected all light, so it was impossible to see through to his eyes.

He spoke in Spanish to his bodyguards. "De el dinero y traiga a las automobiles."

"Si, General," they said simultaneously.

Kennedy knew the general all too well. He had come close to arresting him years ago for allegedly ordering the sadistic murders of several town officials and waging war against the New York Police. He apprehended him at the Miami airport in Florida, but it was all for nothing. Politics had gotten in the way and he was extradited back to the safety of Argentina. It didn't surprise Kennedy that the general was involved with sex trafficking, as no lucrative business was too illegal for him. He didn't gain his political strength from good policy and charitable donations. He gained it from intimidation and the threat of violence.

One of the militants whistled toward the chopper. Four more men came out. Each of them also carrying a weapon. All the firepower surrounding Kennedy—and the lack of stable personalities handling it—made him very nervous.

The general walked directly to Kennedy. "Hola, Señor Kennedy. I hope this goes very smooth, because if not?" The general laughed. "Well, let's just make sure it does."

"Very good, sir. Nothing should go wrong or hold us up."

The general took his glasses down. "Don't think I don't remember you, Detective. Does my standing here offend you?"

Kennedy didn't want to spend any more time talking with Alceveda than he had to for fear he might get aggressive with him.

"No need to call me detective, General. That's the old version of me. The new me is in charge of seeing to it that this operation goes smoothly. So let's hit it."

"Just another mercenary out for money? Fair enough," he said, looking back at his men. "Vamonos, hombres!"

As he walked by Kennedy, he spit on his boots. Fontaine stepped forward to speak with the general and help his men carry the bags of money. The sound of the next helicopter door opening grabbed Kennedy's attention away from his anger. Buyer number two was Julius Fleur. His file had called him a "purebred businessman." He looked the part: nice suit, neatly trimmed dark hair, pale white skin. Kennedy noticed that Fleur's left eye was a brilliant shade of blue, but his other eye was clearly false. It sat in his head, black as midnight, the socket surrounded by scars. It was difficult not to stare at. Fleur walked by Kennedy with his security detail and advisors without so much as saying a word or even acknowledging Kennedy's existence. He was as cold as his soul-less eye. They walked to their assigned car and got in.

The third door opened. Out stepped Jackson Pope—a last name that didn't reflect his actual character. He was pure evil from head to toe. He was of American descent, with wiry brown hair and a mustard stain on his cheek, and loud. He wore a Hawaiian shirt to cover his gut and flip-flops despite the fact that it was wintertime. With him he had two European girls who looked like they were about thirty-five years old...if you combined their ages. He confidently approached Kennedy, which made Kennedy grasp the handle of his weapon tightly.

Just a little bit longer.

"Mr. Pope, how are you, sir," said Fontaine as he ran up from behind. Kennedy had never been so relieved to have Fontaine with him to take the social weight off his shoulders.

"I can't believe I'm in fucking Vermont," Pope belted out. "I can't believe I'm flying into a farmhouse either. And I definitely can't believe I'm about to bring some grade-A American ass back to Europe with me! That shit is pretty rare out there in the world. Can't wait to get this party started!" He slapped the girls on their derrières.

"Excellent, sir, anything you need, you let me know," Fontaine responded as he led Pope to his vehicle. He got him situated and then quickly scurried over to Kennedy. He grabbed him by the sleeve and leaned in close.

"Look a little less like you want to kill everyone here. Come on, Kennedy, pull it together."

Kennedy looked back at Fontaine and gave a big smile. "Better?"

"No, worse. Just get in your car and lead us back."

Kennedy went back to the front car. Once again he was traveling alone, which he thought odd. Marcus' men were supposed to get in his Escalade for the trip back, but he convinced himself they were busy monitoring the cars with the very valuable buyers behind him. Sorenteen rejoined the group and brought his car to the rear. The route back was a bit different. They took the same back road but this time connected with Route 6, which eventually dumped them back to Main Street and then to the casino, where they would walk in the front door. Kennedy had argued it was an unnecessary risk, but Marcus had demanded it be that way so the clients would feel that the entirety of the situation was under control and that they truly were in a safe and private place.

In each of the four cars, there was a tangible nervous energy. Everyone acutely focused on getting all the merchandise and themselves back to Uptown without incident. Missing a turn signal, speeding, a flat tire—these were all variables that could lead to a completely botched pickup.

The cars filed on to Main Street. Kennedy came up to a light that turned red just as he cruised underneath. In his rearview mirror he saw the three other cars slam their brakes.

"Shit!" he exclaimed as he turned the corner. The cars behind fell out of sight.

As per the plan he pulled over next chance he had to wait for the rest of the group to catch up. A few moments passed and the Uptown-embroidered vehicles reappeared and they continued along their way.

As the caravan drew closer, his heart began to race. He could feel the palms of his hands wet with anticipation. Whatever was going to happen in the next couple of hours would change all their lives forever, he was sure. He was very aware of his Glock safely tucked in its holster. He knew everything was loaded and ready to be discharged.

. . . . . .

"Okay, everyone, no one moves until you get my order. Does everyone understand?" Waters commanded over his radio.

There were a handful of affirmative responses, including Sutherland's. Waters had assembled a small field team who were ready and waiting. He had called in every favor he owned and then some to set up such a fast operation. Sutherland had put his trust in Troopers Konine, Dominick, and Smith to commence the high-risk operation. The objective wasn't clear. There were so many variables to take into account that he felt it more prudent to simplify things. Expect the worst, hope for the best. Controlling the situation aggressively early on was the decided-upon approach. Sutherland recognized that this was a once-in-a-lifetime opportunity. Anything short of burning Uptown to the ground was unacceptable.

Agent Waters had been hugely helpful in his cooperation. It was because of him that the opportunity had even been created. He and his team were running point; Smith and Dominick were in charge of securing the perimeter outside of Uptown.

Sutherland waited patiently outside the casino for the caravan to arrive. He was hoping to take down Kennedy first. No matter what, the FBI was going to take Kennedy back into custody.

A moment later, four Escalades pulled up to the casino.

Waters radioed in, "Suspects in sight, everybody hold."

. . . . . .

Kennedy led the transport down the long main entrance driveway and pulled up to the large front doors. For a moment he breathed a sigh of relief that none of the state police had shown up, but then he saw Sutherland standing just a few short feet away from his car amongst a crowd of happy guests.

"Sorenteen, I got Sutherland standing outside. I'm going to try to get rid of him," said Kennedy, a bit panicked, over his earpiece.

"Shit! Stay calm, take him to the main security suite. Distract him there while we get everyone into A-Wing."

"Got it."

Kennedy got out of his car and Sutherland quickly confronted him.

"Will, did not expect to see you here. What can I do for you? You didn't catch me speeding again, did you?"

"No, I'm afraid that would be a much less complicated reason for this visit."

Kennedy could feel the blood rushing to his head, his thought process moving faster than he could interpret. He took a deep breath to try and calm himself as he looked all around him for other signs of movement. He knew Marcus would be watching.

"Well, why don't we talk somewhere with a little bit more privacy. My office sound okay?"

Sutherland thought for a moment while trying to read Kennedy. Waters gave the okay to take him over his radio. It was time to show who possessed the control. "Turn around, Mark."

"You can't be serious."

"Just turn around. Slowly. You have the right to remain silent..." Sutherland started while handcuffing Kennedy.

"Will. Will! Listen to me!"

"...Anything you say can and will be used against you in the court of law," he continued, ignoring Kennedy's pleas.

"Jesus, Sutherland! What are you doing!?"

"It's over, Mark. I don't know what exactly is going on, and I don't know what the truth is. But one way or another, you're involved and that makes you dangerous."

"You are fucking clueless right now. Would you just listen to me for a second?"

"Get in the car."

Kennedy stared at him.

"Now, Mark! Get in the car!" he said, while pushing him toward the backseat.

Kennedy allowed himself to be taken into custody. As he was being secured in the back by another officer, he watched out of the window as Agent Waters appeared and gave the order to check the other cars.

It's over.

Three SUVs pulled up behind the Uptown vehicles, lights flashing. A team exited and approached the caravan.

Kennedy was frantic in the back of the cruiser, trying to get a better look at what was happening.

"Sutherland! Will!" he shouted.

After an eternal moment, Sutherland returned. "The cars are empty," he said with grave disappointment.

Kennedy couldn't have been more confused. He improvised. "Well, what did you expect?"

"They were just valet drivers. Kids. I'd be shocked if they were older than twenty."

"Just showing them some of the local routes. That's what I was trying to tell you."

Sutherland got into the front seat as Waters and his team finished sweeping the vehicles.

"So what, Mark," started Sutherland, "you just wanted to make a fool out of me, make me out to be the crazed cop? Are there even girls inside that fucking casino?"

"I honestly don't know what you're talking about."

Waters came up to the driver's side window.

"Don't worry, Detective, we'll bring Mr. Kennedy back to our Federal building. We'll get him to talk. Not a loss yet."

"It is a loss, Agent. I don't even know if I trust myself anymore."

"So what now?" asked Konine, who joined the conversation.

Sutherland stared forward, not sure what the next appropriate move would be. *What would Mark Kennedy do?* he asked himself.

He looked up at Agent Waters. "With all due respect, sir, I'd like to take him back to our barracks. We'll rendezvous there, we'll talk to my sergeant, put a plan together."

"I don't think that's—"

"I'm not asking, I'm telling," he interrupted.

"Fine, we'll get things cleaned up here and meet you back at the barracks."

Sutherland nodded to everyone and rolled the window up. He looked at Kennedy through the rearview mirror. He was staring out the side window.

"I hope whatever you're into was worth all this."

Kennedy didn't respond. Sutherland gripped the wheel hard to the extent that his knuckles turned a ghostly white while his cheeks flared red.

How is it possible that they keep making me look so fucking bad?

He started the car and began his drive. He got on the interstate and allowed his cruiser to reach seventy, then eighty, then ninety miles per hour, jerking the car in and out of traffic. The faster he drove, the angrier he allowed himself to get—to the point where he couldn't stand it any longer. He pulled off the interstate and onto a parallel route before ducking under a bridge that was out of sight to the public. The same bridge where Liam Robbins confessed.

"Where are we?" asked Kennedy.

Sutherland got out and opened up Kennedy's door. He grabbed him by the shirt and dragged him out of the back of the car. He lifted him up and slammed him against the cruiser.

"Where are the girls?!" he yelled, punching Kennedy in the face. "Where are the girls, you dirty fucking murderer?!" He punched him again. Kennedy didn't know where most of his pain was coming from, his face or his wrists being wrenched behind him every time Sutherland hit him up against the car.

"I don't know. I'm sorry, I don't know." Kennedy wasn't about to ruin the rest of the operation. Sutherland pulled him off the car and then slammed him up against it hard enough to cause Kennedy to drop to the ground.

"Fucking tell me!" he screamed, kicking him in his already injured ribs.

Kennedy doubled over in pain and yelled, "I can't!"

"What do you fucking mean you can't!?" Sutherland said, pulling his gun out and pointing it at Kennedy's head. "You have three seconds to tell me what I need to know."

"Oh great," he responded. "This fucking game again."

Another car came screeching around the corner of the bridge and pulled up several feet away from the two of them. Sutherland pointed his gun at the car. Agent Waters stepped out with his hands up. "Detective, what the hell are you doing?"

"You followed me?"

"Of course I did. Look at you."

"He knows more than he's telling us. This is all a setup!"

"I want to believe you. It's just, when you do things like this, it makes you look—"

"Crazy," chimed in Kennedy.

Sutherland turned back and kicked him square in the chest, making him gasp for air.

"Will!" scolded Waters. "Take it easy! He is our only lead. What do we do when he gets let go because you beat the shit out of him?"

"I'm not going to beat him up anymore."

"Good."

"I'm going to kill him unless he cooperates. That's what you always do, right, Mark?" he said, pointing the gun back at Kennedy. "You know someone is lying to you, that they have information that can make a difference. You don't need the law...you just do what has to be done. If you end up killing the person," he loaded the gun, "just one less dirtbag."

Waters took his gun out. "I am begging you to take it easy, Detective. C'mon, you don't want to go down this road. He's making you act irrationally."

"No, I see it now," Sutherland said with a fire in his eyes. "The system fails. This is the only way to get to those people who are untouchable."

"That's not true, we are above this. We can handle this together. We can let the justice system do what it is intended to do. Show this piece of shit that the system does work."

Sutherland stared down the barrel of his gun as Waters stepped a bit closer, his finger ever so gently caressing the sensitive trigger of his sidearm.

"Will, it's over for him. Don't ruin yourself over a guy like this."

Sutherland's finger trembled for a moment before he eased off. He lowered his gun and took a deep breath. So did Kennedy. So did Waters.

"You take him in your car, Agent. I don't trust myself with him." Sutherland started walking back to his cruiser. Waters came up from behind him, lifted his arm, and smashed him in the back of the head with his gun. Sutherland dropped to the ground instantly. Waters zip-tied his hands behind his back as well as his feet and then secured him to a small tree. He snatched up Sutherland's gun and tossed it in the river.

"What the hell is going on?" asked Kennedy as Waters rushed over to him.

"We gotta get you out of here. Your part here is done. Time to let O'Shea and Sorenteen handle the rest. I've got five million dollars in my car for you from Uptown profits, and I have here a first-class plane ticket out of this country."

"Wait, wait…what?"

"Sorry, let me introduce myself. I'm Mr. X."

"No fucking way. Who else knows?"

"Just Caprizzi."

"Where is he?"

"I can assure you, he's dead, very dead. He needed to be in order to get everything swung into motion, get you released from prison, tie off a loose end as far as his existence. Not to mention he was basically facing life in jail or getting murdered by any one of the dozen or so criminals he'd pissed off. He wanted death on his own terms."

"How did they know to switch the cars on me at the light?"

"I spoke with Sutherland last night. I knew he was going to take you at the casino, so I called your boys at Uptown, as Mr. X, and I told them to switch the cars out. I told Sutherland we wouldn't take your caravan until you were physically at Uptown. By the time he pulled you out and searched all the cars, everyone was already safely back in A-Wing. The show is probably just about to start, and your job with us is officially done. Excellent work, Mark."

"No."

"What do you mean no?"

"I mean no, I'm not going anywhere."

"Mark, there's nothing more for you to do. They will be dealt with accordingly."

"I know you're hearing me, but you're not fucking listening. I made a promise, to one of the girls. I don't know if I'm going to be able to live my life knowing the things I've done, but if something were to happen to her? I just…I can't leave. Not until I know she is all right. And not until I know Marcus and all those involved are dead."

Waters stood for a moment, then popped the trunk of his car. He came back with a silenced nine millimeter in hand. He held it out to Kennedy. "Just remember, this was your choice. Let's go. We don't have a lot of time."

Kennedy grabbed it and examined the weapon for a quick moment. "Thank you," he said sincerely.

"Thank me later. I have a feeling that things are about to get very interesting."

. . . . . .

Marcus sat behind one of the tinted one-way glasses, looking at the stage in front of him. Eugene and Afonos stood behind. All fourteen rooms were full. The three international buyers/distributors held the three biggest viewing areas. The other rooms were taken up by a slew of well-to-do national politicians, gang members, rich men hoping to fulfill their fantasies. The lights were dim; soft music played over the speaker system. Sorenteen, O'Shea, and Fontaine watched from the control room with three of Marcus' guards.

"So, everything should be set then?" Sorenteen asked O'Shea.

"Aye, mates, everything is ready to go. Just a few minutes now."

"Fontaine, did Alceveda, Pope, and Fleur get situated?"

"Yeah, they have the drinks of their choice, a list of the girls for purchase, and rooms at the temperatures they desired. Pope is already having some fun in his room; they should be happy."

While they spoke under the surveillance of Marcus' men, the atmospheres in the buyers' rooms widely ranged. Fleur's room was dead quiet. He had the utmost of focus as he silently reviewed the files of the girls with one of his advisors. General Alceveda was slobbering over a chicken leg, squawking about how lucrative the business was and how he refused to be outbid by anyone. Jackson Pope was hammered and was having his way with the two girls he had brought with him while his men watched and laughed at his degradation of the entertainment.

Marcus leaned into his microphone and called to the control room. Fontaine answered, "What do you need, Marcus?"

"Are we ready to begin?"

"Yes sir, just a couple minutes now." He peered into a video camera where the girls were being held. "The final touches are being put on. They are looking prepped and ready for distribution."

. . . . . .

Rachel's hands shook as she wiped a tear away from her eye to prevent her mascara from running. If anything was out of place, her handler would come over and slave over her for another several minutes, and that was the last thing she wanted in that moment. She caught a glimpse of herself in a mirror, and she was disgusted with what she saw. Underneath her expensive red silk gown, she wore close to nothing. Her makeup had been done to make her look even younger than she already was. She couldn't remember a thing from the last week after what had happened. Marcus had personally come down and started drugging her after he had heard she tried to escape. And then a flicker of a memory shined from the back of her brain. A conversation with Mark in the coldness of her cell.

Had it been a dream?

She tried to remember what he had said. Something about running. Her desperate attempt to access the memory was made difficult by the presence of the other girls. She looked them over. Many of them simply had no more emotion to spill; their faces were flat, doll-like. There were two who began weeping, and they were quickly injected with something by their handlers to make them numb to their environment. Rachel couldn't afford any further impairment, so she held strong, although the effort made her nauseated. She walked up to Theresa, who was standing quietly, dressed like a Barbie.

"Keep your head up. You watch what I do," she said aloud.

Her handler overheard her. "That's good advice," he said, gently touching Rachel. "You should follow her every move, little one. She will sell for a good price, and so will you."

Rachel looked at him and forced a smile. She tried to think about her parents, wondering how long she had been gone. She wondered if they were still even looking.

A light went on above the main door. The guard at the front of the room rang a bell. "No more speaking. Be ready to present yourselves."

. . . . . .

Sutherland came to, his face down in the dirt. It was still light out and freezing. He instantly felt the back of his head throbbing. He went to stand up and realized he was tied down. He spent a few moments rocking back and forth, trying to find a way to free himself, but it was no use. He screamed out as he attempted to break the ties that bound him—a futile effort.

"Help!" he screamed. "Anyone out there!? Help! I'm a state trooper!"

He could hear a car overhead on the bridge. "Hey!" he yelled with all his strength. "I'm down here!"

The car slowly came around the corner. It was a Vermont State Police cruiser and it was followed by another. Out stepped Konine, Dominick, and Smith.

"Jesus, Konine! Over here!"

Konine spotted him.

"How did you know where to find me?"

"When you didn't show up to the barracks, I figured you had taken him to a spot where you could have your way with him. This is where we brought Robbins, so I started here."

Konine looked at Sutherland closely; he noticed the blood. "What the hell happened to you? How did you end up like this? Where's Kennedy?"

Dominick got his knife out and cut him loose.

"Agent Waters, Brent Waters, is helping them."

"What?" said Smith from the back. "How is that possible?"

"He is. They have the DA's office, the prison system, the FBI," replied Sutherland as he stood up and felt the back of his head.

"So it really is just us," Dominick apprehensively said.

"It's all on us and I understand if you don't want to get involved. I don't know what is going to happen back at Uptown, but that's where I'm headed."

"Let's not waste any more time talking. Let's gear up and hit those motherfuckers with everything we've got," Konine demanded.

"I'm in," said Dominick.

"I'm in," replied Smith.

The four of them got in the two cruisers, leaving Sutherland's vehicle behind. Before leaving, he grabbed his bulletproof jacket and assault rifle from his trunk and Konine handed him a spare sidearm. The two cars peeled out and quickly shot over the bridge, back to the interstate, back to Uptown.

. . . . . .

The bright red light that had been staring Rachel in the face finally shut off. The door in front of her swung open, and the music became a more low and seductive tone. The walkway in front took her by several rooms and then into an open circular area. She saw herself reflected off of a dozen or so mirrors that seemed to engulf her. Her cowardly buyers watching safely behind them, treating her and her sisters like filets of fish. All thirty girls entered the showroom as the handlers filed into the last open room to watch the show. The girls each presented themselves one at a time by disrobing. This was perhaps the most important part of the viewing. They could see how popular they were as lights above the rooms indicated the buyers would be willing to put bids in. If no one was willing to bid, you were automatically taken away and sent to Marcus' men where they could do anything they wished. Rachel spun around as she was instructed to do, tears welling in her eyes, all the lights above the rooms brightly lit.

Where was her savior? He promised he'd come back for her.

She started to panic in her own mind.

What if it was all a trick? Another manipulation to make her go along with everything.

She stopped and looked frantically around for an exit, but the only way out was the door behind them that had closed and locked. She stood back in her spot and put her robe back on. She then dropped her head as the next girl stepped forward to show herself off.

. . . . . .

Kennedy and Waters pulled up outside the casino.

"Follow me," instructed Kennedy, running around the side of the casino toward the restaurant.

They came to where the garbage was thrown out. From there Kennedy knew they could make their way across the casino to the vault and to A-Wing. Kennedy went to wave his magnetic key to open the door. It was denied. He tried again; it was denied once more.

"Allow me," said Waters, who took out a magnetic key of his own. He swiped it and the lock clicked open.

"How did you?"

"A gift from Caprizzi."

"Of course. Ready?"

Waters nodded and got himself in position. Kennedy kicked the door open. Two of Marcus' guards were taken by surprise on the inside as they watched the auction on a small receiver. Kennedy and Waters each pulled their triggers once and both delivered head shots to the two guards. They hid their weapons inside their coats, rounded the kitchen casually, and then nonchalantly walked through the busy main dining room to the entrance of the restaurant. Kennedy made it first, took his jacket off, and rolled his sleeves up to allow for better mobility. He peeked his head around the corner. A guard was walking toward them. He motioned Waters out and closed the restaurant doors behind them. The guard walked by and Kennedy silently shot him in the back of the head. Waters grabbed him before he hit the ground and set him down out of view. They began their trek to the vault. About two-thirds of the way through the casino, Waters motioned Kennedy to sit down at some slot machines.

"Damn it," he said at the sight of four armed guards outside the door to the vault with two others up above on the staircase, surveying.

"Any ideas?" asked Kennedy.

"I got it, just be ready to make quick work of these guys."

"What do you mean you got it? We're outnumbered three to one."

"Watch," Waters replied as he took out a remote control. He turned it on and held down a button labeled "Jackpot." All at once the casino floor erupted in lights and sirens. Hundreds of slot machines were rigged to be winners at that moment. People began screaming and cheering and running about the casino floor.

"Well done," Kennedy commended, looking to where Waters had just been a moment ago. He was gone. He looked up and caught a glimpse of him making his way over to the vault.

Kennedy took a few steps forward and saw one of the guards up above taking notice of Waters. Kennedy pierced the man twice in the upper torso. The second guard unleashed a barrage of bullets toward Kennedy, forcing him to take cover. Waters continued his descent amongst the flow of guests running about the area.

Kennedy popped back up and ran straight into the crowd, hoping he'd blend in. His plan fell short as the second guard up above began unloading into the crowd. Several people dropped to the ground around him. He kneeled and fired a handful of rounds into the shooter. He yelled at those who had been struck to get up and get out of the casino. Some of the guests had become panicked, adding to the confusion and chaos, although most others were still oblivious as they grabbed at coins and chips.

Waters got to within a few feet of the guards, who had their weapons drawn and were pushing people away from the vault. Waters withdrew a second gun. He lifted both and shot two of them simultaneously, immediately followed by the other two. Two were dead before they hit the floor, and he made quick work of the other two, who were squirming around on the ground. He looked up to the staircase to see the other two had already been killed. Kennedy came running up to him.

"What the fuck was that? A little warning next time," he said as Waters handed him another clip.

"What? I thought you were right behind me. I told you to be ready to hit it."

"Just give me a clearer heads-up next time please."

"You got it. Ready to get to the other side?"

"Let's do it."

. . . . . .

O'Shea peered into the camera, watching the girls finish up their individual shows. Three hadn't received any votes and were escorted out to the private rooms to be defiled. The time was now. He stood up and went to the back of the room, where a conveniently located water jug was placed. He patted Sorenteen on the shoulder on his way back. Two of the guards sat and intently watched the show; the other was standing by the water tower slowly sipping from his glass. O'Shea poured himself a glass and stood next to him.

"So, does this stuff turn you on or what?"

The guard looked at him disinterestedly, and as soon as he did, Sorenteen spun around and shot the man looking at O'Shea with his M-16. Noise wasn't a concern as the rooms were designed to be soundproof. The two other guards stumbled to take their weapons out, and O'Shea capped both of them from behind. Fontaine immediately got up and flipped open a computer. He put a series of codes into a program. "Lockdown" flashed across the screen. On his monitor, each of the rooms turned red to signify the doors were locked. All but one turned. The room with the handlers remained open.

"Shit, room twelve didn't lock."

"I'll take care of it," commanded Sorenteen. "Fontaine, you stay on the computer, initiate the barbecue."

O'Shea strapped his shotgun around his shoulder and loaded his Glock. "Sammy, let's get to work."

All three of them put on gas masks. Sorenteen and O'Shea left the control room. Sorenteen first went into the private rooms one at a time. In the first, two men were discussing what they wanted to do to their prize. He shot them both at close range. The other rooms were empty.

O'Shea ran to the stage door, easily killing the guard outside it. He flung it open and all thirty girls looked at him, startled.

"Everyone out now, run!"

The girls were stunned, unsure of what to do. Rachel took over and ran to the front of the pack, grabbing Theresa on her way. The other girls instinctively followed. As she ran by O'Shea, he grabbed her. She flailed her arms to break free.

"Hey!" O'Shea shouted. "Take this!" He gave her a security key. "You need it to get out of this room."

Rachel stopped her struggle, took the key, and ran the same way she did in her last escape attempt. The music stopped and the lights turned on. The distant sounds of large men banging on the glass and doors could be heard. Some of the girls trembled with fear as they passed by the rooms. Rachel made sure everyone stayed together and continued to push forward.

O'Shea hesitated to make sure the girls were off in the right direction, then positioned himself with his shotgun in the middle of the stage, ready to clean up any problems. Sorenteen had made his way outside the handlers' room, where the six of them would be fleeing any moment. His M-16 patiently waiting.

Ready for the next phase, Fontaine initiated the second half of the program: "Flash Burn." Each of the viewing room walls burst into flames. Every room had been carefully designed to act as ovens. Smoke filled the air.

Each of the handlers ran from their room, and Sorenteen dropped each one as they exited. Pope's men attempted to grab the chairs to use them as battering rams, but they had been designed to be immovable. One of Alceveda's men took his weapon out and attempted shooting the glass, but the glass had been designed to withstand bullets. O'Shea, content with the theory that the rooms would hold up to the men's desperate efforts to escape, left the stage area and ran up to room two, where he knew Pope had the two young European girls. Fontaine saw him over the monitor and with a key stroke stopped the firestorm in that particular suite. From the computer he unlocked the door and O'Shea stepped inside. He blasted both of Pope's guards with two chest shots. Pope grabbed one of the girls as a shield but couldn't see where O'Shea was due to the smoke. O'Shea appeared from the shadows behind him and knocked him out with a single blow to the head with the butt of his weapon. He pushed the two girls out of the room and gave them another security key card.

"Run around the hall! Get upstairs with the other girls, and you follow them!" he shouted through his gas mask. They did as they were told. They went running from the room and on their way out passed by Sorenteen, who was just entering Marcus' master suite. Eugene was unconscious at the door. Sorenteen put a bullet in him just to be sure there wouldn't be any surprises. He slipped further in where there was little visibility. Afonos, badly burned, tackled him from behind. O'Shea entered just in time and grabbed his head, twisting him off of Sorenteen. After regaining his balance, Sorenteen shot him twice. Marcus was unconscious in the middle of the room. They picked him up and dragged him out.

O'Shea's next stop was Fleur's room. Fontaine opened it for him and oxygen-hungry flames shot out. There would be no survivors their. He thought by now General Alceveda would also be dead. He grabbed the unconscious Pope lying in the hallway and dragged him out behind Sorenteen toward the A-Wing warehouse.

Fontaine shut the computer to let the rest of them burn. He made his way to the warehouse to take one of the many back hallways to get to his office. There he needed to collect two large bags of money and set charges on the thirteenth floor to destroy any lingering evidence.

. . . . . .

Rachel Davis and the other girls managed to get out of the showroom but now were trapped in another hallway. She remembered Kennedy had said something about a vault. But she had no clue which direction that was in. She began to doubt that she had remembered Kennedy's directions correctly.

Where was I supposed to go? Think, Rachel, think!

She couldn't afford running in the wrong direction, not with the responsibility of all the girls looking to her to lead them to safety.

The door to her left made a series of clicking sounds and it began to swing open.

Panicked she shouted, "Run!" The girls bunched together and sprinted in the opposite direction.

"Rachel!" someone yelled behind her. Immediately the sound of the man's voice made her stop in her tracks. A voice that made her heart skip several beats; one that restored her confidence. She spun around to see Mark Kennedy standing in the doorway. She ran to him and threw her arms around him. She looked into his eyes and knew she was safe.

"Are you okay?" she asked, noticing that he had been beaten quite badly.

"Am I okay? Yeah, I'm fine. I'm more worried about you."

"I'm fine, I think everyone is fine," she responded, looking around at the other girls, who all nodded.

"Where is everyone?"

"I don't know, the whole downstairs is on fire. I don't know where anyone ended up."

"Okay. I'm just glad to see you're all safe. Now listen closely. You're going to take these girls and you are going to run through this vault into the main casino. It's pure chaos in there right now, so stay together. You are not going to stop running until you are outside the main doors and with the police."

"What are you going to do?" she asked.

"I'm going to take care of a couple things."

She gave him another big hug. He gently pushed her away. "No time, just go, run fast and run hard." He and Waters began a jog down the hallway.

"Mark!" she yelled, tears of anger swelling.

He spun around.

"You kill him. You kill him and make him feel the pain we all felt."

Kennedy gave a nod and then disappeared into the warehouse.

"Okay, follow me, stay close." she commanded to the girls behind her.

In a tight group the girls, wearing their bright showroom outfits, ran through the vault and into the main casino. Unfazed by the dead men lying on the ground, they scurried along the wall amidst thousands of people running wildly throughout the casino. Like Kennedy had ordered them to, they ran with one goal in mind: Get outside.

"Up there, just ahead," said Theresa. Rachel looked up and could see daylight and blue lights pulling up to the casino. They ran faster, and faster, new life being given to them with the hope of freedom. Through the casino doors they burst and began waving their arms wildly in the air. From the cars came four Vermont state troopers. They controlled the scene and made sure the girls were safe.

From then on Rachel couldn't remember much. The police huddled them together away from the main entrance. A female officer pulled up and took care of them as four troopers ran into the casino. Emotions overwhelmed them all. Some wept; some smiled for the first time in years. Rachel could only recall the novel feeling of safety. Not because she was no longer in captivity, not because she was under the care of the police, but because Mark Kennedy was going to make sure that her captors paid. He was going to make sure they got what was coming to them, and she would be able to sleep better knowing that they could never harm anyone ever again.

. . . . . .

Sutherland couldn't believe his eyes as they approached the casino with a local police unit already on scene. Right in front of him amongst the sounds of a casino melting down, a group of young girls came running out from within. There was no time for distractions, however; he was ecstatic they were safe, but it was time to find the men responsible. Maneuvering through the sea of bodies was proving extremely difficult. Rather than attempting crowd control, they dipped and dodged their way around, looking for clues of where they needed to be.

"Yo, Sutherland! Come take a look at this!" Konine yelled over the commotion.

Sutherland came over to a large door and saw several dead men lying on the ground, then caught the glimpse of two more men dead up above on a staircase.

The door was open straight through the vault and to a back hallway.

"Smith and Dominick, you make your way through here. I'm going to the thirteenth floor with Konine to see if anyone's in Fontaine's office."

"Sounds good; stay in touch over radio."

The two groups split up.

Smith and Dominick ran through the vault to where the back wall should have been. Instead an all-white corridor continued. They came to two doors, one at the end of the hallway and one immediately to their right that was cracked open. They made their way down the dark steps where billows of smoke crept along the ceiling like an inverted avalanche. At the bottom it was dark; just a couple of auxiliary lights were turned on, which merely illuminated the smoky air. Along their way through the room, they noticed a dozen or so doors, all locked but one. Dominick kicked the door in and Smith was first inside. There were three dead men on the ground. They both looked around the room and came across a series of monitors showing each of the rooms to be on fire as well as a laptop computer. Dominick gently opened it and the words "Flash Burn" were rhythmically alarming.

"You see anything?" asked Smith.

"Just a computer. I'm going to unplug it." As soon as he did, the fires immediately stopped. They reviewed the monitors together. Dozens of charred and motionless bodies could be seen through the haze. On the monitor that showed room ten, one body began to move. They both ran for the door, which had been disengaged when the computer shut off. They stepped in and dragged the individual out of the room. The man was barely identifiable, but it was apparent he was some sort of militant. A portly man with the Argentinean flag visible on his shoulder sleeve.

"Let's get him upstairs," ordered Smith. "Radio into the paramedics, have them ready to treat this guy."

. . . . . .

Sutherland and Konine reached the elevators.

"Konine, you stay here, guard this elevator. No one comes up. No one comes down unless you hear from me."

"You got it," Konine responded as he took his stance, gun ready.

Sutherland got in and hit the button for the thirteenth floor. There was no one to stand in his way. As he ascended he checked his weapon and then readied himself for anything. The door opened to emptiness. He looked toward Fontaine's office. It seemed abandoned. He took a step forward and without warning the room exploded, flinging the office door off its hinges. The blast knocked him backward. He quickly scrambled to his feet, and through the smoke he saw a man running from the scene. It was Fontaine with two large duffel bags strapped to his back.

"Fontaine!"

He looked up from the end of the hallway.

"Don't you fucking move!"

Fontaine bolted into the stairwell. Sutherland took off after him, also bursting into the stairwell in time to see a flash of Fontaine's jacket one story below him. He began jumping down several steps at a time. He paused for a moment to make sure Fontaine was still below him; he could hear him clamoring downward. He pointed his rifle down the center of the stairs and hoped he'd catch another glimpse of him. The opportunity didn't present itself.

"Fuck," he muttered as he continued his pursuit. Down and down they both flew. "Konine!" Sutherland yelled over his radio.

"Go ahead."

"Start making your way up the stairs. Fontaine is coming down and he's armed!"

"On my way." Konine ran for the stairs and began his ascent to head him off.

Sutherland passed floor ten, floor nine, floor eight. Finally he heard a door open and close. Sutherland had made some ground up and was just a couple of series of steps behind him. He reached the door, sweat pouring down his face, and kicked it in. He took a quick look, expecting to be shot at, but once again there was nothing. He turned the corner and saw the doors to Club Energized.

"Konine, come to floor seven. Secure the hallway, I'm going into the club."

There were two bouncers standing guard. As Sutherland approached, he raised his AK-47. "I'll only be a minute."

The two bouncers provided no resistance; with their hands up, they stepped aside. Inside the music was overly loud. It was dark, with strobe lights flashing. Hundreds of people were inside partying. With the jazz concert in town, the club was packed all hours of the day. They weren't aware of the disaster going on downstairs. Sutherland walked carefully but briskly with his gun tucked to his side. From close by he saw Fontaine reenter the club from the back door. Fontaine immediately spotted him as he made a run in his direction, pushing through the crowd.

Fontaine disappeared into the exit. Sutherland arrived at the door a moment later and started shooting different spots across its surface with the hope that one would hit Fontaine. He lowered his shoulder and slammed his body against the door, breaking it open. Fontaine was kneeling on the other end of the hallway near the staircase with an obvious gunshot wound to his left leg. Sutherland charged at full speed as Fontaine went to raise his gun, but it was too late. He tackled him and sent them both tumbling down a flight of stairs. At the bottom of the first flight, Sutherland popped up relatively unharmed by the fall. With the amount of adrenaline pumping through his body, he wouldn't have noticed even if he had hurt himself. Fontaine's leg was clearly broken, and the bone was sticking out.

Sutherland picked Fontaine up and held him close. "Where are they, Fontaine? Tell me right now!"

"Where's who?" he answered through bloodstained teeth.

"Wrong answer."

He shoved him down the next flight of stairs. Fontaine's body crumpled next to the outside of an entrance to the back hallways of Uptown.

"All right, Fontaine! You tell me where the fuck they are and you tell me now!"

Fontaine was in excruciating pain. He was whimpering.

"Fontaine!" screamed Sutherland as he lifted him up to toss him down the next series of steps.

"Wait, wait, wait. I'm sorry. I'm sorry. They're headed to the warehouse in A-Wing. I swear. Just please let me go, let me lie here. Please!"

"A-Wing? Warehouse? What the fuck are you talking about? How do I get there?"

Fontaine needed extra motivation to answer. Sutherland placed his gun to the unaffected knee. "One second, Fontaine."

"Go through this door with my key card. Just keep going until it meets up with a hallway, and go through the door at the end of it."

Sutherland knocked Fontaine out. He grabbed his gun and left him there for the police to find. He began the short run toward the basement of A-Wing.

He radioed in to Konine while en route.

"Sutherland? Where are you?"

"I'm headed down toward the vault. I'll meet you there. Let Smith know we need him there now. Tell Dominick to set up a tight perimeter around Uptown. If they're still here, we are not going to let them slip through our fingers."

Sutherland lowered his head and sprinted as fast as he could.

. . . . . .

Kennedy and Waters cautiously swept the giant warehouse and had keyed in on some voices in the far corner where the interrogation rooms sat. Throughout the whole warehouse were crates full of stolen goods and row upon row of ground-to-ceiling shelves. Kennedy noticed a small blue convertible running and ready to go in front of the tunnel. Kennedy moved in first, with Waters covering. As soon as they rounded the corner of the nearest group of shelves, Sorenteen and O'Shea lifted their weapons in their direction.

"Kennedy, you bloody bastard," O'Shea shouted as they all lowered their weapons.

"You used your get-out-of-jail-free card again?" commented Sorenteen.

"Nice to see you too, Sammy."

"Brent Waters? What the fuck is he doing here?"

Waters stepped forward. "I'm here for the same reasons all of you are here. To help make sure that everything is executed properly. You may know me better as Mr. X."

O'Shea let out a laugh. "You're the mystery contact? Only Caprizzi, unbelievable."

"What are you two doing back here?" asked Sorenteen. "You both were supposed to take off."

"I had to be sure the girls got out okay."

"That all?"

"Is Marcus alive?"

"Yeah."

"He held a gun to my head and threatened my life. He is responsible for the death of two of our guys. I want my shot at him."

Sorenteen looked at O'Shea. "Okay, bring him out, then get in touch with Fontaine, see how he's doing. Then we have to go."

Sorenteen patted Kennedy on the shoulder as he went back to work getting everything ready for departure. O'Shea brought out two chairs with Marcus and Jackson Pope tied down, gags in their mouths. Marcus already had an ear cut off, and his nose was crooked. It was eerie how his eyes were still as indifferent as ever. Pope was a different story. His eyes were wide, panicky. He had urinated himself. O'Shea parked them and spun them around so they were facing Kennedy. Kennedy casually put his gun down and ripped the gags out. Immediately Pope started pleading for his life.

"Please, I'll give you anything, all the money you want!"

Kennedy backhanded him as hard as he could. "Shut the fuck up. I'll get to you in a minute."

He menacingly stared Marcus in the eyes. "Are you afraid?"

"You are a fool, Mr. Kennedy, to think that this will have no repercussions."

"Marcus," Kennedy interrupted, grabbing him by the hair, "Marcus, Marcus. That's enough. You're not in a position to be making threats anymore. We have your files; we have the names of your associates. Victor did a lot of work on you. The police are going to find those books. Your entire operation is fucked. Your men are either burned alive or they'll be arrested without the likes of you to do anything about it. The best part is that the story is going to get out about what happened here, and that the people responsible escaped. No one will be able to trust anyone anymore. The news will crumble your empire and those that are involved in it. Of course the most important part is that you are going to get the proper sendoff."

"My business will always run—"

Kennedy grabbed a crowbar from the table nearby and with a hard swing crushed his kneecap. Marcus began screaming and yelling.

"That's better! Your screaming makes me smile."

Marcus' cries turned to laughter. "You know who my favorite girl to fuck was?"

Kennedy's face immediately turned red, and he got in close to Marcus. "I fucking dare you to tell me."

"Marcus, shut up!" yelled Pope.

Marcus looked into Kennedy's eyes. "That Rachel Davis girl. She was so easily manipulated. She truly would have made a great slave."

Kennedy put the crowbar down and grabbed a knife. "You know, I was going to just shoot you in the head, but I think your end deserves something much more theatrical. Something a bit more colorful." He undid Marcus' pants.

"Don't you fucking dare. Don't you touch me—stop!"

"O'Shea, hold him down."

O'Shea came from behind and got control over Marcus' body. Kennedy brought the knife up to his genitals and took one last look at Marcus. "This is for Rachel."

. . . . . .

Sutherland saw a door up ahead and used the key card to enter some sort of storage facility. He didn't immediately see anyone. He crawled his way to what he thought was the main entrance and swiped the card again. The door clicked and he eased it open to reveal Konine and Smith.

"Sutherland, thank God," Konine whispered. "Where's Fontaine?"

"He's out of play. You boys ready?"

They all nodded.

The three of them entered slowly. Crouched down, they walked up to the first set of crates, which were filled to the brim with heroin. They waited a moment in the silence. Light talking could be heard somewhere, but the sounds seemed to echo throughout the large, open space. They slipped in a bit further and held. More voices could be heard, but Sutherland still couldn't determine who it was or what was being said. He dashed for the first of a series of huge shelves with Konine and Smith close behind. He was momentarily distracted by the unbelievable amount of stolen goods and illegal objects that were held there. The sounds of a man screaming recaptured his attention. He made his way to the edge of the shelf and peered around it in the direction of the scream. On the far end of the room, he could make out two men sitting in chairs, their backs turned to him. Kennedy was standing over one of them with a gun to his head. The other had his head tilted back on the chair; he looked dead. Agent Waters was standing off to the side, and Sorenteen and O'Shea were nowhere to be found. As Sutherland continued to survey the room, he noticed the narrow tunnel shooting out into darkness and called Konine's and Smith's attention to it. He signaled to stay low and follow him. They made their way back along the shelf away from the action and snuck a few more sections down, then back to where they could see what was happening.

Sutherland heard the sound of another car starting up somewhere and then O'Shea's distinctive voice somewhere near them. The three of them ducked down.

"Fontaine? Fontaine, are you there?!"

Kennedy called out to him, "Hey, fuck him. Load the car up—we can't wait any longer. If he makes it, he makes it."

There was a series of tall crates scattered between them and Kennedy. Sutherland looked around for O'Shea and Sorenteen, who were still out of sight, and then carefully crept behind the first crate. He moved a bit closer, then a bit closer. He was now within just a handful of yards from the action. Sutherland wasn't sure how many more bullets his assault rifle had, so he set it down behind the crate as a backup and withdrew his Glock.

"Pope, how did you think this was going to end?" he heard Kennedy taunting.

"I'm sorry, I…I need help, you know? I have an addiction."

"No. Not an addiction. Being a coldblooded, evil prick of a human being has nothing to do with addiction. You are a monster. And you will always be a monster. The fact that you're alive makes me itch. Waters, could you hand me a fresh clip?"

With Waters briefly distracted, Sutherland turned and looked at Konine and Smith. With his fingers he motioned one, two, three.

They popped up from behind the crates, guns drawn. Sutherland quickly took several steps forward and got just behind Pope, his gun pointed at Kennedy's chest. Waters was caught completely off guard but was able to lift his weapon up. Waters pointed his rifle at Smith while Konine and Smith pointed their guns back at Waters. Sorenteen slowly slipped in from the room next over with his gun drawn on Sutherland. Everyone was simultaneously yelling for the others to put their guns down.

"Everyone shut up! Everyone just shut the fuck up!" yelled Kennedy. The tension-filled room fell silent, the apprehension so thick it was tangible. "Sutherland, are you kidding me?"

"Well, as far as I'm concerned, you're one of the monsters. I couldn't let you just gallop off into the sunset."

"Get your men, take them out of here, let these ANIMALS get theirs, and I promise you will get more than enough information to take care of the rest of their operations."

"I can't do that, Kennedy. I'm taking this guy back with me, along with the rest of you, dead or alive, to answer for your crimes."

"Sutherland…"

"No more talk from you, Kennedy. You're a liar, a cheater, a murderer! Have you already forgotten you killed a cop? Have you forgotten that one way or another you were involved with sex trafficking? And on top of it all, you tried to destroy my life! And now you have the balls to look me in the eyes and ask me to let you go free?"

"That's exactly what we want," said O'Shea from behind them. Sutherland's eyes darted to the side of his head to see that O'Shea was pointing a gun at his back.

"Easy, Kevin," said Kennedy. He looked back to Sutherland. "Let me kill Mr. Pope here, and then we'll figure the rest of this mess out."

"No fucking chance."

"So in your head this ends with a seven-way shootout?"

"In my head you all surrender, everyone lives. I know you don't want to die. I know you don't want to go back to prison. Cooperate right here, right now, and we'll work something out. I promise. And unlike you, my word counts."

Kennedy pondered for a moment. Perspiration built on the tip of Sutherland's nose and gently fell to the ground below. His arm began to shake. It was becoming evident he had done more damage to his shoulder than he thought when he tackled Fontaine down the staircase.

Where was the backup? he thought.

Kennedy looked at Waters and Smith, their focus immovable. He glanced at O'Shea, who peered down the sights of his gun, still as a statue. His attention fell back on Sutherland. He had come to his decision.

"I'm sorry…"

Kennedy lifted his gun as fast as he could as Sutherland pulled the trigger, and dove off to his right. Sutherland's bullet found its way just above Kennedy's bulletproof jacket; Kennedy's bullet hit Pope in the knee. As soon as the first two gunshots went off, a frenzy of bullets soared through the air. O'Shea's shot missed Sutherland by a hair and penetrated the back of Jackson Pope's head. Konine and Smith both let off rounds that struck a backpedaling Waters in his shoulder and the side of his neck as Sorenteen put a bullet into the side of Smith's abdomen, which made him drop to one knee, gasping for air. O'Shea started shooting in Konine and Smith's direction, making contact with Konine's leg and Smith's vest. Sutherland, from the safety of a crate, took several shots back at O'Shea, which sent him scrambling for cover. Waters got himself to an open grate, one of Caprizzi's escape pathways, and slid halfway down. As Konine went to fire at Sorenteen, who was running over to help Kennedy, Waters sent several shots toward him, making Konine take cover. Konine shot back at Waters, hitting him again and sending him down the grate.

Sorenteen dragged Kennedy as quickly as he could into the interrogation rooms while firing the rest of his rounds at anything moving, but couldn't avoid a shot to his arm from Sutherland. On the other side of the interrogation rooms was a green Jeep waiting to depart. Sorenteen tossed Kennedy in and punched the gas. Sutherland scrambled over to the crate where his rifle stood, grabbed it, and put a handful of bullets into the side of the vehicle. He then fearlessly knocked over the crate where O'Shea had been hiding; he was gone. He looked up just in time to see O'Shea jumping into the back door of the Jeep. Sutherland looked at Konine and Smith, both wounded.

"Go after them!" Konine demanded. "I'll stay here with Smith! Go now!"

Sutherland took off for the blue convertible and jumped in. He threw it in gear and floored it down the tunnel after the Jeep.

He radioed in to Dominick, "Expand the perimeter. I'm in a tunnel headed toward the back of the casino. Get a chopper mobilized to head east from Uptown. Look for back roads and off trails."

"Ten-four," he responded.

Sutherland hit eighty-five miles per hour quickly and could see taillights up ahead. Several shots came whizzing by, one cracking his windshield. He took his sidearm out. He was hoping he had at least one bullet left.

. . . . . .

Kennedy was sprawled out on the backseat moaning. The bullet from Sutherland's gun had shot him clear through his collarbone and out his back. O'Shea was taking turns firing at Sutherland and putting pressure on the wound.

"What do we do!? What do we do, Kennedy!?" yelled Sorenteen.

"Just drive! Find the back road, head north. Try to lose him in the woods."

"C'mon, Kennedy, hang in there, mate," O'Shea begged.

. . . . . .

Sutherland could see the end of the tunnel up ahead. He was within a car length of the Jeep. He took his gun out and carefully pointed it toward Sorenteen. He wasn't a left-handed shooter but had no other choice. He took his most careful aim, and just before pulling the trigger, the Jeep exited the tunnel and slammed its brakes, forcing the vehicle to slide sharply to the left. O'Shea fired several times at Sutherland, who slammed his brakes on and did his best to turn the convertible, just avoiding contact with a tree. He took off after them once again. Where he had the speed advantage in the tunnel, the Jeep was much more suited for the terrain of the snowy back road. Winding in and out of trees and bushes, and running over small branches, Sutherland knew his car wouldn't hold up for long. Overhead a helicopter cruised by. He had no idea how successful they would be visualizing the chase below with the dense forest of evergreen that engulfed them. He decided it was time to make his move. The path straightened out for about a hundred feet, so he geared down and floored it. The convertible shot forward and up alongside the Jeep. Sorenteen turned the wheel sharply to ram him, and as he did, Sutherland raised his gun and put a single bullet straight into his head. The Jeep jackknifed and flipped over several times before coming to a stop. Sutherland went to hit his brakes, but the tires couldn't dig into the snowy gravel hard enough. His convertible began spinning and the passenger side slammed into a tree.

A moment of peace and weightlessness washed over Sutherland. As his reality slowly returned to the surface, he immediately panicked that he may have been seriously hurt. He felt all over and moved his arms and legs. His wrist was killing him and he could taste blood. He looked at himself in the rearview mirror: a deep head gash was gushing, soaking his face. He got out of the car and could see the other vehicle flipped upside down off the road. He briefly searched for his gun but couldn't find it. He decided there wasn't any time to waste, so he descended upon the Jeep without it.

. . . . . .

Kennedy woke up in the backseat. His body in general felt badly injured but nothing as immediately life-threatening as his gunshot wound. He was weak, could barely move his legs or keep his eyes focused. His heart was thumping away inside his chest. The sound of O'Shea's voice gave him a second wind. O'Shea's head popped down from outside. He grabbed Kennedy's hand and dragged him out of the car. O'Shea was shaken up but completely mobile.

"Where's Sorenteen? Is he okay?" Kennedy asked.

"Sorenteen is down, Kennedy. He's finished. Any idea on what we should do?"

Kennedy thought a moment. "You run straight—don't stop until you're safe, and a long ways from here."

"What about you?"

"I'm bleeding a lot, but I can run a short distance. I'm sure he'll follow my blood trail. I'll lead him away from you. Run, now!"

"If by some miracle you make it, mate, I'll find ya. I bloody swear it."

"Don't think it's likely, but I appreciate the sentiment."

O'Shea shook his hand and took off running into the wilderness.

. . . . . .

Sutherland reached the inverted Jeep. He first noticed Sorenteen still strapped in. He was motionless, eyes open; dead. He then squatted down and saw the backseat empty.

"You've got to be fucking kidding me," he muttered.

He ran to the other side where a blood trail dripped its way out into the woods. He followed it cautiously. He tracked it about twenty-five yards from the crash site until the small drops ended. He listened for a moment, gazing around the woods. The snow had begun falling a bit heavier. He took another step deeper into the woods toward a large tree. He crept up as quietly as he could and quickly moved around it.

No one.

As he went to look back toward the crash site, Kennedy came lunging at him, swinging a small log as hard as he was able. Sutherland put his arms up, and the log shattered across his forearms. He was stunned by the hit, and Kennedy managed to tackle him to the ground. Sutherland reached up, doing everything he could to grab something on Kennedy to get some leverage. His hand, freezing cold from the snow, found a wet, warm liquid.

The bullet hole.

He grabbed Kennedy's shoulder, which sent a stabbing pain through Kennedy's entire arm. He pushed Kennedy off of him and got on top, throwing his weight on Kennedy's neck. Looking into the bright sky of the beautiful Vermont woods, Kennedy started seeing the world shrink; his vision narrowed and his body relaxed.

Sutherland gained some control over himself and removed the pressure off Kennedy's neck and rolled to the side. Kennedy was left breathing heavy and fast, blood continuing to spill from his wound.

"Just finish it, Sutherland," he croaked. "You got me, I ruined you. Just finish it."

"Jesus, Kennedy. Listen to yourself. I was never your enemy in this. If you had just told me what was going on, we could have figured something out."

"Just tell me that you know that they got what they deserved. Just give me that."

"Of course I know that. They deserved all of it and a lifetime of hell. But you didn't need to sell your soul for it. Yours, O'Shea's, Sorenteen's, Jules'. None of you did."

"You left out Fontaine."

"I know I did; it was on purpose. I don't really care what happens to him."

Kennedy let out a brief laugh. "Do me a favor…"

"I can't let you go."

"Not that," he said, swallowing hard and taking a moment to catch his breath. "Leave me here. I'm not going back to prison. Just let me be here, please."

Sutherland looked down. "I'm not going to fight you anymore, Mark. I'm going to go back to the road to flag down my people. Whatever happens in between the time I leave and the time I come back happens."

"Thank you, Will."

Sutherland nodded and took a few steps away. He looked back at Kennedy, still breathing fast and shallow, eyes opening, then closing. In that moment he couldn't help but feel great remorse. This had been his mentor, his role model, and he had sacrificed a lot to carry out an operation that would inevitably change the world for the better. He jogged back to the road as the sound of sirens echoed through the woods. He ran to the car wreck and waved his hands so as not to be missed. Exhausted, weak, and fogginess setting in, he couldn't help but think about Jules. Despite everything, he hoped she was okay.

CHAPTER 30

THE AFTERMATH

Rachel had been transferred to Massachusetts General Hospital immediately. She hadn't been in her room for more than five minutes when she heard some familiar voices. "What room is she in? This one here? Which one?!"

Her heart fluttered. She got out of bed and ran outside. "Dad! Mom!" she cried as tears flooded the hallway. They ran to each other and embraced. She truly thought she would never see them again.

"Oh my God, thank you!" Mrs. Davis said aloud. "I can't believe you're here! It's really you!"

"We never stopped looking," Mr. Davis reassured. "We never stopped, honey."

"I know," she responded through waves of emotion. The intense moment brought the three of them to their knees. The warmth of her father's arms and the love of her mother's hugs were instant therapy. She feared the road to recovery and how the experience would change her. But she was so glad that the other girls would get to go back to their families as well. Flashes of Mark Kennedy danced across her mind. The man who saved her life.

"What do you want to eat? Anything you want?" asked Mr. Davis, standing up and wiping his eyes.

"Doesn't matter to me," she responded.

"No, seriously, I mean anything. You want lobster, it's yours. McDonald's, done! World's biggest sundae, I'll have it here in fifteen minutes. Nurse Martha, can you call that ice cream shop—"

"Dad, seriously, you don't have to do that. Anything would taste like gold right now." Her dad's insistence to do something nice brought up old pangs of parental frustration, a feeling she had missed so badly. It brought an ear-to-ear smile across her face.

"I love you both so much," she said as the next wave of tears attacked her eyes.

They put their arms around her once more and as a group made their way back to her hospital room.

. . . . . .

Sutherland woke up from an awful night's sleep in the hospital. It had been a couple of days, and he had been kept in the dark as to what had transpired as he was so closely involved in everything that happened. The pain from his arm fracture, concussion, and bruised spine made him painfully resituate himself in the bed. He called for a nurse. Konine came in.

"You are the ugliest fucking nurse I've ever seen," said Sutherland.

"Nice to see you too, boss."

"Come on, Konine, it's time to tell me everything. Seriously. All details."

Konine carefully closed the door to the room. "Just be sure you tell Sergeant Jennings I was never here. You want the good news or the bad news first?"

"Bad."

"I won't sugarcoat it. Trooper Lance Smith is dead."

Sutherland let his head drop back to the pillow. He was speechless. He felt sadness building from within but didn't have the energy for tears, and the sensation of getting choked up made his head hurt.

"He went peacefully last night; his wife and son were by his bedside. The funeral is next week."

Sutherland kept his head down.

"Agent Brent Waters is gone. Kevin O'Shea is gone. We still have no idea about the whereabouts of Dan Peterson."

"Well, fuck, Konine! How is that not the worst-case scenario? How did Waters get away?"

"We eventually got down into that grate he slipped into. There were a series of complex sewer system paths. He could have gone anywhere."

"Okay, well, how about some good news."

"The department is going to give you a big 'we're sorry' and full reinstatement to your previous position."

"Yippee," he said sarcastically. "That doesn't change Smith's situation now, does it?"

"Of course not, Will. But we have Micky Fontaine in custody. He's not saying much. We'll break him though."

"I hope you have more than that."

"All the girls are okay, aside from the obvious emotional trauma. They're being reunited with their families as we speak. Also, there was one member of the sex trafficking ring that we found alive."

"Who?"

"Well, he was badly burned, but we were able to identify him. General Alceveda."

"You're shitting me. Like the Argentinean warlord General Alceveda?"

"That's right, he's in custody. Doctors think he'll be all right so he'll be able to be questioned by the feds as soon as he's more stable."

"Anything else?"

"Jules Romano wants to see you."

Sutherland thought a moment. "She didn't run?"

"Quite the opposite; she turned herself in."

"I'm just not ready yet, ya know. Can't even think about her right now."

"Understandably. I'll tell you though, she's being fully cooperative and giving us everything."

"Like what?"

"Coordinates of some lake house in the boundary waters of northern Minnesota supposedly full of all of Caprizzi's ideas and operations. Every detail about Uptown and those involved, including Alceveda. We have a team working with the Minnesota State Police right now."

"That's huge," was all Sutherland replied, with a bittersweet smile, glad that something monumental had been obtained from all their painstaking effort and sacrifice.

"One more thing…"

"What's that?" said Sutherland, thankful that Smith hadn't died in vain.

"Kennedy's alive."

. . . . . .

Mark Kennedy came to. Weakened. Frail. Even something as small as moving his hand was a burdensome task. He blinked a couple of times to gain some focus and tried to move his arm up. Handcuffs prevented him from doing so. Dread set in. The thought of going back to prison made him deeply desire death. He closed his eyes, mad at himself for so many reasons. He couldn't stop thinking about how he should have just left with Waters when he had the chance. Or maybe he should have brought Sutherland in on it from the beginning. His mind wandered to what had happened. Where was everyone? Who made it and who didn't?

His ears perked up at the TV's mention of Rachel Davis. It showed her being reunited with her family, a huge smile on her face as she and her parents burst into tears. Her parents holding her so tight. It was all worth it to watch that moment. He closed his eyes to try and get some more rest but was disturbed by the sound of the door to his room opening. Out of the corner of his eye, he could see a white coat approaching him. It was the doctor. He walked to the end of the bed and jotted a few notes into his chart. He walked to the bedside IV and made a few adjustments.

"How are you feeling?" the doctor asked.

Kennedy tried to say something but found he had no voice.

"Oh, my apologies, I forgot your voice is damaged. You suffered a crushing trauma to your trachea right about the level of your vocal cords. No worries, it will improve with time. Just be glad you're alive. It's an absolute miracle the medics were able to get to you in time, and even more incredible you survived to make it to surgery to repair the arteries in your shoulder."

An uneasy feeling crept into Kennedy's stomach. His voice may not have been working, but his ears were fine. That voice was so familiar. He looked at him and despite the disguise realized exactly who stood at his bedside.

"Now," said the doctor, "in case you don't remember, my name is Dr. Balinski." He got down close to his ear and spoke much softer. "But my friends? They call me Victor Caprizzi."

CPSIA information can be obtained at www.ICGtesting.com
Printed in the USA
LVOW12s0014060214

372513LV00001B/2/P